Te...
... Boardroom

...NIFER HAYWARD

...EAH ASHTON

PAULA ROE

MILLS & BOON

® and ™ are trademarks owned and used by the trademark owner and/or its licensee. Trademarks marked with ® are registered with the United Kingdom Patent Office and/or the Office for Harmonisation in the Internal Market and in other countries.

Published in Great Britain 2018
by Mills & Boon, an imprint of HarperCollins*Publishers*
1 London Bridge Street, London, SE1 9GF

Temptation in the Boardroom © 2018 Harlequin Books S.A.

Tempted by Her Billionaire Boss © 2015 Jennifer Drogell
Beware of the Boss © Leah Ashton 2013
Promoted to Wife © 2011 Paula Roe

ISBN: 978-0-263-26633-7

09-0618

MIX
Paper from
responsible sources
FSC™ C007454

This book is produced from independently certified FSC™ paper to ensure responsible forest management.

For more information visit: www.harpercollins.co.uk/green

Printed and bound in Great Britain

TEMPTED BY HER
BILLIONAIRE BOSS

JENNIFER HAYWARD

For Michelle. You've been a rock and an inspiration for me right from the beginning. Thank you for being you.

CHAPTER ONE

ROCKY BALBOA PATROLLED the length of his rectangular glass-encased world with an increasingly agitated fervor, the blinding beam of the overhead fluorescent lights a far from suitable atmosphere for Frankie Masseria's high-strung orange parrot cichlid fish. Used to the cozy confines of Coburn Grant's muted, stylish office with its custom lighting and plentiful dimmers, Rocky apparently wasn't making the transition to Harrison Grant III's cold black-and-chrome domain any more easily than Frankie herself was.

Her mouth twisted in a grimace. She would make the poor joke of being a fish out of water in this startling new development of her as the replacement PA for the CEO of Grant Industries if her stomach wasn't dipping and turning along with Rocky's distressed flips and circles. Harrison Grant, the elder of the two Grant brothers from Long Island, heirs to an automotive fortune, was notorious for his ability to go through a PA a quarter until her predecessor Tessa Francis had taken over two years ago and tamed the legendary beast. Known for her formidable attitude and ability to whip any living thing into line, including even the snooty, tyrannical Harrison Grant, Tessa would have continued to keep the world a safer place for everybody had she not elected to do the very human thing of getting pregnant and requesting a six-month maternity leave. A reasonable request in many parts of the world, but not in the frantic, pulsing-with-forward-momentum world of Manhattan. Frankie had heard of female CEOs texting from the labor room. Yelling orders in between pushes. Not that that would ever be *her*. When she eventually found the perfect man to settle down with, she'd put raising her children first, unlike her parents who'd had them working in the Masseria family restaurant as soon as they were old enough to bus a table.

But that was then and this was now. She sighed and looked down at the massive amount of work sitting on her desk, unsure of what to tackle next. This wouldn't be *her* mess to weed through had Tessa orchestrated the orderly exit she'd been intent on and found a new PA for her impossible boss. But, according to Tessa, Harrison had simply *refused* to acknowledge she was leaving. His eyes would glaze over at the subject every time she brought it up, until finally, with time running out, Tessa had gone ahead and scheduled the interviews.

That's when the unthinkable had happened. Tessa had gone into premature labor last night while Harrison was on a business trip to Hong Kong, the interviews had been canceled and Frankie had been installed in her place by her magnanimous boss Coburn, who had decided his brother could not be without a PA. Without so much as a "would you mind, Frankie?"

"It's the perfect opportunity to shine," he'd told her in that cajoling voice of his. "Six months with Harrison and you'll be back with a whole new visibility within the company."

Or she would be just another piece of Harrison Grant's road kill, Frankie thought miserably. It had been her dream as long as she'd been old enough to apply eye shadow and visited her friend Olga's father in his swanky Manhattan office, to be a glamorous PA. To wear beautiful suits to the office every day, to live in the vibrant city she loved and to work in the upper echelons of power where all the big deals were made.

If that had gone against her parents' wishes to have her remain in the family restaurant business, so be it. She'd put herself through administrative-assistant school with her tip money, graduated top of her class and gone after her dream.

Landing a job with the insanely handsome, charming younger Grant brother, Coburn, had seemed like her dream come true. Working for the legendary Grant family, who commanded one of America's oldest automotive dynasties from one of Manhattan's marquee skyscrapers, was like taking her "what do I want to be in five years" plan and fast-forwarding it *five years*.

She had seized the opportunity with both hands, molding herself into the epitome of efficiency and professionalism in her six months with Coburn. Her boss's flashing blue eyes and easy smile wore his vice presidency with a stark sex appeal few women could resist, but resist Frankie had. She knew he'd hired her for both her skills and the fact she hadn't fallen all over him in the interview like the others had. In return, he'd been a dream to work with. He appreciated every ounce of the tightly coiled efficiency she brought to his office, reining in his tendency to run askew with his passion for his work.

So why throw her to the wolves so easily? She swallowed past the distressed lump in her throat and took a sip of the herbal French lavender tea that was *supposed* to calm her. Harrison Grant was reputed to be as serious and tunnel-visioned as his younger brother was hot-blooded and impulsive. He had a filthy temper from all accounts. She said "from all accounts" because Tessa had always shielded her from her boss, coming downstairs to

Coburn's office if she needed something rather than expose Frankie to one of his moods. Frankie had accepted the arrangement gladly. She could live without having to deal with the massive ego of the man voted most likely to become president by his peers at Yale, his alma mater. Rumor had it that time wasn't far off for the thirty-three-year-old Harrison. Her father had told her he had enough clout within the business community to run as an independent in the next election and, in these disaffected times, he just might win.

If that happened, Coburn would take over as CEO and Frankie would be head honcho admin. The perfect career scenario by all accounts. *If* she survived the next six months.

A throb pulsed its way from her left temple through to the center of her head as she considered the files Tessa had left marked urgent. A key takeover to help facilitate, shareholder meetings to organize, a trip to India coming up in just weeks... It seemed way beyond her means.

Rocky caught her attention out of the corner of her eye, swimming now in faster, demonic circles as if signaling an imminent disaster. His eyes bulged out of his aristocratic head, his expression foreboding. *Yes, I know*, Frankie wanted to reassure him, *but we have twenty-four hours to prepare for his arrival.*

Which meant she needed to get this work done. Despite her misgivings about the whirlwind change in plans, she was determined to prove to Harrison Grant she was the best PA he could ever have behind Tessa, a modern-day version of Wonder Woman. There was no other possible outcome.

The acquisition file was on top of the heap. Apparently Grant Industries was in the midst of attempting to purchase Siberius, a Russian automotive parts supplier. Job number one, Tessa had managed to tell her on the way to the hospital, was to finish the additional background Harrison had requested to support two outstanding contract negotiation points.

She scanned it, decided it was going to be a long night and rifled around in Tessa's desk until she found some takeout menus. The local Thai place appealed. She ordered herself some dinner to be delivered, slipped off her shoes and got comfortable. At seven, the new security guard brought her food up, noticed she was working alone and said he'd check on her throughout the evening. Deciding Harrison Grant owed her a glass of Pinot Grigio for this one, she procured a bottle of reasonably, but not overly, expensive wine from the heftily stocked bar in his office, took it back to her desk with a glass and opened it.

She was about to dig into her noodles when she realized the restaurant had forgotten to include a fork in the bag. Eating noodles with her hands not being an option, she toed her way around for her shoes and came up empty. She stuck her head under the massive desk and looked for them. It was dark under there and it took her eyes a few moments to adjust. Finally she located a shoe she'd kicked to the left and was holding it triumphantly in her hand and reaching for the second when a deep voice laced with an arctic coolness pierced the solid wooden desk.

"It didn't occur to me you were going to like it, Geoffrey. I pay people like you to make things happen, not for your incredibly insightful strategic thinking."

Harrison Grant. Oh, my God. What is he doing back tonight?

She reared her head up, her skull connecting hard with the inch-thick top of the desk. Stars exploded behind her eyes. A curse escaped her as she dropped the shoe, clasped her head in her hands and absorbed the pulsing aftershocks.

"Good God." The harsh-edged voice came closer. "Geoffrey, I'm going to have to call you back."

Frankie was vaguely aware of strong male hands levering her chair away from the desk and lifting her chin. She blinked as he pulled her hands from her head, and tipped her skull back. A clear head might have been a good weapon to face Harrison Grant with for the first time, but her cerebral matter was hazy, her vision shadowy as she took him in at close range. Dressed in a black trench coat in deference to the rainy, overcast New York day, he was tall, imposingly tall. The charcoal-gray suit he wore beneath the trench coat, the amount of rough stubble shading his aristocratic jaw and the laser-like stare of his black eyes under designer glasses made her giddily wonder if he was the devil himself.

Biting out a low curse, he tossed his cell phone on the desk and cupped the back of her head with one of his big hands, his fingers pressing into her scalp to feel for a bump. When he located the growing mass that was causing the deep throb in her head, a furrow ruffled his brow. "What exactly were you doing down there?"

"Shoes," Frankie muttered absently as the world began to right itself. She sucked in a couple of deep breaths and examined him closer. Along with those deadly dark eyes, he had a perfect aquiline nose that framed a firm, wide mouth. Apparently the devil came in extremely good-looking versions that also smelled amazing.

He held up three fingers. "How many?"

"Three."

"What day is it?"

"Tuesday, the sixth of August."

He let his fingers slide from her head. His black gaze, however, remained pinned on her face. "Unless this is *Goldilocks and the Three Bears* redone to feature a brunette, *you* are sitting in the wrong chair."

Her heart sped up in her chest at his low, silky tone, as curiosity radiated from the inky darkness of his somewhat mesmerizing gaze. "What if this is actually the *right* chair?" she offered in an attempt to defuse the tension.

His mouth curved. "Now I know that would have to be a tale, because this chair belongs to my assistant, Tessa, and *you*," he murmured, his sweeping stare taking in all of her, including a rather comprehensive study of her legs, "are not her."

Frankie swallowed hard and followed his gaze. In the commotion, her conservative skirt had ridden up her thighs, baring the lacy black pull-ups that were her one nod toward femininity in her proper office attire. *Oh, God.* She tugged the summer-weight wool back to her knees, so much heat rushing to her face she might as well have been on fire. With difficulty, she moved her gaze back up to his and saw…*disappointment*?

"Tessa," she murmured, searching vainly for a way to rescue the situation, "went into premature labor and had her baby last night. Co—" Her words died in her throat as a flash of silver glinted across the room. She blinked, thinking her swimming head had manufactured it, but when she looked again, the sight of two armed guards bearing down on them, guns drawn, made her mouth drop open.

"Put your hands in the air."

The guards roared the words at them, their attention fixed on Harrison. Frankie stuck her hands in the air, her heart slamming so violently against her chest she thought she might pass out. Her gaze sat frozen on the glare of the lights reflected off the silver barrels.

She tore her panicked gaze away finally, flicking it to Harrison, whose face had a bemused look on it. Instead of following the guard's orders, he put his palms on his thighs and moved to straighten.

"I said put your hands in the air," the guard bellowed, waving his gun at Harrison. *"Now."*

Her boss put his suit-clad arms in the air in a slow, exaggerated movement. He might have acquiesced, but every muscle in his big body was tensed to revolt, his black gaze glittering. They sensed it, their eyes remaining trained on him. "Hands behind your back."

The CEO's mouth parted. "I think—"

"Hands behind your back."

Her boss put his hands behind his back, a dark thundercloud stealing over his face. The guard closest to him holstered his gun, turned the CEO around with a careful appreciation of his powerful frame and snapped handcuffs around his wrists.

Oh, my God. Frankie's frozen brain registered the guards now as Grant Industries security guards. But what were they doing arresting Harrison Grant?

The guard with his gun still drawn crooked a finger at Frankie. "Over here."

The logical part of her brain told her she didn't want anything to do with a man with a gun. Even one in uniform. Maybe these men were *posing* as Grant security guards. Maybe they wanted to *rob* them...

"Move," the guard growled at her. Frankie's behind left the chair in a hurry. She wasn't sure how she did it because her legs were mush, but she wobbled over to where the guard stood, shaking so hard her teeth chattered. His partner pushed Harrison down in the chair she'd vacated.

"What happened?" the guard beside Frankie asked.

She gave him an uncomprehending look. 'Wh-what do you mean? You just came tearing in here..."

"You hit the panic button."

Panic button. What panic button? She vaguely remembered something in her training about an emergency button she could press if anything ever happened, but she'd laughed it off at the time, thinking it would be more useful for handling Coburn's discarded girlfriends than an actual *situation.* Hers had been on the wall beside her desk.

Her gaze slid to the wall beside Tessa's desk. No button. "It's under the desk on the left," the guard said.

Under the desk? Her gaze slid to the big mahogany desk where her new boss sat *handcuffed*. A sick feeling enveloped her. She must have hit the button by mistake when Harrison walked in and startled her.

Oh, good lord.

The guard pointed at Harrison. "Pete said you were up here working alone. *He* had his hands on you when we arrived."

Frankie's stomach rolled. The guards were new. They'd changed to a different company last week. "*He,*" she clarified weakly, "is Harrison Grant, the CEO of this company. I hit the panic button by mistake."

The guards assumed identical gray complexions. Harrison Grant's expression moved from one of disbelief to an even darker countenance Frankie chose to avoid.

The guard beside her turned and surveyed the tall, elegant male in the chair dubiously. "You're supposed to be abroad."

Harrison's dark-as-night eyes glittered back at him. "I parked underground and took the back elevators."

"You don't look like your picture."

Frankie wanted to scream not to poke the beast. The glimmer in the CEO's eyes turned deadly. "I can assure you that she," he said, nodding his head at Frankie, "whoever she is, is telling the truth. Being the workaholic I am, I've acquired glasses since my last headshot."

"You got some ID?"

Her boss dipped his chin. "Front pocket."

The guard closest to Harrison retrieved his wallet from his jacket with a ginger movement that made Frankie hysterically wonder what he thought he'd do. *Bite him?* The man had his hands manacled behind his back. The guard flipped the wallet open, scanned it and went even grayer. Bile climbed the back of Frankie's throat.

"Apologies for the confusion." The guard slid the wallet back into Harrison's pocket. "The situation you two were in, the bottle of wine, we read it wrong."

Frankie's gaze flew to the bottle of Pinot Grigio on the desk. *Oh, heavens.* The way Harrison had been leaning over her... They couldn't possibly have thought this had been an assignation gone wrong...could they?

The grim look on her boss's face suggested that's exactly what they'd thought. He directed a laser-like stare at the guard. "You have exactly five seconds to get these cuffs off me."

The guard retrieved his key and had Harrison stand and turn around while he removed the cuffs. "We work on rotation," he said apologetically as he slid them off. "We're new in this building. So sorry we didn't recognize you, Mr. Grant."

Her boss extended his arms and flexed his wrists to get the circulation going. "Well, now that we've established we're all new, except *me*," he drawled, planting his gaze on Frankie, "and we've also determined this was *not* a romantic encounter with a bad ending for the sake of the gossip mill, perhaps you can tell me who *you* are, Goldilocks not being a suitable answer."

She bit down hard on her lip. "Francesca Masseria. Your brother's PA. Actually...yours now."

"Is that so?" Frankie watched her career hang in the balance of that dark, unfathomable gaze. It occurred to her she'd be lucky to get shipped back to Coburn.

The CEO turned his attention to the guards. "I suggest you start taking some regular walks around the building to learn who people are."

The guards nodded in unison. "Absolutely, sir."

Harrison waved a hand at them. "Go."

Frankie stood quaking in the center of the suddenly silent foyer as the silver-uniformed security detail disappeared toward the elevators. Her boss stood, legs planted wide in front of her, a distinct smoky gray aura surrounding his muscular frame.

She liked him better in handcuffs.

Harrison's mouth curled in a mocking smile. "Despite what you may have heard otherwise, Ms. Masseria, I am not a monster."

The rebuke stung her into silence. "I'm to assume," he drawled, "that you are filling in as Tessa's replacement until we can find someone else?"

"Actually Coburn has asked me to work with you until Tessa comes back."

His gaze narrowed on her speculatively. "Coburn thinks the sun rises and sets with your appearance in the office every morning, Ms. Masseria. How could we possibly expect him to get along without you for six months?"

Warmth stung her cheeks at the unexpected compliment. "I'm sure he'll manage," she demurred. "Nobody's irreplaceable."

"Tessa is."

She flinched. He considered her for a moment, his unnervingly precise gaze seeming to take a visual X-ray of her for further examination. "I need some sleep," he concluded. "Take your dinner and the wine, go home, get some rest and we'll talk about this in the morning."

Frankie took a step toward him. "I have some—"

He lifted a hand. "I have just flown sixteen hours to get home to be told my brilliant right hand and irreplaceable PA is in the hospital having a baby while in the midst of helping me with a crucial acquisition. I've been put in handcuffs by my own security team and had guns pointed at my face. And if that isn't enough, my body is heavily protesting the jump in time zones. The only thing," he underscored harshly, "that is going to make me feel like a human being at this point in time is a good stiff drink and a horizontal position on a bed that is my own. And *you*, Ms. Masseria, are the only thing standing between me and it. So unless you would like to finish this conversation *there*, put your shoes on and let's call it a night."

Her mouth fell open. Had he actually just said that? And why did she find that idea vastly exciting instead of incredibly inappropriate?

His eyes widened imperceptibly, then narrowed. "Joking, Ms. Masseria. Go home."

She looked down at her bare feet on the marble, her muted pink toenails the ultimate in complete humiliation. *Never* in the six months she had worked for Coburn had she ever acted this unprofessional.

But, she told herself lifting her chin, the first step toward redemption was moving on. They would come back in the morning as he'd said, she would show him what she was made of and it would all be fine.

"I will see you in the morning, then. We'll go through the urgent items then."

He inclined his head. She turned and headed toward her desk. Harrison's deep baritone halted her. "Ms. Masseria?"

She turned around.

"Which hospital is Tessa in?"

"Mount Sinai."

The humor that flickered in his eyes then caught her off guard. It made him look almost *human*. "Do you think you can send her some flowers from me in the morning without calling in the cavalry?"

She pressed her lips together. "I'll have it taken care of."

The beast was safely ensconced in his office repacking his briefcase when she ducked her head in to say she was leaving. He wished her an absentminded good-night and told her to take a taxi. Exhausted, she did. When she got home she swallowed down two painkillers for her throbbing head, reheated and ate half the noodles, then immersed herself in a hot bath.

She had just laid her head on the pillow when her cell phone rang. She frowned and pulled it off the bedside table. *Unknown caller.* She was about to decline the call when the thought they'd call back and wake her up made her reach for it.

"Francesca," she murmured sleepily into the phone.

"Just checking that whack on your head didn't do you in."

Harrison Grant's deep voice sent her jackknifing upright. How the heck did he have her mobile number? *The company directory.* Right.

"I was concerned about you. I should have sent you to the hospital to have your head looked at."

"I'm fine," she croaked. Without that arctic chill in it, his voice was the sexiest thing she'd ever heard over a phone line—deep, velvety and laced with a husky fatigue that reached all the way to her nerve endings.

Hadn't he been about to go to bed? *Was he calling from bed?*

She shook her head, wincing as the throbbing reminded her she shouldn't do that. How could she possibly be experiencing erotic images of a man who would likely send her packing tomorrow?

"Do you live with anyone?"

She blinked. "I—I don't think that's the kind of question I have to answer, is it?"

The warm, very masculine laughter that reached her from the other end of the line made the hairs on the back of her neck stand up. "I wasn't inquiring about your dating life, Francesca. I was going to say if you do have a roommate or significant other, you should get them to wake you up every few hours to make sure you don't have a concussion. They can be very serious."

"Oh." Frankie swallowed back a fresh wave of mortification. "That's very thoughtful of you. I do—have a roommate—that is. She's out but I'll do that."

"Good. See you in the morning, then."

She muttered good-night and disconnected the call. Punching down her pillow, she welcomed the breeze that wafted in through her old Victorian window, cooling her heated cheeks. Harrison Grant could add *ridiculously naive* to his new PA's description after tonight's debacle. That was, if he chose to keep her... She wasn't laying odds on it.

CHAPTER TWO

HARRISON'S MOUTH WAS DRY—parched with anticipation. His entire body was rigid with the expectation of physical satisfaction as the beautiful brunette rose from his office chair and pushed him down into it. Her soft, lush thighs hitting his as she straddled him made his heart catch in his throat. The lacy black stockings she wore with garters made an appearance, sending his blood coursing through his veins. *He had to have her. Now.*

Her long, silky dark hair brushed his face as she bent and kissed him. His hands reached blindly for the lace on her thighs, needing to touch. She slapped his fingers away. "Wait," she instructed in a husky, incredibly sexy voice. "Not yet."

He started to protest, but she pressed her fingers to his lips, reached behind her and pulled out something metal that glinted in the dim light of the desk lamp. *Handcuffs. Mother of God.*

He jackknifed to a sitting position. Sweat dripped from his body. Reality slapped him in the face as he discovered he wasn't being seduced in his office chair by a stunning brunette; he was in his own bed. Stunning disappointment followed. His racing heart *wanted* her. His body was pulsing, crying out for her to finish what she'd started...

An appalled feeling spread through him. He only knew

one set of eyes that particular shade of gray. *His new PA. He had been fantasizing about his new PA.*

A harsh curse left his mouth. He swung his legs over the side of the bed and brought his breathing under control. His dream had been wholly inappropriate. Never had he brought sex into the office and never would he. The guns and the handcuffs had truly pushed him over the edge.

And the stockings. That might actually have been the worst.

The birds were already singing. He poured himself into the shower and attempted to clear his head. The dull throb in his temple he'd been harboring for days was still there, reminding him normal human beings needed at least six hours of sleep on a regular basis to function at optimal performance.

His mouth twisted. Not that anyone considered him a normal human being. They thought he was a machine.

He toweled himself off, put his aching body in front of a cup of coffee and the newspaper and tried to focus on the rather mundane headlines. But his utterly incongruous dream kept working its way into his head.

He never had fantasies like that. He identified his urges, satisfied them according to a convenient slot in his insane schedule with a woman who didn't mind his lack of commitment, then he filed them back where they belonged: extracurricular activity that came after work.

His coffee cup went *thump* on the breakfast table. There was no way he could have *that* woman working for him. He took a last gulp of coffee, tossed the paper aside and headed for the gym in his building. He'd talk to Coburn when he got in. Tell him this just wasn't going to work.

Coburn strolled into his office a few minutes after he'd landed there, looking disgustingly fresh and sharp in a navy blue Armani suit. That they were both early risers who appreciated the benefits of physical exercise was about their only similarity. Even their intent in doing it was different. Harrison slotted it into his schedule like any other appointment, because if he didn't he'd be regularly seeing a heart specialist somewhere around fifty. It was in the Grant family genes.

Coburn, on the other hand, pursued mad daredevil-type sports that skirted death on a regular basis. Paragliding, mountain climbing, bicycle racing in European countries with tiny alpine ledges for tracks. Not to mention what it did for his physique, which maintained the steady flow of females in and out of his life so there would never be a dearth where he'd have to consider what the hell he was actually doing. His ex-wife had messed him up and messed him up good. But since that topic had long been considered subject *non grata*, Harrison began with the topic of the hour.

"How selfless of you to loan me Francesca Masseria." He sat back in his desk chair and took his Kenyan brew with him.

"Isn't it?" Coburn grinned. He took the seat opposite him. "Sometimes I can sacrifice for the greater good, H."

Harrison frowned. He hated when Coburn called him H and he knew it. "How many times have you slept with her?"

His brother gave him a look of mock offence. "Not even once. Although it's tempting. If God designed the perfect woman and set her down on this earth, it'd be Frankie and those legs of hers."

"Francesca," Harrison corrected, refusing to go there. "And you don't speak about an employee in that manner."

You just had hot, explicit dreams about them.

Coburn rolled his eyes.

"You've moaned about not having a good PA for years, then when you get one you love, you hand her over to me. *Why?*"

His brother trained his striking blue gaze on him the way he did the board when he wanted them on their knees. "Self-preservation. Frankie is a knockout. Of late, I've discovered she has a crush on me, although not one of her very proper bones would ever admit it. It's only a matter of time before we end up in bed together and I want to *prevent* that from happening because I want to *keep* her as my PA." He shrugged. "So I send her to the school of Harrison for six months, you train her with that regimental authority of yours, and I get her back when I am fully immersed in someone else, better than she was before."

If Harrison hadn't known his younger brother as well as he did, he would have assumed he was joking. But this was Coburn, who possessed every genetic trait the youngest born was created to feature, including an exaggerated sense of the need for his own independence from everything, including serious relationships with females and his responsibilities to Grant Industries.

"You do realize if HR heard even a quarter of that speech, I'd have to fire you."

Coburn lifted a Rolex-clad hand. "Then I retire to the south of Italy, road-race most of the year and manage my shares from there. Either works for me."

Harrison tamped down the barely restrained aggression he felt toward his younger brother. "She's not experienced enough for the job."

"This is Frankie we're talking about. You'll see when you meet her."

"Francesca," Harrison corrected again. "And I met her last night."

Coburn frowned. "How? You've only just gotten back."

"She was working late. Likely trying to make sense of things with Tessa's abrupt departure... I stopped in for a file."

"Your own fault," Coburn pointed out. "You've known for months Tessa was leaving and you did nothing about it."

Because he couldn't bear to be without his mind-bogglingly good PA who made his insane life bearable. Avoidance had been preferable…

"Anyway," Coburn continued, "it's the perfect solution for both of us. Frankie is incredible. Green, yes, but just as smart as Tessa. And," he added, pausing for effect, "she speaks Russian."

"Russian?"

"Fluently. Plus Italian, but I'm thinking the Russian is going to be more useful to you right now."

"How does she speak Russian?"

Coburn frowned. "I think she said her best friend is Russian. Something like that…"

Given his solitary goal in life at the moment was to obliterate Anton Markovic, the man who'd put his father in his grave, and negotiations to make it happen were at an extremely fragile stage with Leonid Aristov balking at the deal to acquire his company, a PA who could speak Russian could be a very valuable asset.

The amusement faded from Coburn's face. "You don't have to keep at this, you know? Father is ten feet under. He's never going to see you bring Markovic down. You're doing this for *you*, Harrison, not him. And lord knows you need a life."

His hands curled tightly around his coffee mug, his knuckles gleaming white. His younger brother's lack of interest in avenging the man who had built this company was a position he had long understood. His personal opinions on how *he* lived his life? Meaningless, when he had always been the only person holding this company together.

He put his coffee cup down on the desk before he crushed it between his fingers, and focused his gaze on his brother. "How about you keep playing with those international markets and making us money like you do and save your philosophical sermons for someone who cares?"

Coburn's easygoing expression slid into one approaching the frigidness of his. "Someday you're going to realize that cold heart of yours has left you alone in this big empty world, H. And when you do, nobody is going to care anymore. But that's okay, because you will have your vengeance."

Harrison flashed him a "see yourself out" look. Coburn stood, straightened his suit coat and paused by the door. "I gave you Frankie because you need her. But if you so much as cause one tear to roll down her face, you'll answer to me for it. You hear me?"

His brother disappeared in a wave of expensive aftershave. Harrison glanced at the clock on the wall. Seven-thirty. It was 7:30 a.m. and already he was exhausted. His *life* exhausted him.

Frankie came to work armed and ready, although that might be an unfortunate turn of phrase given last night's occurrences. "Okay," she admitted to Rocky, who still looked less than thrilled to be in his new surroundings, but marginally calmer than yesterday, "let's just say that *was* a bad choice of words."

She had worn her most expensive suit today, which wasn't very expensive given her limited budget for a wardrobe after paying rent for the brownstone apartment she shared with Josephine. But she'd altered it so it looked custom, the lightweight, charcoal-gray tailored jacket and skirt hugging her curves without broadcasting the depth of them. The color did something for her dark hair and gray eyes she considered inferior to those of her striking female siblings, and her chignon, well, it was the most perfect she'd ever attempted. Geri from Accounting had looked noticeably envious this morning on the elevator, and if there was a morning she needed to win their dueling hairstyle competition, it was this.

She needed all the confidence she could muster facing her new boss this morning. *If* he decided to keep her.

Dumping her purse in her drawer, she ignored her rumbling stomach. She'd tried to eat, but she hadn't been able to get any breakfast down except a slice of toast and juice. She refused to call it nerves because she needed to have full armor on this morning. She'd been noticeably jumpy when the security guard had checked her ID downstairs and that scene of her boss in handcuffs kept replaying itself over and over in her head.

And then there had been his bedroom voice last night on the phone and her resulting descent into lunacy... Her stomach dipped. Today she was going to revert back to her usual, capable self: five steps ahead of her boss at all times, unruffleable and cheerful no matter what the request. And she was going to stay far, far away from that panic button. In fact, she was going to cover it with tape.

Mouth set in a firm gesture of determination, she ran her hands over her head to ensure every hair was in place and, satisfied she was all cool sophistication, walked toward Harrison's office. His brisk, clipped voice directing a conference call stopped her in her tracks. This was good. It would give her time to get organized. Having a boss who came in at 7:00 a.m. left you a bit flat-footed.

She made herself a cup of tea and scanned her email. Tessa had evaded her husband's watchful eye long enough to send her some notes from her smartphone. Frankie sank back in her seat, took a sip of her tea and ploughed gratefully through her list of Harrison rules.

Triage his email first thing in the morning and keep an eye on anything urgent. He's married to his smart-

phone, but the volume is overwhelming. You might have to jump in.

Take his phone messages on the pink message pad on the desk, not the blue one, and don't write on the second half of the page. He likes to make notes for follow-up there.

Fail on that one. She'd put a stack of messages on Harrison's desk last night that had used the whole page. She'd fix that today...

Don't ever put a call through to him from any woman other than a business contact or his mother. Casual dates like to pose as girlfriends when they're not. He hasn't had a regular woman in his life for a while. Apparently, as you likely know from the gossip pages, he's supposed to be marrying Cecily Hargrove to cement the family dynasty, but I have seen no evidence of her of late, so proceed with caution and never talk with the press.

Fascinating. She was nothing if not discreet.

If he asks you to send flowers to a woman, send calla lilies. They're his go-to choice. If he ever asks you to send anything else, you can bet she's "the one."

Frankie smiled. Although she couldn't imagine Harrison Grant ever falling for a woman like that.

Somewhere between eight and nine he will call you into his office to put together a to-do list for the day. Execute the list in the order he gives it to you. He's like the Swiss train system. He needs things done in a certain way at a certain time. Stick to this and you'll be fine.

Wow. He was even more of a control freak than she was.

And, finally, don't ever interrupt him when he's on a conference call. Put a note in front of him if you have to. But since he spends four or five hours on them a day, do bring him coffee. The Kenyan blend—black. He figures out lunch himself.

Ugh. She glanced toward Harrison's office. She hadn't done that. That necessitated facing him.

Getting to her feet, she brewed a steaming cup of Kenyan blend in the kitchen, slipped into Harrison's office with the stealth of a cat and headed toward his desk. He was on speakerphone, pacing in front of the windows like a lethal weapon as he talked. She had almost made it to the desk when he turned around.

Her nerves, the intensity of his black stare and the depth of his intimidating good looks in the pinstriped three-piece suit he wore like billionaire armor set her hand to shaking. *Hard.* Coffee sloshed over the side of the mug and singed her hand. Fire raced along the tender skin between her thumb and forefinger. She bit back a howl of pain, set the mug on the desk, speed walked to the outer office and put it under cold water in the kitchen.

A couple of minutes under the tap made the burn bearable. She spread some salve from the emergency kit on it and retraced her steps into Harrison's office where he was still spewing point after point into the speakerphone. Her gaze locked on the precious dark wood of the desk. A large water ring stared back at her, embedded into the wood. *Oh, no. Please, no.*

She scrubbed at it to no avail. Moved the mug to a

coaster and retreated to her desk. Sat there mentally calculating how long it would take him to fire her. Five more minutes on the conference call, a couple of minutes to think of how he was going to do it and *bam*—she'd be gone.

"Get ready to move again," she told Rocky.

Coward, his elegant snout accused.

"You try dealing with tall, dark and dangerous. Heavy on the dangerous."

Footsteps on the marble brought her head up. Dangerous had emerged from his office and conference call, three minutes early. He was looking at her as if she was quite possibly mad. "Who are you talking to?"

Frankie waved her hand at Rocky. "Rocky Balboa, meet Harrison Grant."

A dark brow lifted. "Rocky Balboa as in the boxer, Rocky?"

She nodded, heat filling her cheeks.

"You talk to a fish?"

"That is true, yes."

There was a profound silence. Frankie closed her eyes and waited for the two words to come. *You're fired.*

"Give me your hand."

She opened her eyes. He was looking at her burnt hand. "It's fine," she refused, tucking it under the desk. "I'm so sorry about the coffee stain. I'll see if the cleaners can work some magic."

"It can be sanded and refinished."

At an *insane* cost. Why was he being so reasonable about it? She swallowed hard. "Do you want to go through the priorities for today?"

"No, I want to see your hand. *Now.*"

She stuck it out. He took it in his and ran the pad of his thumb over her fire-engine-red knuckles. Frankie's stomach did a slow roll at the innocent contact. It didn't seem innocent coming from her fire-breathing boss. It seemed—disturbing.

He sighed. "If we're going to be able to work together, you have to stop being afraid of me."

Gray eyes met black. He *wanted* her to keep working for him?

"I'm not afraid of you."

His thumb settled on the pulse racing at the base of her wrist. "Either you are or you have the fastest resting pulse of any human being I've encountered."

She yanked her hand away. "Okay, maybe I am—just a little intimidated. Last night wasn't exactly a great introduction."

"Stand up."

"Pardon me?"

"Stand up."

She eyed him for a moment, then rose to her full five feet eight inches, which, with the added height of her shoes, brought her eyes level with his smooth, perfectly shaven jaw.

"Look at me."

She lifted her gaze, bracing herself for that intimidating stare of his up close, and it was no less formidable than she'd expected it to be. Except she learned there were exotic flecks of amber in it that warmed you up if you dared to look. They disputed the coldness went all the way through him, suggested if he chose to use the full power of that beautiful, complex gaze on you in a particular way for a particular purpose you might melt in his hands like a hundred-plus pounds of useless female.

His mouth tilted. "I'm intense to work with, Francesca, but I'm not the big bad wolf. Nor am I unreasonable. Especially when I've had a full night's sleep."

Right.

"Now say it again like you mean it."

"Say what?"

"I am not afraid of you, Harrison. You're not that scary." Her mouth twisted. "You're making fun of me."

His sexy mouth curved. "I'm curing you. *Say it.*"

She forced herself to ignore the glitter of humor in his eyes, which took his dangerously attractive vibe to a whole other level. "I am not afraid of you, Harrison. You're not that scary."

"Don't ask me to take that seriously."

She pursed her lips, feeling ridiculous. Injected an iron will into her tone. "I am not afraid of you, Harrison. You're not that scary."

He nodded approvingly. "Better."

His undoubtedly sinfully expensive aftershave worked its way into her pores. They said a person's own chemistry combined with a fragrance to make it what it was and in this case, it was spicy, all male and intoxicating. She wished he would take a step back and relinquish her personal space.

"Francesca?"

"Yes."

His gaze was hooded. Unreadable. "I agree last night was a…disconcerting way to meet. I suggest we wipe it from our memories and start fresh."

The message conveyed was unmistakable. He wasn't just talking about the handcuffs…he was talking about the attraction between them.

She firmed her mouth, taking a step backward. "I think that's an excellent idea. Exactly what I was thinking this morning."

"Good." He waved a hand toward the door. "Back in five. Can we go over the day then?"

She nodded. "Should I really? Call you Harrison, I mean?"

"Tessa does…so yes."

Frankie watched him go, then sat down with the loose limbs of a prisoner who'd just escaped execution and was profoundly grateful for the fact. She found her notebook, carried her tea into Harrison's office and was pondering why Cecily Hargrove hadn't been named Mrs. Harrison Grant yet if he really did have a sense of humor along with the brooding sex appeal, when the phone rang.

She went and picked up the call at her own desk. Leonid Aristov's assistant announced herself briskly and rather snootily. Frankie shifted into Russian, feeling a tug of satisfaction when the other woman paused, took the development in and continued on in her own language. "Mr. Aristov," Tatiana Yankov stated, "would like to have a meeting with Mr. Grant in London next week."

Frankie glanced at Harrison's schedule. "Impossible," she regretted smoothly. If he had time to go to the bathroom it would be a miracle. "Perhaps the last week of August?"

"If Mr. Grant would like to discuss closing this deal with Mr. Aristov, which I believe he is eager to do, he needs to be *in London, next week*," the other woman repeated, as if unconvinced of her command of the language.

Frankie kept her tone perfectly modulated. "Could you tell me what this meeting is to be about? That way I can discuss it with Mr. Grant."

"I couldn't say," came the distant response. "Mr. Aristov simply asked me to schedule the meeting. Call me back when you have a date." Tatiana rattled off a London phone number.

Frankie jotted the number down. "I can't schedule a meeting without knowing what it's a—" A dial tone sounded in her ear. She held the phone away from her and stared at it. She had *not* just done that. She was still staring at the phone when Harrison walked past her desk, a steaming cup of coffee in his hand. "Ready?"

She followed him into his office. "That was Leonid Aristov's assistant on the phone."

He wheeled around, coffee sloshing in his mug. Frankie's gaze flew to the boiling liquid as it skimmed the rim of the cup, wavered there like the high seas, then elected to stay in.

"What did she want?"

Frankie returned her gaze to his face. "Aristov wants a meeting next week."

"A meeting?" A frown furrowed his brow. "He's already agreed to everything in principle. Did you ask what the meeting was for?"

"I did. She wouldn't give me anything. She just said Aristov wanted the meeting and it had to be next week."

"Have you had a look at my schedule?" He trained his gaze on her as if she had an IQ of fifty. "This deal is scheduled to pass regulatory authorities next month, Ms. Masseria. I don't fly around the world on a *whim* because Leonid Aristov wants me to."

Great, they were back to *Ms. Masseria*… She closed her eyes and drew a deep breath. "I'm not suggesting you should. But she was very rude. She hung up on me."

He blinked at her. "Why would she hang up on you?"

"She seemed busy. I was trying to probe for more information when she cut me off and hung up."

He impaled her on that razor-sharp gaze of his that had turned him from beauty to the beast in the space of a round second. Then he thrust out an elegant hand. "Give me the number."

She held on to it. "I can call her back. Just give me some direc—"

"Give me the number."

Frankie went back to her desk, grabbed the pink message pad, marched into his office and gave it to him. And called him a bad name in her head. *A big, bad one.* She had liked him so much five minutes ago. She really had.

He was dialing the ice queen back when she left. She put her head down and started working through his email. God forbid she'd missed something they'd need for their briefing.

He came out minutes later. She suppressed a victorious thrill at the dark scowl on his face. "Cancel everything for Thursday and Friday of next week. We'll fly to London Wednesday night, meet with Aristov Thursday morning then leave ourselves a buffer day in case we have more to talk about with him."

"Did you find out what the meeting is for?"

"No," he said icily. "It's all going to be a pleasant surprise."

Frankie kept her eyes on the notepad she was scribbling on. "You said *Wednesday* night we fly out?"

"Yes. Do you have a problem with that?"

'Yes— No—" She lifted her gaze to his in a pained look. "It's just that I have a special—commitment Wednesday night."

His expression darkened. "Taking into account you actually want this job, Ms. Masseria, you will learn to eat, breathe and sleep it for the next six months. So I suggest you…uncommit yourself."

She bit her lip and nodded. If there was one event this year she didn't want to miss, it was Tomasino Giardelli's eightieth birthday party. But this was her job and she needed it. And it had gotten off to a rocky enough start as it was.

"May I ask a question?"

He waved a hand at her.

"I've been working through that last bit of research you wanted Tessa to compile for the Aristov deal. I get what you're asking for, but, well, Coburn always counseled me to understand the big picture so I can visualize what you need in the end product. Give you my best work… What I don't get," she ventured frowning, "is why Grant Industries is buying a company that mirrors the exact capabilities of one of our subsidiaries…"

His jaw went lax. She had the distinct impression he didn't know how to answer her question from the silence that followed. But of course he did, didn't he?

"Coburn," he rasped finally, "and I have different management styles, Ms. Masseria. Coburn likes to collaborate, to involve people in decisions. I don't. I prefer people to *do what I tell them*. That's what works for me."

Not a tyrant? Blood rushed to her face as if he'd physically slapped her. "Fine," she agreed quietly. "If I have a specific question I'll ask it."

"Excellent." He scraped a hand through his hair, looking weary for a man who hadn't yet hit lunch. "Book us a suite at the Chatsfield so we can work."

She nodded. Then, unable to help herself because she needed to get the rules straight, she asked, "Would you prefer me to use Mr. Grant instead of Harrison now that you seem to have reverted to Ms. Masseria?"

He gave her a long, hard look. Frankie's stomach dipped but she held her ground with a lifted chin.

"My slip," he stated in a lethally quiet voice. "First names are fine."

She nodded and turned back to her PC. Harrison started toward his office, then paused outside it. She looked up expectantly.

"We are pursuing Siberius because it commands alternate markets to the ones we already have control of with Taladan. It makes business sense."

"Got it."

He turned to go. She shifted her gaze back to her computer.

"Oh, and, *Francesca*?"

She looked up.

"Please don't write on the bottom half of these." He waved the pink message pad at her. "It distracts me."

He disappeared into his office. Frankie raised her gaze heavenward. Not only did she have to survive life with Harrison Grant for six months, which must prove she was doing penance for something she wasn't yet aware of, she now had to fly across the Atlantic with him for a crucial meeting that seemed shaky in nature.

Nothing could go wrong with that scenario, could it?

At least there weren't air marshals on privately chartered flights…

CHAPTER THREE

FRANKIE ARRIVED AT Teterboro Airport in New Jersey on Wednesday night of the following week as bruised and battered as Rocky Balboa himself after going fifteen rounds with Harrison Grant over the past week. He'd been tense and edgy ever since that call from Leonid Aristov's assistant, pushing them both to the limits of their endurance in ensuring every *i* was dotted and every *t* crossed in advance of their meeting.

She was dead on her feet *and they hadn't even left yet*. Plus, she didn't sleep on planes…

The limousine pulled to a stop on the runway in front of the black-and-red-logoed Grant Industries jet. She slid out and waited while the driver deposited her luggage on the asphalt. If she was curious as to why her boss was obsessed with a deal that, in the great scheme of things, would be a minor acquisition for a behemoth like Grant Industries, she didn't voice her thoughts. She was paid to *do*, apparently. That was all. And if that made her frustratingly aware she wasn't turning in her best work, if she knew she'd do better had he been just a bit more collaborative and explained things fully, there was nothing to be done about it. She had tamed her natural instinct to question.

Survival was the game of the day.

Hand arced over her eyes, she searched for her boss

in the still blinding final rays of the sun. He was standing by the jet speaking to a gray-haired man in his fifties Frankie thought she recognized as the chairman of the senate committee on foreign affairs. She knew this only because her father loved politics and followed it closely, which meant the entire Masseria clan also did so by virtue of association.

The conversation between Harrison and Oliver Burchell looked like more than a friendly hello. *Was he planning a run for the presidency?* The Grant family was as connected as any family in the upper echelons of political power so it absolutely made sense they could put Harrison on every ballot in the country as an independent candidate. But he was only thirty-three. He had his hands full running a company that had just gotten back on its feet. Was now the right timing?

Her boss registered her arrival with that ever-watchful gaze of his. He held up two fingers. Frankie nodded and took the time to study him in a brief, unobserved perusal. She hadn't yet gotten used to how extraordinarily good-looking he was up close. Today, in dark-wash jeans and a crisp white shirt, sleeves rolled up to his elbows to reveal muscular forearms, he looked like her college accounting professor, except where Frankie had considered him nerdily cute, Harrison was a whole other ball game. He was Clark Kent good-looking with his impressive physique and dark designer glasses, as if he was about to dash into a phone booth to go save the world.

Her mouth twisted. Air Force One was about to acquire a whole new sex appeal.

The senator clapped Harrison on the back and moved off toward the plane sitting behind the Grant Industries jet. Frankie pulled in a Harrison-fortifying breath as he strode toward her. "Ready to go?"

"As ready as I'll ever be," she said brightly.

He lifted a brow at her as he stopped in front of her. "I've been that bad?"

She knew when to keep her thoughts to herself. "I meant I'm not a good flyer. I just need to get this over with."

"So I should tell the pilot to lock the doors to the cockpit?"

She made a face at the amusement twisting his lips. "We haven't had one disaster since the coffee incident. Perhaps we can let that joke lie?"

"I'm still keeping my guard up." He pointed their luggage out to the crew who loaded it on to the plane. "You know, statistically speaking," he counseled, gesturing for her to proceed him up the stairs, "flying is safer than any other form of travel. You should be more frightened of getting on the freeway."

"I *am* frightened of getting on the freeway. And fear of flying is not a rational thing," she countered, climbing the steps.

"Ah, but I thought that's what you are…rational Francesca Masseria, who needs to figure out how things work before she fully commits."

She looked down at him from her higher position on the stairs. Who was he really? The big bad wolf or this intuitive, sardonic version of him who made the occasional visit? And did she dare say what she thought?

She exhaled a breath. "I perform better when I have a clear sense of the objectives. I'm more left-brained than Tessa. I need guidance. I can promise if you offer that to me I will give you what you need."

His gaze narrowed. The undercurrent between them that always seemed to simmer below the surface sprang to life. A tutelage of a far different type was filtering through that brilliant mind… She would have bet money on it. Heat rose to her cheeks. He studied the twin spots of fire. Then he turned it off with one of those dismissive looks.

"All right, Francesca Masseria," he drawled. "We'll give it a shot. You've been a good sport this week. I like that about you. You have a question—a *good one*—ask. I'll do my best to answer it."

He strode past her up the stairs and into the jet before she could close her mouth. No way had the beast just thrown her a crumb. She thought maybe they should break out the champagne, particularly when once seated and buckled in opposite Harrison in a bank of four seats, she realized how *small* the plane was. She'd never flown on a private jet before. Coburn preferred to travel on his own and have her work from the office, and this, *this* little plane didn't look hearty enough to carry them across the Atlantic if a storm hit as it had on her last trip to Mexico.

Her shoulders climbed to her ears in protest as the pilot revved the engines.

"Relax," Harrison ordered, pulling his laptop out of his briefcase. "This is going to be the smoothest ride of your life, trust me."

"Now you've jinxed us," Frankie said grimly. She picked up her cell phone to turn it off. He waved a hand at her.

"Not necessary on this flight. You can use the Wi-Fi anytime."

Of course they could. Why waste one usable moment when you could be poring through the stock market? Checking the price of precious metals? She sighed and settled into her seat. Her hope that at some point Harrison's battery might run out had been wishful thinking.

Her phone pinged with a text message. It was from Danny, who was managing Tomasino's party in her absence.

The cake's not here. When is it supposed to arrive?

Frankie frowned and glanced at her watch. An hour ago. Surely her brother hadn't forgotten?

Call the restaurant, she texted back. I'm sure it's on the way.

Harrison looked over at her. "Problems?"

She shook her head. "Just this thing I'm supposed to be at. He'll figure it out."

The attendant came by to check their seat belts and ask what they'd like to drink once they were airborne. Harrison requested a scotch. Frankie gladly followed suit and asked for a glass of wine. Anything that calmed the anxiety clawing its way up her throat was a good thing.

Another text came in. He hasn't left yet. Dammit. Frankie sent a text to her brother Salvatore. Get that cake there, now. You owe me.

"Men," she muttered. Why couldn't they be as buttoned-down as women?

Her boss glanced up from his laptop. "Trust me, he'll be fine. If he has any sense he'll be waiting with an armful of flowers when you get back."

Frankie gave him an uncomprehending look. "Oh—no, it's not that. It's my brother. He's supposed to be delivering a birthday cake to the party I was hosting and he's late."

His dark brows came together. "You were hosting a party?"

"At the church, yes." The engines roared. She kept talking as her pulse skyrocketed. "I host Wednesday night bingo games for the seniors. I've been doing it since I was eighteen. Tomasino Giardelli, whose birthday it is, is like a grandfather to me. It's his eightieth, so we decided to throw him a party and Mama made Tomasino her special tiramisu cake. Which," she added darkly, "he is going to love if Salvatore gets his behind over there with it before it's over. The seniors are wilting as we speak."

"Salvatore?"

"My brother."

A sober look crossed his face. "I'm sorry you're missing the birthday party."

"You didn't know."

"I didn't ask."

She wasn't sure how to respond to that so she looked down at her hands clasped together in a death lock. His gaze sat on her as the jet taxied off to sit in line behind two others. "You really spend every Wednesday night hosting bingo?"

She tightened her seat belt, her heart going pitter-patter as the captain announced they were two minutes to take-off. "It's always been part of what we do as a family—giving back to the community is important for my parents. It's been good to them."

"Coburn said they have a restaurant in Brooklyn?"

She nodded. 'I'm the youngest of six procreated bus people."

He smiled at that. "Shouldn't you be out on dates instead of hosting bingo? Living the Manhattan single life?"

She made a face. "The last date I was on, the very well-mannered stockbroker I *thought* I was out with accosted me in the elevator on the way down from the restaurant. That was enough for me."

His brows rose. "Accosted?"

Frankie gave an embarrassed wave of her hand. "He kissed me. He wouldn't stop kissing me. And frankly, he was bad at it. I mean, can you imagine?"

The amusement in his eyes deepened. "I can. I mean I *can't* in that he should never have put his hands on you without your permission but the poor guy was probably just desperate."

Frankie crossed her arms over her chest, an image of her flashing him with her lace pull-ups filling her head.

Did he think she usually gave men come-ons like that? She wished she could wipe that entire night from their heads.

"You still don't do that," she said stiffly.

"No," he agreed. "You don't." He gave her a thoughtful look as the jet revved its engines and started down the runway, the speed at which the gray pavement flew by making Frankie light-headed. "Poor-mannered guy aside, there must be a man in your life. You're too attractive for there not to be."

Her chin dipped. "I'm married to my work for the next few years."

"*Or* you're hung up on someone."

The inflection in his voice made her lift her chin and narrow her gaze on him. "No—just not dating."

He shrugged. "Good. Because I'd hate for you to waste your time on my brother, Francesca. He is undoubtedly a magnetic personality and an inspiring leader, but he is not *boyfriend* material by any stretch of the imagination."

Boyfriend material? She blinked at the twin assaults being mounted on her, one from the air as they climbed at a petrifyingly steep angle and one from the man opposite her. "Is that what he thinks? That I have a crush on him?" *Good God.* So she'd responded to a few of her boss's flirtatious smiles lately. She *was* human.

"I can assure you," she said crisply, "I do not have a crush on Coburn."

He held up a hand. "Just a friendly piece of advice. I've seen it happen too many times."

The jet climbed swiftly into the clouds. Frankie gave the receding ground an anxious look, her stomach swooping as the plane rode a current of air. Was that why Coburn had handed her over so easily to Harrison? Because he thought she had a crush on him? That was wrong. So wrong.

A scowl twisted her lips. *Good to know the two Grant brothers both had egos the size of their fortunes...* Her resentment faded to terror as they went through a bumpy patch of cloud, her fingers digging into the armrests.

Harrison sighed and set his computer aside. "You really are terrified of flying."

She clamped down harder on the leather. "Something else to add to my list of eccentricities."

He smiled. "I rather like Rocky. And all joking aside, the seniors, your work in the community, I appreciate your altruism, Francesca. It's refreshing."

"The Grant family does the same."

A cynical light filled his eyes. "There is an intent and purpose behind everything my family does. It's all done with a camera in sight and cleverly crafted messaging at the ready. Hardly the same thing."

His candor caught her off guard. "Hardly surprising with the White House in mind."

He arched a brow at her. "Do we? Have the White House in mind?"

Warmth seeped into her blood-deprived cheeks. "Everyone thinks you do."

He tipped his head at her. "Anyone considering a presidential run spends the years leading up to it coyly denying they're interested. Dropping little hints that never might not mean never, but then again, maybe it does. Then they sit back and take the pulse of every interest group in the nation and see if it's a viable proposition. It's a game, Francesca, a long, bloody battle that would sap the stamina of even the strongest man."

She frowned. So did that mean he was going to or he wasn't?

An elusive smile claimed his lips. "What that means is right now I am focusing on Grant Industries and specifically what Leonid Aristov is going to bring to the table tomorrow."

And with that Harrison Grant cut off whatever valuable insight Frankie might have glimpsed into his psyche and got to work. He pulled up the presentation he'd done for the meeting that addressed two of Aristov's final concerns, asked her to get her notes out and the marathon work session began. This time, however, she was grateful for any distraction that would keep her mind off the fact they were traveling at thirty thousand feet in a glorified tin can.

A couple of hours into their trip across the Atlantic, Harrison thought he might finally have gained some sort of symbiosis with his PA. He could not question Francesca's intelligence after the week they'd just spent together. She was whip-smart, just as Coburn had said, with street smarts to go with it that gave her an uncanny ability to see through people and situations. And now that he'd given her permission to delve deeper with her questions, she was starting to give back to him what he needed—intelligently thought-out ideas on how to present the information she'd gathered to a tricky prospect in Leonid Aristov.

The Russians, he conceded on a deeply exhaled breath, were a thorn in his side. Aristov was playing with him as if he held all the cards when, in fact, he held none. The Russian's fortune was disintegrating in front of his eyes. He *needed* to sell Siberius and yet he was intent on making Harrison's life difficult for a reason he had yet to divulge. Which hopefully, he would wrangle out of him tomorrow.

And Markovic? Well, Markovic was Markovic—an arrogant oligarch with too much money to play with, too flashy a lifestyle and too short a memory to remember the bridges he'd burned. It antagonized Harrison to see him prosper. But soon he would remember what he'd done to his father and he would pay with the same agony Clifford Grant had. With *everything* he had.

Frankie curved one long leg over the other, adjusting her position as he had been over the long flight to keep the blood flowing. It was taking everything *he* had to ignore her five-star legs and keep his mind on work. He might have put a lock on his attraction to her but it didn't mean he wasn't a man with functioning parts. Evidently ones that needed some serious attention.

Coburn would have been highly amused at the situation given his older brother had been born the one with all the self-control and discipline. The one who was not ruled by his emotions. But after a week with Francesca, he almost got why his brother had punted her to him for six months. She was temptation that didn't know it was temptation. And that was the most tempting female of all.

The pilot's voice intruded on his thoughts. *"Hey, folks. We're anticipating some rough weather ahead. I'm going to turn the seat-belt sign on in a few minutes for about an hour so if you'd like to use the restroom, now would be the time."*

A pinched look spread across Frankie's face. "What kind of bad weather?" she asked the attendant as she came to offer them a drink before she sat down.

"A bit of lightning in the area. It could be rough for a while but no worries. Captain Danyon is the best."

Frankie turned a greenish color and unbuckled her seat belt. "Are you okay?" he asked her.

She nodded. "Just going to do like the pilot said."

When she came back, she had a set, determined look on her chalk-white face. They worked through the Aristov presentation. When the captain turned on the seat-belt sign and the bumps began, Frankie kept her gaze fixed on his computer screen and kept talking. As far as storms went, it was a good one. The tiny plane swooped on fast-moving air, then rose again, some of the plunges taking his breath away.

"We can stop," he suggested. "Wait until it's over…"

"Keep talking," she commanded, clutching her seat

with white-knuckled hands. "It's keeping me from freaking out."

He wasn't sure how much she was taking in in her terrified state, but he kept going, working through the back end of the presentation. Forty-five minutes later, they'd finished it and were going through a checklist to make sure they hadn't missed anything crucial.

"We haven't included the most recent market stats," Frankie announced, shuffling through her papers.

"They're on the third slide."

"Oh." She sucked her bottom lip between her teeth and chewed on it. "Do we have that graphic in there, too? The one you asked me to fix and expand?"

"It's in there." He pulled his gaze away from her lush mouth to study her. She didn't look as green as she had earlier, but now she was acting a bit…vague.

"Francesca, are you okay?"

"Perfect." She forced a smile. "I think that's it, then, isn't it? I'll make a note of any questions Aristov asks, although I don't expect he'll have any with this much information put in front of him. Oh—and I'll bring the backup."

The way she said that last part, as if it was a 'nice to have,' alarmed him. "Yes," he said deliberately, "the backup is key. We can't forget the backup."

"No problem." She rubbed her palm across her forehead. "Can we talk about the shareholder meetings now? I really need to get a handle on them."

"If you're a hundred percent clear on the meeting, yes."

"A hunnndred percent, yes." She nodded and tucked the folder in her briefcase and pulled out her notepad. "So for the shareholder thing…"

"Meetings," he corrected. Had she just *slurred* that word? Or was she being funny?

"Right. The meetings… They cover the Monday and

Tuesday, right? With the Wednesday afternoon kept for additional items that come up?"

"The *Tuesday* afternoons are for open items, yes. The meetings are over Tuesday night."

She blinked at him. "That's what I said. Tuesday."

"You said Wednesday. It's *Tuesday* for the open session. Here." He pulled the schedule from her unopened folder. "Look at this."

She studied it with the glazed-eyed look of someone who wasn't taking anything in. "Got it." A sigh escaped her. She put her elbows on the table and rubbed her eyes. "I'm so sorry. My head is very cloudy all of a sudden."

A wave of guilt spread through him. "You're probably exhausted. It's been a long week."

"Yes, but this…" She put her palms to her temples. "I think I might need to lie down."

He pulled her hands away from her face. "You're not feeling well?"

"I'm fine…it's just—" Her bleary gaze skipped away from his. "I—I took a pill my sister gave me for the turbulence. It's making me…"

"Where is it?"

"In my purse."

He grabbed her bag off the seat, opened it up and plucked the pill bottle off the top. Scanning the label he saw it was a sedative.

"Have you taken these before?"

"No. I didn't think they'd hit me this hard." She plopped her chin in her palms, elbows braced on the table, and closed her eyes. "Maybe it'll wear off in a few minutes. Maybe I should have some coffee."

"How many did you take?"

"Just one. But I feel…light-headed."

He uttered a low curse. "It's going to last for hours. You need to lie down."

"I'd rather have some coffee."

He stripped off his seat belt, rounded the table and undid hers. Her eyes half opened. "The seat-belt sign is—"

"Shut up." He slipped his arms underneath her knees and back and lifted her up. She was surprisingly light for a female with her curves, and it should have been an easy carry to the bedroom at the back of the jet, but the plane was dipping and swaying beneath his feet and it was all he could do to keep his balance. Her fingers dug into his biceps with a strength born of fear, her body trembling in his arms.

He kept her braced against his chest as he negotiated the door handle to the bedroom, shouldered himself in and deposited her on the bed with a lucky move that brought him down hard beside her. The jet dropped, this time a good fifty feet, pulling a low, agonized cry from Francesca. He kept a hand on her, his body half draped over her. The jet leveled out. "Swallow," he commanded.

Her throat convulsed as she did. "This is soooo not good."

"It's just turbulence." He recovered his own breath.

"Still." Her eyes popped open, valiantly hanging on to her terror. "Donnn't leave me."

"I can't at this moment." He gave the sky a grim look through the tiny, oval windows. It was an inky, endless black canvas crisscrossed by vibrant streaks of jagged gold lightning.

Francesca pulled him toward her as if he was a pillow. He put a palm to her shoulder to push her back into the bed. A whimper escaped her throat. "Please."

He crumbled. Gathered her soft curves to him and held her while the storm raged on outside. She smelled like orange blossoms—like intoxication and innocence all in one. The plane leveled out and stayed that way for minutes. In the warmth of his arms, Francesca stopped trembling. He tried to remember the last time he'd held a woman like this, for comfort, and didn't have to think long. It would have been seven years ago when Susanna had left.

The thought did something strange to his head. He glanced out the window as the lightning receded and the space between rumbles of thunder lengthened. Having Francesca wrapped around him like this was inspiring the need to find out whether his dream would come anything close to reality... The thought made him hard so fast, comfort was obliterated on a long, potent surge of lust.

He stood and dumped her on the bed. Her eyes flickered open. "It's calming down now." She curled up in the fetal position and used the pillow as a cushion instead of him. He turned and made for the door as a whole lot more creamy thigh was exposed. *Mother of God.*

Back in the main cabin, he buckled himself in and stared out the window at the storm. He'd called this one— he had. It had been a bad idea. A bad idea that was getting worse every minute.

CHAPTER FOUR

FRANKIE WOKE WITH the instinctive feeling something was not quite right. Bright light beat an assault against the throb behind her eyes. Her head felt fuzzy...*heavy*.

She closed her eyes harder against the overwhelming light. She must have forgotten to close the blinds. And on a morning when she had a blinding headache... *Great*.

A low, insistent hum beneath her ear made her frown. Were they renovating the brownstone across the street *again*? The floor dipped beneath her, riding a stream of air. *Floors don't move unless you live in California*. Her eyes sprang open. The light streaming in was coming from tiny oval windows, a world of blue flowing by. She wasn't in her bedroom; she was in the Grant Industries jet on her way to London. And it was morning.

Her gaze flew to the watch on her arm—*8:00 a.m. Oh, lord*.

Pieces of the night before assembled themselves in her head. That awful thunder and lightning storm... The way the jet had been tossed around like a toy airplane, subjected to God's fury. That pill of her sister's she'd taken that had knocked the lights out of her...

Oh, no. Her heart plummeted. The rest of it she didn't *want* to remember. Her boss carrying her in here in the middle of that madness because she'd been half passed out. Him putting her to bed. Him holding her...

She buried her face in the pillow. She'd clung to him like a woman possessed. So far from the independent, strong woman she was it made her cringe to think of it. Made her cringe to think she'd given him yet another reason to think her less than competent.

Heat flooded her face. Tessa would never have put herself in that position. Tessa would have been cool as a cucumber in the face of almost certain aeronautic death.

She got out of bed in a hurry, made it behind her and attempted to straighten her rumpled suit and hair. Deciding nothing was actually going to be accomplished until she changed clothes and redid her makeup, she made her way out into the main cabin.

Harrison looked fresh in a crisp blue linen shirt, tie and pants, his jacket slung over the back of the seat beside him. *Ready to do battle with Leonid Aristov.*

He looked up at her. "Feeling better?"

She nodded. "I apologize for last night. I had no idea that pill was going to affect me that way."

He waved a hand at her. "Forget about it. It was a bad storm." He flicked a glance at his watch. "We're landing in just over an hour. If you want to shower and change, do it now."

She nodded. She wanted desperately to tell him this wasn't *her*, not the way she'd been acting lately. But he stuck his head back in the report he was reading. Not the time to plead her case. And a part of her knew with Harrison, actions spoke louder than words.

She retraced her steps to the bedroom and headed for the shower to make herself into the deadly efficient assistant she knew she was. She could do this. She could.

They landed without incident at London City Airport, where they were picked up by a car and spirited to the Chatsfield. The opulence of the swanky hotel with its reputation for hosting anyone who mattered bounced off Harrison's consciousness as they were ushered up to their luxury suite. His mind was focused on the meeting ahead and getting Leonid Aristov to sign on the dotted line.

He checked his smartphone as Francesca dropped her belongings in her bedroom. An email had come in from Aristov. A feeling of foreboding swept over him.

Grant—Stuck in Brussels. I'm hosting a charity gala tonight at my house in Highgate. Why don't you come and we'll talk there? Two tickets will be delivered to you this afternoon. L

Rage bubbled up inside of him, swift and all-consuming. Was he kidding? He had dragged himself across an ocean, put together an exhaustive presentation that obliterated the Russian's concerns about the acquisition and he wanted to talk at a *party*?

His brain whirred as he struggled to figure out why Aristov was suddenly putting this deal on the back burner when he had been so anxious to sign just weeks ago. Forty million dollars was going to go a long way to pulling the Russian out of the financial mess the oligarch had found himself in recently, bad luck and bad decisions plaguing him in his home country and threatening the empire he'd built.

He shoved his hands in his pockets and walked to the floor-to-ceiling windows with their incomparable view of London, agitation raising his pulse rate. Aristov had told him he was getting out of the automotive business and realigning his assets. *So why?*

A niggling worry entered his head, one he hadn't let himself think of until now. Could Aristov have guessed his true intentions? That acquiring Siberius was only a stepping stone to destroying the man who had killed his father? *Impossible.* He had made sure every company, every lifeline he had snapped up that kept Anton Markovic's automotive empire in business had been buried so deep behind red tape they could never be traced back to him. The one or two deals he'd made publicly could innocently be explained as smart business strategy.

That Siberius was the only supplier in the world left that could keep Anton Markovic manufacturing engines once Grant Industries cut off his other lifelines was something Aristov could not know.

His head pounded with a deep throb, drawing his hand to his skull. If he didn't obtain Siberius as planned, Markovic would continue production, the Russian's company would gain more influence and his plan would be dead in the water.

A fiery feeling stirred to life low in his gut. He would never let that happen, not while he lived and breathed on this earth.

His head took him back to that night. To the horrific scene that had met him when he had walked into the Grant family home on the eve of his father's announcement he would run for governor. The unnatural silence in the house. The eerie feeling that something was very, very wrong. His father's body had been limp and lifeless, slumped over the desk he had created such genius at.

His body went rigid. The beast in him climbed out of the box he had placed it in seven years ago and into his head, blurring his vision. Anton Markovic had been as responsible for his father's death as if he had pulled the trigger himself and he would have a target on his back until he lived his own personal version of hell.

There was no other possible outcome.

The gray mist in his head swirled darker. He pushed it ruthlessly away. If he let the wolves in his head win, if he let the beast rule, he would make a mistake. And any wrong move at this point would bring it all crashing down.

Francesca chose that particular moment to walk back into the room. Her apprehensive expression as he turned to face her had him wiping the emotion clean from his face.

"Is something wrong?"

"Aristov is stuck in Brussels. He wants to discuss the deal at a gala party he's throwing in Highgate tonight."

Her eyes widened. She wisely held her counsel. He turned back to the windows to study the city he'd flown thousands of miles to reach only to be slapped in the face by Leonid Aristov. He could fly back to the States tonight and be done with it, or he could make one more attempt to try and figure out what was going on in Aristov's complicated head.

The thought that regulators would be looking at the deal *in weeks* had him turning around.

"Go buy yourself a dress. We have a party to attend."

CHAPTER FIVE

THE MOST EXPENSIVE dress she had ever bought, *times ten*, floating around her ankles, hair tamed into a sophisticated up-do by the Chatsfield salon staff and some simple makeup in place, Frankie finally allowed herself a look in the mirror. Her eyes nearly bugged out of her head.

The haute-couture-clad, *daring* stranger that stared back at her was not the Frankie Masseria she knew. She would never in a million years have bought this dress if the saleswoman had not insisted it was exactly right for "Leonid Aristov's party of the year."

"Anyone who is anyone is going to be there, sweetheart. Trust me, you cannot be ordinary."

So here she was, anything but ordinary, and not at all sure she could carry it off. Ordinary had been her mantra her entire life. Sure, she had a killer figure; reactions from men had told her that. But she didn't have her two sisters' striking blue eyes to go with her dark hair. She was not a doctor, psychologist, chemical engineer or entrepreneur. She was the girl her mother sent in to calm a particularly difficult customer when no one else could. She and her nondescript GPA had been so good at it her parents had urged her to stay in the family business. But she hadn't wanted to do it. She'd wanted to become a somebody. And coming to work at Grant Enterprises had made her *feel* like a somebody.

She gave her appearance another assessing look. The dress, a stunning, smoky blue color the salesperson had said perfectly matched her eyes clung to every inch of her body as though it had been painted on. But because of the way the beautiful material slipped elusively away from her skin, it was come-hither rather than tacky.

What had sealed the deal, though, and made her set Harrison's black-label credit card down on the counter was the back of the dress. The gorgeous cutout that revealed the graceful sweep of her shoulder blades and much of her back was sexy yet ladylike.

A knock sounded on the connecting door. Her nerves amped up another notch or two. *Harrison.* Tessa had been right. You could have timed the Swiss train system after him, he was that punctual.

Wary of keeping the beast waiting, she picked up her wrap, draped it around her shoulders and swung the door open. Her breath stopped somewhere in her chest. He looked obscenely handsome in a tux that was undoubtedly as expensively made as her dress, the elegant formal wear a perfect foil for his clean-edged, dark masculinity.

She looked up at him before her gaping became obvious. But he was too busy looking at her to notice. His dark gaze seemed to be caught in a state of suspended animation as it moved over her, taking in the daring dress. And he didn't remove it right away. The full-on stare went on for a good three or four seconds, sending a wave of heat through her. Unlike some men's open admiration that had, in the past, made her feel uncomfortable, Harrison's stare made her feel *unbalanced.*

He cleared his throat. "You look…beautiful."

His uncharacteristic struggle for words unleashed a fluttery feeling deep in her stomach. *Stop it*, she told herself. *He's your boss. Now is the time to act cool and collected so he knows you can actually do it.*

"I hope it's not too much," she offered casually. "The saleslady said it was perfect for tonight."

"It's not too much." He looked as if he was going to say something else, then clamped his mouth shut. "We should go."

The ride to Highgate was smooth and quiet as London flashed by the tinted windows of the Rolls-Royce. Harrison was silent, a frown etched in his brow, formulating a plan of attack for Leonid Aristov, no doubt. Her nerves skyrocketed as they entered the exclusive London suburb. Georgian homes shook hands with fascinating Victorian Gothic structures. Not to be outdone, a handful of architecturally brilliant modern homes made their own statement on the tree-lined street.

All impressive, but it was Leonid Aristov's Georgian Revival mansion that was the most impressive of all. Tucked between a canopy of trees as they climbed the hill, the redbrick mansion stood white-pillared and regal on rolling acres. Massive. She'd read it contained fifty-two rooms, including eighteen bedrooms and ten bathrooms, an Imperial-inspired ballroom and an underground bath that harked back to Roman times. As they continued to climb, she stared up at the structure gleaming with light. She'd never seen anything like it.

When they reached the top of the hill, they turned a corner and accessed the property from the official entrance off a quiet road cradled in the branches of giant oak trees. Limousines pulled to a halt in a parade of arrivals in the circular driveway.

Frankie tugged the low bodice of her dress up and checked her hair for the tenth time as they waited in the queue. Harrison shot her a quelling glance. "Stop fidgeting. You look perfect."

She stuck her hands back in her lap. "I suppose you do this once a week."

A fleeting smile crossed his lips. "Not once a week. Remember—they are people like you."

Her heart did a little flip. He was breathtaking when he smiled. How had she ever thought Coburn the better-looking brother? Where Coburn was stunning in a flashy, attention-getting way, Harrison was devastating in a complex, unforgettable way. He had about fifty layers. She wondered if anyone ever got to the bottom of them. It made a woman want to try, that was for sure.

She removed her gaze from him. The only lover she'd had was a year-long relationship two years ago in college. What did she know about unpeeling layers? *Heavens*. She needed to focus on keeping her job, not unraveling her boss in a very distracting way.

The car slid forward to the pillared entrance. A white-gloved, uniformed staff member stepped forward to open the door. "Welcome to Gvidon House."

Harrison stepped out and offered her his hand. She took it and emerged into the flashing bulbs of paparazzi cameras. He leaned down to her. "Gvidon House?"

She blinked against the blinding lights and rested her hand on his arm for balance. "He's a prince from a Russian fairy tale. Apparently Leonid is a big fan of them."

"Fairy tales?"

She nodded, settling her weight firmly on two feet as she eyed the red carpet. It seemed long and never ending.

Harrison set a hand to the small of her back to guide her toward it. "How do you know that?"

"I did my research."

He gave her a measuring look. "Then you know his current girlfriend is Juliana Rossellini, who works for one of London's top auction houses."

"Who is fifteen years his junior."

He nodded. "See if you can gain some intelligence about Leonid from her."

She would, but right now she was too consumed by the distracting feeling of his palm on the bare skin of her back as the handlers indicated they could start down the carpet. It was big and warm. Comforting yet disconcerting at the same time.

His fingers increased their pressure on her skin. "Relax. Pretend it's a walk in the park. You're smelling the flowers…enjoying yourself."

The park didn't have fifty cameras stuck in her face. The park hadn't just realized it was Harrison on the carpet, causing an unexpected buzz. They called his name as they moved forward. Frankie stuck the fakest smile of her life on her lips and held it.

"What if they connect us in the photo?"

His mouth quirked. "It wouldn't do my reputation any harm having a stunning brunette on my arm. I've apparently been going through a dry spell."

A stunning brunette. A flush she was certain would show up in the photographs deepened her cheeks. She was quite sure she didn't compare to any of his beautiful escorts. She'd seen them. They were way out of her league.

"Does it bother you?" she asked. "Being in a constant media spotlight?"

He shrugged. "It's been my life. You get used to it."

They made it down the carpet without incident to the entrance where a queue was forming. People were removing their wraps, shoes… "Metal detector," one of the greeters explained.

A metal detector?

Frankie looked around for something to hold on to while she took off her shoes. Harrison held out his elbow. "Why is it always the women's shoes?" she complained.

His mouth curled. "Because they are weapons. With you, they could be a dangerous thing."

She made a face at him. They made it through the metal

detector unscathed and were directed to the terrace where the cocktails were being served. Frankie was gobsmacked by the scene. Some guests were milling about the exquisitely landscaped, multilevel terrace in the same formal wear she and Harrison had on, jewels dripping from their necks and ears. Others were lounging in the pool in bathing suits, cocktails in hand.

Her eyes widened at the sight of a diamond-encrusted blonde in the pool across the bridge. She was pretty sure those were real diamonds making up the hardly there bikini. They were just too sparkly not to be.

"Apparently," she murmured to Harrison, "I just needed to bring my bathing suit. It would have been a lot cheaper."

He gave her one of his dark, fathomless looks. "I think you're a lot safer in the dress."

The heat that passed between them was swift and unmistakable. She bit the inside of her mouth. *Unfair*, her eyes told him. *I thought we were playing by the rules.*

You asked for that one, his gaze flashed in return. *Be honest.*

She wanted to say she had no experience playing this game. That she was merely attempting to keep her job by attending this party. But he was already scouting the crowd. "Let's make our way to the bar. We can look for our hosts along the way."

They weren't more than a few feet into the crowd when Harrison spotted Aristov. He nodded his head toward the far pool. "He's in a tux, Juliana's in a red dress." Frankie found the couple easily, having also looked at photos of Leonid Aristov during her research. They stood out even among this decadent crowd with their superior, distinctive good looks. A definite power couple.

Harrison acquired a drink for them at the bar, then they wound their way around the candle-strewn lively pools until they were close enough to greet Aristov when he was finished his conversation. It was a good twenty minutes before the Russian made his way over to them with his entourage. She could feel Harrison's powerful body gaining heat beside her with every minute that passed.

Harrison and Leonid exchanged greetings. Leonid, a tall, thin Russian with whiskey-colored eyes and a craggy attractive face, gave Frankie a kiss on each cheek, then introduced his tall, statuesque girlfriend, Juliana, and his second in command, Viktor Kaminski. Juliana was a jaw-droppingly beautiful brunette with just enough imperfections to make her fascinating. She gave Harrison an appreciative look as he kissed her on each cheek, then greeted Frankie. Viktor Kaminski, a ruddy-cheeked, slightly paunchy, not attractive Russian, brought Frankie's hand to his mouth. "How lucky for Harrison," he murmured against her fingers.

She retrieved her hand but couldn't escape Viktor's ardent admiration, particularly when Harrison mentioned she spoke Russian. He insisted she try it out with him while he told her all about the magnificent paintings up for auction that evening, a subject she knew nothing about but feigned interest in.

Thankfully she and Juliana, who was unpretentious and lovely, hit it off. When Leonid offered to introduce Harrison around, Juliana grabbed her hand. "I'll take Francesca to get another glass of champagne. You are so *boring* when you talk business."

"Good thing I shine in other areas," Leonid came back with one of his crooked smiles.

Juliana gave him a saucy look as she took Frankie's arm and led her through the crowd. "Two powerful, delicious men," she murmured. "They look good together."

She couldn't argue with that.

At the bar, Juliana claimed two seats. Frankie sat down beside her. "Poor Viktor," Juliana teased, "he so has the hots for you. But who would be interested in him when your boss looks like Harrison?"

"I'd like to keep my job."

Juliana's dark eyes sparkled. "You can always find another job…"

Not like hers. Not when she'd worked so hard to prove she could be a success. She hadn't performed a groundbreaking open-heart surgery like her brother Emilio had.

Juliana caught the bartender's attention and ordered them champagne. "Leonid says Harrison has big political ambitions…that a presidential run isn't out of the question."

"I wouldn't mention that to him," Frankie said drily. "He'll feed you a whole spiel about how presidential candidates don't really *run*. They *lurk*."

"Still." Juliana gave her a meaningful look. "Power is an aphrodisiac. And *he* is delicious."

"He's not hard to look at."

"There's tension between him and Leonid," Juliana observed.

She kept her smile even. "I think Harrison is just anxious to close the deal. There seems to be a couple of minor sticking points."

Juliana snorted. "I think they're too much *alike*, that's the problem. Leonid likes to be in control. So does Harrison. They're alpha dogs of the highest order. Even if Leonid's empire is crumbling in a very public way, his ego needs to be stroked."

Frankie wasn't sure that was in the cards.

The bartender laid two glasses of champagne on the bar. Juliana slid one over to Frankie. "People might find it hard to believe, but it's not all about business with Leonid. Tonight is about him doing good. He is a *good* man. He needs to feel the decisions he's making are right. So if something is holding him back with Harrison's deal at this late stage, it's not about what's on paper, it's about what's in his heart."

Frankie filed that away for future use. "What's he like?" she asked Juliana curiously. "Leonid? He seems like such an enigma."

The brunette's lips curved. "Very much so. Mensa-level IQ. Hard. Tough as nails. But good to his friends, good to those who work for him and a marshmallow with me despite the fact his ex-wife took half his money and ran."

"One of the good oligarchs, then."

Juliana nodded. "Unlike some. Anton Markovic, for instance." She gave a delicate shiver. "I wouldn't have him in this house if Leonid didn't do business with him."

Frankie knew of Markovic, of course. He was one of the world's richest men, two places higher on the list than Harrison last year. "Is he here?"

"He's out of the country, thank goodness. I don't have to pretend I like him."

"Why *don't* you like him?"

The smile faded from the brunette's face. "He's dangerous. Far too many underworld connections, far too nasty and far too unfriendly to his women."

Frankie made a mental note to avoid Anton Markovic if she ever came into contact with him. Which was unlikely since this was probably the last time she'd ever be at a party like this.

"Anyway," Juliana said, holding her glass up to Frankie's, "enough about business. *Cin-cin.*"

Frankie sipped her champagne slowly as Juliana introduced her around. But the spirit hit her quickly as it always did. By the time Juliana delivered her to Harrison the better part of an hour later, she was in a much more relaxed mood. Harrison, unfortunately, was not. Leonid was not with him and it was clear from the tense set of her boss's jaw he had yet to have the talk he needed to have with the Russian.

Juliana left them to facilitate the auction that was to begin shortly and Viktor disappeared to greet a guest. Harrison threw back the last swallow of whatever amber liquid he was drinking and scowled. "I have no idea why we came. He's been avoiding me, pawning me off on his guests when he knows I want to talk to him."

Frankie thought about what Juliana had said. Did she dare speak up or would that be the last straw for her and Harrison? She pressed her empty glass to her chin and surveyed the beast at his most riled. She had valuable information. She needed to tell him.

She took a deep breath. "Juliana said with Leonid it's not all about business. That he needs to feel good about the decisions he's making. She said if something is holding him back with this deal, it's not about what's on paper, it's about what's in his heart."

The deadly stare he directed at her made Frankie shift her weight to both feet. *"You discussed the deal with her?"*

Her chin snapped up. *"You* asked me to feel her out. She was the one to bring it up. She could sense the tension between you two."

He muttered an oath under his breath. She stood her ground, palms moist, knees shaky as he turned and prowled over to stare into one of the cascading pools. "He doesn't need to feel good about the bloody deal," he growled. "It's going to save his hide."

"And what's going to save his pride?" Frankie returned softly. "Leonid is in financial difficulty. His empire is suffering a very public defeat, yet he throws a party like this one tonight to make a gesture. It sends a message that he is not bowed by it. That he will survive. Let him see you understand that. *Show him* you understand."

He turned around, a savage light in his gaze. "This is all from Juliana?"

She quaked a little inside. "Yes."

He scowled. "Even if I could show him I *understand*, how can I do it when he won't talk? He is never alone. Kaminski hasn't left his goddamned side for a minute."

"There has to be an opportunity." Frankie had always been a glass-half-full kind of person. "Juliana said the auction is very important to Leonid. He wants it to go well. Maybe he's keyed up about it and you'll have your chance afterward."

"Or maybe it's another *giant waste of my time*."

"You won't know until you try."

The glass-half-full part of her hoped she was right.

He stared hard at her. Deposited his empty glass on the table. "Let's go, then."

The over-the-top ballroom done in gold and imperial red was buzzing with anticipation when they arrived. Again, as it seemed with all of Leonid Aristov's estate, it was like nothing she'd ever seen before. Slavic in feel, it dripped with ornate, antique chandeliers, featuring a half-dozen tiny balconies that opened to a view over the man-made lake Leonid had created. All of the little balconies reminded Frankie of the inside of a Russian opera house.

Tuxedo-clad waiters circulated with trays of champagne to whet the appetites of bidders, while staff passed out gold embossed lists of the items up for auction.

The list would have been impressive, she was sure, if Frankie had known anything more about art than Viktor Kaminski had bent her ear with earlier. Her eyes nearly bugged out of her head when she saw the opening bids for some of the paintings. They were in the millions.

"Wow," she murmured. "This is the real deal."

Harrison didn't respond. He was scanning the list with a furrowed brow.

The lights went up. Leonid took the stage and welcomed everyone, Juliana at his side. He made a joke about her not being up for auction with his dry humor that drew an amused response from the crowd. Frankie found his speech about his commitment to the arts and the artists who continued to make the world a more beautiful place heartfelt and eloquent. She could see the goodness in him Juliana had talked about. It made the charismatic Russian even more attractive and compelling.

Leonid highlighted a few of the marquee items up for auction, then exited the stage to be replaced by Juliana's auctioneer. The Brit with his booming voice began the auction with some paintings by a new modern Russian artist. The value of the works continued to go up with every item, with the last painting selling for two million pounds.

A Chagall in brilliant blue tones came next. "I love that one," she murmured to Harrison. It was, according to the brochure, "a piece from one of the artist's most famous series set in Nice, featuring his famous sirens."

Harrison nodded. "I like it, too."

The bidding for the painting started at one and a half million pounds. A Brit in the front row signaled two. A determined look on his face, an American with a Southern accent took it up to two and a half million. The two men went back and forth until the price tag sat at three and a half million.

Harrison raised his hand. "Four million."

Frankie gaped at him. *"Four million,"* the auctioneer crowed, "by the gentleman in the back."

The auctioneer tried to persuade the other bidders to up the price, but the American and Brit weren't biting. *Apparently they were sane.*

"Sold," sang the auctioneer, "for four million pounds to Mr. Grant in the back."

The ballroom was a buzz of conversation. Frankie looked at Harrison, her astonishment written across her face.

"It was a gesture," he said roughly. "And I like the painting."

A four-million-pound gesture. Two more paintings were sold, an astonishing amount of money changed hands, then Leonid appeared back on stage to thank the guests for their generosity and wrap the proceedings. When he stepped down from the stage, said something to Viktor Kaminski and slipped into the crowd, Harrison's gaze tracked him. The Russian was finally alone.

He turned to her. "Can you occupy Kaminski for a few minutes?"

She knew what he was asking, knew it was well past her job description, but tonight she wanted to show Harrison Grant what she was made of. "No problem," she replied crisply, smoothing her dress over her hips. "Leave him to me."

He nodded and strode off after Leonid. Frankie kept her eyes on Viktor as he spoke to the auctioneer. When he left him and headed to the opulent bar, done in exotic dark woods and stone, she headed through the crowd and discreetly shouldered her way to the front of the line. She emerged to the right of Viktor, who had his forearms on the bar and was chatting with one of the attractive servers. She trained her gaze on the bartender as he took her order, hoping Viktor would notice her. But the Russian was lazily engaged with the attractive blonde, chatting for a few moments with her before she heard him order two cognacs. *One for Leonid.*

Adrenaline surged through her. She raised her voice beyond her usual soft, modulated tone as she thanked the bartender for the soda and lime. Viktor glanced over at her, his eyes lighting up as if he'd struck gold in the Yukon.

He wrapped his fingers around the two glasses of cognac that sat on the bar and made his way over to her. "You shouldn't be getting your own drink," he chastised. "Where's Grant?"

"Talking to an acquaintance." She adopted as arch a look as her limited repertoire allowed. "Maybe I can take you up on your offer to show me Leonid's art collection while he's occupied? I'm so inspired after the auction. It's all so beautiful…"

Viktor flicked a glance toward the balconies. His frown belied his indecision. "Pretty please," she murmured, laying it on thick. "I'll never get another chance like this."

He gave her an indulgent look. "Only if you agree to experience what a nineteenth-century Frapin Cuvée tastes like." He held up the cognac. "I was on my way to meet Leonid."

"Done," she murmured. She had one more glass of tolerance in her.

She picked up the glass, took the arm Viktor offered and they made their way through the crowd to the long marble hallway that stretched the second floor of the manor. Aristov's art collection, Viktor explained, was displayed along this and the grand hallway of the third floor. Frankie could see why. The Oriental-carpeted, ornately wainscoted hallways and expert lighting set the artwork off to perfection.

She didn't have to feign attention. Viktor took her through each piece with an enthusiasm that was infectious. His clear love for his subject matter shone through and understanding what she was looking at made it so much more enjoyable for her. She put her hand on his arm frequently to indicate her pleasure, smiling up at him with exaggerated fascination. She could see it was working, from his animated expression and heightened color in his cheeks.

A surge of feminine power heated her veins. She really wasn't half-bad at this femme fatale thing. Why hadn't she tried it before?

Viktor took her through the artwork on the second, then third floors. By the time he stopped in front of what he called the *pièce de résistance*, an exceedingly modern piece by one of the great Russian masters that looked like random splotches of black and green to Frankie, a good twenty minutes had gone by.

"It's so…interesting," she commented, cradling her cognac in her hands. She was sipping the five-thousand-dollar-a-bottle spirit as slowly as she could, but its faint spiciness and floral aroma was delicious, sending a smooth, silky warmth through her bloodstream.

"It's breathtaking," Viktor countered, resting a palm against the wall where she stood. "I really should get back. Leonid is waiting for me."

"Oh," she murmured in disappointment, not sure they'd been gone long enough. "I was hoping there was more."

The Russian's eyes flashed. "There is an even more glorious Chagall in Leonid's personal rooms. I'm sure he won't mind me showing it to you."

Alarm bells went off in Frankie's head. The expression of intent in Viktor's light brown eyes was clear. He was so close she could smell his overwhelming aftershave, a spicy combination that made her want to sneeze.

"Oh, no," she said quickly. "I wouldn't dare intrude on Leonid's personal space."

"Are you sure?" He moved closer. "You've been such a good audience."

"Yes," she said firmly. She put a hand to the wall to lever herself away from it, but Viktor stepped closer, stopping her. *He was going to kiss her.* She'd been flirting outrageously with him to keep his attention, so why wouldn't he?

Her heart raced. "Viktor…this has been so sweet of you to give me a tour but—"

He set his other hand on the wall beside her so she was well and truly captured. "Don't run away," he said in Russian, his voice low and gravelly. "Stay."

Panic sliced through her. He dipped his head toward hers. She ducked under his arm and took a step away from him. He gave her a bemused look. Frankie held up her almost empty glass. "I think I need another one of these first."

He eyed her glass. "Another?"

She nodded enthusiastically. "It was sooo delicious. Just one more."

His generous mouth curved into a smile. "We'll make a full Russian out of you yet with that…*appetite*."

Her stomach did a little churn. Then relaxed as he good-naturedly held out an arm and led the way back down the hallway to the stairs and the ballroom below. He kept a possessive hand on her back as they wound their way through the crowd toward the bar. Frankie searched furiously for Harrison while he got their drinks, but the crowds were thick now, massed on the dance floor with a strobe light passing over them. She couldn't see him anywhere.

Viktor came back with their drinks, handing one to her. "We should dance," he announced.

Frankie thought that might be a good idea because she really didn't need any more to drink. She went to put the glass down on a table. Viktor waved a hand at her. "Bring it with you."

He led her onto the dance floor, where the band was playing a slow enough tune that they could dance and drink at the same time. She fake-sipped the cognac as Viktor's free hand around her waist kept her close. The champagne she'd consumed combined with the first cognac had cast the world in an all-over rosy glow, which would have been nice except *this* was a bit of a nightmare. The dance floor was packed, the heat of hundreds of bodies was magnifying her partner's überstrong cologne and he kept moving her closer with his free hand. She had the feeling he was going to try and kiss her again any minute…

Goddamn you, Harrison Grant. Where are you?

CHAPTER SIX

LEONID ARISTOV WAS a solitary figure on the balcony that overlooked the lake. His elbows rested on the marble ledge that bounded the tiny alcove; his tall, thin body tilted forward as he studied the play of light on the water in the moonlight.

He did not seem at all surprised when Harrison joined him at the railing. His trademark crooked smile flashed white in the darkness. "A Chagall fan? I had no idea."

"Always have been." Harrison rested his forearms on the ledge, mimicking the other man's stance.

"And here I thought you were above trying to impress me."

He lifted a shoulder. "Call it a gesture of good faith. I'm trying to understand the backpedaling, Leonid. I thought we had an agreement."

A laconic smile curved the Russian's lips. "I'm like a bride on my wedding day. I'm having second thoughts."

"About the two insignificant clauses you keep tripping over?"

"I don't care about those."

"Then what?" Harrison kept his temper in check, recalling Francesca's words. "Help me to understand."

Leonid stared out at the water. "A man gets philosophical when his life's work is crumbling at his feet. What was once important to me has become less so."

Harrison's gaze sharpened on the Russian's craggy profile. "You've made a few questionable decisions, Leonid. You're a brilliant businessman. You will rise from the ashes."

"As you did." Aristov flicked him a sideways glance. "My gut tells me this deal is not about Siberius, Harrison. It's about Anton Markovic and your desire to make him pay. The crowning act of your ascension back to glory."

Alarm rocketed through him. *How could the Russian know?* It was impossible. *Impossible.* But somehow, his mind raggedly conceded, he did.

He kept his face expressionless. "Why would you think this has anything to do with Markovic? That's ancient history."

Aristov turned to him, pinning him with the full force of that whiskey-hard gaze. "Because Markovic has become one of the most powerful men in the world. He put your father in his grave...*I* would want him to suffer." His lips twisted at the confusion in Harrison's eyes. "A few questions to a friend in Mergers and Acquisitions at a major investment bank and I had my answers. I know you've purchased another key supplier of Markovic's. I put two and two together."

A red mist descended over his vision, fury mixing with a fear that froze him solid. Heads would roll if it was discovered a banker had divulged that type of information. But that didn't matter now... He had a way bigger problem. Leonid and Anton Markovic did business together. If Leonid chose to, he could blow his entire plan out of the water.

Why hadn't he done so already?

"I can't stand Markovic." Leonid answered his unspoken question. "Yes, I do business with him but you can't always pick your dance partners. My issue," he drawled, "is not what you choose to do to Markovic. I would take pleasure in watching him fall. It's Siberius and your ultimate plans for it I care about."

Relief poured through him, slackening his limbs. He lifted his shoulder in a casual shrug. "It becomes a complementary subsidiary to Taladan that gives Grant International access to the markets we need."

"Or it becomes extraneous. Superfluous...*nonexistent.*" Aristov's gaze narrowed. "The market coverage Siberius brings to the table is not robust beyond the Slavic countries. You may choose to simply fold it into your megalith and it becomes a distant memory."

He kept his expression neutral as Aristov read the situation with deadly accuracy. "That market," he offered, "will become crucial in the next decade. We can't afford not to play in it."

Leonid trained that highly intelligent gaze of his on him with an intensity that would have broken a lesser man. "We have something in common, Harrison. My father built Siberius. It was the foundation for everything that came after it. I *care* about the company. Maybe it's this newfound philosophy of mine clouding my judgment. But I will *not* sell it to you to have it dismantled in an act of vengeance."

A wave of conscience enveloped him. He pushed it away. This deal was not about sentimentality. It was about watching Anton Markovic shrivel up and die a slow death. He would not allow it to be sidelined by emotion.

"This deal is not about dismantling Siberius," he said matter-of-factly. "It's about cutting Markovic off at the knees." If the board insisted he absorb Siberius and its operations within Taladan and wipe out Leonid's legacy as it surely would? Beyond his control...

Aristov turned and rested his forearms on the ledge. "I've been thinking about what I want to be in my second coming, Grant. For you it will be politics, I think. For me? I've been eyeing Manhattan real estate. A couple of penthouses I've been looking at have come on the market and they've agreed to let me see them next week. Present me with a plan for the future of Siberius. If I like it, I'll sign it."

Harrison nodded. It would take some creative positioning but he could make it happen. "I'll have it ready."

Leonid inclined his head. His thin mouth curved in an amused smile. "What have you done to Kaminski? He was supposed to be bringing me a Frapin Cuvée."

"I had Francesca detain him."

Leonid threw back his head and laughed. "How utterly unfeeling of you, Grant."

"On whose part?"

"Why, Viktor's, of course. He is besotted."

Harrison entered the ballroom riding a heady victory that had the blood in his veins pumping in a heated rush. His head felt clearer than it had in months, his walk powerful and full of resolve as he strode through the crowd. All of the low-grade, niggling anxieties he'd harbored throughout Aristov's backpedaling lifted away like dark clouds chased away by clearer skies.

Leonid Aristov had guessed his endgame and was willing to play to make the exceedingly evil Anton Markovic pay. All that was left to do was execute. Every piece, every backdoor would be secured when Aristov signed, and the long wait would be over.

He procured a whiskey at the bar, leaned back against it and drank it down. *Congratulations to me.*

Which reminded him Francesca was likely still out there sidelining Kaminski. She'd accepted the challenge without hesitation. She had risen to the occasion. If he denied that turned him on he would be a liar. The man in him loved the fact she had the courage to stand up to him, that she wasn't afraid to tell him he was a fool. But the employer in him took his attraction to his feisty PA off the table.

He tilted the last sip of his drink toward the light and considered its amber depths. Francesca had a unique ability to read people—to draw them to her with her frank, open—charm and somehow he'd known Juliana would be no different. She had saved the day. Been his secret weapon. But he would be equally well advised to caution himself against falling under the spell of Francesca's seductive charm. It would be all too easy.

He took the last sip of the whiskey, put the glass down and went looking for his PA. Francesca might have taken on her assignment with confidence, but she was a babe in the woods when it came to dealing with men like Kaminski.

He wound his way through the throngs of people on the dance floor. It was hot and sweaty and hard to negotiate. He had just about given up on finding Francesca in the ballroom and was about to search out Juliana when he saw her on the corner of the dance floor with Kaminski.

Kaminski's hand was wrapped around her incredible body, perilously close to her bottom. Francesca had a smile on her face, but it was a hunted, close-to-the-edge smile that made a switch flick in his head. What had he been thinking?

Five long strides took him to the couple. "May I cut in?"

Kaminski gave him an annoyed look. Harrison stared back at him. Luckily Aristov's second in command wasn't a combative personality like his boss and handed Francesca over. "I'll come find you afterward," he told her with a lingering look.

No, you won't, Harrison thought. Francesca nodded to the other man with another of those smiles he knew to be plastic and stepped closer to Harrison. She stood on tiptoe. "I don't need this drink," she whispered in his ear.

The husky whisper went up his spine, then straight back down. He took the glass from her fingers, deposited it on a table and took her in his arms. She flowed easily into him without that awkwardness some women possessed, wrapping one hand around his shoulder and lacing the fingers of the other through his. "Thank God," she murmured. "I think he was about to try and kiss me again."

"He tried to *kiss* you?"

Her hand fluttered from his shoulder in a delicate wave. "My fault. On our tour of Leonid's art collection, I had to lay it on a bit thick to keep him occupied."

He frowned. "What do you mean *a bit thick*?"

"Oh, I just flirted with him…nothing *too* much, you know. It was just at one point, he said he had to go meet Leonid and I was afraid you wouldn't be finished talking so I poured it on a bit and well—maybe he sort of got the wrong idea."

Hell. "I'm sorry," he breathed. "That was my fault. I never should have sent you after him. He's clearly—" he used Leonid's word "—besotted with you."

Her cheeks went pink. "I think that's a bit of a strong word."

"I don't." He tended to agree with Leonid that Frankie had been the dangerous one in that equation. She looked stunning. He'd had to pick his jaw up off the ground when he'd seen her in that dress, not because he hadn't seen a voluptuous woman in a low cut dress before, but because on Francesca it looked like innocence and temptation personified. An irresistible combination that had had his hands itching to touch her all night.

When he had earlier on the red carpet, his palm to her beautiful back, it had been an addiction he could easily fall prey to.

He studied the high color in her cheeks, her lush, beautiful features, the spirited curve of her mouth… It wasn't just her great legs Kaminski had gone wild for. It was the whole vibrant package that made you want to be the one to capture it.

A highly inappropriate wish on his part. Which was not happening.

Her floral, feminine scent drifted into his nostrils. What was it? Orange blossoms? It infiltrated him. Attacked his common sense. It was one thing keeping his brain detached when she was ten feet away from him sitting in her office chair. Another thing entirely when she was in his arms, her ample curves tracing the length of him. She was relaxed now, lacking the tension she'd displayed earlier, her body melding perfectly with his as they moved.

She looked up at him, gray eyes tangling with his in a long, tension-filled moment where he forgot his mask entirely. The jolt of awareness in her smoky eyes marked it a huge mistake.

"Did you at least get to talk to Leonid?" Her hasty words desperately broke the spell.

He nodded. "Because of you, Leonid and I figured each other out."

"What was his issue?"

"Sentimentality. Siberius was his father's company. He's finding it hard to part with it."

"At least he's putting it in good hands…"

Guilt scored his insides. "An acquisition is an acquisition," he said roughly. "There's a lot I can't control."

"He will sign, though?"

"Yes. We need to show him a plan on how we'll assimilate Siberius into the company when he's in New York next week. But that shouldn't be a problem."

"Good, then." Her chin lifted with satisfaction. "I'm glad I could help."

"You did more than help. You were a superstar tonight. I owe you my sincere thanks."

She blinked. "Well, that's…good. You're welcome." She chewed on the side of her mouth in that anxious habit she had when something was bothering her. "I wanted to say on the plane…I mean—I'm normally a very efficient, together person, Harrison, but since I've started working with you, I haven't been myself. I've been…off. I know that and I'm not sure why."

He knew why and he wasn't going there. "Because you're still intimidated by me."

"Maybe." She nodded. "There's a bit of that…"

And a whole lot of something else. He reached his limit. "I think we should go," he announced abruptly. "Before Kaminski comes around for round two."

She nodded, her eyes on his as she stepped out of his arms. She looked as conflicted as he felt.

They said good-night to Leonid and Juliana. Leonid promised to have Tatiana call with his schedule for the following week. Viktor Kaminski looked dismayed they were leaving. Francesca stood on tiptoe and pressed a kiss to both of the Russian's cheeks. He said something to her. Francesca frowned, thought about it for a minute, then replied. Kaminski let her go.

"That was awful," she muttered, climbing into the back of the Rolls-Royce ahead of him. "He wants to take me on a tour of the Met next week when they're in town."

He peeled his gaze off her amazing rear end and got in beside her. "Tell him you're busy. You will be."

She laid her head back against the leather seat. "I will. I just feel bad about leading him on."

"He's a big boy, he'll get over it." Just like he was going to get over his intense awareness of her at the moment.

She was silent, her gray eyes contemplative. He gave the driver instructions, slid the partition closed and the car moved softly off into the night. Frankie turned and stared out at the tall, dark shadows of London as they rolled by, interspersed with bright lights. He directed his gaze the other way. She was as direct and honest as most women were deceptive and ambitious. He'd never realized what a highly attractive quality that was in a woman, when so many in his social circle made game-playing a trait acquired at birth.

Silence fell in the car. He kept his gaze trained on the skyline of London rather than on Francesca's beautiful profile cast in the light of the street lamps. The whiskey he'd consumed, the satisfaction coursing through his veins at the night's success, the attraction he'd been fighting for a week were all too potent a combination to address.

The longer he was silent, the more the tension seemed to rise in the car. Francesca stared out her window, fidgeted with her clutch strap, anything but address it. Finally he felt the heat of her gaze on him. "Harrison?"

He turned to look at her.

"Have I done something wrong?"

He frowned. "No. Why?"

Her gaze fell away from his. "I—I don't know. I feel like I've done everything right tonight and something still feels wrong."

The shadows carved the enticing hollow between her breasts in the low-cut dress. The pout in her amazing mouth had lust snagging at his throat. "There's no issue," he assured her roughly. "I told you, you were perfect tonight."

"Then why have you been ignoring me since we walked off the dance floor? Did I say something wrong to Leonid or Juliana?"

"No." He wanted to leave it at that, sanity told him to leave it at that, but the vulnerable look she wore tore at his insides. He exhaled deeply. "I'm keeping my distance."

That gray stare widened. Her hands fluttered uselessly to her lap. The uncivilized part of him knew he never should have looked at her.

"This attraction between you and me…" He shook his head. "It can't happen. We both know that."

She nodded. But her gaze stayed glued to his as if she

knew the train was running off the track, but was willing to risk full and complete disaster.

"Francesca…" The word was a final, husky plea for her to put some distance between them. She didn't. She moved toward him at the same time he brought her closer with a palm to the bare skin of her back. It felt even sexier than he remembered.

His fingers curved around her delicate jaw, and for the first time in as long as he could remember, he did something for the pure pleasure of it. He kissed the woman he'd been wanting to touch since the night he'd found her sitting in Tessa's chair.

Her lush mouth was every bit as sweet as it had promised it would be. Bare of the lipstick so many women slathered on, her lips were soft, full and edible. He took them in a slow, sensual tasting designed to entice. A soft sigh left her lips as she moved into the kiss, her hands fluttering to his shoulders. The dominant male in him liked her acquiescence. He tugged at her luscious lower lip, sucked it inside of his mouth and savored it. She tasted of innocence and sensuality all at the same time.

He waited, nibbling and tugging on her lip until her response demanded more. She angled her mouth, sought deeper contact and he gave it to her with a rush of satisfaction, slanting his mouth across hers in a kiss that didn't tease, but delivered. He didn't stop until he'd explored every inch of her mouth, drew her out of her inexperienced hesitation until their mouths were sliding hotly against one another.

His body temperature spiked. He couldn't remember the last time he'd felt so…*lost*.

Her innocence should have stopped him. Instead it obliterated his common sense. The palm he held to the small of her back pressed harder, invited her to come closer. She came willingly, her fingers curving around his bicep this time. His hand slipped to the nape of her neck, holding her still as he rocked his parted mouth over hers to request entry. Her lips parted. She tasted of fruit and wild roses. He thought for a moment that might just be *her*, but it was the champagne he was tasting, sweet and inebriating as it combined with the whiskey in his mouth.

He slid his tongue into her warmth to savor her more. Her response was tentative at first, then bolder, meeting the long, lazy stroke of his. When she'd mastered that, he probed deeper, tangling his tongue with hers in the most intimate of kisses. Her quick intake of breath hardened every muscle in his body.

He could take more. So much more… He wanted his fantasy.

That brought him tumbling back to reality. He pulled his mouth from hers and set her away from him with hands that weren't quite steady. His breathing sounded fractured, rough in the silent confines of the car.

The dazed look on Francesca's face turned to horror. "That was my fault," he growled. "Not yours."

She shook her head, her fingers moving to her lips. "I—ah—I was just as much a part of that as you were."

Maybe true, but he was the one in authority here. He had no business *indulging* himself. Being reckless at the most important crossroads of his life. With an *employee* at that. *What the hell was wrong with him?*

He ran a hand through his hair. His brain worked quickly to defuse the situation. "It's been quite a night for both of us," he said slowly. "I think we can agree that was a mistake. A brief lapse of sanity."

Francesca's head bobbed up and down. "Absolutely. It was…" Her voice trailed off, a frown furrowing her brow. "Inappropriate. In every aspect. It will never happen again."

"Good." He rested his gaze on her face. "Tonight you

proved what a valuable asset you are to me, Francesca. You went above and beyond the call of duty. I'm going to need that from you and more over the next few months… It's not going to be easy and sometimes I'm going to be a son of a bitch. But I guarantee if you stick with me you will learn more in six months than you would in six years working for someone else."

A determined light flickered in her gray eyes. "I can be brilliant for you, Harrison, I promise."

"I know that. We make a good team." So no more of *that*.

She bit her lip and nodded. The car traversed the final couple of side streets to the hotel and slid to a halt in front of the Chatsfield. He got out, helped Francesca from the car and ignored the electricity still buzzing between them. It was easy for him to cut off his emotions, what little he had. Francesca, on the other hand, was obviously still processing what had happened as they rode the lift to their suite. He could read it in the myriad of emotions flickering in her gray eyes.

He said good-night to her at the door to her bedroom. She echoed his words, walked through it and closed the thick slab of wood with a soft click. He paused for a moment when he didn't hear her footsteps walking away on the marble. Instinctively he knew she was on the other side of the door, back pressed to the frame. Thinking.

"Forget the kiss, Francesca," he said. "It was nothing."

"It's already forgotten."

Her muffled response from directly behind the door made his mouth curve. Better to put that one to bed entirely. He'd almost capped a hugely successful evening with a mistake that would have cost him dearly. Cost him his focus. And he couldn't allow that. The end was in sight. Time to focus on the master plan.

CHAPTER SEVEN

FRANKIE SPENT THE weekend replanting the flower boxes on her terrace with miniature roses, having brunch with her roommate, Josephine, and generally attempting to restore some sanity to her brain after having *kissed her boss*. She almost would have believed the party at Leonid Aristov's house had been a bizarre and unreal dream that could never have actually happened, except she knew for a fact it *had* happened when at 10:00 a.m. on Monday morning two dozen *full-size* white roses landed on her desk with a card from Viktor Kaminski.

Apparently he didn't intend to take no for an answer. *Allow me to take a treasure to see the treasures of the Met*, the card said. *Friday night? Viktor.*

She winced at the corny line. She'd told Viktor her schedule was impossible this week. She was just going to have to stick to that. And she really *was* too busy. The stack of work she had on her desk was monumental. She was going to have *no* life for the next six months.

The sweet smell of the dove-white blooms filled her nose. A wave of longing settled over her. She would die to receive roses from a man she really liked. Instead, they were from Viktor and she'd kissed her boss.

Stupid. Stupid. Stupid. Just when she'd proven she was a *valuable asset*, she'd gone and done that. She had to wonder if her mind *was* off if she was doing things like this.

She stared grumpily at her favorite flower. The fact that *Harrison Grant*, her stern, sometimes scary, stunningly attractive boss was attracted to her, was irrelevant. As he'd said, the kiss meant *nothing*. *Except*, it had been the most sensational experience of her life. It was one thing to feel chemistry with another person every time you were in the same room together. Another thing entirely to *feast* on it.

Her email pinged. The report she needed from marketing had come in. Josh was coming up to discuss it with her. *Good.* She could definitely use the distraction.

By the time Harrison strolled into the office late afternoon looking every inch the automotive magnate he was in a light gray suit and a white shirt that showed off the color he'd acquired sailing with a business acquaintance on the weekend, she'd made a significant stab at the outline of the Aristov plan.

He shot a pointed look at the flowers. "Don't tell me… Viktor."

She nodded.

He shook his head. "Best to give him the permanent brush-off this time."

"I know. I really wish I didn't have to do it in person."

His mouth quirked. "Oh, come now, Francesca. The art of a good brush-off is an excellent skill to have as a young woman in New York City."

She put her pencil down. "I can't imagine you've ever been on the receiving end of one. I wouldn't think it's very nice."

"The point isn't to be nice. That's what gets you kissed in elevators."

She was considering a clever response when he grabbed the card from the flowers and scanned it. She held out her hand. "Give that back."

He waved it at her. "It's in Russian. What did he say?"

Heat filled her cheeks. "It's a private note."

His ebony gaze sat on her face. "My principled Francesca," he murmured sardonically. "I would expect no less from you. Do you want me to talk to him?"

"*Absolutely not.* I'll handle it."

"Fine." He nodded toward his office. "I need to make a couple of calls then we can start on the plan for Leonid."

"I'm almost done the outline." She glanced at her watch. "It's almost five. Should I order dinner in?"

He flexed his shoulders and frowned. "I've been inside all day. It's gorgeous out there. Why don't we do the work on my terrace and my housekeeper will make us dinner?"

She wasn't at all sure putting them on anything but a business footing was a wise move at this tenuous stage, but she wasn't about to stir the waters of what seemed like an inordinately sunny Harrison day either.

"Sounds good," she agreed. "It'll be much nicer to get out of the office."

He finished up his calls, they collected their work and drove to his penthouse on Central Park West in Harrison's elegant Jaguar. His penthouse was located on the top level of the coveted Central Park West address that everyone who was anyone seemed to be bickering over, but few were lucky enough to obtain. It was beautifully decorated, of course, customized by Harrison's architect during construction so that an entire grand staircase had been moved to one end to create a wide-open floor-to-ceiling-window-lit main level that accommodated his art collection.

Done in sleek, bold colors, with blue and slate dominating, the penthouse reminded her of his office. Sterile and unobjectionable. She slipped her shoes off and wandered over to survey the art. It was not a collection on the scale of Leonid's—maybe twelve pieces in total, but priceless no doubt from Harrison's four-million-dollar Chagall purchase. She walked from one to the next, remembering Viktor's sermon about what to look out for. When she reached a Chagall done in the same vibrant blues as the one Harrison had bought in London, she stopped and took it in. They could be from the same collection.

"It'll have company now…" She jumped when Harrison spoke from behind her. He moved with a catlike grace that made him virtually undetectable.

"Relax," he drawled, his mouth tilting with amusement. "I'm not Viktor Kaminski."

No, he wasn't. He was far more dangerous. Especially when he smiled like that. It was like watching the sun come out on a rainy day. She shifted her gaze back to the painting to get her pulse under control. A bird and a woman were perched in a magnificently colored bouquet of flowers floating over the waters of what must be Nice, with its palm trees and similarity to the one she'd seen in London. Again, as with the other one, the image did not make complete sense. The bouquet had the tails of a fish instead of stems, and the buildings dotting the Riviera were curved not straight.

"It's fantastical, almost supernatural," she murmured. "Things that shouldn't be together are and it seems perfectly natural. Like he envisioned some sort of alternate universe."

He nodded, his gaze moving to the painting. "I think he did. The art historians describe his work as figurative and narrative art. Chagall was embraced by many—the surrealists, the cubists, the suprematists—but he rejected them all. He created a new reality for himself—one that was based on both his inner and outer worlds—the story, the dream he wanted to tell. This series in Nice," he said, waving a hand at the painting, "is always very mystical and inspirational. The colors are incredible."

She got that completely. "Is he one of your favorites?"

"Likely my favorite." The amber flecks in his eyes she found so fascinating glimmered in the expertly angled lighting, giving him a softer appearance. "Some of his later works are much more heartbreaking. They speak of the personal tragedies he suffered before he ended up here in New York."

"I would like to see some of those. I'm sure they'd be amazing."

"They are very moving."

She found herself fascinated by this side of him. The emotion in his eyes when he talked about the artist hinted at a depth to him, an ability to feel he kept hidden underneath the layers.

He read her expression. "You're surprised." His lips curled. "The beast does feel, Francesca. When he lets himself."

Like that night in the car...when he'd let go of that formidable control of his and kissed her senseless.

She couldn't help taking a step on the dangerous side. "Why doesn't he let himself do that all the time?"

He lifted a shoulder. "A beast doesn't need to connect. He lives on another level entirely."

That he did. Her mouth pursed with the desire to speak, but she shut it down. He might tell himself that. But everyone needed to connect, to experience their human ability to feel. Even a beast.

"Shall we get started, then?"

He nodded. "Elisa is making a shrimp-and-lobster paella. Would you like a drink first?"

She shook her head. "Mineral water is fine." Tonight she was keeping this all about business. Every last single minute of it.

The pentagon-shaped terrace, boasting coveted southern, eastern and western views of New York, including one of Central Park, was an amazing space to work in.

Frankie booted up her PC in one of the comfortable seating areas scattered around the space, and took in the view.

"I've received input from Marketing and Sales," she told Harrison when he returned with their drinks.

"Good." He came over to sit beside her to look at the screen. He was overwhelmingly male and distracting with his long legs splayed out in front of him. It was going to take all her powers of concentration to keep her mind where it should be.

"Did we get operations to mock up an organizational structure?"

"Yes, it's here." She flipped to the slide. The drawing illustrated every division of the massive company that was Grant International, including a new parallel subcompany to Taladan for gauges and meters in Siberius. It was mind-numbing to look at, the scale was so vast. Pretty much every piece of a car you *didn't* see on the outside was made by Grant International.

Harrison studied the diagram. "That's fine. Slot an overall positioning slide in at the beginning and I'll give you some points."

She added an up-front slide. He started dictating points, then stopped, backtracked and changed some of his wording. It sounded like semantics to her but she kept typing.

"Point three—the Siberius brand will be maintained as is, pending the outcome of the operations group and consumer research studies."

Frankie started typing. He frowned and waved a hand at her. "Delete that. I want to bury it further down in the plan."

Bury it? Why would they do that?

She kept her mouth shut. He had a reason for everything he did, much of it unbeknownst to her. They finished the opening slides and started on the marketing plan. Frankie thought the team had done an excellent job of making gauges and meters a sexy topic for the industry audience the campaign would be targeted at, but Harrison ripped out two of her favorite ideas.

"Why?" she asked, with her newly granted ability to question. "Those are really smart, creative ideas that work for the target audience. Isn't that key to growing a brand?"

He nodded, his dark lashes coming down to veil his gaze. "But I think it's overkill in this case."

They moved on to the next section of ideas the marketing team had grouped as "core must-haves." The first point included ads in trade publications. "Take that out," Harrison instructed. Now she really didn't understand. When Josh had gone through the ideas with her he had told her advertising was key to creating mass awareness for a product. "If nobody in the North American market *knows* about Siberius's cool products," she asked, "how are you going to expand its base?"

He gave her a pained look. "Expanding Siberius's base isn't an important priority for us right now. It's doing fine in the strength areas it currently occupies."

This was hurting her brain. She put her laptop down and eyed him contemplatively. "Correct me if I'm wrong, but aren't we supposed to be *selling* Leonid on how Siberius will flourish within Grant International? Encouraging him we are the right way to go? He said he had innovative products no one else has. How do we promote those?"

"Every company *says* they have innovative products," he bit out impatiently. "I am conscious of not setting unrealistic expectations when anything could happen when the board gets ahold of this deal."

She frowned. "But of course they'll support the plan if this is the only way you can get Leonid to sign. They'll have no choice."

"That's an idealistic way to look at it, but the reality is they'll do what makes business sense. *I* can only make suggestions. In scenarios like this when we're acquiring similar resources, the board will likely force us to streamline the two companies into one. It's doubtful Siberius will be left standing as its former entity."

"So why are we spending all this time doing a plan?" The words were hardly out of her mouth before it hit her. Harrison had no intention of keeping Siberius intact. He was going to lure Leonid in with this plan and dismantle Siberius when it was done.

Every bone in her body hated the idea. The company had belonged to Leonid's father. He wanted his legacy preserved. That had been his whole hesitation in signing.

She eyed him. "It's a bait and switch."

The impatience in his gaze devolved into a dark storm brewing. "No," he rejected in a lethally quiet voice. "I made a promise to Leonid to do what I can to see Siberius preserved. It is beyond my or any other CEO's control to promise him it will remain intact when business realities say it won't."

Yet he wasn't even giving the company a fighting chance with this plan. She lifted her chin. "I see."

"Francesca…"

She shook her head. This was the part where she needed to stop talking because it got her into trouble. "Let's keep going," she said quietly, looking down at her screen. "Where were we?"

"Francesca," he growled. "This is business. Put the self-righteous look away and be a big girl. You have no idea of the stakes here."

The "big girl" remark did it for her. She looked up at him, eyes spitting fire. "Dictate to me what you want in this plan and I will do it. But do not ask me to say that this is right."

"It *is* right." His ebony gaze sat on her with furious heat. "This is the law of the jungle. Only the fittest survive."

"In your world," she said evenly. "Not in mine."

"And what would your world have me do? Allow some other predator to snap Siberius up because I'm the one *stupid* enough to tell Leonid the truth? Not happening."

"I believe in karma," Frankie said stubbornly. "I know what a good man Leonid is. He's putting his trust in you."

The fury in his eyes channeled into a livid black heat that was so focused, so intense, it scorched her skin. "I know all about karma, Francesca. I know more about it than you will ever want to know in your lifetime. Trust me on that."

She watched with apprehensive eyes as he got up, paced to the railing and looked out at the fading light of New York. Having him ten feet away allowed her to pull in some air and compose herself. This job meant everything to her; she was proving she could make it on her own. But so did the principles upon which she'd been brought up.

"I'm not trying to be difficult," she said quietly to his back. "But my father taught me to treasure my ethics at all costs. That if I was ever in a situation that would make it hard for me to sleep at night, maybe I shouldn't be a part of it."

He turned around, leaned back against the railing and rested his elbows on it. His anger had shifted into a cold, hard nothingness that was possibly even more disconcerting than the fury.

The chill directed itself her way. "Although my grandfather built Grant Industries, it was my father who had the foresight and brilliance to modernize its methods and transform Grant from a successful but stagnant regional player in the American auto industry to a force to be reckoned with worldwide. He spent every minute of his life at the office, sacrificed *everything* for the company and eventually it paid off. When I was ten, my father came home one night with a big smile on his face and told us Grant Industries had made the list of the one hundred most profitable companies in America." He lifted a brow. "Imagine. Coburn and I were only eight and ten—but we got that, we got what that meant."

She nodded. Wondered why he was telling her this.

"As soon as we finished university, Coburn and I joined the business. It was in our blood just like it was in our father's. We had the bug. But neither of us ever expected to take on the mantle so soon."

Because his father had killed himself.

Her insides knotted, a cold, hard ball at the core of her. The skin on his face stretched taut across his aristocratic cheekbones, a blank expression filling his eyes. "One day my father's usual superhuman working day stretched into two. Then three. He looked like a wreck. He would go into the office, put his engineering teams through crazy all-night sessions, then come home and sleep it off. At first we weren't too concerned—it wasn't unlike him to be tunnel-visioned when he was working on a project. But the pattern started getting more and more frequent. More dramatic. One particular night, he came home and he was talking so fast none of us could understand him. We couldn't get him to rest so we called a doctor. He was diagnosed that night as a manic depressive."

Her heart went into free fall. "How old were you?"

"Fifteen."

"Oh, Harrison." She went to get up but he held out a hand, staying her.

"His condition got progressively worse as the years went on. The stress of success and the accompanying pressure made the cycles more acute, sent him into longer bouts of mania. My mother had to focus entirely on keeping him well and ensuring his condition was kept under wraps so the press, the shareholders, didn't catch on."

To the detriment of her boys' emotional well-being.

"We thought we had his condition under control after

handling it for two decades. Then my father made a deal with Anton Markovic to buy one of his Russian-based companies."

Anton Markovic? The sadistic oligarch Juliana didn't like in her house?

For the first time since he'd starting speaking, a flare of emotion moved through his dark gaze. "My father saw the potential in a post-Communist era and knew it would only grow. Buying Markovic's company was supposed to cement Grant as the most powerful auto parts manufacturer in the world. Except Markovic sold us a false-bottomed company that was on the verge of bankruptcy. Under normal circumstances, Grant would have easily absorbed the hit but we were overexposed at the time, in the midst of leveraging capital for an expansion. As a result, the debt from the deal almost crippled us."

She tried to absorb all the information he was throwing at her. "Couldn't you have gone to the courts?"

"We did. His holding company was bankrupt by then."

She swallowed hard, not sure she wanted to know where the story went after this. The emotion in his eyes became hard to watch. "Coburn and I told him it'd be fine. We'd rebuild ourselves stronger than ever. But the miscue threw him into a depressive state he couldn't pull himself out of. There was also the stress of his impending race for governor of New York." His lashes swept down over his cheeks. "My mother left the house for a half hour one day, thinking he was asleep. I came home to find he'd shot himself."

Oh, my God. Her heart broke into a million pieces. It was public knowledge that Clifford Grant had shot himself at the family residence. *But to find your father like that, by yourself?* This time she did get up and walked over to him, setting her hand on his bicep.

"I am so sorry, Harrison."

He looked down at her hand as if it was an intrusive appendage that had crept into his lair and threatened his solitary confinement. She could feel the emotion he declared he didn't have vibrating through him. Then his eyes hardened until they resembled an exotic, impenetrable rock, polished by the elements he'd endured until there were no cracks, no dents, just icy determination. "I'm not looking for your *pity*, Francesca. I told you this because I need you at my side with this deal. I need you to *understand* where *I'm* coming from. Acquiring Siberius is the final piece in my plan to cut Anton Markovic off at the knees for what he did to my father. The company is valuable to me only because it supplies Markovic with vital instruments."

Understanding dawned. Suddenly all of it—Harrison, Coburn, the way they both were—it all made sense. Coburn spent his days running from the truth, Harrison pursuing vengeance.

He wanted her on board so he could land this deal and finish Markovic. Collateral damage in Leonid was inconsequential.

"So we finish the presentation, he signs and it's done. What does this have to do with me?"

His expression was implacable. "I need you to be a part of this until he signs. Leonid likes you. Kaminski likes you. You will smooth out the rough edges."

She turned to look out at the park. It was lit by the skyscrapers surrounding it, a beautiful oasis in a cutthroat city of deal makers. It wasn't lost on her that Leonid was a cutthroat businessman himself who undoubtedly had his share of blood on his hands. No one in a position of power could avoid the gray areas. It was the gray that defined you.

But it was the emotion she'd just seen in Harrison's eyes that clutched at her heart. A raw incomplete grief that was as present now as it had been when Anton Markovic had torn out his heart.

Dampness attacked the corners of her eyes. She blinked

it back and did what her father had always taught her to do. She went with her gut. And perhaps a large slice of emotion. Because no human being should ever have to go through what Harrison had without making it right.

She turned to him and nodded. "Let's get back to work, then."

His gaze darkened. "I'm an honorable man, Francesca. I will keep my promise to Leonid if I can. But it will ultimately be up to the board."

She hoped he could. But sometimes a need for vengeance could wreak havoc on such honor.

CHAPTER EIGHT

HARRISON WAS HAVING trouble sleeping. Dawn was breaking across Manhattan, a vibrant ribbon of burnt orange stretching low across the skyline, casting the base of the skyscrapers in a mist of shimmering fire. It mirrored the turmoil inside of him, the slow burn that threatened to engulf him.

He'd had maybe three, four restless hours of unconsciousness before he'd abandoned his bed and greeted the morning. There was too much on his brain, too much to accomplish, too many decisions that impacted too many people.

He watched the sun, a bright ball of fire, penetrate the mist and make its way into the sky. Today was the day Leonid Aristov would either cement or destroy his seven-year plan to wipe Anton Markovic's empire from the face of the earth. To do that, he must stretch the truth, make a man believe something that was quite likely not possible.

It was eating at him. Plaguing him. He grimaced and set his elbows on the smooth limestone ledge that bounded the terrace. At thirty-three his conscience was making an unexpected appearance and he had little difficulty wondering why. *Francesca*. His personal moral compass who sat on his shoulder, reminding him that the world was not black and white. That one wrong did not right another.

Except in this case it did. Leonid would lose his legacy regardless of who bought Siberius. And he would never let Anton Markovic get away with what he'd done.

He frowned into the hazy pink, orange light. Francesca, on the other hand, was a gray area he couldn't seem to control. A woman unafraid to call him on who he was. The woman whose kiss had woken up something inside of him he'd thought long ago dead…

He didn't let himself think of Susanna, ever, because he'd done what he'd had to do in the months following his father's death. He'd compartmentalized his emotions until there was only rebuilding his father's legacy left, cutting out the rest, including his longtime girlfriend. It had been an act of survival for a twenty-five-year-old who'd lost his mentor and couldn't afford to lose everything else.

Susanna, a smart, young financial broker, hadn't been content to live her life with a shell of a man. And who could blame her? When he'd finally come to terms with his father's death, she'd moved on, found someone who was more "emotionally available." It hadn't just been the last few months, she'd told him sadly, it had been her battle over their entire relationship to get him to open up. "It's never going to happen, Harrison. I give and you take. I need more."

His fingertips dug into the cool stone. He hadn't told Susanna he'd been breaking apart inside, that he didn't know how to let the pain out, because he was inherently flawed by his experiences. He was better off on his own. And his descent into the world of the unfeeling had worked just fine until Francesca Masseria had roared into his life and stamped her do-gooder presence all over his psyche.

He raked a hand through his spiky, disheveled hair and frowned. So that kiss had reminded him he knew how to feel. That he didn't have the emotional IQ of zero his brother thought he had. She was his employee. She was too innocent for a jaded animal like him and she was messing with his head.

If that wasn't enough, he had her tied up in knots over her ethical quandaries. Plenty of reasons to stay away.

The sun rose higher between the buildings, insistently making its presence known to the Manhattan morning. His anxiety rose with it. The political bloodhounds chasing him had stepped up their campaign. Wanted a decision. It made his head want to blow off. To mount an independent run for the presidency meant walking away from Grant. It meant altering his life in a way he could never take back. How could he possibly make such a decision *now* when all he could see was a marker on Anton Markovic's back?

A fatalistic curve twisted his lips. Some would see such ungratefulness at so much opportunity as foolish. Yet it had never been his idea to get into politics. His grandfather had been a congressman. His father had wanted to be governor. Yes, he saw a need for change, but was he the man to do it? Or was he too much of a rebel to make it work?

When his head got too heavy to sit on his shoulders, when he thought it might actually blow off, he headed for the gym. When he got into the office at six-thirty, Coburn was already there.

His brow lifted. "Time change got you?"

"Brutal. But the blondes were fantastic."

He shook his head. His brother had been in Germany for the past week meeting with the manufacturers who built their automobiles with Grant parts. "Try being a little less predictable," he taunted, setting his briefcase down on Coburn's desk.

"I dunno," Coburn came back thoughtfully, tossing his pen on the desk. "I think you're holding your end of the stick surprisingly well lately. You have the political pundits on the edge of their seat."

"Because they have nothing interesting to talk about."

Coburn leaned back in his chair. "Are you going to do it?"

"You'll know when I do."

"Right." His brother's gaze narrowed. "And then there were the photos of you on the red carpet with Frankie in London. When did you start taking your PA to social events?"

"Since she spoke Russian."

"That was quite the dress she had on."

He recognized his brother's predatory look. "She looked beautiful."

"She was a goddamned knockout. But you, H?" His brother lifted a brow. "Haven't seen that sparkle in your eyes in years. Sure you haven't caught the Frankie bug?"

"She was useful, Coburn. That's all."

"I think," his brother ventured thoughtfully, his magnetic blue eyes lighting up, "we should invite her to the Long Island party. She can wear that dress."

"*Francesca?* I don't think that's a good idea."

"Why not?" Coburn challenged. "She's good enough to take to a million-dollar Aristov party, but not good enough to mingle with your Yale friends?"

His brows came together. "This has nothing to do with class. Frankie is an employee."

"You invited Tessa last year."

"Because she'd worked with me for two years."

Because he hadn't wanted to put his hands all over his married assistant...

"I'm going to invite her," Coburn announced definitively. "She's *my* employee and she deserves to come."

He crossed his arms over his chest. "Don't you think she's going to feel out of place with all those people she doesn't know?"

His brother shrugged. "She can come with me."

A discomforting feeling speared his insides. "*You* don't have a date?"

Coburn spread his hands wide. "Dry. Completely dry. I can make sure Frankie has a good time."

He didn't like that idea *at all*. "You said you were going to stay away from her."

"I intend to. But that doesn't mean she doesn't deserve to come." Coburn pursed his lips, his gaze moving over his brother. "Unless you want to take her. Or are you escorting the poor, neglected Cecily?"

"I haven't seen Cecily in months."

"Like I said—" Coburn winced "—poor Cecily. Anyway, Mother would like to know if you're bringing a date."

He was sure she would. It was only then that he realized the party was next week. "I'll invite Francesca," he rasped. "You inviting her would give her the wrong idea. I can position it as a job well done."

"Fine. Aristov sign?"

"Today's the day." He borrowed a page from Francesca's book of optimism. He needed it. Badly.

Frankie took one look at a beautiful, Tom Ford–suited Harrison as he walked into the office and knew she'd never seen him wound so tight.

"Good morning," she said carefully. "Coffee?"

He gave her a distracted look. "Sorry?"

"Did you want some coffee?"

"Oh…yes. Stronger the better, thanks."

She decided that might not be a good idea. She made the cup half strength and carried it into him.

He took a sip. Frowned. "It doesn't taste strong."

"It's strong." She gave the bags under his eyes a critical look. The man didn't sleep. But she was not his mother.

"Tom Dennison called a few minutes ago. He says you haven't responded about the fund-raiser."

Harrison scowled, fatigue creasing the lines of his face. "Tell him I'm in China."

She gave him an even look. Tom Dennison was one of the most powerful businessmen in America, the CEO of a consumer packaged-goods company as well as a highly political animal who liked to shake things up.

"I'll tell him you're occupied with the shareholder meetings," she suggested instead. "And ask him to please send over the details again so you can get back to him tomorrow."

"Brilliant." Sarcasm dripped from his voice.

Leonid better sign tonight. It was her only hope. She took a deep breath. "Have you eaten breakfast?"

"No, thanks."

"I'll get you some granola and yogurt at the deli."

"Francesca," he growled but she was already out the door.

Things went from bad to worse. Leonid's meeting with the penthouse developers was delayed by three hours while he waited to get the paperwork done to buy. Harrison fumed that the Russian clearly didn't have his priorities in order if a penthouse was more important than a *forty-million-dollar deal*. "*Everything* is always more important than a forty-million-dollar deal."

Now Aristov and Kaminski weren't going to be available until after six and Leonid had suggested they meet at the vodka club he frequented for drinks instead.

"How are we supposed to finalize a deal at a *vodka club*?" Harrison snapped.

"Sealing a deal over a meal or drinks is becoming more commonplace in Russian culture," Frankie soothed. "Take a deep breath."

He glared at her from across the desk. "I am not six, Francesca."

Right now you are. Her eyes must have said what her

lips wouldn't because his stare turned positively lethal. *I would prove it to you*, he threw back, *if we didn't have a moratorium in place. But since we do, you are out of luck.*

The electricity simmered and crackled between them. Francesca sucked in a deep breath of her own before it exploded. "I will print copies of the plan to take with us. Anything else we need?"

Closure, his gaze fizzled.

She turned and walked out of his office, heart slamming in her chest.

Leonid's vodka bar was in the heart of Manhattan at Broadway and West Fifty-Second Street. The VIP room the owner directed them to was one of the most unique spaces Frankie had ever seen. A huge cathedral-shaped stained-glass window glowing with a rainbow array of colors that graduated from blue to pink to yellow was the focal point of the room. Green-and-gold wainscoted walls were accented by a vibrant patterned wallpaper in the same colors that climbed up and over the ceiling. A rich, ornate carpet in complementary tones claimed the floor while two stunning chandeliers bookended the room.

She couldn't decide if she loved it or if it was just much too much. "Certainly more interesting than a conference room," she told Leonid as he gave her a kiss on both cheeks.

"I thought so."

Having obtained two of the penthouses he'd had his eye on under fierce competition, Leonid insisted they begin with a celebratory drink. They toasted the deal with vodka that surprisingly didn't taste like rubbing alcohol, but like absolutely nothing instead. Thus the potency, she warned herself.

After a few minutes of real-estate chatter, Harrison went through the plan, his jaw set, expression intent. Leonid stalled at the piece about an operational study of Siberius determining its internal and external positioning within Grant Industries. "You told me Siberius will remain a distinct brand. This makes it sound like it's up in the air."

Harrison regarded him evenly. "I cannot promise you the board will allow me to preserve Siberius's separate identity, Leonid. You know as well as I do these decisions are made with the numbers in mind. I will, however, influence the process as much as I can. But I cannot lead you on and say it's a given."

The room went so silent, so fast, Frankie could hear the ultraquiet fans in the ceiling whirling. Harrison's face was utterly expressionless. Leonid sat watching him, his shrewd eyes assessing. The Russian's fingers ceased their tapping on the table. Frankie's heart stopped in her chest as he placed both palms on the edge. *Was he going to leave?*

After a long moment, Leonid looked at Harrison, his mouth set in a grim line.

"Thank you for being honest with me."

Harrison nodded. Frankie exhaled.

"Continue, please."

Harrison went through the remainder of the plan. It was stripped down, basic and promised very little. When they got to the end, Leonid gave it a long look, flipped it over and threw it into the middle of the table. "Not much there to get excited about."

Harrison eyed him with that deadly, combustive look he'd been carrying all day. "I would say forty million dollars is a great deal to get excited about. As far as a second coming, it's a very nice start."

The Russian was silent. He stood up abruptly, pushing his chair back from the table. "Give me a few minutes. I need some air."

Viktor Kaminski raised a brow as his boss walked out of the room. Harrison's face grew so tight she thought it might snap in half. Since he was like a live bomb right now and she didn't want to encourage Viktor further, she excused herself, saying she needed the ladies' room.

The patio and some air beckoned instead. She stepped out onto it. No wonder Leonid had needed air. He and Harrison had been sucking the room dry since they'd stepped into it.

The patio was packed with people enjoying the steamy summer night. The smell of lilac came from the tree flowering in the garden. Lazy jazz floated on the air from the club next door. Francesca walked to the edge of the garden and stood drinking it in. She wasn't sure when Leonid appeared beside her, tall, thin and contemplative as he smoked a cigarette.

"Don't tell me it's bad for my health." He read her disapproval. "It's one of my few real vices."

"I won't, then."

His eyes glittered with amusement. "I like that about you. This honesty you have. If you don't say it, you can read it in your eyes."

"It's a curse." Her mouth twisted. "Ever since childhood. It got me in a lot of trouble."

"So it is."

He was silent, puffing elegantly on the cigarette. When he finished it he tossed it to the ground and snuffed it out under his foot. "Should I sign it?"

Her breath caught in her throat. "Sign what?"

He turned that hard, whiskey-colored gaze on her. "The deal. Should I sign it? Is Grant the honorable man I think him to be?"

The world closed in around her, the chatter of the crowd, the croon of the music melding together to create a buzz in her ears that seemed deafening. She didn't want to be any part of this. She'd never wanted to be any part of this. And maybe that was what Leonid had sensed.

If she balked now, she would ruin Harrison.

She pulled in a breath, conscious of the Russian's gaze on her face. And said the only thing her conscience would allow. "He's a good man. I wouldn't work for him if I didn't think so."

He watched her. Evaluated her. It was like being inspected by a customs official, the intensity of it. Then he nodded, an expression she couldn't read passing through those cat's eyes of his.

"*Harasho.* Let's go inside, then."

Harrison watched Francesca and Leonid walk back into the room together. Her face was white and pinched, tension stitching her delicate features together. It made the tiny hairs on the back of his neck stand up straight.

Leonid, on the other hand, looked focused and alert. He sat down at the table and signaled for another round of vodka. Harrison's heart pounded in his chest, drowning out everything but what was about to happen. Seven years of waiting and planning could not end in anything but success.

He sat there in agony while Kaminski engaged in small talk with Francesca as they waited for the vodka. The server came back laden with a tray of four glasses. He passed them out. Leonid lifted his glass. "Right, then," he said, looking at Harrison. "We have a deal."

Relief slackened every muscle in Harrison's body. His heart slowed its frantic pace. *It was done.* The last piece was in place. The crystal tumbler felt heavy in his hand as he raised it, eyes on Leonid. "We have a deal."

The vodka slid down his throat and warmed his insides. He had expected a surge of victory. For everything to feel *right* for the first time since he'd started this quest. Instead he felt nothing. Nothing at all except a numbness, an absence of feeling that was almost frightening in its intensity.

He distracted himself by glancing at Francesca. Her long lashes swept down over her cheeks as she took a sip of the vodka then pushed the glass away. Whatever had gone on outside had rattled her. Even in his distracted state, the glitter in her gray eyes burrowed itself beneath his skin. What had gone on between her and Leonid?

They finished the vodka. Leonid requested a fully executable contract be sent to his lawyer the following morning. If he got the green light that Harrison was sure he would because the lawyers had already scoured the document, he would sign.

He kept waiting for the euphoria to hit him. While he smiled at Leonid's joke about missing their personal chess matches each day. As they said goodbye to the two men and climbed into the car, Francesca stopping to speak to Viktor. While he stared out at a now dark New York. It never came. Why wasn't he on top of the world? Why didn't the victory feel sweet instead of bittersweet? He could close in on Anton Markovic now and bring it all full circle. Make him understand his pain. Wasn't that what he'd always wanted?

It made no sense.

He glanced at Francesca. The pinched look hadn't left her face. If anything it was worse. "Did you let him down easy?"

She turned a conflicted gaze on him. "I told him I was hung up on someone else. It seemed nicer to do it that way."

He wondered if she meant him. He could not deny he was more than a little hung up on her. And fighting it bitterly.

Her gaze fell away from his. He rested his head against the back of the seat. "What did Leonid say to you outside?"

Her mouth pressed into a straight line. "He asked me if he should sign the deal. If you were the honorable man he thought you were."

His head came off the seat. Her gaze moved back to his, stark and most definitely under siege. *Aristov had asked her that?*

"What did you say?"

"I said you were a good man. That I wouldn't be working for you if you weren't."

It had cost her integrity a great deal to say that knowing the scenario he'd painted. He closed his hand over the fist she had curled on the seat. "Thank you."

Her gaze dropped to his hand. "It's the truth. You are a good man."

With a cross to bear she didn't agree with... His hand remained closed over her fist. He fought the desire to bring it to his mouth, to press his lips to her skin until she released the tension and he could taste the salt on her skin. He wanted her. He wanted her so badly he could taste her already under his mouth. But she was unavailable to him.

He released her hand before he did it. His skin pulsed with the need for more because that touch, *her touch*, was the only thing making him feel alive right now.

He brought his back teeth together. Fought it. Recited to himself all the reasons he couldn't have her. *Good* reasons.

Derrick slid the partition open and asked, "Where first?"

He gave him Francesca's address.

She shook her head. "We're closer to you. I need the papers for the Detroit project to work on while you're out in the morning. I'll come up, get them, then Derrick can drive me home."

It made sense. It would also get him out of this car sooner. "Fine. That works."

Derrick stopped in the circular driveway at the side of the building. They rode the elevator to the penthouse in silence, neither of them about to address the tension and push things over the edge.

He found the papers she needed on the desk in his study and carried them out to the living room. "Text me if you need any clarification." The delicate fingers he'd just held closed around them. Her gaze fastened on his, probing, seeking. "I'll see you tomorrow afternoon then."

"Yes." He willed her out of the apartment with a curt, dismissive look. He needed to be alone or he needed to drown himself in her, but he couldn't do anything in between.

She was halfway to the door when she stopped and turned around. "Harrison, are you okay?"

"I'm fine. Thank you for your help today."

She nodded and left. When the door closed behind her and he heard the sound of the elevator whishing its way toward ground level, he poured himself a drink he knew he didn't need and took it out onto the terrace. The moon was a perfect, giant orb in a sheet of black. Luminous; full of promise. It should have been another signpost of where he was headed. Vengeance. Yet he continued to feel nothing. The fear he dreaded always found a way in, insidious as it was, worming its way into his consciousness.

He lifted his palms to his temples. Willed it away. It was nights like this, nights when he scaled Mount Everest and won, when any other human being would have been basking in the glory, that he wondered if the darkness would claim him, too.

There had never been any sign he had picked up his father's genetic markers for mania, but the depression beckoned, whispering along the edges of his mind. He raised his eyes to the Grant tower, a shining beacon of what made America great. Had his father known how close to the flame he was flying? Or had he been blinded by the heights he ached to achieve?

Would it be too much for *him*? His head pounded with

the weight of too many decisions. Too many paths that were no longer clear. *Too much, too much.*

A jet banked over the Hudson, the lights on its wings flashing in the darkness. He stared at it, hypnotized by the pulsing flares. *Is destiny the fate of every man? Is your path irreversible no matter how you pursue it? Or is there a way to rise above it? A way to blaze a path that is yours and yours alone?*

The throbbing in his head intensified. He needed to escape, but he didn't know how.

CHAPTER NINE

FRANKIE COULDN'T GET into the car. The haunted, hunted look on Harrison's face when she'd left, the way he'd been ever since Leonid had agreed to sign the deal, was gnawing at her. She'd expected him to be victorious and superior. Instead she'd found him dark and introspective.

Working nearly 24/7 with someone meant you were in tune with their moods, and the Harrison she'd witnessed tonight was one she hadn't seen before. One that scared her. Leonid might have passed it off as exhaustion, distraction, but she knew it was much more.

Derrick gave her a quelling look. He wanted to get home to his family. He thought she was nuts standing here on the sidewalk, utterly caught in limbo.

She got into the car. They pulled smoothly away from the sidewalk, weaving into traffic. Her stomach churned in big, conflicted circles. She had led Leonid to believe he could depend on Harrison when in reality he would likely be bitterly disappointed. Whether Leonid had read between the lines or taken her words at face value was something she would never know.

A soft curse left her lips. She didn't want anyone's future revolving around her. Then to make her choice only to have Harrison turn into a stone wall when he had been handed everything he'd wanted? *What is going on?*

She clenched her hand into a fist and pressed it against the seat. Was he feeling guilty for what he was about to do to Leonid even though he'd laid his cards on the table? Or had he finally realized, with the final piece in place to destroy Anton Markovic, that vengeance was a poor substitute for a broken heart? That it would never bring his father back?

Or was it something else entirely? That call from Tom Dennison today? The twisting in her gut intensified. She couldn't do it.

She tapped on the screen. Derrick opened it. 'Yes, ma'am?"

"Can you take me back? I've forgotten something."

He gave her a supremely patient look. "Of course. Let me just find somewhere to turn around."

When he deposited her on the sidewalk outside Harrison's building once more, she thanked him and told him to go home. "I may be a while."

Derrick nodded. "Call me if you change your mind."

She was out of her mind. Setting her jaw, she entered the building through the side entrance. The door required a thumb scan to get in but Harrison had taken care of that for her last week when she'd had to come collect some documents for him. She rode the whisper-quiet elevator to the penthouse, heart pounding in her ears.

The doors of the elevator swished open. The apartment was eerily silent as she moved through the entrance way and into the living room. The precious artwork glowed silently on its perfect cream backdrop. No Harrison.

His study was in darkness. A glow from the terrace suggested he was there. She walked through the living room and stepped outside. Harrison was standing at the railing, looking out at the skyline. Her heels clicked on the concrete as she walked toward him. He turned around, frowning. "Did I forget to give you something?"

"No." Her knees betrayed just the slightest wobble as she took the last few steps toward him. "I just—" Her voice trailed off. Just what? What the heck was she doing here?

She came to a stop in front of him. Her gaze rose to his. He was as tall and commanding as ever, as stomach-clenchingly beautiful, but the tormented look dominated now. It emanated from every pore of him, blanketing her in his desperation. She pulled in a breath.

"I wanted to make sure you were okay."

The shadows in his face darkened. "I told you I was fine. Go home, Francesca."

"But you aren't." The words spilled from her mouth. "Ever since Leonid agreed to the deal, you've been off."

"I'm *fine*."

She frowned. "It's what we've been working toward. I thought you would be happy."

"I *am* happy." The emotion vibrating in his voice sent a shiver down her spine. He turned to look at the skyline again. "It's none of your concern, Francesca. Go home. I'll see you in the afternoon."

She stood her ground, legs shaking now. For a man who claimed to feel little emotion it was written in every taut muscle of his body. In the rigid column of his back, his neck. In the barely leashed confusion that surrounded him. It reached out and wrapped itself around her, pulling her toward him.

"Sometimes," she said quietly, laying a hand on his arm, "the things we want the most, the things we think are going to make us feel better, don't. *Can't* because they were never the solution in the first place."

He spun to face her, dislodging her hand. Antagonism poured off him in waves. "Nailing Anton Markovic to the ground is going to make me feel better, Francesca. *Much better*. Make no mistake about it."

Her heart thudded against her rib cage. "Then why? Why are you like this?"

"Because I have too much going on in my head." He practically yelled the words at her. "This is not another case of you saving the day, Francesca. It's far more complex than one of your little sermons can fix."

Her stomach lurched. "I didn't suggest that."

His mouth curled. *"Go."*

"I won't leave you like this."

The deliberate way he looked at her made her pulse buzz in her ears. "You would be very wise to do so," he suggested in a low, deep voice that made her insides liquefy. He lifted a finger and dragged it across her cheek, watching as she shivered in reaction. "Otherwise I will do what I was aching to do in the car and drown myself in *this*. And I think we've both agreed it's an unacceptable result."

His touch felt like fire on her skin. The kiss from London sizzled through her head, beckoning her on to sure destruction. They were like hot and cold fronts converging in a storm it seemed impossible to outrun.

But he was her boss. She loved her job. She really must go.

He slid his thumb down to her lips, his gaze holding hers as he traced the trembling outline of her mouth. *"Go,* Francesca. You're the only thing making me feel alive right now. If you don't, I can't be responsible for what happens next."

Run, her sensible side commanded, hurting man or not. But the other side of her, the one pulsing with an awareness of him so strong it made her mouth dry, wanted him to drown himself in her. Wanted to experience that type of passion. Because *he* made her feel more alive than she'd ever felt in her life. Being the center of his attention was *hypnotizing.*

The tremor in his hand as he stroked the pad of his

thumb over her bottom lip made her heart turn over. She couldn't go.

His dark gaze glittered. *"Out. Now."*

"No."

The word hung on the air between them, defiant and crystal clear. She watched the control fizzle in his eyes at the same time he reached for her hand and brought it to his mouth. He pressed his lips to her palm in an openmouthed kiss, as if tasting her very essence. Her pulse ran wild.

"You have five seconds to leave," he murmured. "Or you *don't.*"

She closed her eyes as he pressed another kiss to her palm. Counted out the seconds in her head. His soft curse split the night air.

"Francesca."

She brought his hand to her mouth. Found his palm with her lips. *He* tasted hot, salty and hedonistically male. She wondered if he'd experienced the same stomach-churning intensity of it. The way he went completely still said he might have.

He let her play for a while, to know him. Then he curled his fingers around her wrist and brought her the two steps forward he needed to let her feel the heat his tall frame emanated.

"You're sure?"

She nodded. His fiery, conflicted gaze scoured her face. "I won't take an innocent."

"I'm not." She didn't need to tell him there had only ever been one, awkward and disappointing as the sex had been.

The warm night air heated up around them, like it was catching fire, too. He slid his fingers into her French twist and started pulling pins out. The buzz in her ears was so loud she couldn't hear them hit the concrete, one by one. She should have been terrified with what little she had to bring to this insanity. Instead she trusted him on a level she didn't understand.

He pulled out the final pin. Her hair fell loose around her shoulders. He lifted a hand and fingered a silky strand, a curious look on his face.

"What?"

"I can't figure you out," he murmured. "Honest, fearless, unsure of yourself at times yet so sure of so many things on a bigger life level." He wrapped a chunk of her hair around his finger and let it slide through his hand. "It's why Leonid asked you that question tonight. Because the essence of you is good. It emanates from you."

Her lips pursed. "It's the way I was brought up. I don't know any different."

"I do." He bent his head and put his mouth to the hollow between her neck and shoulder. "You don't seem real to me."

She wasn't sure if that was a good or bad thing. But then it didn't matter as she abandoned herself to the sensations his lips were evoking on her skin, the warm slide of his mouth across her heated flesh sending sparks to every inch of her body. He savored the hollow he'd found, pulled every reaction out of her with his lips and teeth. The arch of her neck, her soft sighs, guided him. *More.* He set his hand to her jaw, moved it to the other side and did the same masterful job to the matching sweet spot between her left shoulder and neck. It made her weak in the knees. She curled her fingers into his waist and anchored herself to him.

He slid his hand to her nape and took her mouth then. Hot, possessive and never-ending, it wasn't like his kiss in the car. It promised carnal, exciting things to come and it made her rational brain shut down.

He pushed her jacket off her shoulders and threw it over the railing. Dispensed with the buttons on her blouse so expertly it made her wonder what the heck she was doing, thinking she could play in Harrison's sandbox. By the time he'd undone the last button and bared her to his gaze, her cheeks were scarlet. The look of pure lust that crossed his face sent that thought flying off into the nether.

"You are so beautiful," he murmured, absorbing her with his eyes. "I swear to God I thought you were an apparition the night I walked into the office and you were sitting in Tessa's chair."

She bit her lip. Remembered her complete mortification. How shameless she must have looked, her skirt riding up her thighs, her lace stockings on display...

"Oh, yes." His gaze was on her face. "I had dreams about those. That and the handcuffs... They did me in."

She covered her cheeks with her hands. He shook his head and pulled them away. "It was the sexiest thing I've ever seen..."

Her heart beat a wild rhythm in her chest. The decadent, openmouthed kiss he pressed against her lips almost felled her unsteady legs. The thought she could never sit in that chair again without blushing, that *this* would change *everything*, crossed her mind as his palms closed over the weight of her breasts and his thumbs slid across her hardened nipples. "Don't," he growled in her ear as she stiffened beneath him. *"Not tonight. Feel."*

She obeyed his command, because even in her inexperience, she knew only Harrison could ever make her feel like this. It had been that way from the beginning.

The pleasure he was lavishing on her as he rolled her nipples between his fingers with both hands unearthed a low moan from her throat. Sharp, urgent need lanced through her, sending her fingers to his biceps to curl into taut, hard male muscle. He rewarded her by sinking his teeth into her shoulder in a gentle bite that promised more was coming. *Much more.*

Oh, lord. She was so, so out of her depth.

His knee nudged her legs apart. She anchored her palms against his chest as he ran his hands up the back of her thighs. She had left the lace stockings off for an entire week after the *incident*, she'd been so mortified. But habit was habit and she loved feeling feminine. His swift intake of breath when he found the lace edging reverberated through her head. "You're killing me."

He slid an arm under her knees and picked her up. She had a vague memory of him doing that that night on the plane, but she'd been half unconscious then. Now she was fully alert, fully aware of the power caged in his muscular frame. Her heart raced in her chest, slamming against its containing walls. He was insanely strong. She had handed herself over to him to do what he liked. It inspired a feeling of mild panic.

He nudged the French doors shut behind them and carried her through the dimly lit penthouse and down a dark hallway toward the bedrooms. His was the big master suite at the side of the apartment. Her heart reached up to tattoo itself against her eardrums as he set her down in the middle of the lushly carpeted floor and switched on a lamp. She distracted herself with the jaw-dropping view of Central Park while he stripped off his tie and tugged his shirt collar open with a sense of purpose that made her heart stutter. Digging her toes into the plush carpet, she avoided the urge to turn and run out the door of his very expensive penthouse.

The deliberate way he moved back toward her almost rattled her poise completely. It must have shown on her face because he stopped in front of her, captured her hand and lavished another of those erotic, tongue-infused kisses to her palm. "Trust me."

Everything inside her melted. Her gaze fused with his dark, tormented one. "I do."

He curled her fingers around the top button of his shirt. She latched on to the direction like a lifeline, slipping the buttons free with hands that shook slightly but managed the job in a far less efficient process than his had. When she had them undone, he yanked the shirt from his trousers and threw it to the floor. He had the most amazing chest she'd ever seen on a man. She rocked back on her heels to take him in. Hard, muscled, honed by the hours he put in at the gym every week, he was the most perfect example of masculinity she'd ever seen. It was almost intimidating to touch him, but she couldn't help herself. Her hands moved by instinct, sliding up and over him, wanting to learn every inch with this liberty she'd been given.

Everything about him was impenetrable, indestructible, except tonight his vulnerability allowed her a way in. *It was intoxicating.*

She slid her palms over his nipples. He tensed under her touch but held himself still. Fascinated by how rock hard the hair-roughened peaks were underneath her fingertips, like tiny pebbles, she explored them with the pads of her thumbs.

He groaned. "More."

She wasn't sure what he meant until he covered her hand with his and slid it down over his trousers. The scalding contact with the hard, thick length of him made the blood roar in her head. Eyes closed, she traced him, learned him. He leaned into her caress, his growl sliding into a velvety moan of approval. It made her feel empowered, emboldened. She stroked him more firmly, pressed her palm against the impressive bulge of him and felt him grow harder beneath her touch.

His palms returned to her thighs, sliding up the back of them. This time he slipped his fingers beneath the lace and caressed the ultrasensitive skin there with fingers that burned her skin. "These stay on."

Frankie forgot her task completely as the raspy timbre of his voice shot through her. He slid his palms higher until he reached her lacy panties. Her hands fell to her sides, her head dropping to his chest as he nudged her legs apart with his knee, moved his fingers beneath the lace and touched her so intimately her back arched in pleasure.

"Harrison." His name slid from her lips on a groan of pure pleasure. He repeated the caress again, his fingers sliding against her slick skin. Leisurely at first, he stroked her like he might a cat, caressing her nerve endings. Then he deepened it, intensified it. She let him take her weight as her knees buckled. His voice was a husky demand in her ear asking if she liked it. Commanding her to tell him when she wanted more. She did because this was beyond anything she'd ever experienced, it felt that good.

His hands left her aching flesh. She wanted to scream greedily that it wasn't enough, beg for more, because she'd never experienced the type of pleasure he was giving her. But he was disposing with his trousers, intent on another kind of pleasure entirely. He slid off his briefs and kicked them aside. Her mouth went dry, her palms sweaty. She could have expected he'd be big because of his size but his arousal, proud and daunting, kicked her heart into a whole other gear.

He was as aroused by her as she was by him.

He pushed her blouse off her shoulders, found the back button of her skirt and undid it. She swallowed hard to inject some saliva into her mouth as her zipper went the way of her button and he nudged the skirt off her hips. Self-consciousness would have overwhelmed her then, as she stood there only in her lacy underwear, if she hadn't been utterly fascinated by the ruddy color staining his cheekbones. The tortured look was gone. Urgent, compulsive desire was plastered across his face. He was totally and utterly fixated on her, as if he couldn't believe she *was* real.

Her gaze tracked him as he backed up and sat down on the bed. He pulled a foil package from the night table drawer and rolled a condom on his impressive erection. She watched him, finding his beautiful body such a turn-on it was impossible to look away. His gaze lifted to hers when he'd finished, his eyes telling her exactly where she was supposed to be. She moved to mere inches in front of him.

"In my fantasy you had me in handcuffs." His hot gaze singed her from head to toe. "But you didn't need them, you had me totally under your control."

Her legs felt as though she'd done a seven-hour shift at Masserias. He reached up, slid his fingers in the sides of her panties and stripped them off. She almost lost her footing when he moved his hand between her thighs and cupped her aching center. Squeezed. It was a blatant act of ownership that made her stomach dip. Sent her fingers clutching the hard muscles of his shoulders for support.

"I'm not averse to a woman tying me up," he continued, easing his grip on her to fill her with a long finger instead. "But then you wouldn't get this. And I want you as hot and wild for me as you were in my fantasy."

Frankie closed her eyes at the seductive heat in his voice. It raked over her nerve endings and sent warmth flooding to the very place he was caressing. She couldn't help her response, couldn't help moving her hips against his hand every time he filled her. It was *incredible*.

He added another of those amazing fingers, palming the soft flesh of her buttocks with his free hand to hold her where he wanted her. A low moan escaped her lips.

"That's right," he murmured, spreading the fingers he had inside of her to maximize her pleasure. *To ready her.* "That's exactly how you were."

He withdrew from her. Left her hot and aching again, but only to shift both his hands to the backs of her thighs and lift her on top of him. She wrapped her legs around his waist, her thighs making contact with his hot, aroused body. Too many contact points fried her nerve endings. The unleashed power of him beneath her made her pulse speed up into an almost impossible awareness of his masculinity. But most intense of all were his eyes. Dark and full of want, she felt him all the way inside of her.

"You do something to me," he rasped. "I can't explain it."

She couldn't, either, but she felt it, too. She watched the desperation flicker back to life in his eyes as he fought it, fought the physical and mental connection they shared. The lack of control…it was a last-ditch effort to hold on to the darkness and she wouldn't allow it. She brought her mouth down on his in a kiss so intimate, so soul-consuming, she was sure she would never forget it.

His hands bit into her bottom as he lifted her up and brought her down on the hard column of flesh that telegraphed his desire for her.

"Tell me," he muttered against her lips, "if I'm hurting you…"

But he had brought her to the edge, to a greedy, grasping place where he was all she wanted. Inside of her. *Exactly like his fantasy.* Her body was malleable, soft as she accepted the tip of him. He was big; he stole her breath as he brought her down on him with firm hands. It was a tight, exquisite fit, one she almost couldn't stand. But when he had filled her completely, she wanted more.

"*Then what did I do?* In your fantasy…?" she whispered.

He took the weight of her hips in his hands, his eyes locked on hers. "You rode me like an angel."

Oh. She went down then, lost in the way he made her feel. She circled her hips around him. Took him deep inside, then retreated. His eyes caught fire. His hands helped her move. Then there was nothing between them except the sensation of being impaled on him. She took him again and again until her body was all soft heat, grasping him, *needing* him.

It was unmistakable, the sweet intensity that built inside of her then as his size, his girth touched a spot that promised heaven. She gripped his shoulders harder. He slid a hand between them and rubbed his thumb against her center. Back and forth in a path of fire that had her limbs clenching around him. "Give yourself to me," he commanded roughly.

She closed her eyes. Let his thumb take her over the edge. Her back arched, white lights exploded in her head as an orgasm racked through her. Her gasp as it tore into the night was raw and pleasure-soaked. Animalistic.

It was hot and amazing and never-ending. When she finally came down. Harrison was watching her, a deadly heat in his eyes. Her lashes lowered. "Don't," he commanded, his thumb claiming the curve of her lip. "You were spectacular."

She opened her eyes. Allowed him to part her mouth with his thumb, her breath coming hot and hard against his skin. She could taste herself on him. Taste what he'd done to her. It was too much. *Overload.*

He rolled onto his back and took her with him. He was buried deep inside of her, pulsing and rock-hard. *Unsatisfied.* His gaze morphed into the darkest, deepest granite as it ate her up. He wanted her to blow his mind. To obliterate his thoughts.

She leaned forward, pressed her palms to his chest and rotated her hips in a slow, grinding circle. His hands tightened around the flesh of her bottom. Faster, harder, he urged her down on him until his eyes were glazed and she knew he had lost it completely. But she drew it out, knew he wanted her to. He drove up into her with awe-inspiring stamina, again and again, his erection sending sparks of aftershocks through her. Slowly, amazingly, she felt her pleasure build again, hovering over the edge of another sweet surge of heaven. This was why he'd made it last. Because he could give her this.

He read the tautness of her body, his face blanking as he took her hard and fast, fully in control now. *"Again."*

She gave herself into the deep, piercing release, lost to him as he came with a hoarse shout, his hips bucking against her. Aftershocks jerked his powerful body. They racked through her as she dropped her head to his chest and tasted the salt of his skin. Nothing had ever felt so right. So perfect.

And yet it was so wrong. The cool night air sent reality flickering across her sweat-dampened skin. He was her boss. At least her temporary boss. And she'd just had scorching, wild sex with him.

Harrison rolled her beneath him, his big body holding her captive. His gaze found hers. Narrowed. "Stop thinking."

"I can't think," she muttered. "My brain is mush."

"Good." He left the bed, disposed of the condom and came back to her, hooking a finger under the front closure of her lacy black bra. "How did this stay on?"

Her cheeks flamed. Because they'd been in such a hurry?

He lowered himself back onto the bed beside her. Her cheeks heated as she absorbed his magnificence. It was a bit overwhelming. Dark amusement gleamed in his eyes as he captured one of her hands, pressed his thumb to her palm and worked the tension from it.

"It bothered you to say that to Leonid tonight..."

She closed her eyes as the magical pressure of his fingers made her tingle right down to her toes. "Not because I don't think you're a good man. You are. It's what happens to Leonid's legacy that I have an issue with. You tearing his company apart like that... My family has owned Masserias for thirty years. If someone bought them out and changed everything I'd be brokenhearted."

He pressed his thumb into the joint between her thumb and forefinger. Frankie almost moaned out loud. "So why didn't you go into the family business if you love it so much?"

"My parents wanted me to. *I* wanted to forge my own path. I've wanted to work as a PA for as long as I can remember. I always thought it was so glamorous, but challenging at the same time."

"Glamorous? With a tyrant like me?"

She opened her eyes. "*You* are a different case."

His gaze darkened with intent. "Okay," she admitted, "I love working with you when you're not in one of your moods. You have an amazing brain."

He grabbed her other hand and started working on it. "Only my brain?"

"And the rest of you…" she conceded. "I appreciated all of you from the beginning, much to my dismay. That is so utterly unlike me."

"You had a thing for my brother…"

She gave her head a shake. "Why do you keep saying that? Coburn is attractive and charming and I like working for him, but I've never had a *thing* for him."

"You idol-worship him."

His tone was decisive. She put a hand on his chest and levered herself up to look at him. "My lord, you Grants have the biggest egos. I do *not* idol-worship Coburn. He is an inspiring, wonderful person to work for. He treats me like I'm an equal, valued partner. A somebody…but that's it."

He frowned. "Of course you're a somebody. You're excellent at your job."

She glowed at his praise. Harrison meant every word he said. "I was a disaster with you at first."

"Because your mind was in the gutter. Exactly where mine was."

The warmth in her cheeks intensified. "Sometimes you need validation," she told him. "My parents didn't think a career was the right place for me. I never had a good GPA. It was average, if that. They thought I should be managing Masserias because I'm so good with people." Her mouth curved. "My dad says I have the magic touch."

"You certainly do."

The meaningful tone in his voice made her swat him. "Harrison."

He unsnapped her bra. She arched away from the mattress to allow him to strip it off, although that proved to be a bad idea because the slide of his fingers over the bare curve of her breast, over its taut center, were infinitely distracting.

"What about your brothers and sisters? Did they go into the family business?"

"I have five." Her mouth twisted in a wry smile. "One's a neurosurgeon, one's a psychologist, then there's the chemical engineer, banker and if you like the nontraditional route, my brother Salvatore is an entrepreneur with a state-wide series of fitness clubs at twenty-six."

"The one who forgot the cake?"

She nodded. "So you can see why I was the obvious choice to take over Masserias… The unspectacular one of the bunch."

His chin lowered. "I think that's an inaccurate description. You handle people with a deftness I've rarely experienced, Francesca. You have great natural instincts for business and you speak three languages."

So did her sister Federica: English, Italian and Spanish. *And* she was a psychologist.

She gave him a pained look. "You don't need to try and make me feel better. I'm at peace with who I am."

"Are you?" She didn't like how his far too perceptive gaze seemed to look right through her. "You should shift some of your absolute truths into the department governing your opinion of yourself. Ten minutes with Juliana and she's explaining the psychology of Leonid to you. That's a *gift*."

"Speaking of Leonid," she offered casually, "care to talk about what's making your head too full?"

His eyes flashed. "No, in fact."

The intimacy of their position, the way the hard muscles of his stomach quivered as she traced her way down toward the sexy dip between his abs and leg spurred her to dig a bit more. "Could you put up enough of a stink with the board that they would maintain Siberius as a separate entity? Keeping in mind, of course, we're only talking in hypotheticals."

His gaze narrowed. "Perhaps. But when you only have so much political capital with a board, you choose your battles wisely."

"Right." She left that hanging in the air between them because she wanted him to think about it.

"Francesca," he growled. "Stop meddling."

She followed the sexy dip down over his muscled thigh, luxuriating in the hard, densely packed muscle beneath her fingertips. "Juliana says Anton Markovic is an evil man. That he has underworld connections that make her wish Leonid didn't do business with him." She looked up at him. "Does he know you're after him?"

"No." He captured her exploring hand in his. "And you can put his name out of your head. Juliana's right. Anton Markovic is not a man to be played with."

"Yet you are…"

"Francesca." He bent his head and put his mouth to the curve of her breast. "I think I'm going to have to silence you."

That might be fine, too. His mouth closed over her hardened nipple, scoring it with his teeth. The way he used those sharp incisors was truly…remarkable. A moan broke from her throat. "That is not fair."

He drew her nipple into his mouth with a hard suction that made her whole body go rigid. The slide of his hair-roughened leg as it parted hers rendered her distraction complete. He really *wasn't* finished with her.

She moved against him, her smooth legs luxuriating in the feel of his harder male limbs. His teeth and lips teased her other nipple into a hard, aching button. It took him about five seconds to drag her back into the maelstrom.

"Now we go freestyle."

Freestyle? Oh, the fantasy. That was apparently over and they were onto a very vivid, very real exploration of her stomach. The tender, vulnerable skin of her lower abdomen… She clutched his coarse hair in her fingers. He couldn't do *that*. *Not after what they'd just done.*

She tugged on his hair. "Harrison." He made a low sound in his throat and nudged her tensed legs apart. She jammed her eyes shut as his fingers parted her and he slid his tongue against her slick flesh. The way he savored the essence of them was too intimate. Too much. But then again everything about tonight had been too much.

He rasped his approval as her legs fell open and she surrendered completely. His licks turned long and languorous, intent on waking her body up. Then they became purposeful, *unrelenting.* He waited until her limbs stiffened, she dug her hands in his hair and came, shuddering against his mouth before he moved his way back up her body, slid another condom on and took her with a deep, breath-stealing thrust. She threw back her head and reveled in his possession. In the hot, sweet perfection they made together.

When he sought his release with a ragged groan and buried his mouth in her throat, she held him to her while the storm they had created together unleashed its final fury. His breathing slowed, evened out. It was long minutes before she levered herself up onto her elbows and saw that he'd passed out in her arms.

A primal instinct, a need to nurture, stirred deep inside her. It was stronger than the magnitude of what she'd done with her career tonight. Stronger than all of it. Because in that moment, she knew no matter what the morning brought, *this* had been right. She had pulled him back from the edge.

If it had also tipped her feelings for him, a man she could never have, into dangerous territory? If her own emotions were wildly out of control? That was the stuff of tomorrow.

CHAPTER TEN

IT WAS THE LONG, elegant leg thrown over his that convinced Harrison something was very off in his universe. The floral perfume hit him next…heady and distracting. It occurred to him he might be having another of his very inappropriate dreams about his PA and he latched on to the desperate appeal of that thought with gusto. He opened one eye to verify. No, he was not dreaming and yes, that was Francesca sprawled on top of him, the tantalizing floral scent of her mixed with something that could only be described as steamy hot sex.

That she'd had *with* him in *this* bed *last* night.

Mother of God.

He closed his eyes. Traced the steps back in his head. Leonid had agreed to sign the deal and for some bizarre reason instead of feeling elated, he'd felt curiously dead about it inside. The darkness had descended to take the place of the numbness, the monsters in his head had roared to life and it had all become much too much.

Francesca, somehow sensing, with that bizarre intuition of hers, how low he'd sunk, had returned. At his weakest point. When he hadn't been able to do anything but take her apart like he'd wanted to for the past two weeks. He had seduced her, *drowned himself* in her. And when it was done, he'd still felt like he'd only skimmed the surface of what they were.

His hand clenched around her smooth thigh beneath his palm. Francesca murmured and moved against him. He extracted himself from her, his guts turning in a slow, discomforting twist. The intimacy they had shared had been overwhelming and unexpected. But far more damaging had been what he had revealed. The scary depths his mind could scale if he let it... The tortured part of him. The man no one knew.

A cold layer of perspiration blanketed his skin. Never did he let anyone see his vulnerabilities. His weaknesses. Yet Francesca had walked in here last night and smashed through his defenses with one sexy kiss to his palm. He shuddered to think what she'd witnessed. His was not a darkness he chose to show to anyone. And he'd been darker last night than he had in ages. Completely inside his head.

He ran a palm over his damp brow. It didn't surprise him that it had been Francesca who'd broken through to him. What shocked him was how completely he had fallen under her spell. How thoroughly she had pushed the torment away. Until there had only been the purity of her to ease his troubled soul.

And she had. He may have made a huge mistake with her, his head might still be buzzing from it, but the heaviness had lifted. The darkness had gone.

Her scent drifted to him again, evocative and oh so feminine. His body reacted immediately. You would think after not having sex for months and having her twice last night, he'd be out of gas. His body, apparently, begged to differ.

If he laid one hand on her now he was a goner. He knew that as certainly as the sun came up in the morning. His only hope was to get out of bed, shower and make a plan for how to handle this. He might then have a chance of escaping with his head intact. *Might*.

He reached down and slid her leg off his with the subtlest of movements. Francesca sighed and curled up in a ball. *Perfect*. He shifted his weight to the outside of the bed, eased himself sideways until he could throw his legs over the side. Another sigh. He looked back. Big mistake. If there had ever been an angel in his bed it was Francesca. Her long dark hair was tangled around her face, she had the body of Venus and goodness shone from her like a beacon to come to the light.

His mouth firmed. *Not a bloody chance in hell.*

He threw himself under a cold shower. He would get the contract over to Leonid this morning, the Russian would sign and he would execute his long-awaited confrontation with Anton Markovic. Markovic was making it easy on him with a planned trip to Washington to lobby the government. Except he would never be able to deliver on that contract because his supply chain was now owned by Grant Industries.

How unfortunate.

He stepped out of the shower and dried himself off. Francesca was still dead to the world when he slipped into the bedroom. He grabbed a shirt and trousers from the walk-in closet, dressed and made for the kitchen and coffee. A steaming cup of sensibility in his hand, he walked out onto the terrace and watched Manhattan stir to life. The lights had gone off in the park, the day-shift cabbies were taking over from the night shift and he could already see the powerful cars of the die-hard financial brokers on the road ready to get a jump start on the day.

A low oath escaped him. Things always looked better in the morning, but what had happened between him and Francesca last night? It had been such a huge error in judgment on his part, he couldn't even fathom it. They could not continue to work together after last night. She would be the end of him. If he'd been distracted before, he hated to think what he'd be like now knowing what it felt like to take her. To have all that sweetness and fire underneath him, begging for his possession.

It would make him crazy.

Except giving her back to Coburn also inspired that same feeling. His brother could seduce a woman without even using a tenth of his charm. But Francesca had declared herself not interested…

His mind slammed the door shut on the subject with a definitive thud. It was the right thing to do.

The fact that she was naked sprawled across Harrison Grant's bed hit Frankie before she registered he wasn't anywhere to be seen. *Thank God.* Pieces from the night before circulated through her head like the View-Master she'd had as a kid, except this show was not her favorite fairy-tale princesses, this was her and her *boss* acting out their deepest, darkest fantasies.

Oh, dear lord. Adrenaline fast-circuiting through her veins, she pushed off the massive bed, rustled around on the floor for her underwear and slid it and her dress on. Her lace stockings sat in a pile beside the bed. She picked them up and balled them up in her hands. No way was she going there today.

A covert operation to the living room turned up her purse where she'd dropped it on a chair last night. She shoved the stockings in it and went in search of her more gut-churning target. The compassion she'd been intent on honoring last night was fading fast, replaced by the utter horror of what she'd done. Yes, this might have been inevitable between them, but this was her *job*. When had she decided that was less important than mending Harrison's broken spirit?

Her teeth sank into her lip. Right around the same time he'd kissed her again. But it didn't negate the facts. She didn't for one minute think they could carry on like normal after *that*. Facing him was going to be hard enough.

She fortified herself with the thought she would do the same thing if presented with the situation all over again. Leaving a human being in agony wasn't an option. How she handled things now was.

The smell of coffee drifted through the penthouse, guiding her to the kitchen. When she didn't find Harrison there, she crossed the living room to his study. He was working, looking fresh as a daisy in a crisp shirt and pants. She winced as he looked up, his gaze moving over her tangled hair to her rumpled dress to her stockingless feet.

"I'm going to shower and change at home," she said hurriedly. "I was just coming to tell you I was leaving."

His gaze settled on her face. "Go get a cup of coffee and we'll talk first."

No. No talking. Just escape. His eyes narrowed. "Get the coffee *now*, Francesca."

The order brought his others from the night before back. Exciting, *forbidden*. She turned around abruptly and headed for the kitchen. *That* was not the way to handle this.

He had pulled his chair out from the desk and was sitting facing the sofa when she returned. She handed him a new cup of coffee, noting the look of absolute control on his face. The beast was back. *Good.* That would be helpful.

She sat down on the leather sofa, legs arranged in front of her like she was at a tea party. His gaze held hers. "We can't just avoid what happened last night."

"I know."

"It was bound to happen, we both know that."

She nodded again. Set the coffee on the table before she spilled it.

He steepled his fingers against his thigh and studied the arrangement. "I wasn't in a great place last night. My head wasn't right."

Tell her something she didn't know. "It shouldn't have happened, regardless of our chemistry. It creates real issues."

"I get that." Her words came out sharp and singed.

He looked up at her, his hard gaze softening into something more human. "It was amazing, Francesca. *You* were amazing. I—" He stopped, frowning, as if looking for exactly the right word, like a man on the witness stand. "I needed to escape. I needed to not be in my head. And you helped me do that."

So she was the nonrational choice. Fury fired her veins. She knew exactly what she'd been to him last night. She was shocked, however, by how much more she wanted him to say. How she wanted him to admit the undeniably special connection they shared. That last night had been as unforgettable as she'd thought it was. Even though she knew that was ridiculous. Harrison didn't commit. Last night had illustrated the demons that drove him—demons that had shut him down this morning.

She'd be so smart, so wise, to stay away. He was right.

"You needed to be with someone," she said quietly. "It's fine."

His gaze sharpened on the stubborn upper curve of her lip. He looked as if he was going to say something, then his mouth tightened. "We need to decide where we go from here. I don't think it's reasonable to expect us to keep working together under these circumstances. I'm going to send you back to Coburn after the Aristov deal is signed. I can use one of Tessa's replacement candidates until she's back."

Her shoulders rose. She knew it had been coming, but he threw it at her like one of the painful, ruthless decisions he made on a daily basis.

"And what will you tell Coburn?"

His jaw hardened. "I'll tell him it was a personality clash. My fault. He knows I'm a son of a bitch. It won't be hard to believe."

It wouldn't. But she wasn't sure Coburn would buy it. He knew she wasn't a quitter. He knew she would have made it work. However, right now, none of that mattered. All that mattered was getting out of here before he made her want to say something completely out of character. Something *angry*. Because although this was her fault, even though she had made her own bed, it was clear it was never going to be Harrison Grant's.

And that hurt in a way she didn't want to examine.

She lifted her chin, gray eyes clashing with black. "Are we done here? I'd like to go home and shower."

His eyes flashed. She watched him bank the heat down into that cool, calm control of his. "Two things. Can you call the agency and get the replacement candidates in for interviews next week?"

Wow, he wasn't wasting any time getting rid of her. "Of course."

"Good. I've sent a note to the lawyers telling them to forward the Aristov contract to Leonid. I may need your help this morning facilitating things while I'm in my meeting. Stay close to your phone."

When was she ever not close to her phone? She nodded and got stiffly to her feet. She was almost to the door, still full coffee cup in her hand when he spoke.

"Are you all right?"

She turned around and gave him her iciest look. "Perfectly fine. I'll see you this afternoon."

Harrison spent the rest of the morning in an industry meeting with various automotive groups from across the country, trying not to feel like the cad he was. He knew what Frankie had wanted to hear. He couldn't deny he'd felt it. He'd *told* her he'd felt it last night. *You do something to me... Give yourself to me...* But he would never admit it in the cold light of day.

He reached for his coffee cup, then shoved it away before he developed caffeine poisoning. He'd never had that kind of a connection with anyone, *ever*, not even with Susanna, whom he'd loved with what he'd later learned had been a surface, selfish kind of it. But it didn't mean he had the ability to offer Francesca anything, even once he shipped her back to Coburn. He couldn't even table the idea of an affair to see where things would go. That would only be cruel of him when he knew where it would lead. *Nowhere.*

He sat back in his chair and tried to focus on what the chairman of an industry group was saying. But his thoughts kept drifting back to the woman who had stormed his defenses. So Francesca had proven he had the ability to feel when he'd thought that emotion long ago gone. He would bolt at the first sign of commitment if they did pursue something. It was his history. Last night had been a window, not a door. He'd needed to make that clear and he had, hurtful or not.

The meeting dragged on until they broke for lunch. He headed back to Grant instead of socializing. Coburn was in his office working when he arrived. His brother gave him a careful look. "I thought I heard via the grapevine Aristov signed. Didn't you sleep well with your revenge plot wrapped up tight around you last night?"

Heat stained his cheekbones. "He signed. I'm here to talk to you about Frankie. *Francesca.*"

His brother's eyes narrowed. "Don't you dare back out of taking her to the party, H. She's looking forward to it."

Hell. He had forgotten all about the party. That was a problem.

"It isn't about that," he said roughly. "I think she should come back to work for you. Our styles are too different. It isn't working out. I'll find someone from the agency until Tessa's back."

Coburn sat back in his chair, his blue eyes spearing him. "You stood here yesterday telling me how fantastic she was in London. What's changed?"

He lifted a shoulder. "I don't want to strip the spirit out of her."

How true that was.

His brother got to his feet and walked around the desk. His usual urbane charm took on a dangerous edge. "It's funny all this would come to pass when I saw Frankie in the elevator this morning looking like crap. What the hell did you do to her, H?"

His hands curled into fists at his sides. He had not been the only adult present last night.

"I'm suggesting you take her back, Coburn." He gave his brother a cool look. "Do it. It's better for everyone."

His brother's eyes glittered with incredulity. "You have a thing going with her...I *knew it* when I saw those photos."

The accusation bounced off him like the far too late summary it was. "She's going to finish the Aristov contract with me this week and get the shareholder meetings sorted. We'll interview candidates for her replacement next week and you can have her back by the following Monday."

"Then what? You sleep with her a few times like you always do, then brush her off like lint on your sleeve? Frankie isn't one of your sophisticated, heartless types, H. You will *crush* her."

"Exactly why it's not happening." Or at least it wasn't ever happening again. "Take her back," he said roughly. "And spare me the sermon. You are one to talk."

"*I* was the one smart enough to stay away from her." His brother shook his head. "What about the party?"

His lips thinned. "I'll escort her like I said I would." He had a week before he had to figure that one out.

CHAPTER ELEVEN

"So you are alive..." Salvatore's deep baritone reached over the phone line, familiar and comforting. "I was instructed to check."

Frankie tossed her pencil on her desk and sighed. "Just. My boss is a slave driver. It's been nuts. One more week and I'm going back to work for Coburn and life will return to normal."

And why did that hurt so much to say? Was she a total glutton for punishment?

"You should come for a drink at Masserias tomorrow night. A few of us are going."

"I would love to but I am attending the Grant Long Island party."

Salvatore whistled. "Exalted company."

She chewed on her lip. "I'm not really *going* going. My boss asked me to be nice."

"Still, that's a score. Maybe you can net yourself a millionaire."

Unlikely. The only *billionaire* she wanted wasn't on the market for her.

"Who are you taking?"

Her teeth burrowed deeper into her lip. "No one. Harrison is escorting me. To be nice...like I said."

There was silence on the other end of the line. She could

hear her brother's protective instincts silently shifting into gear. "That's…interesting."

"Quit it, Salvatore. He considers it a *reward*. I promise I will come out next week."

"I'm taking that as a solid, set-in-stone kind of promise."

"You got it." She tapped her fingers on the desk, fighting the urge to confide in her closest sibling. "Look, I really should get back to work."

"Franks…" A pause. "You okay? You sound funny. I'm not far, I could drop by for coffee."

She shook her head. Then realized he couldn't see that. "Sorry, too busy. And I'm fine, really. Just tired."

Better not to tell him her problem was a man and that man was her boss. He'd be over here in ten minutes flat, Harrison on the other end of his black-belt-trained glare. Salvatore always brought out the real Frankie. The emotional side of her that right now felt curiously close to tears. She had been so happy here at Grant. Now it felt as though everything was falling apart. Coburn couldn't help but think she'd failed when she was getting shipped back to him, although he'd been seemingly thrilled at the idea. His temp was messing up his filing *and*, he'd added, she didn't bring the sunshine in with her.

Her heart sank another foot. Somehow that didn't make up for the fact that Harrison was clearly washing his hands of her, now that she'd soon cease to be useful to him, with the Aristov contract signed. The bright, shiny glow of her new life was fading fast and she didn't want any member of her family seeing her like this when they so clearly felt she belonged at Masserias.

"All right, then." She heard a horn sound in the background as Salvatore negotiated traffic. "Next week for sure or I come find you."

She hung up to find Jack Robbins, the head of Grant's legal counsel, at her desk. He eyed Harrison's closed door, dropped the Siberius contract in front of her and gave it a satisfied look. "Fully executed, sealed in stone. The bear will be happy, no?"

"No doubt."

Jack glanced at his watch. "I have a lunch meeting. Could you ask him to call me if he has any questions? It should be as discussed."

"Will do."

The lawyer made his way out the door whistling. Frankie could have used a bit of his good cheer. The past five days had been as bad as the pre-Aristov deal era. Only for a completely different reason. She and Harrison had been trying so hard to stay out of each other's way that it had become excruciatingly awkward to be anywhere near him. His curt, near polite behavior was so odd, it was disconcerting. Perhaps because when they came within five feet of each other, neither of them seemed able to keep their cool.

That's what happens when you have hot, sweaty sex with your boss. When you connect on a level that's way beyond the physical, putting your feelings in distinctly dangerous territory. You avoid.

She picked up the contract and got to her feet. She was so tired of avoiding she wanted to scream. At least when she was back with Coburn she could get back to normal. She wouldn't be dreaming about that night with Harrison. She wouldn't be wondering about her boss's every mood and she wouldn't be feeling the irresistible desire to comfort the beast even though he was making that hard. It would no longer be her job.

She headed toward his office. The worst was the party. She had to attend the damn thing with Harrison when she'd rather spend the night washing dishes at Masserias. And that was saying a lot.

He was on the phone when she knocked and entered.

She waved the contract at him. He motioned for her to stay and wrapped the call.

"That's it?"

"That's it. Fully executed and ready to go. Jack said to call if you had any questions."

"Good." He laced his fingers together and pressed them to his chest. "You've been such a huge part of this. Why don't I take you to lunch?"

Lunch? She stared at him as though he was nuts. "You have a lunch meeting."

"So I'll cancel it. You deserve some appreciation for the great job you've done."

She eyed him. *She'd done her job and this was his kiss-off lunch.* It was guilt talking. Looking at that contract in his hands, knowing what he was going to do with it, knowing thousands of people were likely going to lose their jobs when he folded Siberius into Grant made her feel *unwell*. Angry. *Used.*

"No, thank you," she said stiffly. "I appreciate the offer, but I seem to have lost my appetite today."

His black eyes glittered at her. "You okay?"

"Perfect. Would you like me to go down to the deli for you?" She gave the clock on the wall a pointed glance. "Your meeting starts in ten minutes."

"I'll get it myself afterward."

She spun on her heel and walked.

"Francesca."

She held up a hand and kept going. Last week it had been him on the edge of an explosion. This week it was *her*.

Harrison dressed for the annual Grant summer party the next evening with the grim determination of a man who'd been through the interminable small talk and politics so many times he could have run it in his head before it had even started. Divorces would be announced, affairs would surface and rumors would abound about everything from political campaigns—namely *his* or his lack of one this year—to high-profile job losses and corporate defections. The only thing that changed was the players. And sometimes, if they were misguided or unlucky enough, they stayed the same, too.

He'd been in a filthy mood ever since Francesca had walked out of his office, her back ramrod-straight, her icy look telling him exactly what she thought of him. Which was so *unfair.* They were adults, they'd done what they'd done and sulking wasn't going to help the situation.

Meanwhile, he was struggling. Did she think this was easy for him? He had done everything, *everything* to put her out of his head and move on, including setting up his "accidental" meeting with Anton Markovic with exquisite care. He had buried himself in work, used the nights to consider his future and refused to think about how much he craved Francesca's level set outside the office as much as he valued it inside.

While he attempted to deny that that night with her had changed everything.

He muttered an oath. Picking up his jacket, he rode the elevator to the parking garage and drove the short distance to Francesca's apartment on the east side.

Something inside him did a slow roll when he saw her standing on the sidewalk, glowing in a crimson-colored gown that was less body-hugging than the one she'd worn to Leonid's party, but still heart-stoppingly sexy on her hourglass figure. She was an unattainable goddess for a man still mired in his head.

He got out, walked around the car and stopped in front of her. He couldn't help taking a long look. Her hair was up, done in a million curls caught on top of her head. Sparkly earrings dangled from her perfect ears. Her feet were encased in dainty silver shoes that accentuated the arch of her delicate foot. But it was her eyes that tugged at his heart. They were a deep, unsure gray, so unlike her usual spirited self.

It was going to be a long, long night.

"Hi." His voice when it rumbled from his chest was rusty and not his own. Frankie's eyes flickered. How insanely articulate of him. That was the way to handle a tough crowd.

He cleared his throat. Took another stab at it. "You look stunning."

"Thank you." Her stiff demeanor wasn't bending one bit. *Fine*. He could play this game. He put her in the car, walked around to the other side and started driving. Relentlessly he plied her with small talk. Frankie gave one-word answers, sometimes a handful. It was a ninety-minute drive to Long Island and that got old fast. She was angry, concluded the male in him. Women didn't know how to separate the emotional from the rational while men were rarely in touch with their feelings. He wondered how it actually ever worked.

He even asked her how Tomasino and the gang were doing at the church. Instead of scoring him points, it made her mouth tighten even more. So he shut his mouth, turned on the radio and drove.

They arrived at the Grants' redbrick Georgian mansion on Long Island Sound just in time for cocktails. Dropping their bags in their rooms, he gave her a quick tour of the elegant, dark-paneled house with its checkerboard marble grand hallways and massive tapestries. He could tell instantly Frankie liked it more than his penthouse.

The minute they appeared in the back garden, his mother pounced on them, emerging from a crush of people gathered under the fairy-light-strung trees with her usual gray-haired, impeccable elegance. She had Frankie summed up in three seconds flat, her keen blue gaze sliding over the brunette who bested her petite frame by a good six inches.

"So you're the Frankie my boys are so enamored with."

Frankie blushed. "*Enamored* is hardly the word. You have lovely sons, Mrs. Grant. I'm lucky to have my job."

"They're lucky to have you," Evelyn Grant countered smoothly. "Every powerful man needs a supporting cast."

Harrison kept a supporting hand at Frankie's back, even though it was clear she didn't want it there. If anyone knew the value of a supporting cast, it was his mother. She had been that her entire life as the matriarch of this family, these days focusing far too much of her attention on her sons' careers.

His mother gave him a pointed look. "Tom Dennison was asking after you. Perhaps I can introduce Francesca around?"

He didn't know why it bothered him to let Frankie go. It was better that way, keeping their distance from each other, and his mother would undoubtedly do a superb job being the social queen that she was.

He glanced at Frankie. "Okay?"

She nodded, but he knew her well enough now to catch the trace of trepidation in her eyes. His mother had a reputation, no doubt about it, but Frankie was more than up to it handling her. She had no problem handling him.

He left the women and found Tom Dennison enjoying a drink on the far end of the patio with a couple of other power-broker CEOs. Dennison made a joke about him being a mirage, then folded him into a tight-knit discussion of politics and current affairs. It was clear Dennison was offering him his backing and that of his political side-kicks if he elected to run. He kept his poker face on and tested the waters.

His mother, true to her word, introduced Frankie around. At some point she handed her off to Coburn, who kept her at his side as he moved from group to group, his usual life-of-the-party self. As the night wore on, he watched Frankie's sparkle return. Her eyes glowed, and as Coburn's eligible friends flirted with her, she smiled often with that combination of shyness and pleasure he found so damn appealing.

A knot formed itself in his chest. More than a few of the single, imminently successful types seemed interested in the beautiful brunette. *And why not?* She was everything a man could ever want in a woman. Gorgeous, smart and witty. The type of girl they could put a ring on and know they were damn well lucky to have her.

He grabbed a glass of wine from a passing waiter's tray, the tightness in his chest growing. He was not those men. No man could ever really change his spots for a woman. Not even for one who'd turned his mind and body upside down in the space of a few weeks. If the darkness in him didn't destroy her, his life would. Because after he'd brought Anton Markovic to his knees, he might enter the nastiest arena of all—a place he could never imagine good-hearted, ethical Frankie in.

Hors d'oeuvres were served and the champagne flowed. The four-piece band who'd been playing the Grant party for almost two decades struck up a tune. He had just extricated himself from a long discussion with one of his father's oldest friends when Cecily Hargrove found him in all her bubbly blond enthusiasm.

"Harrison," she admonished, giving him a kiss on the cheek. "You didn't return my phone call."

When had that been?

"A month ago," Cecily clarified, shaking her head at him. "Daddy is a workaholic, but you are worse."

He studied her with fresh eyes, this socialite from a family so connected she could ease the way for a presidential run in multiple eastern states. Perfectly straight hair with clever highlights, big blue eyes and a stick-thin figure that wore clothes perfectly, she did nothing for him. She would make the ideal wife for a governing official. She would never say the wrong thing, she would never counsel him to be anything he wasn't or question his intentions.

She would never make him feel as alive as Frankie did.

"Let's dance," Cecily insisted, tugging on his arm. "I've just been horsing in Montana. I have to tell you all about it. The skies were amazing."

Frankie watched Harrison escort a beautiful, petite blonde onto the dance floor set among the twinkling fairy lights. It was like a dagger to her heart watching him emerge from his political networking only to immerse himself in the blonde. *Which was nuts.* They didn't have anything according to Harrison. She was better off paying attention to one of the good-looking men chasing her who actually might send her roses. Who might not kick her out the morning after as if she was a piece of unwanted furniture.

She could not, however, contain her feminine curiosity. "Who is that?" she asked Coburn, posing the question with the casual air of someone who'd just spotted a nice-looking car and wondered what brand it was.

"Cecily Hargrove." Coburn made a face. "I'm surprised it took her this long. She's usually on him like paint."

If Frankie's mood could have sunk even lower, it did. The woman Harrison was supposed to marry, according to the oddsmakers. She was *perfect.*

Coburn's eyes went a mischievous, vibrant blue. "Want to have some fun?"

She forced a smile to her lips. "I am having fun."

"I mean some *real* fun." He grabbed her hand and started walking toward the dance floor, a series of flag-stones set under the trees. "Play along with me."

Doing what?

Coburn took her in his arms on the dance floor, where the band was playing a Frank Sinatra classic. At least she didn't feel so barefoot watching Harrison dance with Cecily when she was in the arms of handsome Coburn. He was a great dancer, better than Harrison, his smooth lead easy to follow. It would have been lovely, enjoyable if she didn't have to watch Cecily smiling up at the man she was obviously crazy about.

She averted her eyes and focused on what Coburn was saying. Another song started. Everyone stayed on the dance floor. Coburn pulled her closer. She looked up at him, startled. "Relax," he murmured. "I'm having some fun with my brother."

The glitter in his eyes made her wince. He knew. She'd been sure he was smart enough to figure out what had happened between her and Harrison, but the verification was mortifying. *Oh, lord.*

She thought about denying it, then sighed. "He isn't going to care. Forget it."

"You don't think so?" Coburn's gaze was pure wickedness. "Give me five minutes."

Frankie started to protest. Then defiance kicked in. *Pride.* When Coburn pulled her into a closer hold, his cheek against hers, she let him. His hand moved to the small of her back, his lips to her jaw. The couple beside them gave them an interested look.

"Coburn…"

"Wait."

The band belted out the high notes of the sultry Ella Fitzgerald classic. A dark shadow fell over them. Coburn lifted his lips from her jaw as if pulled from a particularly delicious moment. "H?"

She turned her head. Harrison stood beside them, Cecily Hargrove in tow, a dark cloud on his face. "My turn, I think. We should switch."

Coburn didn't release her right away. The stare between the two brothers dragged on. Cecily bit her lip and stood there watching. "Only," Coburn murmured finally, releasing her, "if you bring her right back."

"Not bloody likely."

Frankie's head spun as Harrison took her hand and pulled her into his arms. Coburn did the same with a bewildered Cecily. Her new partner did not have the same smooth rhythm as her previous one. His steps were forced and jerky. *Angry?*

She looked up at him. "Harrison, what's going on?"

"I could ask you that." His voice was clipped, ruddy color striping his cheekbones. She stared at him, about to confess Coburn had been having some fun with him. The words died in her throat.

"I was simply dancing with Coburn."

"He was *kissing* you."

"Oh, not really," she denied. "What does it matter anyway? You've made it clear we aren't going to pursue what's between us. I'm a free agent."

"So you move from *one brother to another*? I thought you had better morals than that, Frankie."

He was calling her Frankie. He was also jealous. Extremely jealous. The knowledge hit her like a ten-table arrival on a busy Masserias Saturday night.

The opportunity to make him admit his feelings was too tempting to resist.

"Maybe I'm taking your advice. After all, I was a big mistake. You said it yourself."

A lethal glimmer stoked the heat in his eyes. "I was trying to be *smart* for the both of us."

"Fine. Take me back to Coburn. Go dance with Cecily. It's probably for the best."

The heat in his gaze overflowed. She watched it unleash itself, swirl through the air like a wisp of smoke coming off a fire. His hand tightened around hers, just short of making her yelp as he turned and headed off the dance floor, dragging her behind him. She half ran to keep up, Coburn watching the whole thing with an amused, satisfied look on his face.

"What are you doing?" She dug her heels into the grass when they'd cleared the dance floor and pulled to a halt.

He gave her a hard look. "We are going to the boathouse to talk. The only place no one will be. You want to walk or do I carry you?"

Her heart tripped over itself. She wasn't sure she wanted to be alone with him like this. And he would not do that. Not in the middle of all these people. She drank in his stormy demeanor. The deadly intent raging in his ebony eyes. *Then again, maybe he would.*

He started walking. She followed, conscious of more than a few curious looks following them. "You're making a scene."

"Does it look like I *care*?"

Uh-oh. Her heartbeat sped up into an insistent staccato as he skirted the house and took a pathway through the forest down to the water. The farther they got from the crowds milling around the property in loose-knit groups, the worse her trepidation became. Finally, they reached the boathouse, which looked more like a full-fledged house to her with its clapboard walls and big windows. An outside lamp at the front sent a swath of light spilling across the water.

"Harrison—"

He pulled to a stop on the dock and let go of her hand. "You are *not* interested in him. You told me that."

"No, I'm not," she fired back, trying not to be intimidated by his aggressive stance, feet spread apart. "But I thought it might be nice to have a little honesty between us. You are jealous, Harrison. You are feeling things for me you won't admit, not even to yourself."

His eyes flashed. "Oh, I've admitted them to myself. I'm way past that."

She blinked. Swallowed hard as he took the two steps between them and glared down at her with the full force of his fury. "You want honesty, Frankie? Yes, I hate the look of you with Coburn because I know you don't want him. You want me. And he is a *predator.*"

"He is not. He was just having some fun with you."

His jaw hardened until his face took on the consistency of granite. "You think that's a good idea?"

She shook her head. "No, I—" She put her palms to her temples. "It wasn't."

"You don't want me, Frankie." He kept going as if he hadn't heard her. "Tell yourself that. You want a tidy little relationship with a nice guy who will treat you well, give you the requisite two-point-one kids and take you to church on Sunday." He shook his head. "That's not me."

"I never said that." A funny feeling unfurled inside of her. "Why don't you tell me what these feelings are you're having before I make a decision like that?"

He shook his head, a wary look in his eyes. "It won't accomplish anything. I have nothing to offer you."

Frustration burned through her. "I swear I will turn around, go back up there and find one of those eligible men and flirt like crazy if you don't start talking."

His throat convulsed. For a minute she thought he was going to walk away. Then he took the last step toward her, his gaze dark and tormented. "You make me want things I can't have."

"Like what?" She was hypnotized by the confusion in his gaze. The honesty.

He cupped her jaw in his hands. "You make me want you. *Need* you. Crave to be with you. I don't do relationships. That's why I walked away. Not because I don't have feelings for you."

Having his hands on her again felt *so* good. She wanted to purr into him like a cat. Her gaze held on to his. "Maybe you don't know what you're capable of."

"Even if I was," he said harshly, "you are goodness, Frankie. I am the darkness. I would only drag you down there with me."

She moved closer because she was melting inside. "I can handle myself quite nicely, Harrison. I did the other night."

He looked down, as if he was studying the heat drawing them together. "You can't handle my life as it is. With Leonid. Siberius. I could be walking into a whole other playground in a few weeks, one I'm *sure* you couldn't handle."

A presidential campaign. Rumors had been swirling all night about it. Everyone expected him to do it. But she didn't care about that. She cared about the man.

She swallowed hard. "That night at your penthouse… I've never felt like that about anyone. I've never had that kind of a connection with anyone. It was—" She shook her head, stumbling over the words. "My feelings are scaring the heck out of me, too, Harrison. I don't know how to handle them. But I won't deny them." Her gaze clung to his. "You said I make you feel alive…*you* make *me* feel alive."

His gaze darkened. He was silent for a long moment, long enough for her to hear her heart beating in her ears. "You'd be smart to walk away. If I don't break your heart now, I will later."

"You don't know that." She stepped closer until the heat of their bodies melded into one another. "There are no sure things in life. You can't insulate yourself against pain. It's impossible."

She thought she might see a flicker of awareness in his eyes. That she was right. That he'd been locking his feelings away for far too long. Her heart thrummed in her chest as he brought his mouth down to brush against the corner of hers. "There are far better bets than to take a chance on me. I'm not going to lie."

"I don't think so." Her soul reached out for his. "Let yourself go. Follow your instincts. I'll jump if you will."

He murmured something unintelligible against her mouth. Sparks flew between them, their bodies too close, too aware of their wanting not to seize it. Take it. His mouth shifted to cover hers more fully. She moved into him, like water finding a path again. After the uncertainty of this past week, she wanted comfort. She wanted to know she was right.

He kissed her hard, his mouth hungry, lacking in finesse. She had pushed him out of his comfort zone. His hands moved restlessly down to shape her breasts, the curve of her thighs through the silky material of her dress. "You look so good in this," he muttered when they came up for air. "I almost knocked Coburn senseless."

She smiled against his mouth. "He was provoking a reaction."

"He succeeded." The hand that shaped her hips pulled her hard against him. His arousal lay between them, potent and ready. Frankie gasped. "Harrison."

He grabbed her hand and walked toward the boathouse. She tugged on his fingers in a halfhearted protest. "Not here."

"You wanted me to go with my instincts. Live with it." He pulled open the door and tugged her through it. The interior of the boathouse was dimly lit, wooden seating surrounding the empty slip where the water slapped against the boards.

"Isn't everyone supposed to be down here soon for the fireworks?"

He backed her up against the wall, his gaze dark and

dangerous. "We have a good twenty, twenty-five minutes. More than enough time."

Fire raged in her belly, a forbidden, excited pull tugging at her insides. *Really? He was really going to do this?*

"People saw us leave." She attempted a last-ditch effort at sanity.

He pushed the straps of her dress off her shoulder and put his mouth to the rounded curve. "This would not be the biggest scandal in history. Trust me."

That didn't actually convince her, but his hands peeling her dress to her waist distracted her enough that she forgot all about it. She was braless beneath it, the style making undergarments impossible. His rough rumble of approval reverberated through her head. He cupped both breasts in his big hands, bending his head to capture one in his mouth. His lips and tongue played with the hard peak until it was distended and throbbing. Until she was aching inside. Then he switched his attention to the other.

His palms made a foray under her dress and pushed it up her thighs. Her silk panties were a mere wisp of fabric under his heated gaze. He left them on and dropped to his knees. His rough command to hold her dress up was all that proceeded the hot possession of his mouth on her.

Oh, dear God.

Frankie leaned back against the wall, hands clutching her dress, eyes closing at the long, lush strokes of his tongue. Her fingertips dug into the wood on either side of her. His strokes moved deeper, came harder. The only sounds in the boathouse were her breath coming in quick pants now and the water slapping against the wood.

"Harrison."

He nudged her legs farther apart with his elbows. His big hands held her thighs wide as he took her apart with deep, urgent strokes. With a tunnel-visioned focus on the throbbing center of her that shattered her completely. Her moan as she came was so loud in the echoing space, it froze her in place.

What if someone had heard?

Harrison rose. His expression was beyond caring, beyond anything except his end goal. He picked her up, braced her back against the wall and released himself, his strength, the bulging muscles of his biceps as held her in place, a massive turn-on. He moved the fabric of her panties aside and notched his erection into her hot, aching flesh. A low groan tore from his throat. "Please tell me you're protected." She nodded, not sure she would have stopped him even if she hadn't been. She was that far gone.

He buried his face in her neck. Took her with a forceful thrust that stole her breath. She pressed her head against the wall. "God—that's…"

He withdrew and thrust into her again. And again. She dug her nails into his biceps and held on. She wanted everything he had to give her, every piece of the wildness, because it gave her hope he could let go. That he would give in to the magic that was them.

Strain wrote its way across his face as he increased the pace, chasing his pleasure. Frankie brought his mouth down to hers. "Now."

He took more of her weight in his hands, ground his hips against her until his movement set her flesh on fire. She writhed against him, helped him reach the spot she needed. He didn't stop until she groaned in his mouth and sensation ripped her apart again. Then he tightened his hands around her hips and found his release. Hot, hard and uncontrollable, his orgasm sent a flood of warmth through her. It was the most complete she'd ever felt in her life.

It was long seconds later, minutes maybe, before either of them moved. Harrison let her feet slide to the floor, his face buried in her neck. A thin layer of perspiration blanketed his brow. Her heart struggled to find its normal rhythm.

Voices outside ripped them out of their stupor. Her heart crashed against her chest. *Oh, my God.*

Harrison recovered before she did, pushing her dress down over her hips and sliding the straps over her shoulders. "Fix your hair," he muttered, reaching down to make himself decent. She moved her hands up to smooth it but so many curls had escaped, there was no way she was getting it back the way it had been.

The voices got louder. They were directly outside. She threw Harrison a panicked glance. "I can't fix it."

He ran the back of his hand over his brow. "Forget about it. It looks windswept."

He straightened his jacket and reached for her hand. "The side door. We can slip into the crowd."

They exited the door, emerging into the cool night air to find most of the party had moved down to the shore for the fireworks. Any hope she had of stealthily merging into it was crushed by the appearance of Evelyn Grant, a frown on her face, Coburn directly behind her. Coburn's eyes went to her hair, which was always perfectly in place. Widened. Then it traveled to Harrison who looked utterly cool and collected. Coburn's gaze dropped lower. Frankie's followed. *Oh, dear lord, no.* Harrison had a dirt smudge on the knees of his trousers. *Both knees.*

Coburn turned away. Frankie saw his shoulders shaking. Evelyn Grant waved a finger at her son. "Honestly, Harrison. The only thing I asked you to do was round up people for the fireworks."

He lifted a shoulder. "Frankie hadn't seen the view. Apologies, forgot all about the time."

Evelyn's mouth pursed. "Can you at least ask them to start?"

Harrison kept her by his side as he walked over and

gave the instructions to the crew. He tucked her in front of him, arms around her, as the fireworks exploded across the sky, crackling into a starburst of red, blue and white, the brilliant stars falling down around them. She leaned back in his arms. The dazzling display felt like a stunning new beginning of something. Harrison lowered his mouth to her ear. "We made better ones."

The display went on for almost twenty minutes. The Grants had spared no expenses tonight in this marquee party of the year that celebrated the end of summer. She glanced around at the crowd. Looked directly into a pair of big blue eyes on their left that looked utterly shattered. *Cecily.*

There are far better bets than to take a chance on me.

A knot formed in her stomach. Was she being incredibly foolish taking this jump? Utterly naive? Because that sandbox Harrison had talked about…it wasn't her world. *This* wasn't her world. She could easily get eaten alive.

His arms tightened around her. She nestled into him as the fireworks came to an end. Faith required a whole lot more determination than that type of thinking.

She stood by Harrison's side as he and Evelyn waved the guests off in the driveway. If his mother thought her presence there of interest, she didn't show it.

When most of them had left, except for a few stragglers still partying on the dock with Coburn, Harrison clasped her hand in his and they walked toward the house.

The big mansion was silent after the noise of the crowd. They climbed the stairs to the guest rooms, but Harrison didn't stop there; he kept going up the next flight toward his.

"Tongues are wagging," she said quietly as they walked down the hallway toward his suite.

He twisted the knob on the door to his room, opened it and pushed it in with his palm. "Let them."

The room was impressive and warm with its elaborately carved wood fireplace and king-size bed. Harrison came up behind her, put his lips to the nape of her neck and sent shivers down her spine. She leaned back into the heat of his mouth, into the storm they had unleashed. Because she was most certainly in love with him. And she'd been brought up to trust her heart. She only hoped she could trust Harrison with hers.

CHAPTER TWELVE

ROCKY ADJUSTED TO his former home far more easily than Frankie did. He'd resumed his habit of swimming lazy circles to show off his magnificent burnt orange color, his elegant snout pitched in her direction to make sure she was watching, as well as his more frequent naps on the enticing, mossy crystalwort that lined the bottom of the tank.

He'd also clearly taken a cue from the more relaxed demeanor of his owner. Frankie was happy to be back with Coburn where she knew exactly what was expected of her. The work was challenging and satisfying and if there was a part of her that missed the excitement of working with a man whose multiple facets posed a different challenge every minute of the day, she had more than enough of that to contend with in her burgeoning relationship with Harrison outside the office.

He was complex and intense in everything he did, including the bedroom, where he was demonstrating just how passionate and multifaceted a relationship between a man and a woman could be.

Heat drew a curtain across her cheeks. That was where she liked him the most: in bed, where he couldn't get enough of her; where he showed how he felt without the words he couldn't seem to find. He had awakened a side of her she hadn't known existed. A confident, vital part of her that suggested maybe she wasn't so ordinary as she'd always suspected; that maybe she was much more than that. And although she still wasn't completely sure he wouldn't break her heart, she grew more confident every day in what they had. And one day at a time was how she'd promised herself she was going to play this.

Rocky swam another lazy circle in front of her, his beady eyes staring at her. "Yes, you're gorgeous," she told him, shutting her computer down as Coburn put on his coat. "But now I must leave you for a glass of wine and a good book."

"Not with my brother tonight?" Coburn came to stand by her desk.

She shook her head. "He's having dinner with Tom Dennison."

His mouth lifted in a wry tilt. "A full-court press, I'd say. They want him badly."

But did Harrison want them? It was a question she kept asking herself as she got to know the enigmatic man better and better—one she hadn't been able to answer yet. "Far more illustrious company than I," she offered drily, pulling her bottom drawer open and reaching for her bag as the elevator chimed its arrival.

Coburn's eyes moved past her to the elevators. "I think you underestimate your appeal."

She turned. Registered the dark and dangerous presence of the man who was her lover striding toward them. Her pulse shifted into overdrive. Although his eyes had the bruised look of someone who had slept even less than usual of late, undoubtedly due to his showdown with Anton Markovic next week, and the frown that marred his brow made him look forbidding, he was still the most handsome, electric man she'd ever encountered.

The trace of suspicion in his ebony eyes as his gaze flicked to Coburn's position beside her desk sent a warm, heated feeling through her. She liked him jealous. It made him just that little bit vulnerable she needed to get inside.

"H," Coburn greeted him. "Dennison stand you up?"

"I canceled."

Canceled?

Coburn straightened, moving away from her desk and the line of fire. "I'm taking it you aren't here for me. In which case, I'm going to get going. I'm meeting friends."

Harrison nodded. "I'll see you tomorrow morning."

Frankie caught the flash of emotion that passed through Coburn's eyes as he said good-night to her. He wished Harrison would confide in him. The distance between the brothers was becoming so clear to her. She waited until Coburn had stepped on the elevator and left before turning her gaze on the man who'd taken his place. "You know it hurts him when you shut him out like that."

He wrapped his fingers around her wrist and brought her to her feet. "Coburn and I are complicated. Don't get in the middle."

But she knew he didn't bite now, despite his reputation. "Was it always like this?"

His ebony eyes flattened into a matte black. "No. We were close once." He slid an arm around her waist and pulled her close. "We took two different paths. It's years of history. Stop digging."

"Okay," she murmured, suddenly feeling out of breath as he bent his head toward her. "There are security cameras here…remember?"

He kissed her anyway, the heat of his mouth burning through any resistance she had. She curled her fingers into the lapels of his jacket and kissed him back. He didn't stop until she was fully distracted, a deep sigh pulling from her throat.

"Have dinner with me tonight," he murmured huskily against her lips. "Unless you have plans…"

"With a pizza box and a book." She pulled back and studied his weary face. "Why did you cancel?"

A grimace stretched his lips. "I can't think when they're all over me."

Yet he'd chosen her to be with. Heat radiated from her chest, spilling into every part of her. "Yes," she accepted, running her fingers over the taut skin of his cheek. "If you agree to order pizza."

He produced the pizza and a bottle of Chianti, an easier battle than it might have been given it was Elisa's night out and his food snob tendencies couldn't take over.

"You know," she murmured when they'd demolished the pizza on the sofa in the showpiece of a living room, "this decor doesn't suit you at all. It doesn't say anything about who you are."

His lips curved. "I could tell you hated it from the minute you walked in."

"I don't hate it. I think it looks like an art gallery, not a home."

"It's supposed to be an investment."

"Do you plan to live here for a while?"

"Unless plans change."

Unless he ended up in Washington...

He waved an elegant hand around the space. "What would you do, then, with it?"

She gave the open-concept, stark room a critical once-over. "I would add some of that color you love, maybe a gray blue for the walls. Carpets to give it warmth, definitely. And maybe some exotic accents."

He cradled the big wineglass in his palm. "You think that's me?"

"I think it's complex like you are... You aren't cold like this, Harrison. You're layered, you have great depth of feeling when you allow yourself to experience it."

Suprisingly, he didn't back away from the assessment.

His face was lost in thought as he sat there in a rare still moment. "I can't afford to be emotional right now," he said finally, his dark lashes coming down to veil his expression. "Too many things depend on me being level-headed."

"My father always taught me to go with my gut," she countered. "He said the rest will come if you start with what's in your heart."

He lifted his ebony gaze to her. "What if your heart's conflicted?"

Her heart squeezed at the admission. "You need to find out why."

He rested his head against the sofa and stared over at the beautiful Chagalls, both of them in place now. Frankie swallowed hard. "Where is the push for politics coming from? Is it your dream or is it your father's unfinished one?"

He blinked as if he couldn't believe she'd said it. Her hands tightened around the glass, her pulse speeding up. The moment hung in the air between them like an irreversible stepping stone to an intimacy he didn't know how to traverse. Then he sat back and swirled the wine in his glass, his eyes on the ruby-red liquid. "It's both," he said finally. "Politics is in my blood. In my family's blood... My grandfather was a congressman, my father would have been governor had he not taken his own life. You talked about giving back to the community on our flight to London... *I* want to do that. There are so many things I want to change, things I know I *can* change. But am I the right man for the job? This isn't about what I want. It's about what this nation needs."

Frankie felt the overwhelming sense of responsibility coming off him in waves. She couldn't imagine how he felt, but she could try. "I think the country needs hope and vision," she said quietly. "People need someone to believe in. I've seen you lead, Harrison. You've turned a company that was on the verge of disappearing into one of the most powerful in the world. You know how to do this."

He was silent for a long time then. His eyes when he looked at her held that same darkness she'd seen that night she'd rescued him from himself. "Sometimes too great an ambition can destroy a man."

He's worried about becoming his father. Suddenly she understood what had been eating him that night, what had been eating him ever since he'd signed that contract with Leonid. *I am the darkness*, he'd said to her that night in Long Island, *I would only drag you down there with me.* He was afraid of being consumed by the same disease that had taken his father. And who wouldn't be?

She put her wineglass down, got up and settled herself on his lap, knees on either side of his muscular thighs. "You are not your father," she said, cupping his jaw in her hands. "He was sick. You are strong."

His body tautened beneath her like a big cat ready to spring free, but she held his gaze firm in hers. He inhaled deeply, then exhaled, a warm rush of air brushing her cheeks. "He fell apart the night before he announced he was running for governor. I think after what Markovic did, the pressure was too much for him."

Her heart ripped to shreds. "He was on the verge of losing everything. It's understandable. *You*, you are walking into this having conquered. That's a whole different thing. I've watched you do superhuman things. You do what the analysts say can't be done."

His mouth twisted. "Expectations are a bitch, Frankie."

She smiled at that. "I know all about expectations. I'd be running Masserias right now if I'd done what everyone expected of me, and it wouldn't have been the right road for me." She fanned her fingers over his beautiful, tense face, so full of everyone's expectations but his own.

"Figure out if this is *your* dream. If it is, make it happen. If it isn't, walk away."

He captured her fingers in his own, the depth of emotion in his dark eyes making her heart turn over. "I'm done lecturing," she murmured, tugging her fingers away to start undoing the top buttons of his shirt. "Should we discuss the weather now?"

A new emotion joined the ones spiraling through his conflicted gaze. *Desire.* "Only if the forecast involves all my clothes coming off," he said roughly.

"Eventually." She dropped her mouth to his hard, muscular torso as her fingers worked the last buttons free. He shrugged out of the shirt and sat back. Her fingers went for his belt, sliding it free from the buckle with industrious swiftness. Her lips and tongue made a foray down over the hard wall of his abdomen. The muscles beneath her lips contracted with every inch she traveled, until she reached the waistband of his pants. His breath was faster now, his anticipation firing her blood.

"*Hell*, Frankie…"

She undid his pants. Slid the zipper down and released him. He was all hers, this powerful man, and she wanted all of him. *All* of him.

His intake of breath drowned out the blood pounding against her eardrums. She had never done this for him, had never done it for any man. But he was too intoxicating to resist. She bent her head and took him into her mouth.

He cursed and arched beneath her. She refused to let him hurry her, taking her time exploring every musky, potent inch of him that knew how to give her such pleasure. He was big and beautiful and she was shocked at how much she loved touching him like this. Tasting him. It was such a potent turn-on it threw her right into the melee with him. When his hands bit into her biceps and he lifted her from him to rid himself of his pants and then her of her underwear, she didn't protest. Her dress bunched in his hands, he brought her down on him in a joining so fierce, so complete, it stole the breath from her lungs.

"Was that enough of the angel for you?" she murmured when she finally recovered enough to meet his dark, bottomless gaze.

His eyes glittered back at her. "*You* are my angel," he murmured in a gritty voice that made her heart swell. "I love how you rescue me."

She closed her eyes as his hands on her hips guided her down over him again. "You make me crazy," he told her on a half groan. "I can't make this last."

She dug her fingers into the hard muscle of his shoulders to tell him he didn't need to. His fingers clutched her hips in an almost painful grip as he took over the rhythm, driving them both to a powerful climax. It rocked her, taking her apart from the inside.

Shivers snaked through her as he stroked his hand down her spine, his touch on her skin a sensory overload. Emotional overload.

He carried her to bed and made love to her again. Frankie thought that finally, in the aftermath, her head on his shoulder, she had cracked the beast. That she had found what it was inside of him that had needed to be found. *Healed*. For if she hadn't, she had most certainly just sealed her own fate.

CHAPTER THIRTEEN

THE NIGHT BEFORE Harrison confronted Anton Markovic in Washington, Frankie's family invited them to dinner at Masserias. She was concerned, he knew, about how tunnel-visioned he'd become in the past few days and was attempting to distract him. It was a good attempt, her boisterous clan loud and entertaining, but tomorrow was weighing heavily on his mind.

He should have felt settled, confident, with everything in place. He'd brought Siberius under the Grant fold with what looked as if it was going to be minimal intervention from the regulators. He knew exactly when and where he would intercept Markovic. But still the rush wasn't coming. The bloodthirsty urge to tear the Russian from limb to limb that had fueled so much of his adult life hadn't materialized. Instead grim determination defined him. A desire to put a chapter of his life to rest. To avenge the honor of his family. His father.

Frankie's clear, perfect laughter filled the table. Salvatore was teasing her about her taste in music. The happiness written across her face touched something deep inside him. He knew it was she who was changing him. She who was balancing out his extreme emotions. Every day he spent with her he felt more whole, more at peace. She was more than he ever could have anticipated having.

Wanting. He couldn't feel numb with Frankie in his life. She surrounded him in emotion. But having lived so long without it, it was as if he was in the middle of a maze with untold treasures at the end of it, but if he took a wrong turn, it could all end in disaster.

Terrifying.

He took a sip of his Chianti. Forced himself out of his introspection. The Masserias were a fascinating clan to watch as they interacted. He'd never seen such a close-knit unit. Even though all of them were different, from psychologist Federica, with her dry wit and calm demeanor, to Salvatore, Frankie's favorite, with his aggressive, acerbic personality, the depth of caring between the siblings was obvious. They may not all be close—indeed Frankie had filled him in on the tensions between the different factions—but he had the feeling they would all do anything for one another if push came to shove. The bonds were that strong.

A pang seared his heart. He had never had this, a family unit to support him. Not even before his father had gotten sick. It had all been about building the empire for Clifford Grant. About ascending in society. Family had taken a backseat. But he did have Coburn, whom he'd once been close with, the only warmth that had existed within the cold, formal Grant family walls. But his brother's attempt to party and daredevil his way out of his grief had pushed them far apart, a gap that had grown with every year.

He took another sip of his wine and set the glass down. It was eating away at him, had been ever since Frankie had offered that observation about them that night at the office. He hadn't realized until then how much he had missed his brother.

His gaze collided with Vanni Masseria's across the table. Frankie's father was watching him with a probing look: measured, assessing. As if he was weighing his intentions. Harrison met his gaze evenly. It was easy to see where Frankie got her charm and wisdom. Vanni was a charismatic, self-made man who knew himself. Who knew the world from the perspective of a successful man who'd worked hard and prospered just like Harrison's own father had. He also knew Harrison was older than his daughter and much more worldly. That if he put himself in a presidential race it would thrust Frankie into a cutthroat, very public world she'd never known.

Harrison shifted his gaze to Frankie, wondering how she would handle the pressure of being a politician's wife. Would she carry that effortless charm and composure of hers to the role as easily as she'd slipped into his life and found her way inside him? Inside his heart? Or would it drown her? *Would being a Grant make her lose herself?*

He didn't blame Vanni Masseria for being wary. He was, too.

Frankie followed Salvatore into the kitchen, dishes in hand. Her brother set his stack of plates down, turned and leaned against the counter. "I like him."

A weight lifted off her chest. She set her pile of plates down beside his, realizing how nervous she'd been bringing Harrison here for this impromptu dinner. Things were still so new between them, and her family meant everything to her. If they hadn't liked Harrison it would have put her in a turmoil.

Even more so than she was in right now.

Salvatore eyed her, his guarded expression suggesting that *liking* wasn't all that mattered. "You know what you're doing? He's a bit out of your league, Franks."

She chewed on her lip. Why was it every time she was around her family, she ended up feeling insecure? Unsure of herself? She loved them, adored Salvatore, but she hated the feeling she got in the pit of her stomach when they questioned her actions.

She lifted her gaze to her brother's. "Apparently he isn't since we're together."

He shook his head. "You know it's true. Two weeks ago you're telling me he's escorting you to a party but he's not your date. Now you look like you're head over heels for him." He rubbed a hand over his goatee. "You work for him, Franks. He's a Grant. A hard, ruthless businessman. It's worth keeping your head is all."

"I'm happy with him."

"That doesn't change the fact he knows his way around a woman." His eyes lost their aggressive edge. "Look, I am happy for you, sis, I am. Nobody likes to see the sparkle in your eyes more than I do and he gives that to you. But I'm a man. I can see when a guy's got a lot going on in his head. Just take it slow."

Harrison did have a lot going on in his head. He was flying to Washington tomorrow to confront Anton Markovic. It made her sick thinking about him coming face-to-face with the man who'd destroyed his father.

"It's complicated," she told Salvatore.

He grimaced. "That's a fancy word we men use to define *unsure*."

The knot tying itself in her stomach grew tighter. And larger, as she and Harrison said their goodbyes and drove to the penthouse. He was quiet in the car, quiet as they rode the elevator up to the swish, elegant lobby. She could feel the tension gripping him, watched him retreat into his head. She'd wanted to be here for him tonight because she'd known he'd be keyed up about Markovic. And he was.

"They liked you," she murmured when he rose, went into the kitchen and came back with coffee for him and herbal tea for her.

He gave her one of those blank looks he'd been wearing all evening. "I liked them, too. You're lucky to have them."

Something he didn't have. She curled her fingers into his thigh. "What's wrong?"

He looked down at her fingers. "I'm just distracted. A million things on my mind."

"Are you sure you still want to do this?"

His gaze lifted to hers, fiery now. "No sermons, Frankie, I can't take it tonight."

She bit her lip. Tomorrow he was going to take his revenge on a man who had stolen his father from him. It wasn't the answer to his anger, but he couldn't see it.

"It won't bring him back." She dug her fingertips deeper into his thigh. "Nothing is going to bring your father back, Harrison. Nothing is going to right the wrongs Anton Markovic did. The only way forward is for you to forgive him. To move on and honor your father like you have been."

"Forgive?" His mouth flattened into a straight line, his thigh tensing beneath her fingers. "That's what your *new-age advice* would tell me to do? What exactly is that supposed to accomplish, Frankie? I'm supposed to become at peace with the world by doing it?"

She winced, but his anger no longer had the power to silence her. She knew he didn't bite. "You're making it sound too simplistic. You have to let go to move on. Hatred is toxic. Hatred is what gives you these black moods. They aren't going to go away unless you get rid of the poison behind them."

He stood up. His gaze was beyond lethal as he pinned it on her. "*He* is the poison. *He* is the toxicity. *He* needs to be broken."

"And then what? You destroy him and take everything? You think you are going to miraculously feel better because you did the same thing to another man that was done to your father? Did you ever think that he might have a family, too? That he might have children who will be as broken as you and Coburn if you do this? If you take away their livelihood?"

He lifted a shoulder. "He should have thought about that before he played so cavalierly with other people's lives. You can bet if he conducts business this way we were not the only victims. There are others, and I want him gone so he can never do it again."

She couldn't argue with that point. Juliana had told her what an evil man Anton Markovic was. But evil had nothing to do with this. In taking Markovic down, Harrison would give his own soul away. He was halfway there now.

"Ask yourself," she said quietly, "if you can handle the guilt when it's all over. Ask yourself if it's worth it. Because I saw your face after Leonid signed that contract. You are an honorable man. But you won't consider yourself that if you do this tomorrow."

An expression she'd never seen before passed over his face. Shock that she'd said it? Anger that she'd dared? Fear she was right? Her blood raced in her veins, making her feel light-headed. She had gone too far. But she'd never have forgiven herself for not saying it before it was too late.

He turned and walked away from her, out onto the terrace. She gave him a few minutes, then followed. He stood looking at the smoky skyline of Manhattan, shrouded on a smoggy, summer night.

"You think you know me," he rasped when he sensed her behind him. "But you don't. You think everyone is good like you are, but they aren't. You're an anomaly in a world where greed and selfishness rule."

She moved beside him so she could see him, see the torment on his face. Her blood pounded hard in her ears, warning her to stop, warning her she'd already pushed him far enough and he was letting her in slowly but surely. But she couldn't because he needed to hear this.

"You tell yourself that because it's easier to believe. Because it's easier than admitting the beautiful human man that you are inside that cast-iron exterior. I can't watch you do it, Harrison. I am beyond that."

"Then leave." His harsh words hit her like a slap in the face. She braved his anger and put a hand on his arm. He shook it off, his eyes cold. "It was a mistake thinking this could ever work, Frankie. I told you that in Long Island, but you wouldn't listen."

"Harrison—"

"Leave." His gaze tangled with hers, like polished stone. "I don't want you here."

Her heart fell apart. She should be used to how brutally cold he could be but it didn't prepare her for the way she shattered, tiny fragments of herself raining down over her until she felt as though nothing was left. Only a searing pain that seemed to transcend her body.

He had the ability to make her feel everything. And nothing.

Her hands shook as she pushed her hair out of her face and looked up at him. "You're right. I don't know you, then. Because I thought you were more than this."

She turned and left the penthouse, tears threatening to penetrate her numbness. She'd thought she'd been getting through to him, that something was clicking in that closed-off brain of his. But she'd been wrong. The beast could wallow in his self-imposed misery. She was done.

CHAPTER FOURTEEN

THE PRIVATE CLUB in the heart of downtown Washington where Anton Markovic was meeting a senior government official had been described as "the closest thing to the unofficial heart of the city's intellectual elite" that existed. Housed in an elegant Louis XVI–style townhome on Embassy Row that had once been a private residence, it had been the meeting place of presidents, Supreme Court justices and Nobel Prize winners over its history.

It was the type of place that, should he run for office, would define Harrison's life. He entered the wood-paneled library with its refined decor and elaborately carved fireplaces and took a seat near the windows. You could almost *feel* the backroom conversations that had shaped a nation. It was that steeped in tradition. *Prestige.* He felt underdressed even in a suit.

Locating his target sitting across from a salt-and-pepper-haired bureaucrat near one of the fireplaces, he took the opportunity to study him. Anton Markovic was in his late fifties, graying at the temples, handsome by anyone's standards. But it was the cruel edge to his mouth that drew his eye. The knowledge of how much devastation he had wreaked with a calculated move to save a failing empire.

His body went ice-cold, as if it had been February, not

the last sweltering days of August in a town built on a swamp.

He was not letting him walk out of here intact.

Markovic gave him an absentminded look, as if he half recognized him but was too wrapped up in his conversation to pursue the thought. Harrison sat down in a chair beside the fireplace and waited. It was another half hour before the two men stood, shook hands and walked toward the stairwell. Harrison unfolded himself from the chair, intercepted them at the door and held his hand out to Markovic. "Harrison Grant."

The bureaucrat looked intrigued to see him there. A wary glitter appeared in the Russian's eyes. "A pleasure," he said, shaking his hand.

Bile pooled in the back of his throat at the touch of the other man's hand. He brought a practiced, easy smile to his lips. "Could I steal you for a drink? I had something I wanted to discuss with you."

The suspicion in the Russian's eyes intensified. "I'm afraid I have dinner plans."

"Ten minutes." Harrison made it rude not to accept. *You'll want to hear what I have to say*, his eyes told the Russian. *And not in front of your companion.*

Markovic nodded and said his goodbyes to the bureaucrat. The Russian waited until the other man had cleared the landing and was walking down the lower stairs before he spoke.

"I had the feeling our paths might cross someday."

The way he said it in an almost casual tone, the complete disregard for the tragedies he'd instigated, brought Harrison's breath to a halt in his throat. The man was a monster. Without feeling or soul. He'd heard he was this way but it was something else to see it in the flesh.

"Sit down." He bit out the words before he clawed the other man's eyes from his face.

The Russian sat, his expression still that cool, controlled mask. "So?"

Harrison sat down. His disbelief overrode the speech he had rehearsed in his head hundreds of times. "You don't care, do you? What you did to my family?"

Markovic's eyes flashed a frigid blue. "I didn't kill your father, Grant, he did. Things happen in business… He could have done what you did—moved past his mistake and rebuilt. Instead he was weak."

Harrison's rage descended to a bone-deep level that scared even him. It made it almost impossible to move, to speak. "You don't feel the slightest bit of remorse," he managed finally, "for what you did?"

The Russian shrugged. "I'm sorry you lost your father. I'm sorry he had a disease. But he chose to make the deal."

"*He didn't know what deal he was making.* What you did was amoral and illegal. Today you would be prosecuted."

"Good thing yesterday isn't today. And we all know I suffered, too, Grant. I failed. I lost everything. I was going through my own personal hell."

"Get ready to go through it again."

Markovic's eyes flickered. "How do you figure that?"

Harrison leaned forward and rested his forearms on his thighs. "I've bought up every single one of your key suppliers. Through offshore entities, subsidiaries, friends. When I flick a switch tomorrow morning, you will be missing one part, then another. Production will be delayed, then delayed some more. Until one morning you wake up and your entire operations have ground to a halt and you are *paralyzed*. And then I don't care if you feel remorse. I only want you to experience the *hell*."

The Russian's face went gray. "It's a global economy, Grant. There are any number of other suppliers I can turn to."

Satisfaction lanced through the numbness blanketing

Harrison. "Try it." He nodded in the direction the bureaucrat had taken. "But I advise you do it before you sign your contract. You might find yourself *unable to deliver*."

A sick realization spread across Markovic's face. Harrison stood up. His skin felt too tight to be in the presence of such ugliness any longer.

Not one more second would he let this man rule his life. "Enjoy your dinner."

He walked past the tapestries, the paintings three presidents had considered while they had changed a nation. Away from his past. Toward his future. And wondered why it still didn't feel right.

A whisper-quick flight later, the Grant jet deposited him back in Mahattan just before eight. Standing on his terrace with a whiskey in his hand, watching the lights from the skyscrapers cast the city in a glow of prosperity versus the history of Washington, New York seemed a lifetime away from Anton Markovic. From his past.

Someday you're going to realize that cold heart of yours has left you alone in this big empty world, H. And when you do, nobody is going to care anymore.

The empty feeling in his gut so perfectly matched Coburn's prediction it was like a knife twisting a particularly painful path through him. How his brother and Frankie had both known so clearly that vengeance was never going to give him the satisfaction he craved made him wonder how well he knew himself. Avenging his father's honor was the phantom, the mirage that had kept him going all these years, but when it came down to it, Markovic had been right: his father had been sick; the Russian had not been responsible for his death.

The whiskey burned as he took a long slug of it, but not enough to ease the self-knowledge that seared him. He had wanted to hate Anton Markovic rather than acknowledge the disease that had ravaged his all-powerful father. Because if it could happen to a force like Clifford Grant, it could happen to him.

He cradled the crystal tumbler in his palm and watched the light bounce off its carefully crafted edges. Funnily enough, what was hurting him most wasn't the past, which he knew now he needed to let go. It was Frankie. He was afraid he was that cold-hearted monster Coburn had painted who had driven away the woman he loved for good.

That he loved her his heart had acknowledged weeks ago. His head had simply refused to follow. The question now was whether he deserved a chance at happiness. Was he *enough* to make her happy? Would the darkness continue to move away with her in his life or would he destroy her?

His fingers tightened around the glass. He wished he had a crystal ball that would give him the answers he needed. He was terrified instead that putting his heart on the line was the only thing that might save him.

Something latent but still alive stirred inside him. He had to try.

CHAPTER FIFTEEN

"I'M BANKING ON the fact you have beer in this bachelor pad."

If Coburn found it odd that his older brother, who rarely drank beer and even more infrequently dropped by for a chat on a Wednesday evening, was standing on his doorstep, he refrained from commenting. His expression, though, as he stepped back and Harrison walked in, was wry. "You're going to have to let me finish up. Carole is here."

"Finish up?" Coburn glanced in the direction of the bedroom. Harrison ran a hand through his hair. "Good God, Coburn." He turned around and headed for the door, but his brother stopped him with a hand on his arm.

"She's getting dressed. She has an early yoga class. Stay."

Harrison went to the kitchen, grabbed two beers from the fridge and headed for the patio. He tipped the beer back and drank a long swallow while he watched what appeared to be a raucous party on the patio opposite Coburn's in the trendy Chelsea neighborhood.

His brother came out, pulling a T-shirt over his head. Harrison handed him his beer and nodded toward the door. "You know you're going to have to get rid of *that*."

"When I'm seventy, maybe yes."

"Sooner than that. That type will get far too attached to the idea of bedding a CEO. Of being *the one* beside all that power."

The bottle stopped halfway to Coburn's mouth. "You're going to run."

He nodded. "You think you can take over without driving us into the ground?"

His brother put the bottle down. Iron determination filled his face. "You know I can."

"I do." Harrison tilted the bottle at him. "The press conference is tomorrow to announce my candidacy. I'd like you to be there with me."

To any other brother, the command would have sounded arrogant. But Coburn knew what it took for him to ask for support. His brother's eyes glimmered with an emotion he hadn't seen him exhibit in a very long time. "I'll be there."

They drank in silence for a while. An ache filled Harrison's chest. He'd missed this. More than he'd known. "How do you even sleep with that racket going on?"

"I don't...much." Coburn turned to him, resting his hip against the railing. "What happened with Markovic?"

"I took away enough of his suppliers to hamstring him but not kill him. He's going to spend the rest of his days remembering what he did." He shrugged. "Or maybe not. The man has no conscience."

"Why didn't you do it? Why didn't you annihilate him?"

He lifted a shoulder. "Because you were right. Doing that isn't going to bring back our father. And at the end of the day, the fact is, Dad was sick. Markovic didn't kill him, the disease did."

"And you are better than that." His brother's look was pointed. "I was waiting for you to realize that."

"Someone else helped me realize it."

Coburn's eyes sharpened on him. "She's miserable, H. You did a number on her."

His heart turned over in his chest. "I know. I plan to fix it." He just wasn't at all sure what the outcome would be. It had his insides tied into a knot.

They talked about tomorrow. About the future of Grant and their roles in it. Harrison would stay as involved as he could for as long as he could. But the CEO role was Coburn's—permanently. If politics didn't work out for him, well, they'd cross that bridge when they came to it.

Coburn walked him to the door. His eyes were full of life. Full of challenge. He'd been needing it for a long time.

Harrison did something he hadn't done in as long as he could remember. He wrapped his arm around his brother and hugged him hard. Then he walked out into the night before Coburn saw the tears stinging his eyes.

Masserias was buzzing on a Thursday night with every table in the restaurant taken and the overflow spilling to the bar. The patrons were in a universally upbeat mood, it seemed, enjoying good food and wine before the weekend.

Frankie took the order from her table, walked to the computer and punched it in. She was grateful for the infusion of energy, had volunteered to take this shift from a sick waitress to help her parents out, because if she stayed at home and moped for another night she was going to turn into a permanent case of pathetic.

"Well, I'll be damned." Her father's voice carried to her from the bar where he was mixing drinks with Salvatore. The bemused tone in his voice drew her eye.

"What?"

He pointed at the TV mounted on the wall to one side of the bar. Frankie skimmed the headline. *Harrison Grant to join the presidential race as an independent candidate.*

She moved closer, her heart stirring to life in her chest. Her father turned up the volume so the announcer's voice could be heard over the crowd. *"Grant confirmed the long-*

anticipated news today that he will run as an independent candidate for president. The CEO, whose grandfather was a congressman and whose father took his life the night before his announcement he would run for Governor, of New York, gave an emotional speech about the financial well-being of a nation he described as 'struggling to find its identity.'"

Her heart, which hadn't come close to repairing itself, swelled with an ache so painful it winded her. A clip of Harrison at the podium filled the screen. "I believe in a nation where things can be better. Where we can all believe in who we are again, where we can have faith in the principles this country was founded on. And that starts with the people." He paused, his gaze trained on the cameras. "Someone recently reminded me of the goodness of people—how every decision we make impacts not only us but the people around us. And that goodness—that caring for each other—is what the fabric of this nation was built on. It's what we need to go forward. My vision is about putting the people first again with a back-to-basics fiscal policy shaped by the principles that created this country. We all want to contribute. We all want to make our mark. And we will."

Her heart throbbed in her chest. The announcer wound up the story and invited a panel of guests to discuss how Harrison's entry into the race would affect the dynamics. Her father slapped his hand on his thigh. "Well, I'll be damned," he said again. "He's actually going to do it."

Her eyes were burning. She turned away from the screen, but not before a tear slipped from her eye and eagle-eyed Salvatore saw it. A dark look spread across his face. He knew how badly she was hurting.

"Franks—"

She waved him off. "I need that Bellini."

An order was up for her in the kitchen. She waited

for the chef to set the last plate on the counter. *Someone recently reminded me of the goodness of people.* He'd been talking about her, she was sure of it. Tears streamed down her face. She grabbed a napkin from the counter and mopped them up. She was so happy for him and so utterly miserable at the same time. She wanted him to heal, wanted him to move on, but she wanted it to be with her. She might only be twenty-three but she knew when someone was your soul mate. The problem was, you couldn't make someone love you. She knew that, too.

She composed herself, picked up the plates and headed back into the dining room to deliver them. Table served, she went to collect her Bellini at the bar. It was waiting for her. She slid it onto her tray.

"Aww, hell."

"What?" She turned in the direction of Salvatore's scowl. A dark-haired male clad in a black trench coat was talking to her mother. He was too arresting, too handsome to ignore. He looked exactly like he had the night he'd walked into the office and all hell had broken loose. Except he had a bouquet of red roses in his hands.

Her mind lost all conscious thought, including the fact she was holding a tray. The Bellini hit the floor with a loud crash that had all eyes on her.

It was the roses that did her in.

Her gaze locked with Harrison's. He looked so serious, so intent it stopped her heart in her chest. You could hear a pin drop in the room as eyes moved from her to the man who'd just been on TV. The need to escape the attention, *to do something*, sent her to her knees. She right-sided the tray and started picking up the pieces of glass. Salvatore dropped to his knees beside her and brushed her hands away. "Forget about the goddamned glass," he muttered. "Go talk to him before I kill him."

She got to her feet. Most of the crowd in the restaurant

had gone back to their conversations, but there were a few who were too interested in the news of the day to want to miss a thing. Her pulse fluttered wildly in her throat as Harrison headed toward her.

He stopped in front of her, his gaze eating her up. "My effect on you hasn't seemed to change."

She swallowed hard, pride kicking in. "Don't be so sure about that."

"Oh, I *am*."

Heat invaded every cell of her body, thrumming through her veins. "Congratulations on your announcement," she said stiffly. "You have everybody in a flutter."

He reached out and ran a finger down her cheek. "The only one I'm interested in having in a flutter is you."

She flinched away from his touch. "You ended that on Monday or have you forgotten?"

His gaze darkened. "Do you think we can have this conversation in private?"

"No." She shook her head, too hurt, too unwilling to go there with him when he'd made it clear they were over. "You can't push me away then expect me to fall into your arms again when it's convenient for you, Harrison."

"That's not what this is."

"Then what is it? You told me it was never going to work. Don't come to me on some high then break my heart again. I can't take it."

"I've changed." His voice vibrated with emotion. "*You've* changed me, Frankie. You've made me see how wrong my thinking was. How capable I am of feeling."

Her heart started to melt despite herself. He saw it, pressed his advantage. "Give me another chance. I promise I deserve it."

She crossed her arms over her chest, holding in the surge of hope that took ahold of her. "Why should I? What's going to be different this time?"

"Me." He stepped closer until he was occupying her personal space. Every cell in her body reacted to him. Begged her for him. His eyes were the deepest black she'd ever seen them, except now, she realized, they were clear, without a shadow of doubt in them.

"My head has been so messed up. I've had so many decisions to make, so many ghosts to put to rest, I couldn't think straight. But you," he said, reaching for her hand, "you are the only thing that's been right."

She shook her head, wanting him so badly it hurt. "I can't be a part of your endless circle of revenge. It will eventually tear you apart and me along with it."

"It won't. I'm stepping down as Grant CEO. But I have gained the board's assurance that Siberius will remain a separate company. Leonid's wish will be fulfilled."

Something shifted inside her. She had dangled that possibility in front of him that night in bed, hoping he would see he had alternatives. But he had shut her down so completely she had given up hope. "And Markovic? What did you do with him?"

His jaw hardened. "I put him on notice that if his behavior ever gets beyond my tolerance, I will take him apart. Meanwhile, I left him enough lifelines to stay alive."

"Why?" She could hardly get the word past the lump in her throat.

"Because one tragedy does not equal another. Of all the crimes Anton Markovic has perpetrated on my family, killing my father was not one of them. My father was teetering on the edge. I needed someone to blame instead of facing my own rage. My sadness."

She saw for the first time the vulnerable edge to his decisive, steely exterior. It was there just behind the blazing confidence in his eyes, that soft amber light she'd discovered in the office that day. She swallowed hard as she digested it all. The things he'd done had proved beyond words that he did want to move beyond the darkness. That he meant what he was saying.

But she had no idea where to start. He did. He put the roses on the bar, took her hand and dragged her from the room.

"Harrison…"

"Where?" he growled. "I've had enough of an audience today."

"The staff room," she offered weakly, pointing at a door past the kitchen. He opened the door, but there was someone in there. Cursing, he found the next available door and yanked it open. It was a supply closet. He pulled her in and closed the door behind them. She was too full of emotion to do anything but stand there, back against the wall in the tiny space as he curled a hand around her nape and brought her to him. The glitter in his eyes made her insides contract. "I love you, Francesca Masseria. Your goodness, your passion, everything about you. You have healed a broken part of me I thought forever lost."

Her heart leaped into her mouth and stayed there. She couldn't get a word past her lips. Not one.

"The next year is going to be crazy," he continued, "and I know it's a lot to ask of you, but I want you by my side during this. Actually," he amended, "that's not true. I want you by my side always."

Her breath escaped in a long, harsh expenditure of air. "Harrison—"

He let go of her, reached inside his jacket and came out with a box. Her brain went haywire. "You aren't going to—"

"Propose in a supply closet?" He dropped to his knee. "I tried to go somewhere private."

"Yes, but—"

He flipped the box open. A sparkling sapphire winked back at her, surrounded by the most perfect row of white fire. She stared at it. Stared at the powerful, ruthless man at her feet who'd just declared his intentions to run this country.

"Marry me," he murmured. "Be my anchor in this storm because I need you there."

Could she be a Grant? Could she be a politician's wife? He was asking her to take a leap just like she had asked him that night in Long Island. And although the idea scared the hell out of her, her heart wouldn't let her do anything but follow it.

"The answer is yes," she said softly, "if you promise me that when things get dark, you won't shut me out. You will talk to me."

She thought she saw moisture build at the corner of his eyes. It made hot tears gather in hers. "I promise," he said, his voice steady and sure.

She stuck out her hand. Held her breath as he slid the sapphire on her ring finger. Because it had to fit. *They* fit perfectly. She was strong where he was weak and he was all-powerful in the spaces between.

It fit.

He rose to his feet. She threw herself into his arms, every bit of pent-up emotion bursting out of her as he anchored her against him and kissed her. Sure and never-ending it was heaven.

His palms moved lower on her hips, settled her more intimately against him. Frankie drew in a breath at the white-hot heat that consumed her at his blatant arousal. "We are *not* doing this here."

"No," he murmured against her lips, "I value my life. But I need five more minutes."

When way more than five minutes had passed, they emerged from the closet, clothes intact, a bloom in Frankie's cheeks that made Salvatore's face darken when they walked back into the dining room. She held up her left hand and the glare faded. "You are a lucky man, Grant. By the skin of your teeth."

Her brother's face relaxed into a beaming smile as he stepped forward and shook Harrison's hand. The bubbly came out and the night devolved into a restaurant-wide celebration, on the house.

Her father and Harrison spent the night talking politics while her mother plied her about dress choices between customers. But Frankie wasn't ready to think about any of that. She wanted to savor every minute of the weight of Harrison's ring on her finger.

She heard her father say something about hosting a rally here at the restaurant for Harrison's campaign. "We've created a monster," she said rolling her eyes.

Salvatore gave their father an amused look. "He should have run a long time ago. Let him live vicariously through your fiancé."

Fiancé. The glow lasted all the way home to Harrison's penthouse. In the elevator where they almost lost control completely, then in the bedroom where her *fiancé* disposed of her clothes so fast her head spun. She lay back on the bed, watching him as he prowled toward her. "Maybe you should come work for me on my campaign. I can live out my fantasy. *Daily...*"

She dug her fingers in his hair as he pressed a kiss to her throat. "I have never dropped a drink in my life until tonight. I'm done working for you, Harrison. You have me entirely on edge."

His gaze glittered. "Actually," he murmured, "I completely agree. The only place I want you off balance is here. *Under me.*"

She could offer her full cooperation on that. Her insides contracted with the need to have him after a week full of misery. But it was his clear, unclouded gaze that touched her the deepest. In that moment, she knew she could do it.

She could be a Grant, and maybe, if the stars aligned, she could be a president's wife. Because she was the woman who'd conquered the heart of the beast. The woman who'd helped heal him.

She smiled and closed her eyes as he dragged her down into the tempest with him. They'd said it was impossible. What did they know?

* * * * *

BEWARE OF
THE BOSS

LEAH ASHTON

For Isla,
welcome to the world, honeybun!

CHAPTER ONE

WITH A GASP, Lanie Smith sat up abruptly, her floppy straw hat dislodging onto her lap and her towel a tangle amongst her hastily rearranged legs.

What on earth?

A shockingly cold nose pressing insistently against her knee answered that question. The large dog, its long red coat soaked in salt water and decorated generously with beach sand, nudged her leg, then flicked its liquid chocolate gaze hopefully in her direction.

'You lose something, buddy?'

Lanie leant forward, searching amongst the folds of her towel. The dog found its soggy-looking target first and snatched the ball up, backing a quick handful of steps away before going still and staring at her again.

'You want me to throw it?'

Knowing there was really only one answer to that question, Lanie pressed her hands into the sand and climbed to her feet. She shook her head a little, still fuzzy from her impromptu nap.

One minute she'd been reading her paperback…the next… She glanced up at the sky, looking for the sun, and breathed a silent sigh of relief when she realised it was still low and behind her. At least she hadn't slept for long.

Not that sleeping the day away would have been such a disaster. It wasn't as if she had a million other things to do.

The dog came closer and dropped the ball with a dull plop at her feet.

Hurry up.

Lanie couldn't help but smile.

'Okay, okay, buddy—here we go.'

With barely a grimace as her fingers wrapped around the slobbery ball—there was enough water here at North Cottesloe beach to wash her hands, after all—Lanie weighed up her throwing options. Back towards the water, from where the dog had obviously come? Or along the shore…?

'Luther!'

The deep voice stilled Lanie's movements. The dog momentarily glanced in the direction of the obviously familiar voice before refocussing his rapt attention on the ball.

A man loped across the blinding white sand towards her. He was shirtless, wearing only baggy, low-slung board shorts and a pair of jet-black sunglasses. The morning sun reflected off toned olive skin that glowed with exertion, and he ran a hand through slightly too long dark brown hair as he approached, leaving it standing in a haphazard arrangement.

Lanie found herself patting uselessly at her own brownish hair—which, in contrast, she was sure had *not* been rakishly enhanced by the combined effects of sand, wind and the fact that she'd done no more than loop it into half a ponytail before walking out of the house this morning.

'*Luther!*' the man said again.

The dog moved not a muscle, every line of his body focussed on Lanie's hand.

For the first time the man glanced in her direction.

And it *was* only a glance—as brief and uninterested as Luther's when he'd heard his owner call his name.

'Are you planning on keeping his ball?' the man asked, shifting his weight from foot to foot as he waited for her response.

Lanie blinked behind her own sunglasses. 'Pardon me?'

He sighed, twisting his wrist to look at his watch. 'Can you please give Luther his ball? Soonish would be great.'

The ball dropped from Lanie's fingers, but the big red dog pounced as excitedly as if she'd thrown it miles away. Now he crossed the short distance to his owner, and moments later the ball was whizzing through the air and into the shallow waves. The dog followed with huge, galumphing, splashing strides.

The man left too, without a backward glance, jogging the exact parallel distance from the lapping waves as he did every single morning.

'You're welcome,' Lanie said to his rapidly retreating broad shoulders.

What a jerk.

She knelt to stuff her towel and book into her canvas tote bag, and covered her windblown hair with her hat.

Well, at least now she knew.

In the past weeks she'd come to recognise most of the early-morning regulars at the beach—the dedicated open water swimmers who swam at seven a.m. every day, come rain, hail or shine. The walkers—both the walking-for-exercise and the walking-because-the-beach-is-gorgeous types. The joggers, the surfers, the sunbathers—and of course the dogs.

That man was also a regular. Unlike the others, who would greet Lanie with a familiar nod or smile each morning, this man appeared to be absorbed completely in his own world. He went for his run, his dog zipping about the shore in his wake—and then he left. That was it.

Dark and interesting, Lanie had thought whenever she'd seen him. *Private. Intense.*

Gorgeous. Obviously.

She wouldn't have been human not to wonder about a man like that. What did he do? What was his name? Was he married?

Not that she'd harboured any ridiculous daydreams. Lanie was, if nothing else, pragmatic.

But still—she'd wondered.

And now she had the only answer she needed. So, what was he like? *Rude*. Definitely.

Oh, well. No great loss—he could still add to her beautiful view each morning. A personality deficiency wouldn't impact on that.

With her shoes dangling from her fingers, Lanie followed a path through the green scrub-tufted dunes towards Marine Parade. Small white shells mixed amongst the sand dug into the soles of her feet. When she hit the footpath she dropped her shoes to the ground so she could step into them. The concrete was surprisingly warm, despite the lukewarm winter day.

It was Tuesday, so the Norfolk-pine-lined street was mostly empty, not crammed with cars fighting for every available space as was typical throughout summer weekends. Across the road, multi-million-dollar homes faced the cerulean ocean, with a single café nestled amongst their architecturally designed glory. The café's white-painted tables and chairs spilled outside, protected by brightly covered shade cloth sails and decorated with blue glass bottles filled with yellow daisies. Lanie's house was a two-minute walk up the hill—but a wave from the grey-haired man amongst the empty tables drew her attention.

'Lanie!' he called out, pausing his energetic sweeping to prop himself against a broom. 'Morning! Did you swim today?'

She smiled as she shook her head. 'Not today.'

'Tomorrow?'

They followed this script every day. 'Maybe.'

The man grumbled something non-distinct, but his opinion was still crystal-clear.

'Tell me what you *really* think, Bob,' she said dryly.

'Such a waste,' he said—just as he had yesterday—then patted one of the table tops. 'Coffee?'

Lanie nodded. Along with her early-morning beach visits, coffee at the eponymous Bob's Café had become part of her daily routine.

She slid onto the wooden chair, careful to avoid Bob's scruffy-looking apricot poodle who slept, oblivious, at her feet. Bob didn't wait to take her order, just shuffled inside to brew her 'usual': flat white, no sugar, extra shot of coffee.

On the table was today's newspaper, and automatically Lanie flipped it over as she waited.

A giant colour photograph almost filled the back page: a familiar, perfect, blinding white smile; slicked back, damp blond hair and eyes identical to those she saw in the mirror each day—except Sienna's were a sparkling azure blue, not brown.

'Hazel,' her mum always said. *'Not brown. If you only made more of them, Lanie, they'd be your best feature.'*

'Another gold medal,' Bob said, sliding a large mug and saucer onto the table.

Lanie shrugged. 'I know. She's doing really well. This is a great meet for her.'

Meet. Quite the understatement.

Bob raised his white-flecked eyebrows.

'I mean it,' Lanie said—and she did. 'I'm thrilled for her. Very proud of her.'

Her sister was in London, living Lanie's dream.

No, *Sienna's* dream. Lanie's dream had ended months ago, at the selection trials.

Lanie held her mug in her hands for a few moments, then raised an eyebrow at Bob, who still hovered.

'It's the relay tonight,' Bob said.

'Uh-huh.' Lanie took a too-quick sip and the hot liquid stung the roof of her mouth. She pressed her tongue against the slight pain, dismissing it.

Bob didn't push, but she felt the occasional weight of his gaze as he swept around her. He was a sports nut—pure and simple. Fanatical, actually—he had to be to have recognised her that first morning she'd emerged from her mother's house. *Lanie Smith* was far, far from a household name. *Sienna Smith*—well, that was another story. A story that could be read in the sports pages, in gushing women's magazines, or even in lads' mags accompanied by pictures of her in far more revealing bathers than her sister wore at swim-meets.

It didn't bother her. Her younger sister was suited to the limelight and she deserved it. Lanie was much happier in the shadows and perfectly satisfied with her accomplishments as a world-class relay swimmer. Besides, she certainly didn't crave the adulation that Sienna seemed to draw like a magnet.

Mostly satisfied. Lanie mentally corrected herself. *Mostly satisfied with her accomplishments.*

Absently she flicked through the sporting pages, full of photos of winners on podiums.

'Wish it was you?'

She hadn't realised Bob had approached her table again, and she glanced up in surprise. 'Of course not,' Lanie replied—snapped, really. Immediately she wished she could swallow the words. 'I'm retired,' she clarified, more calmly.

He nodded and drifted politely away again—but Lanie didn't miss the questions, and maybe concern, in his eyes.

She stood and left a handful of coins on the table, trying to ignore how her eyes had started to tingle and squint.

It was the sea breeze.

She slung her bag onto her shoulder and took big, brisk strides to exit the café and get home as quickly as possible.

She'd walked past three huge mansions, heading towards the street where her mother's small neat cottage was, when something caught her eye.

The glint of sun off a sweaty, perfectly muscled chest.

That man.

He jogged along the footpath on the opposite side of the road. His dog was now on a lead, intermittently gazing up at his owner in adoration.

Lanie felt herself tense, for no reason she could fathom.

She'd slowed her walk, but now she deliberately sped up—back to the pace she'd been before.

She didn't care about that guy. Didn't care if he was rude. Didn't care what he thought of her.

Didn't care what Bob thought.

Didn't care what her sister thought. Didn't care what anyone thought.

She held her head high and walked briskly past. With purpose.

But out of the corner of her eye she couldn't help but watch the man.

And notice that he paid her absolutely no attention at all.

It was as if she were invisible.

The knock on Lanie's front door later that night was not unexpected.

She headed down her narrow hallway, her slippers thudding against the hundred-year-old floorboards.

She flung the door open, and—as expected—behind the fly screen stood Teagan. Her long black hair was swept off her face and semi contained in a messy bun on the top of her head, and her eyes sparkled behind red-framed glasses.

Her oldest friend held up a plastic grocery bag. 'I have four types of cheese, olives, sundried tomatoes, and something I believe is called quince. The guy at the deli told me it was awesome, but I remain sceptical.'

Teagan bounded up the hall, as comfortable in this house as her own. As kids they'd split their time between their family's homes, although Teagan's family had long upgraded and moved on, while Lanie's mum had quite happily stayed put in the house she'd grown up in.

Lanie watched as Teagan pottered around the kitchen, locating a large wooden board and helping herself to cutlery.

She didn't bother asking why her friend was here as it was so obvious. Equally obvious was the fact that Teagan had ignored her when she'd politely declined her offer to hang out with her tonight.

'It's just another race, Teags,' she'd told her. *'I'll be fine.'*

Apparently she'd convinced Teagan about as well as she'd convinced herself.

Soon they'd settled on the rug in front of the TV, red wine in hand, cheese platter set out in front of them.

'You *do* know the final isn't until, like, two a.m.?' Lanie asked, her legs sprawled out in front of her.

'That's what coffee is for,' Teagan said between sips of wine. 'Besides, this current job I could do in my sleep. Hardly anyone calls Reception. In fact I'm starting to think they don't have any customers at all. You know...' Teagan paused, leaning forward conspiratorially. 'I reckon it's possible that it's all an elaborate front for something dodgy. I've always thought that my boss has shifty eyes...'

Lanie laughed out loud as Teagan outlined a typically outlandish theory. More than once Lanie had suspected that Teagan's preference for temping over a more permanent job was purely to get new material—whether they caught up for coffee, dinner or a drink, it was guaranteed that her friend would have a new story to tell.

As they ate—and polished off the bottle of wine—Lanie flicked from channel to channel of the sports coverage—heats of rowing, horses leaping over huge fences across country, cyclists whizzing around a velodrome.

'So, have you made a decision?' Teagan said a while later, her tone much more careful than before.

Lanie shifted uncomfortably. 'Has my mother been in touch?'

Teagan pulled a face. 'God, no. And it isn't like your mum's not capable of nagging you directly.'

Lanie's lips quirked unevenly.

Teagan drew her legs up so she sat cross-legged. '*I* was just wondering.' She paused. 'Worrying, maybe,' she added softly.

Lanie found herself biting the inside of her lip. When it happened twice in one day—first Bob, and now her best friend—that look really couldn't be misinterpreted.

They felt sorry for her.

Her whole focus had been aimed in one direction for so long. But now the pool wasn't calling her to training each morning. Her coach wasn't yelling at her. Her times weren't creeping down—or up. She didn't have another meet to aim for.

She had no goals.

Even though she wasn't the slightest bit hungry she reached for the cheese platter, busying herself with slicing bread and cheese and then taking her time to chew and swallow, not looking at Teagan

She mentally pulled herself into shape.

'I've decided not to go back to my old job,' she said, finally answering the question. 'It's time for a change. Managing the swim school is too much the same thing I've been doing for ever.' She attempted a carefree laugh. 'Although I can't imagine a job where my office doesn't smell of chlorine!'

Teagan, ever the good friend, smiled back, but she wasn't about to let her off the hook. 'So, the new plan is…?'

On the TV a rider toppled off his horse when the big grey animal slid to a stop before a hulking log fence. Lanie watched as he immediately jumped to his feet. She could see what he was telling everyone with his body language—*I'm fine!*—but the commentator was explaining in a clipped British accent that this meant he was disqualified. His dream was over.

The man patted his horse's neck, then leant forward until his silk-covered helmet rested against the horse's cheek.

Lanie knew *exactly* how he felt.

'I don't know—maybe I'll finish my business degree,' she said with a shrug. Three-quarters finished years ago, she'd abandoned it leading up to the national titles, intending to defer only for a semester or two. But then she'd made the Australian team, and everything had changed.

'Still living here?' Teagan's wrinkled nose conveyed exactly what she thought of that idea.

Lanie didn't know. She'd moved back in months earlier, after the selection trials. At the time it had seemed sensible—she'd taken extended leave from her job, needed a break from swimming entirely, and without an income she couldn't afford the rent on her little one-bedder in Scarborough without putting a huge dent into the savings she had earmarked for a house deposit. Her mum and sister had been focused on Sienna—not unusual in itself—so she'd reasoned that it wouldn't be too bad.

But they'd both be back soon.

'Maybe.'

Teagan raised an eyebrow. 'Hmm. You're always welcome to crash at mine. Or I can put a good word in for you at my temp agency?'

'And I can inadvertently work for an international drug cartel?' she asked with a smile.

Teagan stuck her tongue out at her.

So the conversation was over—for now.

Some time during one of the rowing finals Lanie noticed Teagan had fallen asleep sprawled against the front of her sofa. She padded over to extract the empty wine glass from her friend's hand, and then took her time washing up and tidying the kitchen.

She wasn't at all tired. Quite the opposite. In fact with every passing minute she felt more alert, more awake.

Before Teagan had arrived she'd considered not watching

the race at all. She'd told herself that it wasn't as if anyone would know—and she'd find out the result tomorrow, anyway.

But she hadn't really believed she could do that, and now she *knew* she couldn't. It wasn't quite the same, but she recognised how she was feeling: as if *she* was racing today.

The anticipation, the adrenalin, the nervous energy. Muted, but there.

From her kitchen bench Lanie watched the swimmers walk out for the men's hundred-metre breaststroke final. Watched them stretch and roll their shoulders, wiggle their legs about.

Then she watched the race—listened to the crowd, to the increasing hysteria of the commentators, and then watched the moment the winner won gold.

Automatically she smiled in reaction to the winner's smile, and then grinned to herself when she realised what she'd done.

See? She could do this. Tonight was just like any other night in front of the television. She'd watched her sister win two medals and been genuinely nervous and then over the moon for her. If she was going to have regrets, or be overwhelmed by jealousy or resentment or something equally unpleasant and inappropriate, she would have done it by now.

It really was just another race.

On the screen, groups of swimmers began to walk out to the pool. Sweden, in their uniform of vivid blue and gold. Japan, with all four women holding hands as they waved to the crowd. The Dutch in orange and grey.

And then the Australian team.

'Lanie?' Teagan poked her head over the top of the couch and blinked sleepy eyes in her direction.

'Perfect timing!' Lanie said, managing to sound remarkably normal. 'The race is just about to start.'

Her friend raised an eyebrow.

Okay. Maybe she didn't sound totally normal. But surely a little bit of tension was to be expected?

The swimmers had all discarded their tracksuits and onto

the blocks stepped the lead-out swimmer. Australia was in lane four, sandwiched between the United States and the Netherlands.

Teagan's eyes were glued to the television when Lanie sat beside her, but her friend still managed to reach out and grab her hand. She shot a short glance in Lanie's direction as she squeezed it—hard.

'You okay?'

Lanie nodded. 'Totally.'

'Take your marks.'

Pause.

Complete silence.

BEEP!

And they were off.

The first leg was good—strong. The United States touched first, but there was nothing in it. By the end of the second lap Australia had drawn level.

Then the third Aussie girl dived in, sluicing through the water like an arrow.

This was *her* leg. The girl was just like her—the fastest of the heat swimmers, awarded with the final relay berth amongst the more elite girls.

She was doing a brilliant job. Holding her own.

Would Lanie have?

She closed her eyes, squeezing them shut tight.

She imagined herself in the water. Remembered the way her focus became so narrow, so all-encompassing, that she didn't hear the crowd—didn't hear a thing. It was just her body and the water, and all she could control was her technique.

Stroke, stroke, *breathe*. Stroke, stroke…

The crowd—a world away—was suddenly much louder, and Lanie's eyes popped open. The anchor swimmer was in the water, and Great Britain had a chance for a medal. The crowd had gone wild.

Teagan squeezed her hand again, harder, and Lanie blinked, refocussing her attention.

Australia had pulled ahead. They were going to win.

And just like that—they had.

The girls had done it, and done it in style—in record time. They deserved every accolade the over-excited commentator was bestowing upon them.

They filled the television screen, swim caps stripped off, damp hair long around their shoulders, as they completed the standard pool-side interview.

'Lanie?' Teagan's voice was full of concern.

Despite her own mental reassurances that she was fine, and the many times she'd told herself she was a bigger person than to be jealous or resentful or whatever, she suddenly realised she wasn't.

A tear splashed onto her hands, and she looked down to where her fingers were knotted in the flannelette of her pyjamas.

She'd been wallowing. Treading water until this moment—waiting for tonight, for this race.

Why?

Because tonight was the end. The end of her swimming dream.

Teagan silently shoved a handful of tissues in front of her and Lanie dabbed at her cheeks. Blew her nose. And considered what to do next.

She needed to do something—anything. And she had to do it *now*. She couldn't wake up tomorrow and be the also-ran swimmer.

She turned to face Teagan on the couch. Her friend was so close to be as good as shoulder to shoulder with her, but she'd wisely not made a move to comfort her.

'I need a job,' Lanie said.

Teagan's eyes widened, but then she smiled. 'But no drug cartels?'

'Or anything involving swimming.'

Her friend's smile broadened. 'Consider it done.'

CHAPTER TWO

GRAYSON MANNING SHOVED his chair away from his desk, then covered the generous space between the desk and the door in quick, agitated strides.

Outside his office, his assistant's desk was empty.

He glanced at his watch, confused. It was well after nine a.m., and Rodney was always on time. Gray insisted upon it.

He frowned as he walked into the hallway. Thankfully a woman sat behind the glossy white reception desk. Behind her, 'Manning' was spelt out in ridiculously large chrome block capitals.

What was her name again? Cathy? Katie?

'Caroline,' she said, unprompted, as he approached—reminding him he'd guessed wrong last time he'd asked her a question, too.

'Caroline,' he repeated. He'd been told doing so was useful when remembering names—not that it had helped him so far. 'Where's Rodney?'

The woman blinked. Then bit her lip, glancing away for a moment. 'Um…Mr Manning, Rodney resigned…' A pause. 'Yesterday.'

Gray's jaw clenched. 'Our agreement with the agency specifies at least two weeks' notice must be provided.'

The woman nodded, her blond ponytail bouncing in agreement. 'I believe he asked your permission that his resignation be effective immediately.'

'I didn't agree to that.'

Caroline's lips twitched. 'I'm pretty sure you did. Rodney forwarded me your e-mail so he could organise cancellation of his building access and so on. It was there in writing.'

Gray pulled his phone from his jacket pocket and quickly scrolled through yesterday's sent messages. Yesterday had been stupidly busy—back-to-back meetings, a major issue with one of his contractors, and a lead on a new investment opportunity in South East Asia.

Even so, surely he would have noticed if... *Letter of Resignation.*

It wasn't even a vague subject line. He really needed to start paying more attention to his inbox. But then, that was one of the reasons why he had an assistant: to prioritise his mail, to nag him to respond to anything important, and to allow him to pay no attention to anything that wasn't.

The irony was not lost on him.

Without another word he headed up the hallway to the opposite end of the floor. To his father's office.

A mirror image of his own, Gordon Manning's office also had a smaller adjacent waiting area—although his was complete with an actual assistant.

'Marilyn—'

Unlike Caroline, the older lady didn't even attempt to hide her smile. She shook her head. 'Gray, Gray, Gray...'

'I need a new assistant.'

'So I hear.'

His lips thinned. 'Does everyone but me know that Rodney resigned?'

'A group of us had farewell drinks last night. Lovely guy.'

'I was unaware you were so close,' he replied dryly. 'He was only here a couple of weeks.'

'Two months,' Marilyn corrected smoothly.

Really? Since his father had announced his impending retirement six months ago, Gray could barely remember what day it was. He was working seven days a week, and easily twelve-hour days.

'Is my father in?'

'No, not today.'

His father hadn't been into the office in months. Initially his transition to retirement had been gradual—and Gray had been unsure if his father was capable of retiring at all. But soon Gordon's days in the office had been reduced to only a few hours, and then to nothing. And while Marilyn continued to manage his dad's life, now she did so exclusively via e-mail.

A month ago Gordon Manning had had his no-expense-spared retirement party and that had made it all official. But Gray wasn't silly enough to clear out his dad's office just yet—apart from the fact it contained about forty years' worth of god-knew-what paperwork, it would be a while before Gordon—or Gray, come to think of it—could imagine a Manning Developments office without a desk for its founder.

'So you can help me today? Fantastic. I need you to accompany me to a meeting in West Perth. And to sort out my flights for next week. And—'

But Marilyn was shaking her head. 'No need. Your new assistant should be here soon.'

Oh. The agency must already be on to it. Even so...

'I'd rather not have someone completely new to Manning with me today. This is a very important meeting. It's essential that—'

Marilyn's look froze him mid-sentence, exactly as it had frozen him many times before—although the vast majority of such glares had been twenty-five years ago. A kid learnt quickly *not* to mess with Marilyn.

'If you don't want a new assistant, be nice to the assistant you have.'

'I *am* nice.'

Her eyebrows rose right up beneath her dead straight fringe.

'Be nice to this one, Gray. Let's try for three months, this time, hey?'

* * *

Almost an hour later, Caroline ushered Gray's new assistant into his office.

'Mr Manning?'

He was just finishing an e-mail, so he barely glanced in the direction of the figure in his doorway and instead just waved an arm in the general vicinity of one of the soft leather chairs in front of his desk.

Absently, he heard the door thud quietly shut, and then the click of heels on the marble floor—but all his attention was on the e-mail he was composing:

I look forward to discussing the proposal further...

No. He hit the delete key half a dozen times, maybe a little harder than was necessary. He didn't want any discussion. He wanted a decision. The deal was already behind schedule. He needed a *yes* and he needed it last week.

I trust you'll agree...

That was even worse. He held down the delete key again, thinking.

But that was the problem. He was thinking too much. It was just an e-mail—an e-mail to an investment partner with whom he already had an excellent rapport. The proposal was little more than a formality.

Or at least it should be. But their last meeting had been... *off.* It had been subtle—more questions than he'd normally expect, more careful perusal of the numbers Gray had shown him. All perfectly normal things for a wise investor to do. The thing was that *this* particular investor had so much confidence in Manning that he was usually rather relaxed about conducting his own due diligence.

Quite simply—he'd trusted Manning.

But now...

Maybe it was a coincidence that this new-found caution coincided with Gray's father's retirement...

Gray didn't believe that for a second.

And it was damned infuriating.

Gray glanced up. His eyes landed on the woman's hands—long, elegant fingers, unpainted, neat, short tips. She was sluggishly rubbing each hand down her thighs, the movement slow but clearly triggered by nerves.

She wore trousers, not a skirt, he noticed.

'How do I finish this e-mail?' he asked. His tone was sharper than he'd intended, and Marilyn's words echoed momentarily.

His gaze shot to the woman's face.

As their eyes met her body gave a little jolt and she gasped—quite loudly.

Immediately one of those long-fingered hands was slapped to her mouth.

Her eyes widened as she looked at him.

And they were very lovely eyes, he acknowledged. Big and brown, framed by dark lashes—even though he was almost certain she wore no make-up. They watched him with unexpected intensity and an expression that was impossible to read.

He didn't understand. Surely his request wasn't so shocking? Abrupt, maybe, but hardly earth-shattering.

When the silence continued he shrugged, his temporary interest in her reaction rapidly morphing into frustration.

He didn't have time for this. The agency would just have to send someone else.

'I don't think this is going to work out,' he said, very evenly. 'Thanks for your time.'

He didn't bother to wait for her to leave, just gritted his teeth and got back to his e-mail.

Again he only half listened to the sound of her heels on the marble—although soon he realised she was coming closer, not going further away.

'Regards,' she said, from right behind his shoulder.

'What?'

He looked up at her. She was somehow bigger than he'd expected—taller, and wider through the shoulders. She leant forward slightly as she studied his computer, her long hair shining in the sunlight that flooded through the office's floor-to-ceiling windows.

'I'd delete all that stuff at the end, and just say *Regards*. Or *Sincerely*. Or however you normally sign off your e-mails.' She met his eyes, and this time she didn't look like a deer caught in the headlights. She watched him steadily, and there was a sharpness to her gaze that he appreciated.

Her eyes were definitely hazel, he realised. Not brown.

When he didn't say anything, she explained further. 'Judging by the e-mail trail beneath this one, you've been having this conversation for a while.'

Gray nodded.

'And you want a resolution? But you don't want to be seen as pushy?'

'Exactly,' he said, surprised.

'Well, then,' she said, as if it was the most obvious thing in the world. 'Sometimes saying less is more.'

She straightened up and took a step away from his chair.

Silently, he deleted his half-written sentence, ended the e-mail as she'd suggested, then hit *'Send.'*

Good. It was gone.

He stood, and with this action, the woman took another rapid step away. Then she rolled her shoulders back, and thrust out her hand.

'Elaine Smith,' she said, very crisply. 'Lanie.'

Automatically he grasped her hand. It was cool and delicate. And she *was* tall. But even in heels she was an inch shorter than him.

Her suit jacket was a dark grey and a little tight across the chest—and her soft pink shirt wasn't sitting quite right, with one side of her collar higher than the other. Combined with her loose, wavy hair and lack of discernible make-up, no one would call her perfectly presented.

He would call her pretty, though. Very pretty.

Gray rapidly dispatched that unexpected musing. The appearance of his employees was irrelevant. All he cared about was their ability to do their job.

And, despite her slightly odd initial reaction to him, there was an air of practicality to this woman that was appealing. Plus she'd been right about the e-mail.

Most importantly he needed an assistant, and she was here.

'I have a meeting in half an hour in West Perth.'

For a moment she looked at him blankly. 'So I have the job?'

He nodded impatiently. 'Yes, of course.'

A beat passed.

He sighed. 'Anything else?'

'Oh,' she said. 'No.'

He turned back to his computer and a moment later she walked away, her heels again clicking loudly.

He briefly wondered if she needed help figuring out how to log into her computer or anything—but then another e-mail popped in that he urgently needed to attend to, and that was that.

Surely it wasn't that difficult? She seemed smart. She'd figure it out.

Lanie almost collapsed into her new, plush leather office chair.

Her phone trilled its musical message notification from within the depths of her bag, but for now she ignored it.

Of course she'd forgotten to put it onto silent mode prior to her interview.

Thank goodness she hadn't received that message a few minutes earlier. She could just about imagine Grayson Manning's reaction to *that*.

But then would that have been such a bad thing?

If he'd stuck with his original conclusion—that she wasn't suitable—she'd have walked out of this office no worse than how she'd walked in: without a job.

With the added benefit of *not* working for Mr Grumpy Pants.

No. Not a bad thing at all.

And yet she'd had her chance to leave. She had her chance still to walk away. No one would force her to stay. Not even the employment agency she was working for.

Which reminded her...

Lanie fished out her phone. As expected, the waiting message was from Teagan. As she'd been whisked up to the twenty-fifth floor in a seriously shiny mirrored lift she'd tapped out an urgent message to her friend:

What did you do??!

Because this building was definitely not what Lanie had been expecting of her first assignment with the agency. Yes, she'd known the role was as a personal assistant, but after seven years managing the swim school she'd been unconvinced she really had the skills for such a role—but Teagan had been adamant. *'You'll be fine,'* she'd said. *'Piece of cake,'* she'd said.

Given her lack of relevant experience, Lanie had imagined she'd be working somewhere small. Somewhere that couldn't afford a true executive assistant. Somewhere she could kind of figure it all out as she went along.

Manning Developments was *not* that place.

Teagan's text message therefore did not surprise her at all.

I spruced up your CV. Just a little.

Right.

Lanie rolled her head backwards until it rested on the high back of her chair and stared up at the ceiling.

The sensible thing to do would be to leave. She didn't have the experience for a role like this, and if she stuffed it up then the agency, Teagan *and* herself would all look pretty bad.

It was sweet of Teagan—annoying, inappropriate, and dishonest—but sweet.

It should end here.

But she remained at her vast new desk. For the same reason she'd stayed in Grayson's office after she'd recognised him as the man from the beach.

For long seconds she'd searched for the cutting comments he deserved after his performance at the beach—but then, before she'd gathered her thoughts, she'd realised he'd just *dismissed* her.

Again. Just as he had at the beach, he'd carried on as if she was irrelevant to his world. Why on earth would she want to work for someone who would treat her like that?

But she couldn't let that man—*Grayson*—ignore her again.

So here she was. With a job she didn't really want, working for a man she didn't like.

Lanie wiggled the wireless mouse on the desk and the large flatscreen monitor blinked instantly to life, revealing a login screen.

Her gaze flicked to the still open door to Grayson's office, but then immediately away. That he would be of no help at all was obvious.

She stood and headed for the hallway—Caroline, the little plaque on the reception desk had proclaimed. She should be able to point her in the direction of IT Support or something.

She could do this. It couldn't be too difficult.

She'd figure out *why* she was doing it later.

CHAPTER THREE

THE LITTLE GREEN man started blinking, so with a coffee cup gripped firmly in each hand Lanie made her way across a very busy St Georges Terrace.

'Lanie!'

A fierce breeze whipped between the high-rise buildings, blowing her loose hair every which way and partially covering her eyes. Not that she needed a visual aid to identify that particular deep and demanding voice.

Calmly she stepped onto the footpath and Grayson met her halfway, jogging down his building's steps and deftly negotiating the sea of lunchtime pedestrian traffic.

'We're going to be late,' he said. 'Why didn't you say something?'

Lanie tossed her hair out of her face and met his gaze as she handed him his triple-shot latte.

'I did mention that there may not be time for a coffee.'

Grayson blinked. As always, he seemed genuinely surprised. 'Oh...' he said.

In the week she'd worked for him this routine had already become familiar. He was rather like a mad scientist—so utterly focussed on his work that the practicalities of life seemed beyond him.

It would have been endearing—except...

'Well, make sure it doesn't happen again.'

Lanie bit her lip.

Remember the money. Remember the money...

It was the money, Lanie had decided. The reason she hadn't already quit.

Thanks to Teagan's creativity with her CV, and her ability so far to fudge her way through the job, she was earning almost twice what she had at the swim school. And she needed the money so she could move out of her mother's place as soon as possible—before she and Sienna returned from Europe, preferably.

That was the only reason she was here. Nothing to do with that morning on the beach.

Lanie nodded tightly. 'I've got a car waiting for us.' She gestured with her spare hand in its direction, and to the driver idling illegally in the clearway. Grayson opened his mouth, but Lanie jumped in before he could get a word out. 'The laptop, projector and business specs are on the back seat.'

In response his eyebrows rose, just slightly. 'Good,' he said.

Again Lanie bit her lip. *How about a thank-you, huh?*

She pivoted on her heel and strode towards the car.

Remember the money. Remember the money. Remember the—

The toe of her shoe caught on something and Lanie stumbled. But before she had much time to register that the grey pavers of the footpath were rapidly becoming closer her descent was suddenly halted.

Grayson's arm was strong and solid and warm around her waist. In an effortless movement he pulled her upwards and towards him, so she was pressed against his impeccably suited body.

She tilted her chin to look up at him.

He caught her gaze—*really* caught it—and for a moment Lanie was completely speechless.

His eyes weren't just grey—they were flecked with blue. And with his face now arranged in concern, not hard with tension, he was somehow—impossibly—even more handsome.

Of course she already knew he was gorgeous. To pretend otherwise would be ridiculous. And, frustratingly, beautiful people didn't become less beautiful simply by their unlikeable behaviour.

Less *attractive*, though. They did become less attractive. He'd proved that, that day on the beach. And each day since then.

But right now Grayson did *not* seem unattractive. Right now, with the subtle scent of his aftershave and the warmth of his arm and body confusing her, he was anything but.

The side of her body he touched…no *everywhere* he touched, reacted to him. Electricity flooded through her.

'You okay?'

Because it was all she could manage, she simply nodded mutely.

He took a step away from her and amazingly she had the presence of mind not to follow him. She took a deep breath, rolled her shoulders back, and rebalanced on her own two feet.

She realised she was gripping her coffee cup hard enough to slightly crumple the cardboard, and made herself loosen her grip.

Then he smiled. It was a subtle expression—far from broad—but it was the first Grayson Manning smile she'd witnessed.

Once again her ability to form words evaporated.

He covered the short distance to the car and opened the door for her.

She slipped past him, not catching his gaze. With every moment she was increasingly aware that she *really* needed to pull herself together.

If she was going to keep working for Grayson she needed to erase completely from her subconscious even the smallest skerrick of romantic daydreams involving her boss.

Obviously the agency would not approve.

Secondly she—*Lanie*—did not approve. She might not

have extensive experience in the corporate world, but even she knew getting involved with your boss was…well, pretty dumb.

And thirdly, Grayson was not about to be overcome by lust when it came to Lanie Smith.

Lanie's lips quirked up at the idea of Grayson arriving at her front door to take her out to dinner. It was laughable.

She settled into the soft leather of the back seat as Grayson closed her door, and moments later he was sliding into the car from the opposite side.

Lanie took a good long gulp of her coffee, hoping that the addition of caffeine would help get her brain back to speed.

She fully expected Grayson to flip open his laptop as the car pulled way, or to make another one of his seemingly endless phone calls. But instead he turned towards her.

He cleared his throat, the sound unexpected and awkward in the quiet vehicle.

'Thank you for the coffee,' he said gruffly.

Lanie shot a look in his direction, not immediately sure she'd heard him correctly.

But his expression was genuine. Not quite contrite—that wouldn't be Grayson Manning—but still…

'Not a problem, Grayson.'

He nodded, then glanced away through his darkly tinted window at the passing traffic.

Without looking at her, he spoke again.

'You can call me Gray.'

The beach was near deserted the following morning. Gray's bare feet smacked rhythmically against the wet sand, his progress only occasionally punctuated with a splash when the waves stretched across his path.

Luther was well ahead of Gray, having abandoned his ball to begin enthusiastically digging a hole to China. Beyond Luther rocky fingers of coastline stretched into the ocean, and distant cranes for hoisting shipping containers formed blurry silhouettes against the sky.

It was cool—it was only July after all—and all but the most dedicated swimmers had abandoned the beach on such a dull and overcast day.

But today Gray needed to run.

Maybe he'd hoped the bite of the frigid air in his lungs would help. Or, more likely, it was that heavy ache in his legs that he craved.

Because out here he was in control. He could run as far as he wanted—further even than his body wanted to go.

And Gray liked being in control. He was used to it. Expected it.

He was in control of everything he did in both his business and his private life. He knew what he was doing and could plan with absolute confidence how things were going to work out.

By Gray's reckoning, his father's retirement should be no more than a blip on Manning's radar—after all, it had been many years since Gordon Manning had spearheaded a project. For the past five years Gray *had* been Manning's CEO in all but name. So Gordon's retirement was nothing more than a formality. Nothing would change except he'd eventually have to repurpose his dad's offices.

That was how it was supposed to be happening.

It was still how Gray thought it *should* have happened.

But it hadn't.

Things *had* changed.

That irritating e-mail from the suddenly cautious investor was just one example. Not of many—far from it—but enough to frustrate the hell out of Gray.

An extra question here or there shouldn't bother him. Or decisions taking longer than he felt they should. Or even that subtle, almost but not quite imperceptible shift in the atmosphere at meetings...

Even Gray had to smile at that. Since when had he been so sensitive to a change in *feel*?

Well, whatever it was that had changed—it *had*. And it did bother him. Because it wasn't just an irritation…all these questions and atmosphere-shifts …it had the potential to impact his bottom line.

In fact it already was.

And Gray was *not* going to tolerate that.

In his peripheral vision, Gray noticed a lone figure walking near the dunes. As he glanced in her direction the woman waved, while her other hand firmly held an oversized floppy hat to her head.

Automatically Gray waved back, then refocussed. Deliberately he crossed from the wet sand to the dry, wanting the extra demand on his muscles the deep, soft sand forced from his body.

It turned out that, despite the many years since his dad had actually led a Manning project, for some of his clients Gordon Manning had been a very real and very important presence—somewhere behind the scenes.

The reality that it had truly been Gray they'd been working with—not Gray as Gordon's mouthpiece—didn't matter, and that exasperated Gray.

He deserved the trust he thought he'd already earned. He deserved his stature in Australia's business community.

A larger wave pushed far up the beach and Gray's bare feet splashed through foamy puddles as the water slid back into the ocean.

It also annoyed him that he hadn't realised this reality. That he hadn't fully understood what it meant to be Gordon Manning's son, regardless of his own track record and years of success.

So it was frustrating and exasperating and irritating…

But it was also…

Gray's time.

Now was his time to prove himself.

And nothing could be allowed to stand in his way.

Lanie dropped her arm as Gray disappeared into the distance. He'd waved each morning since she'd started at Manning, although he'd shown no sign of realising she was the woman he'd been so rude to on the beach that morning of the relay final. Now, knowing Gray, she doubted he ever would.

She'd considered telling him—but what would that achieve?

Lanie knew the answer to that: a blank stare, followed directly by a look that said *Why are you wasting my time with this?*

That was a look she was quickly becoming familiar with. At least now she didn't take it personally. Pretty much everything not immediately related to Manning and preferably relevant *right at that moment* elicited exactly that look.

'*Which hotel would you like me to book for you in Adelaide?*'

When he'd discovered he was not, in fact, booked into his favourite hotel, he'd booked himself in, then sent Lanie a helpful e-mail with the name of the 'correct' hotel for next time.

'*For that presentation tomorrow, would you like me to include the numbers from the Jameson project?*'

Turned out she'd guessed right with that one…

So a returned wave each morning was both unexpected and welcome. Although ignoring the woman he worked with every single day would have been quite a stretch—even for Gray.

With Gray and Luther little more than specks in the distance, Lanie started walking again and allowed her thoughts to circle back to where they'd been before the flash of Luther's red coat against the sand had distracted her.

It would be odd, she'd just decided, if she wasn't jealous of her sister.

Wouldn't it?

She didn't know. It was what had got her out of the house so ridiculously early on a work day. She needed the beach. The space, the salt and the sound of the waves… It was all as familiar to her as breathing.

Water had always helped her. Whether chlorinated or not, it was where she gravitated at times of stress. When her dad had left it had seemed natural. He was, after all, the reason she loved water. With an offshore mining job he'd rarely been home—but when he had he'd spent all his time at the beach.

As an adult, she looked back and wondered whether he'd simply tolerated the fact she'd clung to him like a limpet when he was home—rather than her more romanticised version in which she'd told herself she'd been his swimming buddy.

Because surely if he'd really wanted her there he would have bothered to stay in touch after he'd left. Or not left at all.

But if nothing else he'd given Lanie her love of water and the genes that helped her swim very quickly through it.

It had been a mistake to skip the beach earlier in the week. She needed to rectify it. Even today, with the wind whipping off the waves and gluing her long cargo trousers and thin woollen jumper to her skin, it was the right place for her to attempt to organise her thoughts and her reactions.

Sienna had e-mailed her overnight, full of post-championships euphoria. From the magnificence of the closing ceremony to how much fun she was having, through to how she was dealing with the rabid tabloid press after being seen out on a date with a British rower.

Lanie had seen the photos—and the headlines—as they'd made it to Australia too. 'Golden couple'. 'Winners in love'.

Jealousy? Whatever it was she was feeling, she hadn't defined it.

Until Sienna's e-mail.

It hadn't been until right at the end, amongst all the glitz and excitement, that her sister had acknowledged how Lanie might be feeling. Her sister wasn't stupid, or heartless. A bit oblivious at times—but then, that was Sienna.

Somehow, though, Sienna's awkward attempts at making the contrast in their situations seem somehow okay had hit home harder than anything else.

How are you doing? It wasn't the same without you. You should be so proud of your personal best, though. Any other year you definitely would've made the team.

And so here she was, at the beach.

Walking today, not swimming—but the scale and scope of the ocean helped, just as she'd known it would.

She envied Sienna. She *was* jealous.

Today she allowed herself to be.

CHAPTER FOUR

THE UNEXPECTED SENSATION of warmth against his chest snatched Gray's attention from the report he'd been reading. He glanced downwards, to discover a trail of pale brown liquid trickling in multiple rivulets down his front.

A brief perusal of the obvious culprit—the takeaway coffee cup in his hand—revealed a leak beneath the lid.

He swore. Loudly. He had a meeting right in this office in less than twenty minutes.

Tossing the defective lid into the bin beneath his desk, Gray downed the rest of his coffee as he tapped a short message into Manning's internal instant messaging system.

Moments later his office door swung open, although Lanie paused before walking in. 'You said you had a problem?' she asked.

He stood, his gaze moving downwards as he surveyed the damage to his shirt and pulled the damp fabric away from his skin. With the other hand he gestured for Lanie to come closer.

Moments later her long, efficient stride had her by his side. 'Nice one,' she said, a hint of a smile in her tone. 'I don't suppose you have a spare shirt?'

'If I did,' he said, for the first time transferring his attention from the shirt to Lanie, 'would I—?'

His eyes met hers and he momentarily had absolutely no idea what he'd been about to say.

She stood closer than he'd expected. Or maybe it was just her height. When she was in her heels they were very nearly eye to eye, and he still wasn't quite used to that sensation.

Plus today she looked…*different.*

Her hair, he realised. It was tied back. It highlighted the striking structure of her face—the defined cheekbones, the firm chin—and her skin's perfect golden glow.

He'd thought her pretty when he'd first met her, but right now she looked…

As he watched she raised an eyebrow.

Gray blinked. 'If I had a spare shirt…' he tried again '…would I need you?'

He looked down at his ruined clothing again, yanking his mind back on track. So what if he'd noticed Lanie looked nice today?

Lanie crossed her arms in front of herself. 'What size are you?' she asked.

Not for the first time she'd pre-empted his next question. 'I have no idea.'

She didn't bother to hide her sigh. 'How can you not know that?'

Gray shrugged. 'I shop in bulk. Those couple of times a year I shop, I figure out what size I am then.'

He reached for his shirt, automatically sliding button after button undone. He'd tugged it off his shoulders and gathered the fabric in his hands before he noticed Lanie had backed off a few steps and was currently staring out the window.

'This is how I normally work out my size,' he explained, finding the tag beneath the collar. 'There you go. Turns out I wear a forty-two-inch shirt.'

'And you'd like me to go buy you a replacement?'

'Exactly.'

Not meeting his eyes, Lanie turned away from the window and took a step back towards the door. 'You know, I could've just checked the tag for you. No need to...' a pause '...undress.'

For the first time Gray noticed the tinge of pink to her cheekbones. He suspected the right thing to do would be to apologise. But with the words right on the tip of his tongue he paused.

'My shirt was covered in hot coffee,' he said, instead. 'And this way you can take the shirt with you. To check the size or whatever. Here.'

He thrust the shirt out in front of him.

Now she met his gaze, and hers wasn't bashful any more. It was razor-sharp and most definitely unimpressed.

He just shrugged. He'd done too much second-guessing recently. The equation was simple—he needed a new shirt and quickly. That was it. Anyone walking down the beach most mornings in summer saw a heck of a lot more skin than he'd just revealed to his assistant.

He steadfastly ignored the subtlest echo of Marilyn's words in his head. *Be nice to this one.*

Lanie reached out and their fingers brushed as she snatched the shirt away. Gray watched as her blush spread like quick fire across her cheeks, but her gaze never wavered from his.

'Thank you,' he said.

She raised the subtlest eyebrow, but remained silent.

See? He was nice. He checked his watch. 'You've got about ten minutes.'

Gray thought he might have heard Lanie muttering something as she strode out of the room.

Something about remembering money?

'He took off his *shirt*?'

Teagan's voice was incredulous as she raised the pizza slice to her lips.

'Uh-huh,' Lanie said, rounding her kitchen bench to join

Teagan at the dining table. 'I guess it's not that big a deal.
I've seen it all before at the beach.'

Teagan chewed thoughtfully for a few moments. 'You don't
think he was…like…coming onto you or something?'

Lanie just about choked on her own mouthful of pizza.
'*No!* I told you. This guy looks like he just walked off a
catwalk.' She shook her head in a decisive movement. 'It's
more likely he happily whipped of his shirt because he forgot I was female.'

Her friend narrowed her eyes. 'That's a pile of crap and
you know it. You're gorgeous.'

Said with the certainty only a best friend could manage.

'I'm not gorgeous,' Lanie said, and waved her hand dismissively when Teagan went to speak again. 'Not in the way
people like Grayson Manning are. Or my sister. My mum,
even. I'm just not one of the beautiful people. And, honestly,
if it means I'd carry on like Gray does, I really don't mind
my ungorgeousness.'

Teagan shook her head in disagreement, but thankfully
kept silent.

It had been a great disappointment to Sandra Smith that
her eldest daughter had inherited not only the height and ath-
leticism of her ex-husband, but unfortunately also the strong
features that were arresting in a man but not exactly beautiful in women. Thankfully two years later Sienna had come
along, and was every bit as beauty-pageant-pretty as Sandra.

'So what are his latest efforts?' Teagan asked, picking up
the unspoken cue to change the subject. 'Other than the emergency shirt-shopping expedition?'

Lanie shrugged. 'Same old, same old. Letting me know
he needs me to write up a report five minutes before five—
so I'm there until seven. Or asking me to book the best restaurant in Perth that is fully booked, for a very important
lunch meeting—so I have to go down there and sweet-talk a

table out of them. And then cancelling said meeting. Plus, of course, just the general expectation that I can read his mind.'

Teagan shook her head. 'You shouldn't put up with this, you know. I'm starting to feel bad. This guy isn't normal—trust me.'

An unwanted flashback to that more-than-a-glimpse of incredible bare chest she'd seen in Gray's office very much underlined that comment. No, Gray was *not* normal. She didn't understand why, but somehow in his office his chest had been just so much more *naked* than at the beach. It had felt personal.

Intimate.

She put her half-eaten pizza slice back down on her plate, suddenly no longer hungry.

'You *can* quit, you know. I'm sure the agency would find you something else—no problem.'

'I know that,' Lanie said. 'But it's not so bad. It pays almost double my salary at the swim centre, and I wouldn't get that anywhere else—anyone but Gray would see straight through my total lack of experience.'

Teagan's eyes narrowed. 'There you go again. Underselling yourself.'

Lanie snorted with her wine glass in mid-air. 'No. You were the one that *oversold* me, remember?'

Teagan rolled her eyes dramatically. 'A small detail. The fact is this guy has an awesome PA and he should know it. He's taking you for granted. Most people would've quit by now.'

Based on what she'd learnt in the Manning lunch room, most had. Lanie had a sneaky suspicion that one of the guys in Legal was running a book on how long she'd last.

'Teags, I could deliver his twice a day triple-shot latte nude and he wouldn't notice.'

Disturbingly, her friend's eyes widened. 'That's *it!*'

'I'm not flashing Gray Manning, Teagan,' she said dryly.

'No, no. Not that—at least not exactly.'

'Partial nudity, then?' Lanie said. 'You know, I reckon if I borrowed one of Sienna's skirts it would be so short and so small that—'

'You're not taking this seriously.'

Lanie raised her eyebrows. 'I didn't realise *you* were.'

Teagan's wine glass made a solid thunk as she placed it firmly on the table. She leant forward, meeting her eyes across the half-finished pizza.

'*Make* him notice you. *Make* him appreciate you.'

'And what would be the point?'

'Because you deserve it.'

It was lovely, really, what Teagan was doing. Lovely, and kind, and all the things that Teagan's friendship always was. Plus also one of the things it occasionally was.

Misguided.

'I'm fine, Teags,' she said. 'Really.'

She didn't need Teagan—or Gray as her proxy—to be her cheerleader.

She knew Teagan was worried about her—worried about how she was handling the continuing publicity around Sienna and her success.

But she was fine. She had a new job that paid well. A fresh start.

Not that working for a grumpy property magnate had ever been a particular dream of hers.

She looked across at Teagan. 'So you can put the pink hair dye or whatever you were planning on hold for now.'

'I was thinking more along the lines of a gorilla suit, but...'

And then they both laughed, and Gray and his shirtlessness was—mostly—forgotten amongst talk of Teagan's latest disaster date, the cooking-related reality TV show they were both hooked on, and anything and everything else.

Except, of course, swimming. Or Sienna.

* * *

Lanie's phone rang far too early the next morning.

She rolled over in the narrow single bed she'd grown up in, reaching out blindly with one hand towards her bedside table. Typically, she managed to knock the phone to the floor rather than grab it, so it took another twenty seconds of obnoxious ringing and fumbling around on her hands and knees in the inky darkness before said phone was located.

'Hello?' she said.

She'd been too disorientated to read the name on the screen, and besides it was most likely Sienna. Her sister hadn't quite managed to figure out the whole time difference thing.

'I need you to come over.'

The voice was deep and male. Definitely not her sister.

Lanie blinked in the semi-darkness. Dawn light was attempting to push its way under the edge of the bedroom's blinds with little effect.

'*Gray?*' she asked, although it was a rhetorical question. Of course it was. 'Do you know what time it is?'

'I have a flight to Singapore that's boarding in a few hours' time—so, yes, I do.'

There was a long moment of silence as Lanie considered hanging up on him.

'Oh,' he said eventually. 'I'm sorry. I woke you.'
Lucky.

'Can you come over?' he repeated. 'Now?'

'I'd rather not,' she said honestly. 'What's the emergency?'

Now it was Gray's turn to go silent. 'Oh…' he said again, and his surprise that she hadn't just dropped everything to come to his aid was apparent even in that single syllable.

At work Lanie could roll her eyes at his unreasonable requests—probably not as subtly as she should—or she could tell herself it was her job or whatever. But just before five in the morning…

No. There was a line, and Gray had definitely just stepped over it.

'It's my dog,' he said.

Instantly Lanie felt terrible. 'Is he okay?'

'Yes,' Gray said. 'But I forgot to organise someone to walk and feed him. Rodney used to sort it out for me, but I guess I didn't mention it to you.'

Lanie supposed he got points for not making *that* somehow her fault.

'And you couldn't e-mail me about it?'

'No,' he said. 'I need you to come over now so I can explain what he eats and where to walk him, and—'

'Okay, okay,' she interrupted on a sigh. There was no point asking him to write it down. Gray just didn't work— or think—like that. In his head it would be far more efficient for her to come over and for him to tell her. 'I'm coming over.'

Ten minutes later she knocked on Gray's front door. He lived only a few kilometres away from her, but unsurprisingly his house was right on the beach. It was gorgeous in an angular, modern, mansion-like way. At this hour of the morning the street was silent, save for the muffled crash of waves.

The door swung open, but before she could even say hello his back was to her as he walked away, already shooting out instructions. Luther, at least, bothered to greet her. He sat obediently for his welcome pats, then pressed his head against her thigh as she followed Gray down the hall. Lanie had thrown on an old tracksuit, and her sandals thwacked loudly against the pale, glossy porcelain tiles.

'So, Luther is a red setter,' Gray was explaining. 'And he's on this special prescribed diet as he has a few allergies. It's *essential* he only eats this food…' Gray opened up one of the many, many drawers in a huge granite and glass kitchen to point at neatly labelled tubs of dog biscuits. 'Otherwise he gets sick and—well, you don't want to know what sort of mess that makes.'

Lanie raised an eyebrow as she considered the size of Luther and the fact that every bit of the house she could see was decorated in shades of white and cream. 'I can imagine.'

Gray met her eyes for a second and one side of his mouth quirked upwards. 'I'd advise you not to.'

Automatically, she grinned back.

When he smiled, his face was transformed. She wouldn't say his expression softened—there was something far too angular and intense about Gray—but there was certainly a lightness, a freshness. And a cheeky, intriguing sparkle to his gaze.

Lanie took a step backwards and promptly walked into a tall stainless steel bin. Some sensor contraption obediently flipped the lid open, and the unexpected movement made Lanie jump and bump her hip—hard—against the benchtop.

'You okay?' Gray asked.

'Other than it being far too early in the morning for me to be co-ordinated?' she replied, raising a pointed eyebrow.

Nicely covered, she thought, giving herself a mental shake. The last thing she needed was another confusing beside-the-taxi or shirt-off moment.

'Sorry about that,' he said, not sounding sorry at all. He'd already walked off again, continuing his monologue.

Lanie rubbed the small, rapidly forming bruise on her hip as Gray described how this section of the house was secured separately from the rest and about some nifty automatic heating and lighting system he'd had installed so that Luther would be comfortable. Plus there was a Luther-sized door to the landscaped pool and garden that Lanie could now just see in the very early rays of sun.

At the end of his explanation, in front of a neat row of hooks hung with multi-coloured leads, Gray finished with a flourish, 'So Luther is *totally* fine whenever I go away.'

But Gray wasn't looking at her, he was looking at Luther, who had stretched himself out, oblivious, at their feet.

'You don't sound all that convinced.'

This whipped Gray's attention back to her. 'Of course I'm—' he started. Then, suddenly he crouched down and rubbed the big dog's head right behind his ears. He looked up to meet Lanie's gaze. 'No, you're right. I hate leaving him behind. Leaving him here is better than boarding him, but not much.' Another pause. 'I'll give you a list of walkers I've used before, and a couple to avoid—'

'I'll look after him,' Lanie said. She'd assumed she would be, anyway. Another invisible line on her job description: *Responsible for the care and walking of Mr Manning's red setter as required.*

'Are you sure?'

Lanie nodded. 'No problem. Although I'd rather take him home to my place, if that's okay? Easier than coming here twice a day.'

Gray smiled, again—a big, genuine smile—and Lanie found herself smiling back almost as hugely. It was impossible to do anything else in the presence of such high-wattage charm.

But then his brow furrowed. 'Do you have any experience with dogs?'

His obvious worry for his pet was beyond endearing. Luther rolled onto his back, baring his pale golden tummy in a silent plea: *scratches, please.*

'I grew up with a collection of my mother's small, fluffy lapdog terrors—honestly, anything Luther throws at me will be child's play. Besides,' she said, dropping to her knees to administer the demanded tummy-rubs and directing her next comment to the dog, 'Luther and I have an understanding— don't we, mate? I am the thrower of the ball—but he owns it.'

She grinned as she darted a glance at Gray.

'That's about right,' he said. 'He'll also love you for ever if you walk him down at North Cottesloe beach. It's his favourite.'

'I know,' Lanie said, slowing her hand's movement down to a glacial pace.

Gray's brow had refurrowed and he looked at her quizzically, as if she'd just said something very odd. 'How do you know?'

Lanie blinked. Her hand had gone completely still, and Luther writhed about on the floor a bit, apparently hoping to somehow wring another pat from her listless touch.

'Because I walk down at North Cottesloe beach. *All the time.*'

'Really?' Gray said. He was so close to her, kneeling by Luther's head.

He bumped his shoulder slightly with hers as he stood, and reached out to steady her. Instantly her skin went all tingly and warm.

'Yes,' she said, quite firmly. 'I walk most mornings. I see you and Luther a lot. You wave.'

At some point Lanie had stood too, and Gray dropped his hand from her upper arm.

'Oh…' Gray said, no longer in concerned-and-rather-adorable-dog-owner mode, but in vague-when-it-comes-to-everything-but-Manning mode. 'To be honest the beach is kind of my time out. I don't really pay attention to much at all.'

No. Definitely no points for that total lack of an apology. She'd convinced herself it was okay that he'd never connected her to that original morning they'd met because he'd noticed her now. He made the effort to wave. It had felt friendly—like a form of camaraderie or something. As if they were a team.

It was that guy on the beach with his dog that she reminded herself of when Gray was being particularly unreasonable, or autocratic, or pushy—or whatever other negative phrase she wanted to use to describe her boss.

But it wasn't even real.

Lanie was silent as Gray handed her a dog lead. He was

saying something about how he'd go and grab Luther's bed, and bowls and food to put in her car.

She watched his retreating back. He was in casual clothing for his flight—a faded old T-shirt, jeans that rode low on his hips. His shoulders were broad, and he had the type of strong, muscled legs that could never wear the currently fashionable, hipster skinny-guy jeans.

He was gorgeous and perfect—the type of guy that you didn't forget.

But the girl he worked with eight hours a day was evidently not worth noticing even when he looked directly at her and waved.

Gray had made her feel invisible that first day at the beach *and* ever since.

And Lanie Smith was *not* going to let that happen again.

CHAPTER FIVE

A MAKEOVER WAS not particularly original, Lanie knew. And Teagan had insisted it wasn't necessary—but she was just being kind.

Lanie did know—in an absent, better-get-round-to-it-at-some-point way—that she needed a haircut. And that the few suits she owned were nearly five years out of fashion and better suited to her at her race weight—not with the extra five odd kilos she was carrying now. *And* that it probably wouldn't hurt to slap on some make-up each morning. There was no chlorine fog to make her eyes water and her mascara run at Manning, after all.

So—a makeover it was.

Lanie twisted to slide the skirt's zip closed, then fussed for a few moments, tucking and plucking at the cream silk blouse.

She smoothed her hands down the fine wool fabric of the skirt, enjoying how it felt against her palms. The price tag dangled just above her hip, and she traced the sharp edges of the thick card with her fingers.

It was silly to delay the inevitable, but she wanted to enjoy how the clothes felt for as long as possible. Right now, before she turned to face the mirror, she could pretend she looked as good in this outfit as the mannequin also wearing it on the shop floor.

She wouldn't say she hated to shop—not exactly. She appreciated beautiful clothing, and was regularly tempted to try on the clothes displayed in shop windows—although she rarely did.

Like Gray, she had a tendency to shop in bulk—but unlike Gray she didn't do it in the name of efficiency. It was more that clothes and Lanie just didn't get along.

The way she imagined she'd look when she first saw the dress, or top or jacket on the rack and the way she *actually* looked never quite matched.

But this part she liked. Before she turned to face the mirror. The possibility that *this* outfit might look as amazing as she'd hoped.

'Come *on*, Lanie!' Teagan knocked on the change-room door impatiently. 'How does it look?'

Lanie shook her head as if to clear her thoughts. She was being ridiculous. Melodramatic. 'Just a sec.'

She spun around.

She looked…not bad.

Intellectually, she knew that.

The slim cut skirt helped emphasise what waist she had, and the delicate embroidery around the V neckline helped draw attention away from her broad shoulders. She stood up on her tiptoes to mimic heels and noted that her legs looked good—long and athletic.

Which, of course, was the thing. No matter the clothes or the shoes she was still tall, still strong and still slightly awkward. That was how people described her: *athletic*. Not elegant, or beautiful. And definitely not willowy—a descriptor regularly associated with Sienna.

But I'm lucky to be so tall, to have such strong shoulders. It's why I swim so fast…

She flung the door open, striking a pose. 'What do you think?'

Teagan clapped her hands together. 'Fabulous!'

It took a huge effort not to raise a sceptical eyebrow, but she managed. Teagan would only argue with her, anyway.

Her friend had a small mountain of clothes in her arms and she shoved them in Lanie's direction. 'Here—try these.'

'You know,' Teagan said through the door when Lanie was back in the change-room, 'it seems a shame to waste all these outfits just on Grayson Manning.'

'They're not really *for* Gray,' Lanie said carefully. She absently assessed the charcoal-coloured shift dress she wore—not good: it made what shape she had disappear entirely—before meeting her own gaze in the mirror. This and her upcoming visit to a hairdresser and beautician wasn't about looking good for Gray. It was about her not feeling invisible any more.

Teagan made a dismissive noise. 'Whatever. You look hot. You should come out with me one night.'

'I don't know—'

'And you can't use the early-morning training excuse any more.'

'It wasn't an *excuse*,' Lanie corrected gently. 'It was a fact. I was training to make the Australian team—not the local swimming carnival.'

'But you're not training now,' Teagan said—not unkindly, but with some emphasis. 'And you definitely need to start dating men who aren't *swimmers*.'

Lanie grinned at Teagan's tone as she tugged the dress off over her head. 'You make it sound like they have gills or something.'

'It's all that waxing they do,' Teagan said, and Lanie could just imagine her friend's look of distaste. 'It's not natural!'

Lanie laughed out loud. 'Fair point.'

She grabbed the next piece of clothing from the hook—another dress, this one in shades of chocolate, with a peplum detail at the waist.

'Although,' Teagan continued, 'I reckon I'd be happy if you dated *anyone*. It's been far too long. It can't be good for you.'

Lanie laughed again, but it was a touch more forced.

'What? A date a month keeps the doctor away or something?'

She stepped into the dress and tugged it upwards a little roughly.

Teagan snorted. 'Honey—a *month*? That would be awesome. But I reckon we're talking a year since that guy...what was his name?'

'Dominic. And it's not been a year.'

Although as she contorted herself inelegantly in front of the mirror to do up the back zip, Lanie did the calculations. Teagan was right—it *had* been a year. Fourteen months, actually.

And it had hardly been some amazing love affair. A guy she'd met at the swim centre. A good handful of dates over a month or so. He'd stayed over a night or two—but then she'd ended it.

She'd wanted to focus on her swimming—in fact she'd *needed* to. She'd known how hard she'd have to work to make the team and she hadn't been able to afford any distractions. Especially the distraction of a relationship in which she felt they were simply going through the motions.

Swimming had come first. *Always.*

Dress finally on, she pushed open the door to show Teagan.

'Oh, this is *definitely* my favourite!' her friend gushed.

Lanie turned this way and that in front of the mirrors that lined the wall across from the change room. She still looked like a tall, slightly gawky Amazon—but the dress worked her curves for all they were worth. 'It's nice...'

Teagan rolled her eyes. 'You're a lost cause, Lanie-girl,' she said. Stepping forward, she reached out to grab her hand. 'But I meant it before—you need to get out more. You've worked so hard for so long, you deserve to have some fun.'

'Mmm-hmm,' she said, and ignored Teagan's raised eyebrow. 'But for now I'm focussing on exorcising Ms Invisible, okay?'

* * *

Gray kept staring at their hands.

One was young, pale and perfect. Tipped with subtle pink polish, the fingers were laced through her husband's much larger, much *older* fingers. His nails were cut short and straight across in a neat contrast to the skin of his hands, which looked slightly oversized and baggy, scattered with the occasional sunspot—gained golfing, Gray could only presume, as his father hadn't exactly spent his working days outside.

Their hands lay linked on the crisp white tablecloth, between the fine china and sparkling cutlery of the table settings.

Tasha laughed musically at something Gordon had said, staring up at him with adoration. Gordon smiled back—a familiar smile. Loving and equally adoring.

Gray had seen it all before.

He looked back at their hands. Somehow it was *their hands* that surprised him.

He shouldn't be surprised. Tasha was wife number seven. Yes, *seven*.

He'd been here before—to dinners just like this one, organised by the eager new wife, keen to establish a relationship between herself and her new 'son'. Not that any in the past twenty years had been stupid enough to refer to him in that way.

He knew this dinner—knew the infatuated smiles, knew he'd drive home tonight and wonder where exactly his father would buy this latest wife's new home when they inevitably divorced. He might even wonder whether his dad ever worried that his ex-wives would bump into each other at the local, ritzy, over-priced organic grocery store.

Gray knew the answer to that: *no*. His father had perfected the art of the amicable divorce. A multi-million-dollar home as a parting gift possibly expedited that goal.

Yet tonight he was surprised.

Because tonight his dad looked old.

Not just older-than-his-new-wife old—he'd been that for the past three wives, quite spectacularly—but just plain old, *old*.

He looked like a man with a thirty-five-year-old son who'd had said son when pushing forty himself. He looked retired. He looked like a smartly dressed, smartly groomed *old* guy.

Gray's eyes were drawn back to their hands again. Tasha was rubbing her thumb back and forth along his dad's knuckles.

It should have looked loving and sweet. Maybe it did.

To Gray, it looked obscene.

With a glance and a nod in Tasha's direction he excused himself from the table. He wouldn't leave—he'd done that once before, years ago, and the wife of that moment had been devastated. It had *not* been worth the subsequent months of that wife trying far too hard—and his father being angry with him.

He couldn't even remember why he'd walked out that time. This time he just needed space, some fresh air. His dad's place was a penthouse at the opposite end of the terrace to the Manning offices. The balcony was huge, but mostly empty, with moonlight reflecting off the panes of the bifold doors and something sparkly mixed into the pavers.

Gray walked to the railing, wrapping his fingers around the smooth, cool metal, and stared out, unseeing, to the spectacular Swan River. On the other side of the water streetlights edged the South Perth foreshore, and to his right headlights glowed as they crossed the Narrows Bridge in a steady stream.

'What was that about?'

His father's voice was gruff, but not angry, behind him.

Gray turned slowly and shrugged. 'I'm tired.'

He'd flown in from Singapore only hours before. His meetings hadn't gone as well as he'd expected. He'd hoped he'd be flying home with a signed contract. He wasn't.

Was he different without the reassurance of his father in the background? He didn't really believe that. He'd never needed his dad to hold his hand.

Next week he'd fly out again, this time to Vietnam: a new resort on China Beach and a tour for potential investors of the villas already built. He was determined to be on his game. To be the Grayson Manning he'd been the rest of his career.

'What do you think?' his dad asked.

It took Gray a moment or two to work out what his dad meant.

Oh, Tasha. He shrugged again. 'She seems nice.'

He'd never met her before. His dad didn't have elaborate weddings any more—he did Las Vegas, or Bali or—as this time—Fiji. He didn't even bother telling his son about it.

Not that Gray telling his dad what he *really* thought would have made any difference.

Why are you doing it, Dad? What's the point?

He knew the answer to that question, too: *Why not? I love her.*

Right.

And that theory had worked so well the previous six times.

For a brilliant businessman, renowned for his hard bargaining and measured decisions, Gordon Manning's approach to his love-life made absolutely no sense.

It went against everything Gray had been taught. He modelled his business manner on his father's—the way he never let emotion cloud his decisions. The way he always took the time to fully understand or analyse everything. His steely, unflappable nature in the boardroom. And yet Gordon had retired and walked out of that boardroom and—it would seem—straight into the arms of sales assistant Tasha. Three months later they were married.

Gray shouldn't be surprised.

But he was disappointed.

This obsession with the idea of love—and not just any love, but insta-love—and his bizarrely unwavering faith in the idea of marriage despite all evidence to the contrary, was his dad's quirk.

Quirk? Weakness would be more accurate.

'Tell me about Singapore,' his dad said.

Gray propped his weight against the balcony railing. Even in the limited light out here it was clear that his father was in default mode. The sharp, shrewd, intelligent mode that Gray was familiar with. The one that he understood, admired and respected.

Not sooky, moony, head-in-the-clouds mode, while his much younger wife caressed his weathered skin.

That version of his father embarrassed him.

'Singapore was fine,' Gray said.

He wasn't going to elaborate. He didn't even consider it. He'd had almost twenty years of grooming from his dad and he'd just been confirming Gray's instincts for much of the past decade. Whatever his clients and investors might think, he *didn't* need his father's advice.

Gordon raised an eyebrow. For the first time Gray noticed that it was made up of more grey than raven-black.

'You're retired, Dad. You've got more important things to worry about,' he said. He even nodded meaningfully towards the kitchen, where he could see the slim figure of Tasha as she fussed about busily.

It wasn't sincere and Gordon knew it.

But still his father didn't push. Instead he reached out and gripped Gray's upper arm. Gray was wearing a T-shirt and jeans—straight off the plane—and his dad's touch was surprisingly firm and warm where it overlapped cotton and skin.

He met Gray's eyes. They were a near mirror image of his own, the colour an exact reflection. His expression was intense and knowing.

But he wouldn't push. He never had. He'd once said Gray did enough pushing on his own.

'You're right there, son,' he said with false heartiness. 'But I've got to tell you, Gray, you're missing out. About time you settled down.'

Gray pasted on a false smile, managing a laugh, even. 'Maybe one day, Dad.'

But Gordon knew that was false and insincere too.

Because Gray had worked too hard to risk all that he'd achieved on something as fleeting, as distracting and as superfluous as *love*.

His father's relationships—and his own—were yet to convince him of anything different. At least he had the good sense to end his affairs after a few weeks or months, rather than taking his father's rather extreme option and getting married.

Together, Gray and Gordon walked back inside, their joint re-entrance eliciting a mega-watt grin from Tasha. This was familiar too—the new wife's concern that she had somehow formed a wedge between father and son.

Gray should tell her she had nothing to worry about.

Gordon and Gray's relationship never changed. And so it would remain—long after Tasha, in a shower of expensive parting gifts, was gone.

'Now, don't you look lovely!'

Bob grinned down at her, order notebook in hand. Lanie leant back in her chair to smile back up at him. Beside her Luther sat obediently, his liquid brown eyes beautifully pleading in Bob's direction.

'Thanks.' She reached up to tuck a strand of newly highlighted hair behind her ear. 'Just the usual,' she said. Bob didn't take the hint.

'Guess you didn't swim today if your hair's still looking fancy?'

Lanie forced her smile to remain in place. 'Nope,' she said firmly. 'Haven't swum in months. And you know what? I don't miss it at all.'

Bob's mouth formed into a perfectly horizontal line. He took a deep breath, as if he was going to speak again—but then didn't. Instead he slowly—he wasn't young, after all—dropped down to a squat in front of Gray's dog. As he'd done on each of the four days that Gray had been away, Bob miraculously produced a small bone treat—which Luther took, very politely.

The speed which he ate it was less so.

Bob headed back to his shiny chrome coffee machine without another word, and Lanie shifted in her seat so she could stare back out across the street to the ocean.

She could make a good guess at what Bob had been about to say. That he believed she should still be swimming was obvious. It was bizarre. Everybody else—the selectors, her coach, her team mates…heck, *herself*…had known it was the right time for her to retire. She wasn't going to be making some great comeback. She was done.

Everyone knew that—except for the kind old man who worked at her local café.

It was sweet, she supposed. Well intended. She was sure he didn't mean to make her feel uncomfortable whenever he asked his daily question.

And, to be honest, she didn't have a clue why she *did* feel uncomfortable. If anyone asked her if she'd made the right decision she'd answer immediately and honestly: *Yes, I have.*

So, yeah—it was a bit weird…that he asked her and that she reacted as she did.

It was getting warmer now—not summer-warm, but warm enough that in the sun like this, summer didn't feel quite so far away.

More people were at the beach each morning, too. Not Gray. He'd flown back from Singapore yesterday and then gone straight to a dinner. He'd wanted to come and collect Luther afterwards, but Lanie had been clear that it really was no trouble having him another night.

Besides, she hadn't really wanted Gray turning up at her house late at night. Her flannelette pyjamas did *not* feed into her plan.

Flannelette pyjamas were Ms Invisible.

Next time she saw Gray she was determined he'd be paying attention.

Also—she really didn't want to give Luther up just yet. Lanie reached out to rub him behind his ears and the big dog leant immediately—blissfully—against her.

She'd loved looking after Luther. Loved having a silent companion on her daily beach walks and the way he lay on her kitchen floor as she cooked.

She'd never considered a pet before—between her rigorous training schedule, her full-time job, regular travel for swim meets and the tiny apartment she lived in, it just hadn't been possible.

Lanie's lips quirked upwards. Except for the size of her place, they were exactly the same reasons she'd remained mostly single her entire adult life.

But she guessed things were different now.

Everything was.

Gray was already in his office—door closed—when Lanie arrived at work an hour and a half later.

She felt good. So far Caroline at Reception had complimented her on her new suit, while Marilyn had said lots of nice things about her hair—wanting to know the name of her salon, no less.

Not that she'd gone crazy with her efforts today. Some women looked like different people when they were made up—but Lanie wasn't one of them. She'd been genetically blessed with a few good things—long, thickish eyelashes, for one, and clear, smooth skin, for another. A bit wasted on her average-coloured eyes and too strong features, she felt—but hey, she wasn't complaining.

But even though she was wearing mascara and foundation today—and even a bit of eyeliner—Lanie didn't feel she looked all that stunningly different.

The clothes she'd bought with Teagan were probably the bigger statement. Well-fitting, and a size larger, her new pencil skirt and pretty salmon-coloured blouse flattered her shape rather than pulling against it. And combined with her hair—now cut in layers and with generous splashes of blond—it *was* quite an improvement.

So, while she hadn't exactly turned up as a different person—she didn't aspire too, anyway—she *did* look good.

Lanie was putting the finishing touches on a report—some impressive statistics related to the success of Manning's Singapore residential developments over the past five years—when the little instant messenger bar at the bottom of her desktop screen started to flash impatiently.

She clicked on it and a window popped up.

IMON

This was Gray's very own acronym: *In My Office Now.*

No *please*, of course. As usual, her jaw clenched and she silently seethed.

She'd come up with a series of her own acronyms, and her fingers itched to type them as they hovered just about the keyboard: *WPF—When Pigs Fly.* Or… *SYASNN—Since You Asked So Nicely, No.*

But instead she stood, straightened her shoulders, and brushed her hands down the fabric of her blouse and skirt. For now, this job was serving a purpose. So she held her tongue/fingers.

She grabbed a notepad and walked in her shiny, trendy new heels into Gray's office.

As usual, he didn't look up when she walked in. He was focussed entirely on his computer screen and instead simply waved vaguely in the direction of one of the chairs across from his desk.

This was part of the routine. The alternative was that he'd just start talking—or rather, barking directions. The fact he'd waved at the chair simply meant this was going to be longer than a ten-second conversation.

Lanie smiled. *Conversation.* Right.

Her tummy felt unexpectedly light and butterflyish as she walked to the chair.

Nerves.

She did her best to ignore them.

She settled into the chair, notebook at the ready. 'How can I help?'

Now Gray looked up. A quick glance—lightning-quick. He barely met her gaze before his attention returned to his computer.

'Have you booked my flights to Hoi An for next week?'

'Last week,' she said. 'You're flying direct to Ho Chi Minh, then a second flight to Da Nang. A car will meet you at the airport.'

She waited impatiently for him to look up. To notice the changes—to, for once, properly look at her.

He nodded, still staring at the screen. 'Do you have a passport?'

Lanie blinked. 'Yes.'

She'd renewed it leading up to the championships, so it was perfect and stamp-free.

'Right. I want you to come with me. Can you sort that out?'

'You want me to come to Vietnam?'

Finally he glanced up, as if surprised by her question. 'Isn't that what I just said?'

This time he did pause for a second, to catch her gaze.

Then his attention flicked over her—her hair, her face, maybe her clothes. Very brief.

Had he noticed?

Anything?

He typed something on his keyboard, the subtle click of each key seeming particularly loud today.

She knew what this was: she'd been dismissed.

She was supposed to go away and book her flights and that was that. Gray's brain had already ticked over to his next task.

He probably wasn't even entirely aware that she hadn't left the room.

'Why?' she asked.

Gray's head jerked up. As expected, his expression was very much: *Why are you still here?*

'Because I want you there.'

Again back to his screen and his oh-so-important e-mail.

'What if I have plans?' Lanie asked. 'The trip is over a weekend. I could have somewhere terribly important to be.'

Gray pushed back his chair a little and leant back. His gaze shifted a little. Focussed.

'Do you?'

Lanie shrugged. 'That isn't the point. If you can explain to me the reason why I need to jet off across the world at a moment's notice, I can then weigh up whether or not I'm able to do it.'

'Vietnam is hardly across the—'

'That isn't the point either,' she said.

Did his lips quirk up just momentarily? Lanie couldn't be sure.

'I thought everyone wanted to go to Vietnam. It's very beautiful.'

Lanie shrugged. 'I'd love to go to Vietnam—' she started, and immediately saw Gray's eyes unfocus. He thought it was sorted. The issue filed away. 'On a holiday. *Not* with my boss.'

The glint returned to his gaze. Another blink-and-you'd-miss it sense of a smile flicked across his lips.

'Right,' he said. He crossed his arms, but his attention remained on her. He cleared his throat. 'I'd like you to accompany me as this project is particularly important to Manning. We require further investors for a new luxury beachfront hotel. Interest hasn't been as I'd hoped, so the purpose of this trip is quite simply to convince a group of wavering investors that there is nothing better they could do with their money than hand it over to us for this project. I'll be there for three days—wining, dining, etcetera, etcetera.' His lack of enthusiasm for this task was obvious. 'I need you to keep me organised, to deal with the details I tend to forget. You did a great job while I was in Singapore, but our being in different countries is not ideal. It would be much more efficient to have you there with me.'

That was about the most Gray had ever said to her at once. He tended to talk in soundbites, and very much on a need-to-know basis.

Something else occurred to her. 'I assume I'll be paid overtime?'

He nodded. 'Of course.'

Lanie narrowed her eyes as she looked at Gray, as if she was carefully considering his request.

He held her gaze the entire time.

'Okay,' she said, after what she figured was enough time for him to stew about it. 'I'll come.'

Gray nodded sharply, then stood—and surprised her by holding out his hand.

She stared at it for a moment, before making herself step forward and reaching out her own hand to grip his.

His touch was firm and warm. Lanie felt a blush start to build somewhere around her chest and begin to creep upwards. No slower than the day when he'd stripped off his shirt and definitely no less heated.

And a blush just wouldn't do. Not now. She made sure
her gaze remained firmly trained on his. Clear and direct,
not flustered.

'Thank you,' Gray said.

Lanie dropped her hand from his as soon as she could.
Immediately it was easier to think, and for the cogs to start
moving again in her brain.

'Not a problem,' she said, although her voice cracked a little and she needed to clear her throat. 'I'll get back to work,
then. I'll need to sort out my visa immediately.'

But now she was speaking to the top of his head. He'd sat
back down.

'Mmm-hmm,' he said, reverting to the Gray she was familiar with.

Although that was okay. Because today she certainly
hadn't been invisible—and it had *nothing* to do with her new
hair or new clothes.

But what had she hoped to achieve, really? Did she want
Gray to think she was attractive?

No. He was her boss.

Liar.

It was like that first morning at the beach. She wouldn't
be human if she hadn't noticed Gray Manning running along
the shore with the sun glistening off his sweat-sheened biceps. And wondered...

She wouldn't be human if she didn't want to impress a
man like Gray.

And today he had noticed her—when for the first time in a
very long time she'd said exactly what she was thinking. She
hadn't censored herself—not for Gray, and not for herself.

Not the way she did when she told people she was okay
after missing out on team selection. *'I swam a personal best.
I did everything I could. I'm proud of getting this far. Of
course I'm okay.'*

Not like telling Sienna how happy she was for her, telling her not to waste any time worrying about her. *'This is your moment, Sienna! I'm so proud of you, and that's all that matters.'*

And not like telling Teagan that she was fine working in a job that was so far removed from her dreams and aspirations that it was laughable—and that she was frankly terrified that she had nothing new on the horizon. Nothing new to strive for. *'It's actually really great, Teags, to have this time to re-calibrate. To think. I feel really relaxed, really calm—don't worry about me!'*

Today she'd spoken her mind—over something trivial, but still—and it had felt *great*. Better than the way she'd felt when Caroline had admired her suit or Marilyn had been sweet about her hair.

It was a tiny thing. A baby step.

But she knew she was going to do it again.

CHAPTER SIX

THE HUMIDITY, THICK and cloying, enveloped Lanie as she stepped from the plane onto the mobile staircase that led to the Tarmac. She'd worn jeans for the flight—perfect for Perth in August, but not ideal for Vietnam at the very beginning of the wet season. She could feel the heavy fabric clinging to her with every step as she headed for the bus that would whisk them the short distance to the terminal.

'Don't worry, we're about two minutes away from air-conditioning,' Gray said beside her, rolling up the sleeves of his shirt as he walked.

Lanie nodded, glancing in his direction. She'd half expected him to be completely unaffected by the weather—one of those perfect people who were always effortlessly cool and stylish, as if in their own separate temperature-controlled micro-climate.

Although she supposed she was already quite aware that he did, in fact, sweat. A disturbingly photographic memory of Gray running shirtless along the white sand of North Cottesloe beach flashed unhelpfully across Lanie's brain. She gave her head a little shake and cleared her throat.

Focus.

The small bus was almost full of tourists. Backpacker-types with nut-brown tans, families from toddlers up to grandparents, and a few couples that Lanie would put good money on being honeymooners, with their arms intertwined and bodies touching, despite the oppressive heat.

It was a different crowd from the arrivals in Ho Chi Minh a few hours earlier. There the plane had also had its fair share of travellers in business attire—quite fitting for Vietnam's bustling, rapidly developing economic centre and its population of more than twenty million. All Lanie had seen was the airport while in transit, but even so the sense of sheer activity had been apparent, and she wished she'd had the opportunity to venture outside and witness the uniquely crazy street traffic for which Vietnam was famous.

But Da Nang airport served a tourist centre and here life already felt slower. Although when she walked into the terminal Lanie quickly realised that *slower* was relative.

She'd expected something smaller. She'd been told by friends of a single baggage carousel and walls plastered with posters for local hotels and the tailors that Hoi An was famous for. Instead she was greeted by what seemed like acres of shiny tiles and high raked ceilings. Very modern, very international—not at all the regional Vietnam she'd expected.

'The new terminal opened about a year ago,' Gray explained as they waited to collect their bags. 'You could say that this area has well and truly been discovered by tourists. It's no longer a closely guarded secret.'

'That's why we're here,' Lanie said.

'Exactly.'

And although it was silly—after all, she didn't know any different—she felt a little disappointed that she hadn't been here earlier—before tourism and investors just like Manning had swooped.

Once they had their bags they headed outside into another wall of heat, and a crowd of neatly dressed men touting their taxi services. Many came right up close, offering to take their bags, wanting to know where they were staying, and insisting they could offer *'a very good price.'*

Everyone was smiling, and no one touched her—and yet it wasn't what Lanie had expected. She found herself shifting nearer to Gray as they walked—close enough to bump into him.

'Oh!' she said, stepping away. 'Sorry.'

But a moment later she bumped into him again, just as Gray told yet another extremely keen driver that they already had a car organized. This time as she went to apologise she felt Gray's hand on the small of her back.

Not wrapped around her. Not pushing her or directing her. Just *there*.

In the heat his touch was—of course—warm. Very warm. It went right through her thin T-shirt to her skin, and his hand felt strong and reassuring.

She let out a breath she'd had no idea she was holding,

His hand didn't move until they arrived at their car—which was low and white and expensive-looking.

A man in a crisp shirt—who *did* look completely unbothered by the weather—opened the rear door for her just as Gray's hand fell away.

'Thank you,' she murmured.

He just smiled and shrugged in response. *Not a problem.*

Gray walked around to the opposite side of the car as Lanie slid onto the creamy leather back seat.

When Gray joined her, the driver—who introduced himself as Quan—presented them both with small, chilled white towels and bottles of icy cold water. The car slid away from the airport almost silently as Lanie and Gray took advantage of both.

'So, what do you think so far?' Gray asked.

Lanie twisted the cap onto her water bottle and placed it back in its little tray between the front seats.

'Overwhelming,' she said, then grinned. 'Although it is kind of silly to be, I guess. I'm taller than *all* the drivers.'

This had only occurred to Lanie as she'd stood directly beside Quan—who was clearly inches shorter than her.

Gray tilted his head as he looked at her. 'Why would that make any difference?' he said. 'It's overwhelming for everyone the first time they come here—me included. I'm a lot taller than you and, trust me, I almost turned around and went back into the terminal the first time I visited.'

The image was so unexpected—tall, strong Grayson Manning hightailing it back into the glossy new terminal—that Lanie laughed out loud. 'Right. Besides, you aren't *that* much taller than me.'

Gray shifted in his seat to face her. 'What are you? Five-eleven?'

She nodded, surprised he'd noticed. 'Exactly.'

'So I've got three inches on you. I win.'

There was a mischievous hint to his tone that was new, and Lanie couldn't help but laugh again. Normally her height triggered comments like *Wow, that's really tall!*—and not in a good way. During her swimming career her body had been her tool, and the breadth of her shoulders and lankiness of her limbs a positive. She'd made herself look at her body objectively and monitored her weight, her skin folds and her lung capacity as if she were a racing car engine.

Yes, she had moments where she envied her more petite sister—when she went clothes-shopping, for instance. Sienna was more reasonably tall, at five foot eight, but with long, narrow feet like flippers and a freakishly good technique. Sienna had an elegance and a *normality* to her—no one ever made jokes about the air being thinner up there, or guessed that she must play basketball or something.

But overall she'd always seen her height as a good thing, and had told herself—firmly—that her moments of self-consciousness were a total waste of time.

More recently she was finding that more difficult. Now she was tall, quite frankly *not* a small person, and she wasn't even an athlete any more. Her size didn't make her special, and it didn't make her a potential champion. It just made her different.

And Gray didn't seem to think it was all that unusual. At all.

Lanie, for the first time since she'd arrived, felt the tension ease from her body. She settled back into her seat, and watched Da Nang city fly past her.

Growing up in Perth, she'd travelled to nearby Bali before, and to Singapore—and her swimming had taken her to Rome a few years ago, and to China. But as the car whisked them through the city the architecture was like nothing she'd ever seen before.

In pretty pastel shades the buildings were sandwiched together—the fronts tall and narrow but their structure stretching out long behind. Above them, power lines criss-crossed each intersection, looking rather alarmingly messily arranged and remarkably copious—as if every home's appliance had its own personal power supply.

Around them, the traffic mingled indiscriminately—luxury cars amongst rusted old overloaded vans—and everywhere, motorbikes. No one, including their own driver, appeared to pay too much attention to the road's lanes, or to progressing in single file. At each stop sign multiple scooters would surround their car and then shoot off ahead, two or three abreast.

And then, just occasionally, Lanie spotted a glimpse of the Vietnam she hadn't even realised she'd been searching for: a man walking along the footpath balancing two baskets from a pole across his shoulders, a woman on a pushbike in simple clothes of beige and brown, her face shaded by a traditional conical hat.

'Oh, did you see her?' she said enthusiastically, when she first saw the woman on her bike, and Gray leant across to see where she was looking. Soon she was asking him questions as Gray pointed out some of the French influences scattered throughout Da Nang—from the red-roofed architecture to the baguettes for sale at cafés alongside traditional Vietnamese *pho* soup.

Soon they'd left Da Nang and joined a busy road towards Hoi An. To their left was the ocean—China Beach—and to the right the marble mountains. More like hills than mountains, they thrust out abruptly from a flat landscape, covered in greenery and dotted with colourful pagodas visible even as the car zoomed past.

The traffic had thinned—not that that stopped the driver of every car or motorbike that came anywhere near them from leaning heavily on his horn. It seemed in Vietnam the horn was more about *Here I am!* rather than *Watch out!*

But soon their car was escaping the noise and the glare of the sun as it turned from the main road down a grand cobble-stoned driveway, lushly shaded with towering palms.

Moments later the car came to a stop before a sprawling double-storey building—and here the French influences that Gray had mentioned were immediately apparent. Painted in shades of cream, the red-roofed building boasted elaborately moulded columns and a balcony that stretched across the entire second floor.

The hotel reception area was open-sided, with oversized wicker fans spinning languidly overhead. They were greeted by two women in traditional attire and handed seriously exotic-looking juice concoctions, and watched as their bags were unloaded and silently whisked away.

Gray's phone rang almost immediately. He answered it, making vague hand gestures as he disappeared outside that Lanie could only guess meant he'd be a while. She already knew she had the rest of the afternoon free, so she checked in and then followed another crisply shirted hotel employee to her villa.

It was one thing for Lanie to be familiar with this development through her work with Gray back in Perth—on paper, multi-million-dollar pricetags for a luxury beachside villa weren't all that meaningful—but here, surrounded by this opulent reality, it was something else altogether.

From Reception they passed the main pool area—a series of infinity pools built on different levels, each with uninterrupted views to the private beach. No one swam today, or lay in the canopied daybeds. The hotel was not yet open for business, and none of the private residences had been sold.

Beyond the pools was the beachfront, and here Lanie was deposited at one of the smallest villas—after all, she had no need for multiple bedrooms. Entry was through a private courtyard, lush with thick grass and edged with palms. Inside, the open-plan space was dominated by a raised central section topped with an extravagant four-poster bed. Bifold doors opened out from a small, exquisitely decorated living area to a private deck and then to perfect white sand and the ocean beyond.

It was absolutely beautiful.

Although it had only been a short walk from Reception to her villa, the car's air-conditioning felt like a forgotten memory. Lanie's skin felt over-warm again, despite the cool sanctuary of the villa. There was an obvious solution to that, so she unzipped her suitcase and pulled out a bikini.

With the two pieces of fabric in her hands, she paused.

The swimsuit was new, purchased with Teagan on their shopping trip. The violet-coloured fabric was gorgeous, and it flattered her now slightly less than super-fit shape. It was the perfect bikini to wear at a place like this, but when Lanie thought of the perfect, untouched, unused pools she'd just walked by it didn't feel right at all.

Not the bikini's fault—but she didn't want to laze by a pool, she realised. She didn't even want to simply splash around in the shallows or order a cocktail while she relaxed in crystal-clear water.

She wanted to *swim*. For the first time in ages. And a bikini simply wasn't going to cut it.

Minutes later she'd changed into the plain black one-piece suit she'd packed almost automatically. It was one of her training suits—built for efficiency, not glamour. But it wasn't about to worry her with the possibility of parting from her body at an unfortunate moment, so it was definitely the right suit for today.

She grabbed a fluffy white towel and hit the beach. To her right she could see activity in the distance, but here, on the resort's own beach, there was not another soul. Even the lifeguard's tall white chair was empty. She dumped the towel but resisted the temptation to hit the water immediately—instead she stretched, as she had every morning prior to training for as long as she could remember.

But then—finally—she was in the water. It was warmer than she'd expected, and shallower, so she ducked beneath the water and put further distance between herself and the shore with strong, easy underwater breaststrokes.

Breaking the surface, she treaded water momentarily, looking back towards the shore and the perfect white sand to her beautiful villa.

Lanie grinned. This was surreal—this was *not* where she was supposed to be right now. She and Sienna had had plans to travel together through Europe after the championships—but now it was just Sienna doing the travelling.

And here she was—in Vietnam for *work*, no less.

She was not supposed to be here, but she was unexpectedly glad she was.

Then, with one last look, she turned in the water and with a sure stroke and a powerful kick began to swim.

Gray swiped the phone to end the call, then placed it not entirely gently on the small writing desk in his villa.

Then he swore.

An investor who'd been booked in for the weekend had cancelled.

It should be okay—after all, the personalised tour of the residential properties that Gray had planned for this weekend involved a group of investors. Losing one was no disaster. He knew that, and yet it still bothered him.

Not that the guy had cancelled—it didn't even matter why—but because it had rattled Gray.

On the flight over he'd busied himself on his laptop while running through in his mind exactly how this weekend was going to proceed. In itself, that was not unusual. What *had* been unusual was his demeanour—he'd been tense and fidgety. Fidgety enough to be irrationally annoyed at how Lanie had so obliviously read a paperback for the entire flight, as if she had no idea how much was riding on this trip...

Which, of course, she didn't. And she'd offered numerous times to help during the flight. He'd assured her that she couldn't.

The fact was he'd had nothing to do on the flight either. Everything was sorted. Everything was planned to the nth degree. It *would* go off without a hitch.

There was absolutely no reason why it wouldn't.

He realised he was pacing the floor of his villa from one side of the room to the other, his gaze directed blankly to the limestone tiles.

This was a waste of time.

He needed to go for a run.

Gray's chest heaved as he slowed to a walk. He leant forward, his hands just above his knees, as he took in great, big gulping lungfuls of air.

His body was coated in sweat thanks to the still intense humidity even now, as the sun was just beginning to consider setting. The solution to that problem was obvious, and he'd turned to step towards the welcome waves...when he noticed her.

A long way out a woman was swimming. Her arms moved in confident, practised freestyle movements, her feet kicking up a neat stream of bubbles.

It must be Lanie, he realised—it could be no one else.

He watched her for a few long moments, surprised. Maybe he shouldn't be. She had such a tall and athletic frame it really shouldn't be unexpected that she swam—and swam well.

Not for the first time since that morning after he'd arrived back from Singapore he wondered about her. What did he know about Lanie? She'd shocked him that day with her forthrightness. No one had ever questioned him at work before—at least, not so blatantly. He realised it didn't reflect well upon him—and Marilyn's damn words again came to mind—but, honestly, people didn't say *no* to him. Ever.

But Lanie had. And that intrigued him.

She'd worked for him for weeks. And she'd always been obliging.

Although maybe she hadn't always been. He had a sudden flash of memory of just slightly narrowed eyes, a glint to her gaze. Subtle, but there.

Yes, she'd been obliging. But maybe she hadn't always been happy about it. Or with him.

Actually, that was disingenuous. He *knew* she'd been unimpressed with him at times—the days when he was particularly busy or distracted—and he *knew*—normally some time later—that he'd been less than polite.

But he hadn't really cared.

He'd figured she was being paid to do a job and that was that.

But now...now he was wondering what she really thought.

And as he watched her swim he wondered who she really was.

She'd told him that morning in his house that they'd shared

the beach many a time. He hadn't realised. Even now, considering it, he couldn't remember seeing her. But then, even if pressed, he probably couldn't describe *anyone* he saw at the beach each day. When he ran, he used the time to think. And the times when he couldn't face thinking he'd focus on his breathing. Or the thud of his feet on the sand.

It was just him and Luther and his thoughts—or lack thereof.

It wasn't personal that he'd not noticed her, which is why when he'd seen her reaction that morning—her shock and, hurt—he'd dismissed it.

Gray straightened and ran a hand through his damp hair. Lanie was pretty quick, he'd give her that—she cut through the water effortlessly.

As he watched her he wondered *how* he couldn't have noticed her.

Yes, he'd been focussed on the business. *Entirely* focussed on the business—it was all he did and all he thought about. Except for running.

He prided himself on his focus. Honed it, in fact.

But Lanie somehow—at least momentarily—had him questioning it.

He was intrigued.

In a single movement he pulled off his soaked T-shirt, dumping it on the sand, and—given he ran barefoot—he was instantly ready to swim. He didn't mess around with wading into the water. He simply dived into the shallows, the cool water a welcome relief to his heated skin.

Then he surfaced, spotted Lanie, and began swimming in her direction.

CHAPTER SEVEN

HER STROKES WERE easy. Relaxed.

She wasn't training today. She certainly wasn't racing.

She was just swimming.

Stroke, stroke, stroke, *breathe.* Stroke, stroke, stroke, *breathe.*

Slow. Easy. Effortless.

She wasn't wearing goggles so she kept her eyes shut in the water—besides, there was no blue line for her to watch at the bottom of the ocean.

Every now and again she'd remember to look up between strokes, to check where she was going. But really—aside from the risk of accidentally swimming too far—she was safe. She wasn't about to swim into a stray surfer or a boat.

It was just Lanie and this perfect, gorgeous slice of the South China Sea.

She let her mind wander to anything and everything.

Some of it was silly. She found herself wishing that Bob's little café would miraculously appear on the beach, just so when he asked *'Did you swim today?'* she could declare *Yes!*

But at other times her thoughts turned more serious corners.

Within the reassuring, regular rhythm of her breathing she let herself consider stuff that was far from controlled. Stuff she hadn't let herself consider in weeks. Mainly, *What was she going to do?*

Because—nice and unexpected as this trip to Vietnam was—a career as a personal assistant was not her dream.

She'd spent her life for as long as she could remember striving for her swimming goals. She'd put everything into it and shaped her world around it. She'd been driven and dedicated and *obsessed*, quite frankly. She'd had to be to get up at four-thirty each morning and head for the pool. To stare at that line on the bottom of the pool for lap after lap. To maintain the strict training regime and the diet and the lifestyle.

She'd known she wasn't as naturally talented as other swimmers, but she'd had the raw elements—the height, the shoulders, the legs—to propel her bloody fast through the water. But without quite the same intrinsic talent as her competitors she'd had to work harder. She'd rarely let her hair down. Rarely taken a day off.

Her life had revolved around swimming and her goal.

And now she needed something else to fill it.

Stroke, stroke, stroke, *breathe.* Stroke, stroke, stroke…

She looked up just prior to taking her next breath—and just about sank to the bottom of the ocean.

Ahead of her—within a handful of metres, basically in the middle of the South China Sea—was Grayson Manning.

Her lips must have dropped open because salty water filled her mouth, making her cough and splutter.

'Hey!' Gray said, swimming closer. 'Are you all right?'

He reached out towards her but Lanie shooed him away, treading water. 'Of course I'm fine,' she said.

She'd stopped her swim so abruptly that her hair half covered her eyes. Automatically she dipped beneath the water and then ran her hands through her hair as she resurfaced, so her hair was slicked back from her face.

The action had moved her closer to Gray—really close, actually. Close enough that she could see the water droplets on his eyelashes.

She'd meant to say something—something inane to fill

the slightly odd silence. But as she looked at him—treading water before her, with the remnants of the sun, making him squint in an unfairly attractive manner—she found herself swallowing her words instead.

And saying nothing at all.

Gray hadn't really thought too much about what he'd do once he swam out to Lanie. Just that it seemed the logical thing to do.

Lanie was swimming, he was surprised and curious about that fact, plus it was hot and he wanted to swim—so he'd swum out to her.

But now he was here he wasn't sure what to do next.

Right now his body seemed quite content just to stay here, simply *looking* at her.

When she'd done that thing—that neat little dive and elegant reappearance with her hair slicked away from her face in shades of dark blond and brown—it had been as if he was seeing his assistant for the first time.

There'd been moments, of course, when he'd noted Lanie's attractiveness. Her eyes he'd noticed immediately—right back at her interview. And then the first day she'd worn her hair tied back in a ponytail, rather than spilling forward and covering her face. He thought she'd changed her hair again the other week too—her hair framed her face rather than shrouding it. And she did have a nice face—a strong jaw, defined cheekbones and a long, fine nose.

But that was the thing—he'd noted these things and had thought them nice. That was it, no further consideration. But right now she looked a heck of a lot better than *nice*.

Her deep brown eyes seemed huge, set off perfectly by her lovely, lightly tanned skin and the hint of freckles across her nose. Without her hair as a distraction her face was revealed for what it was—striking, defined and different. She wasn't model-beautiful, but she was...*distinct*. Much more than pretty. Much, *much* more.

'I'm sorry I don't remember seeing you at the beach,' he said.

He hadn't planned to say that, and Lanie blinked at him for a moment.

'You swam out here to tell me that?' she asked, raising an eyebrow.

'Yes,' he said. Then, realising that wasn't true at all, added, 'No. Of course not.'

Lanie tilted her head, studying him as if he was a very, very strange sea creature.

He didn't even bother to explain.

'I didn't know you swam,' he said instead.

Her eyes widened dramatically. 'You didn't know I *swim?*'

He would have shrugged if it had been easier to do while treading water. 'How would I? We've already covered the fact that I've been oblivious to your presence at North Cottesloe beach for weeks, so I wouldn't expect me not knowing your extracurricular activities to be a surprise.'

Lanie's lips quirked up in a bemused-looking smile. 'Okay.'

They really were very close to each other. Lanie wore what he was pretty sure was a simple one-piece swimsuit, its practical looking shoulder straps visible above the waves.

'So you swim,' he said. 'What else do you do?'

'Is this *Get to Know your Employees Day* or something?'

Gray laughed. 'Not officially. Let's just say I meant it before. I'm sorry I didn't recognise you at the beach. It's not personal. I've been particularly...distracted these past few months.'

That last bit he hadn't meant to say at all.

But Lanie nodded. 'You spoke to me once, too. Before I started working for you. You weren't happy when I took too long to throw Luther's ball.' Her expression was unreadable as she waited for his response.

Gray grimaced. He didn't remember the incident specifically, but it sounded about right. 'I'm sorry about that, too.'

She nodded again, this time with a subtle smile. 'Thank you.' A pause. 'You were very grumpy that day.'

'I've been told I can be,' he said.

Lanie's smile broadened. 'Your sources are onto something.'

He couldn't help but grin back.

But then that slightly tense silence descended again. Water lapped against them both, making them bob up and down amongst waves that would not fully form until much closer to shore.

Gray caught Lanie's gaze, meaning to repeat his earlier question: *What else do you do?*

But she was still smiling, her eyes sparkling. She looked like—Gray didn't know what mermaids were supposed to look like, or water nymphs, or whatever, but he'd guess they looked like Lanie. Glistening with tiny droplets of water, she looked entirely natural in the ocean.

Much, much more than pretty.

His attention now was far from abstract. More so than even five minutes earlier.

He was looking at her not as his assistant but as a woman. Out here, both of them without the accoutrements of their roles—no suits, or laptops, or smart phones—it was impossible to think of her and of himself as anything but a man and a woman. It was all they could be out here.

Just a man and a woman. Alone.

Lanie's smile had fallen away and the sparkle in her eyes had shifted to something far more intense. Far more compelling.

One of them—her or him?—had moved a little closer.

He could see flecks of emerald in her eyes.

Something else he'd never noticed before.

As he watched she licked her lips, a bead of salt water disappearing with that little movement of her tongue.

Then, in a sudden splash of water, Lanie was not so close any more.

'Race you?' she said. Her voice was high-pitched.

'What?' He was trying to gather his thoughts, far from certain he had any idea *what* he'd just been thinking.

'Back to the beach.' Her voice was steadier now. She gestured parallel to the shore with one arm. 'Swim straight this way till we're in line with the lifeguard's chair, then first one out of the water wins.'

'And the winner gets…?' he prompted.

'I'll decide what I want later,' she said with a cocky grin.

Gray made a show of sizing her up. 'You sound extremely sure of yourself.'

Remarkably so. Sure, she could clearly swim, but he was taller and stronger.

'I am,' she said.

He considered offering her a head start but from the steely look in her gaze decided that would be a very bad idea. He guessed Lanie was the type of person who wasn't interested in winning any way but fair and square.

He could understand that.

'And if *I* win, I want—' he began.

'Doesn't matter!' Lanie said. 'You ready? Let's go!'

And just like that they were off.

He did better than she'd expected. Lanie had to give him that.

For the first half of the hundred-metre-odd swim he was her shadow.

But gradually—completely as she'd expected—she pulled away.

In fact by the time he emerged from the water in all his bare-chested glory she was already on her feet, hands on hips, waiting for him.

The sun was rapidly setting behind her and long shadows were thrown by the backdrop of towering palms. Gray walked in and out of these shadows as he moved towards her, water sluicing down his long, lean body.

Unlike that day in his office, this time Lanie properly looked. She looked at the heavily muscled width of his shoulders. At the defined—but not overly so—shape of his pectorals. The lightest sprinkling of dark chest hair. The ridges of his belly. The way his shorts clung very low on his hips.

He was gorgeous. She already knew that. She always had.

Her gaze travelled upwards again to meet his own.

He was looking at her as he had when they'd been treading water in the ocean. How to describe it? Maybe as the opposite of the way he usually looked at her—or rather the way he usually *didn't* look at her.

This look wasn't dismissive, or uninterested, or brief.

It was intense. Interested.

In what?

The same question had triggered their impromptu race. The race that had been supposed to clear her thoughts, to give her time to realise that she'd imagined whatever it was she'd seen in his gaze.

Standing here staring at him like this was not conducive to that goal.

She gave herself a mental shake before taking two steps towards Gray and holding out her right hand, as if they were meeting for the very first time.

'Elaine Smith,' she said, then added proudly, 'Retired Member of the Australian Swimming Team.'

'This is not what I expected,' Lanie said.

Gray paused in the narrow laneway. 'You said you wanted me to take you to my favourite place in Hoi An.'

Her prize for winning their race. Although he *had* pointed out that he felt he'd agreed to the race under false pretences.

She'd countered by mentioning that, had he bothered to read her CV when she applied for her job, he would have known exactly who he was swimming against.

Which was a good point.

Lanie smiled up at him. She wore a long, summery dress with thin straps that revealed sunkissed shoulders. 'I was imagining a temple. Or a view from a mountain. Or maybe a fancy pants restaurant.'

'So you're not the only one surprising people today?'

'I guess not.'

They *were* at a restaurant—although the word could only be used loosely.

At the end of a long lane—which itself stretched down from the main street of Hoi An town, about ten minutes' drive from the resort—was a collection of mismatched plastic chairs and metal tables. The lighting was provided by naked bulbs strung across the back of a pale yellow two-storey building with dark green shutters and a red-tiled roof that was about five hundred years old.

The contrast between the ancient and the new was stark, and should have been ugly. But somehow this place—completely packed with locals—wasn't ugly at all.

It was vibrant and authentic.

And, besides, the food was amazing.

Gray led Lanie to a spare table—no one greeted customers at a place like this—and then left her for a minute to pay. You also didn't get to order here, either.

As he walked back with a couple of cans of soft drink sold from a bucket full of ice, he watched Lanie, observing this place.

She looked relaxed, leaning back comfortably in her chair. Her gaze was flitting everywhere, as if she was trying to see and absorb everything: the details of the ancient houses that surrounded them, the raucous laughter from a table of Vietnamese women all dressed in modern Western clothes, the older woman who was yelling directions at the restaurant's staff as they ferried oversized tin or plastic plates to table after table.

He'd decided to come here without much thought, and really it wasn't the most logical choice. He'd meant for them both to eat dinner at the resort tonight, alone in their respective rooms, as he'd had plans to work late into the evening.

If he'd properly considered taking her out to dinner it wouldn't have been to this place. He would have taken her down to the banks of the Thu Bon river, where the streets on either side where lined with cafés and restaurants, all serving incredible food at tables located perfectly for hours spent watching the world go by.

Lanie smiled as he approached. 'This place is awesome,' she said. 'Like nothing at home.'

And instantly Gray was reassured. He'd been right to bring her here. She got it.

'Tourists don't come to this place,' he said. 'Quan, our driver, brought me here one night last year. It isn't the sort of place that appears in guidebooks, or in a glossy pamphlet at a hotel reception.'

'That's probably a good thing,' Lanie said as she poured her iced tea into a glass. 'If this morphed into a tourist trap it wouldn't be the same.' She took a sip of her drink and met his gaze over the rim of the glass. 'This way I feel like I'm in on a secret.'

Their food arrived—banh xeo: crispy deep-fried pancakes with a pork and mushroom filling baked into the batter. Gray showed Lanie how to add lettuce and roll the pancake before dipping it in a lime and chilli sauce.

He waited for her verdict as she took her first bite.

'Delicious!' she declared, and Gray felt as stupidly pleased as if he'd cooked the meal himself.

'I looked you up on the internet,' Gray said, after polishing off his first pancake. 'Elaine Smith, member of the Australian swimming team.'

Lanie met his gaze. 'And what did you learn?'

'That you were aiming for this year's championships.'

She nodded. 'That's correct.'

'And your sister is Sienna Smith.'

'So's that.'

Now she did break eye contact, her attention suddenly focussed on a stray beansprout she was twirling between her fingers.

'It must have been hard, watching her win after you missed out on the team.'

Lanie looked up and raised an eyebrow. 'You don't beat around, do you?'

He didn't bother to answer that question.

'That's not very sensitive of you, you know,' Lanie pointed out. 'Most people would assume that's a delicate subject for me.'

'Is it?'

Lanie shook her head, but said, 'Yes.' Then blinked, as if surprised by what she'd said.

But she didn't correct herself.

'Of course,' she continued, 'I'm absolutely thrilled for Sienna. It's amazing to see someone you love achieve their dream.'

'That sounds scripted.'

Lanie's eyes narrowed. 'I meant every word. What sort of person would I be if I didn't?'

'I didn't say you didn't. I'm just not sure why you mentioned it. We were talking about you, not your sister. I don't really care about what she did or didn't win.'

He reached for his can of drink, enjoying the play of emotions and reactions across Lanie's face. Shock, affront—and then careful consideration.

How had he not noticed how transparently expressive she was?

Well, the same way he'd not noticed that he'd hired a world class athlete. It was apparent such an oversight was not difficult for him.

'So you're saying it wouldn't bother you if I was insanely jealous, overwhelmingly frustrated and more than a little bitter that my baby sister—who only began swimming to copy me—has just gone ahead and done something I've spent my whole life dreaming about?'

'No,' he said.

Lanie gave a little huff of protest. 'Right. I—'

'I'd call you honest.'

Her mouth snapped shut.

She reached for her own glass and downed the remainder of the sparkling liquid in a single gulp. 'For the record,' she said eventually, 'I don't feel that way.' A long, telling, pause. 'Most of the time.'

Gray nodded. He believed her. 'Do you want to go for a walk?' he asked.

'Definitely,' Lanie said, already on her feet, as if keen to escape from the conversation as quickly as possible.

Minutes later they were heading down Le Loi Street, which stretched all the way down to the river. Red paper lanterns were strung across the street, and with motorbikes parked along the footpath the narrow street itself was full with foot traffic—only the occasional swift-moving bicycle or a motorbike heralding its arrival with a toot of its horn wove amongst the crowd.

It wasn't late, and many of the shops remained open. Each flung light across the street, and the walls of colourful fabrics inside drew tourists towards them like moths.

Lanie's walk had slowed almost to a standstill. 'Can I have a look?' she asked.

Gray nodded. Even he with his bulk-purchasing approach

to clothing had been attracted to the famous Hoi An cloth shops. Le Loi Street was almost entirely full of them—and this was far from the only street in Hoi An like this. From suits to shirts to evening gowns, tourists could have almost anything made to measure—generally overnight.

If he'd had more time on his fleeting business visits he might even have had a suit or two made. But he hadn't, and he definitely wouldn't have time this trip, either.

For the first time in hours—since he'd dived into the ocean, actually—the real reason for this trip rushed back to fill his brain.

Temporarily he'd felt as if he was on holiday. A tourist, not a businessman.

He'd followed Lanie into a shop, but now he turned and walked out the way he'd come.

Lanie ran her hand down the wall of neatly folded silks and satins. Here they were organised in shades from the palest pink to a blood-orange-red, and the textures beneath her fingertips varied from silkiest smooth to roughly textured to delicately, prettily embroidered.

The fabric covered all three internal walls of the small shop. Suiting fabrics—pinstripes, wool and houndstooth— were just across from her, but it was this pretty wall that interested her. It was funny, really, she'd never been a girly-girl, yet it was this rainbow wall of pastels that had drawn her from the street.

A young woman had approached her as soon as she'd stepped inside, her black hair shining beneath the bright shop lights. Now she followed Lanie with a thick file full of pages carefully torn from top-end fashion magazines. She kept flipping to a new page, pointing at some amazing dress and ensuring Lanie they could make it for her, saying how beautiful she would look in it.

Lanie tried to explain that she was just looking to little effect. She knew Gray's schedule for the weekend inside out, and there was *no* time for this—no matter how remarkably fast the tailors in Hoi An were.

Lanie smiled to herself. Her sister would think this hysterical—that *Lanie Smith* was disappointed she wouldn't have a chance to shop. Combined with her makeover expedition, she was practically a shopaholic!

But here—with this wall of fabrics and the stack of fashion books and files on the battered-looking wooden desk in the middle of the shop—there was a possibility that maybe she could get something made just for her. Something perfect and custom-made that would...

What?

That would make her beautiful?

Lanie's hand stilled on a roll of fabric and she realised she was digging her fingers into it—hard. Enough to tug it a little out of its shelf. The shop girl watched her warily, as if she was about to fling the defenceless fabric onto the floor.

'Sorry,' Lanie murmured.

She turned, searching for Gray. He'd been standing amongst the mannequins at the front of the shop, but now he was nowhere to be seen.

She strode outside, negotiating the parked motorcycles to stand in the middle of the street. Gray should be easy to spot—and he was, way down the street.

Now she didn't bother looking into each shop. Instead she walked far faster than the groups of turtle-slow tourists, her flat sandals slapping on the bitumen.

Gray stood outside a café, his full attention on his phone. Behind him a blackboard sign proclaimed free wi-fi with any purchase and an untouched frosty colourful drink in his spare hand made it pretty easy to put two and two together.

'Gray?' she said.

He glanced up. Not a glance like earlier today, but the

type she was far more used to. The type that seemed to look straight through her.

It was so unexpected she took a step back.

'I need to get back to the resort,' he said, eyes still on his phone. 'I need to deal with this.'

They were supposed to be continuing their walk down to the river. He'd told her of oversized, giant *papier-mâché*-like sculptures that floated along its surface in the shapes of dragons and fish. And a market across the bridge entirely lit by thousands upon thousands of paper lanterns.

But she didn't bother mentioning it to him.

It was a timely reminder, really. A necessary one.

Gray was her boss and nothing more.

Whatever she'd thought had happened down at the beach clearly hadn't.

It was as silly and misguided as the idea that somehow just the right outfit could make Lanie Smith beautiful.

That was never, ever going to happen.

Just as Grayson Manning would never look at her as anything more than his personal assistant—who had used to be a swimmer, once.

CHAPTER EIGHT

GRAY WAS TENSE. Very tense.

Lanie sat at the end of a long table, her laptop set in front of her as she took notes.

There were no conference facilities at the resort, so one of the function rooms had been converted into a meeting room of sorts. Although—wisely, she thought—Gray had decided to leave the floor-to-ceiling windows uncovered. Subsequently there was no mistaking where they were, with a sweeping view over the pools all the way down to the gently swaying palm trees and the pristine private beach.

For the investors gathered around this table today there would be no forgetting that they were sitting amidst paradise.

The goal was that all of them would find it impossible not to buy a slice of it for their own—either as a private retreat and long-term investment or to visit a handful of times a year and rent out to the fabulously wealthy for the remainder.

It was what Gray did—invest in construction and development and then sell the completed properties. The Vietnam-based corporation with which he'd built this resort—necessary due to Vietnamese law—would retain ownership and management of the main hotel-style half of the complex, while it was the private villas Gray needed buyers for.

Lanie had kept an eye on the five groups of investors throughout the meeting—on the sharply suited couple who made absolutely no concession to the heat, through to the maxi-dressed, tattooed woman with crazy, curly red hair whom Lanie knew had made her fortune shrewdly on the stock market. She watched their gazes drawn back time and time again to the view—to the promise and the possibilities that Gray was spinning for them.

She reckoned two of the five groups were already ready to sign on the dotted line—no question. The others—particularly the suits and Raquel of the maxi-dress—needed more work.

That Gray could convince them she had no doubt. She'd seen him in action before—he was good. Very good.

But today…

He was tense. Definitely.

Gray abhorred the type of presentation in which someone talked at words on a wall or screen. Sure, he'd show short movies, or photos, or the occasional chart or whatever—but generally his skill was talking. That he genuinely believed in the property he sold—his 'product', so to speak—came over loud and clear to anyone who met him.

He was passionate about what he did. Lanie was sure that that alone sold many of Manning's properties.

So, as usual, he wasn't standing at the head of the room and presenting. He was sitting at the table, having a conversation with the investors and answering questions while cleverly weaving his sales pitch into everything he said. Occasionally he'd stand and walk over to the windows to draw further attention to the view, or he'd ask Lanie to hand out yet another glossy photograph, or the impressive projected rental return figures, or research on the estimated growth in tourism in Hoi An over the next five years.

He was as smooth and as polished as he always was.

But he was tense. It was subtle—very much so. When he stood and walked around the room Lanie could see the stiffness in his shoulders beneath his cream business shirt. When he answered pointed and at times abrupt questions he would pause just that little bit longer before responding. And today, rather than *I know* or *This will* he was saying *I believe* or *Expectations are*.

She hadn't really believed him when he'd told her last week that this trip was particularly important, and that was why she needed to accompany him. She'd figured they were basically throw-away words, because she knew at Manning *every* project was important—particularly from Gray's point of view.

But now she'd revised her opinion.

She didn't really understand. Based on her knowledge of Manning's financial state—admittedly gained more from osmosis than anything concrete—everything was going incredibly well. Manning had ridden the Western Australian mining boom over the past decade to remarkably profitable effect. The company had developed and sold the flashy head offices required by the mining conglomerates in the Perth CBD, and had also diversified to invest and build in the mining centres dotted across the state. With the boom, by all reports, now gradually dying down, this new push into tourism and South East Asia was somewhat of a risk, Lanie assumed, but as far as she was aware it was a calculated one.

Nothing Gray had said or done in the time she'd been working with him had ever indicated that the company was in trouble.

But today, for the first time, she wondered.

The meeting ended and Gray left with the group briefly— the resort chef was conducting a special Vietnamese cooking class for their guests. When he returned he closed the door behind him and Lanie watched as he let out a long breath— as if he'd been holding it for some time.

'What's wrong, Gray?'

She asked it automatically, without thinking.

Gray's gaze snapped up to meet hers. For a moment he

looked as if he was actually going to tell her—although maybe that was just wishful thinking.

Then his eyes went cold and flat.

'I have no idea what you're talking about,' he said.

Then, as if the exchange had never happened, he walked over silently, pulling one of the chairs away from the table to sit beside her.

He began talking, his attention on her laptop screen—certainly not on her—without any expression at all.

But every inch of his body radiated tension.

Not that Lanie had any intention of asking him about it again.

Gray knew he'd stuffed up with Lanie.

He walked along the path to her villa, rehearsing what to say. He wasn't getting very far.

She'd thrown him before. Her question—asked so matter-of-factly—had felt as if it had come from nowhere.

He'd told himself that this first day had gone well.

That he had nothing to worry about.

But then Lanie had asked her question…

No. That was unfair.

He'd known he'd been off since he'd left Perth. He'd just been refusing to acknowledge it.

It didn't mean it had come as any less of a shock that Lanie had noticed.

Had the table of investors noticed too? The possibility had floored him. Made him re-evaluate every moment of the day so far.

So, yes, he'd been rude to Lanie. He knew it.

But how to explain?

As if he could just come out with it: *You see, it turns out the reputation I've built over the past fifteen years isn't as rock-solid as I thought.*

It bothered him enough that *he* was bothered by all this.

That he clearly hadn't been able to shake off his frustration as completely as he'd intended.

Who cared that some of Manning's clients would apparently much rather his dad was still around?

It turned out *he* did.

He shouldn't be dealing with it at all.

So, no. He wasn't going to tell Lanie the truth.

But a simple apology wouldn't cut it either. It had become clear that his assistant was not about to nod and agree to everything any more.

And he needed her help tonight.

Gray jogged up the steps to the front door of Lanie's villa, but just as he raised his hand to knock it swung open.

Lanie stood before him in her one-piece bathers, towel in hand—and nothing else.

'Oh!' she said, taking a step back.

His gaze travelled down her body—he was male and breathing, after all—and confirmed that she looked equally amazing in her swimsuit today as she had yesterday.

Tall and athletic, with never-ending legs, she looked like the world class swimmer he now knew she was. One with subtle curves in all the right places and—his gaze made it back to her face—blush-red cheeks and a furious expression.

'What do you want?' she asked. Her tone was pure frost. 'I believe I've finished work for the day.'

The combination of a near naked Lanie and his lack of preparing anything reasonable to say meant he blurted his words out.

'How did you know something was wrong today?'

Instantly her eyes softened, but she crossed her arms across her chest, her towel hanging forgotten from one hand.

She raised an eyebrow, and what she was thinking was obvious: *Seriously?*

Gray ran a hand through his hair. 'If I was rude to you before, I'm sorry.'

Silence.

He tried again. 'I apologise for my behaviour earlier. You've been a huge help to me this trip, and it was unfair of me to lash out at you about something which is not your fault.'

Lanie raised her chin slightly. 'Better.'

Her arms had uncrossed, and now she was fiddling with the towel in her fingers. 'Do you want to go for a walk?' she asked.

Not particularly. But he wasn't about to quit while he was ahead. 'Sure.'

Lanie had hoped the addition of a summery dress over her bathers and swift exit from the too-cosy confines of her villa would help. She'd felt far too exposed—both literally and figuratively—in her swimsuit, and had figured the beach would give her the space—mental and physical—she needed.

It was only somewhat successful. Having a business conversation while half-naked and in what was effectively her bedroom was clearly not an optimum scenario. But likewise walking along China Beach with six feet two inches of Grayson Manning with his suit trousers rolled up and his dress shoes in his hand didn't feel anything like a meeting in his office back in Perth, either.

But still, it would have to do.

As usual, the beach was deserted. The lapping waves nearly brushed their bare feet and a gentle breeze ruffled the dense line of palm trees. The sting of the sun had lessened, but it was still warm against Lanie's skin.

Gray cleared his throat. 'Why did you ask if something was wrong today?'

It was obviously difficult for him to ask, and no less the second time around.

Part of her wanted to push—to make him tell her what was wrong first. She shot a glance at him as they walked side by side and noted the hard edge to his jaw, and the way his gaze was remaining steadfastly ahead.

No, he wasn't going to tell her.

'Well,' she said after a while, 'it wasn't any one obvious thing.'

Instantly she sensed Gray relax, and that reaction surprised her. What had he expected?

'I doubt anyone else noticed,' she continued, and now Gray's attention moved from something in the distance back to her. 'I've just watched you in so many meetings that the subtleties stood out for me.'

He nodded. 'Like what?'

So she explained.

At some point they both came to an unspoken agreement to stop walking, and sat in the shade beneath a palm tree, their legs stretched out in front of them.

Gray didn't interrupt as she spoke, and it didn't take all that long, really.

'Thanks,' Gray said when she'd finished.

They were both staring out at the ocean as the sun set behind them.

Lanie was making a move to stand up when Gray spoke again.

'It's about my father,' he said.

Lanie sat down again, looking directly at Gray. He'd gone tense once more, almost as if he was angry.

'Okay...' she said.

'You wanted to know,' he said, with an edge to his tone, as if she'd somehow forced it out of him.

She went to stand again. 'Don't do me any favours, Gray. You can tell me if you want. Or not. Up to you.'

He stood too, and in silence they headed back to the villas. Gray was walking much faster than before—big, generous strides. Certainly not leisurely.

Halfway back, he spoke again. 'My dad retired a few

months ago,' he said. 'For years he's been little more than a figurehead. He's been my mentor, I guess, but not active in negotiations or anything like that. So, logically, his official retirement shouldn't have made a difference to anything.'

'Has it?'

Gray came to a stop. He shoved both his hands into his pockets as he faced her. 'That's the stupid thing. It *hasn't*. At least I don't think so. Everything's fine. Manning's fine.' He seemed to realise something. 'Is that what you're worried about? Job security? There's nothing to worry about on that front.'

She should have been worried about her job, but no. She'd been worried about Gray.

Ha! How stupid. As if Gray would worry about *her*.

A memory of Gray's hand at the small of her back at the airport, and his concern that day when she'd tripped on the street, momentarily confused her. It was easier to think of Gray as her grumpy, unreasonable, thoughtless boss. Not the man who'd raced her to the beach, or who hadn't judged her when she'd revealed more than she'd meant to at dinner last night.

Certainly not the man who was talking to her so openly now.

It was disconcerting.

'It's good that Manning is okay,' she said. She blinked, trying to get her thoughts back in order.

Gray studied her for a long moment. 'It doesn't make any sense. If the business is okay, if I know what I'm doing, and if this particular project is no more of a risk than any other significant new venture for Manning, then *why on earth* am I second-guessing myself?'

Lanie met his gaze. 'Because you're human,' she said, echoing his words of the night before.

His attention flicked over her shoulder, maybe to the waves beyond.

She spoke carefully, not even sure herself what she was trying to say. 'It's difficult to be so directly compared to someone else. When your father retired it was natural that people would search for change. That they would judge you and weigh up your achievements against what had come before. You'll be benchmarked against him for a very long time.'

'Is that what people *really* do?' Gray said, a derisive edge to his tone.

Lanie shrugged and her gaze dropped to her feet.

'It doesn't matter if they do it or not. Maybe they don't. Probably they don't—not all of them, anyway.' She curled her toes in the sand. 'All that matters is that you *think* they do.'

The touch of Gray's fingers beneath her chin shocked her.

Slowly, he tilted her face up again, so she was looking straight at him. Into his eyes.

'Who are we talking about here?' he asked gently. Too gently.

She took a step back, annoyed. 'You. Me. Does it make any difference?'

His hand fell away. The sea breeze was cool against the skin he'd touched.

He started to walk again. Whatever had happened then—if it had been *a moment* or whatever—had clearly passed.

Lanie took a second to follow him, but he paused a few metres away to wait for her.

Together, they walked again, the quickening breeze whipping long strands of Lanie's hair out of its ponytail.

'So what do we do about it?' Gray asked at the base of the steps to Lanie's villa.

Lanie laughed out loud. 'I wish I knew.'

A moment later Gray followed suit, and they stood there laughing together about nothing really funny at all.

When they'd both gone silent again Lanie gestured towards her front door. 'I'd better get inside. Sort out some room service or something.'

In response, Gray looked at his watch. 'Damn, I lost track of time.' He looked up at Lanie. 'Can you be ready for dinner in fifteen minutes? We're having dinner in Hoi An town with the investors.'

Lanie grinned. *This* Gray she was comfortable with. 'So what you're saying is that you'd like me to accompany you to a business dinner tonight, *please?*'

He nodded, completely oblivious. 'Yes. I realised today that it would be good to have you there. I should've included you from the beginning.'

'Okay,' she said.

But Gray had already turned down her steps, never even considering she might decline.

'Don't be late!' he called out, not bothering to look over his shoulder.

And that was just so quintessentially Grayson Manning that Lanie was laughing again as she closed the door.

CHAPTER NINE

THAT NIGHT WAS the full moon festival in Hoi An town.

Gray explained the celebration as the group had dinner in a café overlooking the Thu Bon river. On the fourteenth day of the lunar month the streets of the ancient town were closed to motorised vehicles and the street and shop lights switched off. The result was a world lit only by lanterns and candle-light—and, of course, the light of the moon.

It was a night during which the locals celebrated their heritage, and Lanie and the investors all got to experience this first-hand, with a dragon dance on the street outside the open windows of the café: three young boys—one beneath the elaborate dragon's head, another as its body, and the third providing the beat with a makeshift drum.

Amongst the celebrations, and at this simple café where each meal cost only a few dollars, they were a million miles away from the luxurious resort where the investors had spent the day.

It was a beautiful spot. Across the river the ancient build-ings also housed restaurants, all with packed chairs and tables spilling out onto the street, dark except for the smattering of lanterns. The temperature was balmy but far from unpleas-ant, and the locals and tourists were out in earnest. A gentle buzz of happy chatter spread from the street to the shops and restaurants and back again.

Lanie thought Gray had chosen well. *This* was what Hoi

An was about for tourists—amazing, authentic Vietnamese food served in the ancient town without any airs or graces. As lovely as the beach and the five- and six-star hotels that were popping up along it were, it was Hoi An itself that had originally drawn people, and it was this town that would continue to do so. She'd been here two days, and that *this* was what it was all about was already clear to her.

Hopefully the group of investors would see that too.

After dinner a line of cyclos arrived to whisk them out of the ancient town to where three cars waited to drive them back to the hotel. Lanie had enjoyed her ride down to the river in the three-wheeled bicycle taxi, seated ahead of her driver between the front two wheels on a canopied bench seat padded in shiny red vinyl. One by one each investor climbed into their own cyclo and were driven away two abreast, so they could continue their conversations as they sped across the cobblestones.

Lanie and Gray had sat at opposite ends of the long table at dinner, Lanie's role simply being to keep the conversation going—especially with Raquel and another investor who was travelling alone. Unsurprisingly the evening hadn't been about business at all—a few cocktails and their guests had seemed to forget about work entirely.

Raquel grabbed Lanie's hand as she stepped into her cyclo. 'Thanks for a fun night,' she said, squeezing her hand. 'I've never had dinner with someone famous.'

Lanie laughed. 'Not quite famous.'

'Pfft!' the older woman said with a dismissive gesture. 'Famous enough for me!'

And then with a wave Raquel was on her way.

Lanie was still smiling as she turned back to the road, but it fell away when she realised how close she was standing to Gray. It was the closest they'd been all night—almost as close as they'd been that afternoon down at the beach.

Her skin goose-pimpled, even though it wasn't even close to cold.

Gray studied her steadily. His face was shadowed, but the full moon overhead and the lanterns that edged the street provided more than enough light for Lanie to see he was truly meeting her gaze.

'Famous?'

'Uh-huh,' Lanie said with a grin. 'Haven't you heard? Raquel thinks she might remember watching the women's relay final four years ago, and she might also have seen me on television. Therefore—apparently—I'm a star.'

'She's right,' Gray said, very matter-of-fact. 'You are.'

Then he immediately turned away to speak to the driver of the waiting cyclo.

Lanie blinked at his back for a moment or two, not quite sure what to say.

Tonight had been the first night in ages—months, even—that she'd really, truly enjoyed herself. Just as Raquel had said, it *had* been a fun night.

Of course amongst the plentiful food and drink her swimming career had come up in conversation. Lanie had forgotten how normal people reacted to it. To her family and friends—even in her old job—her achievements had long ago become part of the wallpaper. But Raquel had been impressed—seriously impressed. As had the others seated near them.

For a little while she had felt a like a star.

So she couldn't really tell Gray he was wrong.

'Lanie?'

Belatedly Lanie realised that only a single cyclo remained outside the restaurant.

'Are you walking back to the hotel?' she asked with a grin.

Gray smiled back—the first time she'd seen him do so all evening.

'No,' he said. 'That market I mentioned last night… We…'

a pause '…we ran out of time yesterday. But I think you'd like it.'

Lanie smiled again. 'Sure.'

He gestured at the cyclo for her to climb in.

'So you *are* walking, then?' Lanie asked, confused. 'I can walk with you. I don't—'

Gray shook his head. 'There's heaps of room,' he said. 'We can share a cyclo.'

Lanie took another look at the bicycle-like vehicle. It was admittedly slightly wider than the one she'd been driven in on. But still…

'Maybe for two *normal*-sized people.'

'Don't be stupid,' Gray said. 'Trust me—we'll fit.'

He neatly ended Lanie's protest by grabbing her hand and tugging her into the cyclo behind him. The driver started pedalling the instant they were seated, and for a few moments they were both silent as they turned off from the relatively busy road along the river to an empty back street.

Silent and…squished.

From shoulder to hip to toe they were pressed tight against each other. The skin of Gray's arm was hot against hers, and their knees bumped awkwardly with every jolt in the road.

And then Gray started laughing. Laughing so hard his whole body vibrated—and consequently so did Lanie's.

'So it turns out,' he managed eventually, 'we *don't* fit.'

It was impossible not to laugh with him.

Their detour took them past a street corner crowded with tourists. Amongst the throng a small band played traditional Vietnamese songs and women in beautiful sashed dresses danced with oversized fans that flicked and flickered in time with the music. As they headed back to the river Lanie began to relax just a little—or as much as was possible given their proximity.

After their laughter faded away they didn't talk for the remainder of their trip—although it wasn't an awkward silence.

Lanie had expected Gray to ask what she thought about the dinner. She'd definitely noticed a subtle difference—not so much in the stuff he couldn't control, as she'd still seen the hints of tension in his posture, but he'd shifted his language, reverting to the more confident phrasing that she was more familiar with.

But she was glad he didn't ask. It was nice to play tourist for just a little while.

She risked a glance in his direction.

His gaze was directed outside the cyclo at the many shop fronts and the boats moored along the river. In profile, Gray was every bit as handsome as he was from other angles. Although this close she noticed he wasn't quite as perfect as she'd suspected. His nose *wasn't* quite straight, and had the smallest bump near the bridge. His just-too-long hair had a couple of flecks of grey, and he'd even managed to miss a section while shaving. The tiny patch of stubble was unexpectedly endearing.

He must have sensed her attention because he turned to meet her gaze with a smile. Of course she smiled back.

It turned out that even now—when Gray's smiles were *almost* a regular occurrence—they had just as much impact on her. It was near Pavlovian—one smile from Gray and her insides went all gooey, with a dopey smile to match.

Of course she knew this wasn't a good thing. She'd told herself that many times—particularly in the past twenty-four hours and *especially* since he'd dragged her onto this cyclo. But what she needed to remember was that it was natural for the two of them to feel some sort of temporary closeness, given how much time they were spending together.

That was what this was. Nothing more.

The cyclo came to a stop at the base of a wide pedestrian bridge. On either side floated giant lantern-like sculptures—far taller than even herself—bobbing amidst the boats on the river. A tiger, a serpent, a fish and more—all glowing in shades of gold, red and green.

'Come on,' Gray said. 'We'll walk this last bit.'

He stepped out and then reached out a hand to help Lanie. Once she was standing, and while he asked the driver to wait for them, he kept right on holding her hand.

Lanie looked stupidly down at their joined hands, but let him tug her behind him as they crossed the bridge. His touch did such strange and crazy things to her. This was different from how she'd felt in the cyclo because—like down on the beach—she couldn't interpret it as anything but deliberate. Sensations fluttered in her belly that she really had no business feeling.

He was her boss, after all.

And he wasn't interested in her.

Are you sure?

More than once now she'd thought she'd seen something when he'd looked at her. As they'd swum together in the ocean. When he'd surprised her at her villa door in her bathers. That moment he'd raised her chin with a tender touch... And maybe now...

No. No, no, no, no, *no.*

She was being fanciful. Imagining things.

She should pull her hand away from his immediately.

But she didn't.

She wanted to kick herself for her weakness. What was she going to do next? Swoon at his feet?

They emerged from the crowd on the bridge to a wide expanse of road on the other side. As the crowd parted their destination was immediately obvious: the Night Market.

It was so beautiful that Lanie came to a sudden halt right in the middle of the street. Gray's hand dropped from hers, and with the removal of his touch he returned her capacity for speech.

'Wow!' she said. Which pretty much said it all.

'I thought you'd like it,' Gray said, looking pleased. 'Do you want to go explore?'

As if that question actually required an answer.

The market was small—only a single row of stalls, plus a line of freestanding carts and stands selling jewellery and souvenirs. But what it did have was an abundance, or even an overabundance, of light. Each and every stall sold lanterns— lanterns in silks and chiffon and lace and cotton and in every colour under the sun. And all were lit—rows and rows of them. Pendant shapes and diamonds, columns and spheres. Some with golden tassels, others without. Some delicately painted, others tiny and strung together on delicate strings.

All beautiful, all bright, all magical.

There was no other light in the market but that thrown by the lanterns—but it was enough. Lanie approached one stall and a woman immediately offered to make her a lantern on the spot, in any design she wanted. Any colour, any size, any painted decoration.

Lanie turned to Gray. 'I don't actually *need* a lantern...' she began.

Gray laughed. 'Neither do I. But I have two from here at home, in a cupboard somewhere.'

Once again he'd surprised her, and she found herself laughing back at him. 'Grayson Manning the impulse shopper?'

He slanted her a look. 'Do you honestly believe you're leaving here without a lantern?'

'Good point,' she said, and then embraced the inevitable by weighing up her many, many lantern options.

In the end she kept it simple—a sphere-shaped silk lantern in a blue that reminded her of the South China Sea, with today's date painted in delicate script at its base. What she'd do with it when she got home she had no idea—it wouldn't exactly blend in with her mother's décor. But of course that wasn't the point.

Directed to return in half an hour to collect her new lantern, Lanie took her time browsing the other stalls, exploring even more lanterns, plus jewellery, trinkets and silk fans. Tonight Gray didn't disappear. He didn't hover over her shoulder, either, but browsed the stalls with her, occasionally drawing her attention to the weird and the wonderful—like the unexpected discovery that one stall was selling, of all things, cheese graters.

Eventually they reached the edge of the Night Market. They stood together in a puddle of light thrown by the final stall's lanterns, both of them looking back the way they came.

'I read your CV,' Gray said out of the blue. 'I figured I should check for any other hidden talents I was unaware of.'

Lanie shifted her weight a little uncomfortably. 'Um…' she began. How to explain?

'For an elite athlete,' Gray went on, 'you've managed to squeeze a heck of a lot into your business career.'

Maybe she'd imagined his questioning tone, but regardless she needed to tell him. 'My CV—excluding the swimming part—is a little…uh…*creative.* A friend of mine made some adjustments without my knowledge.'

'So you lied to get your job?' he said. But his tone wasn't accusing.

'In a way…yes.'

A long pause. 'I should probably be pretty angry about that,' Gray said.

Lanie met his gaze, and even in the lantern light a sparkle was unmistakable. 'Probably,' she said. 'But you're not.'

He studied her. 'No.' A shrug. 'You're doing a great job. And you haven't quit. So that's in your favour.'

'I've heard you have an issue with people doing that.'

Gray sighed. 'Marilyn says I need to be nicer to my staff.'

'Marilyn is a very wise woman,' Lanie said. 'Although you *are* improving. You've been almost nice at least once this weekend.'

Actually, many more times than that.

'Have I—' Gray began, but then a couple with a huge, fancy-looking camera began talking to them in a language she didn't understand—although their hand gestures soon made their intentions clear. They wanted to take a photo down the length of the market and she and Gray were in the way.

So they stepped aside—around the side of the last stall and into almost darkness, with only a few lonely-looking lanterns hanging above their heads. The move had brought Gray closer to her—close enough that she needed to tip her head up to look at him.

'What was I saying?'

'Something about being nice,' she said.

'No, not that,' he said. 'Your CV. If all that experience isn't accurate, then what *have* you been doing for work? Or were you paid to swim?'

Lanie gave a brief laugh. 'No! Surprisingly, an unknown relay swimmer is *not* a target for lucrative sponsorship deals.' She briefly explained her old job at the swim-school, which she'd taken to support the limited government funding her swimming had received.

He looked at her curiously. 'Why are you working for me?'

'Because you're such a nice guy?' she said, trying another laugh. But this one was even less successful.

'No, I'm serious,' he said. 'Is this what you want? A career in business?'

Lanie wrapped her arms around her waist. Her stomach was feeling strangely empty, despite their recent meal. 'Why not?' she said.

Gray shook his head, and the small action made Lanie's jaw go tense.

'You're not young for a swimmer,' he said, oblivious to Lanie's narrowing eyes. 'So I'm guessing swimming has been your life for—what?—ten years?'

'Longer,' she said.

'So after all those years focusing on and striving for one

thing—being completely driven by your own goals and aspirations—you walk away to be my assistant?'

Lanie felt her nails digging into her waist. 'It was the right time for me to retire,' she said very tightly. 'And there's nothing wrong with being a personal assistant.'

'Of course not,' he said. 'If that's what you want.'

She couldn't listen to this. 'I don't have the luxury of *doing what I want*, Gray. Not many people do.'

Lanie didn't want to stand still any longer. She stepped away, needing to walk somewhere. Away from Gray.

But his hand, light on her upper arm, slowed her. Then his voice, quiet but firm, stilled her. 'What *do* you want, Lanie?'

She shrugged his touch away, not needing the distraction. Gray was standing directly below the small cluster of lanterns. Their light was inconsistent, putting his face into flickering shadow. She couldn't quite make out what she was seeing in his gaze—but she could guess.

Concern.

Pity.

'I wanted a gold medal, Gray,' she said. She spat the words out, as if it was a dirty secret. 'But you know what? I soon learnt not to be fussy. Then I just wanted a medal. Later it was enough to be on the team, to swim in a final. Then just being a heat swimmer was okay.' She paused, taking a step closer to Gray. 'I've got pretty good at downgrading my dreams. And how is it any of *your* business what my new dream is? Maybe I've just figured out that it's better to choose a dream I've got some hope of actually achieving.'

She dropped her gaze, staring at nothing over his shoulder. Somewhere at the back of mind she didn't understand her reaction. Wasn't this question exactly the one she'd pondered as she'd swum yesterday?

But then, maybe that was the problem. Yesterday she'd had no answers.

Today she still didn't.

She wasn't going to admit that to Gray.

She didn't even want to admit that to herself.

Gray shifted closer, and now the lantern light revealed his expression to her more clearly.

'Lanie...' he began, then paused.

If his gaze had held the pity she expected she would have walked away. If it had been compassion, or worry—everything she saw in Teagan's eyes and heard in Sienna's voice—she would have been gone. Out of there.

But it wasn't there. None of it was. He looked at her with... *something.* A mix of understanding and maybe respect?

Could you even *see* that in someone's eyes?

He reached for her again—this time for her hand. His fingers were warm and firm as they wrapped around hers.

'Don't do that,' she said, although she didn't pull away.

'Touch you?' he asked.

She nodded. 'You keep doing it. At the airport, the beach, just before...'

Lanie realised it sounded as if she'd burned every instance of his touch into her brain, and she felt a blush steal up her cheeks. He probably had no idea. It had probably all been subconscious actions—nothing to do with her.

'Why is that a problem?' His voice had become very, very low.

She was looking down again. At their joined hands. She had pretty big hands—they were in proportion with the rest of her—and long fingers. But Gray's made hers look normal.

Almost, but not quite, small.

'I can't concentrate when you do,' she said. And then immediately wanted to whisk those words away. She tried to make a joke. 'See? I don't know what I'm saying.'

But the atmosphere didn't lighten. If anything, the shadows in which they stood felt even more intimate.

Here at the end of the stalls there was no one. No tourists, no shopkeepers—nothing.

They were alone.

'Really?' he said. His grip shifted, moving a little way up her arm so his fingers brushed the sensitive skin of her inner wrist.

The tiny, delicate movement made her breath catch.

'You don't have to hold my hand, you know,' she said, her voice not sounding at all like her own. 'I'm not going to walk away. Not because you don't deserve it, but because I don't know how to get back to the hotel.'

Gray's lips quirked upwards.

'Maybe I'm not touching you for purely practical reasons,' he said.

Lanie didn't know what to say to that.

Her instinct was to argue. To say, *Don't be stupid.*

But as she looked up into his eyes, as she felt the gentle touch of his fingers and realised it was most definitely a caress, words failed her.

Electricity was shooting up her arm and her whole body felt warm. Different. Certainly not entirely her own as she felt herself sway towards him.

He was looking at her as he had in the ocean. With an intensity and a certainty that she didn't know how to handle.

She was familiar with a Gray who barely registered her existence. This Gray, who was making her feel as if she was all he was capable of looking at…whose gaze she felt travel from her eyes slowly, slowly to her lips…this Gray was completely overwhelming.

But, unlike that afternoon at the beach, she just couldn't make herself look away.

It was crazy. It was stupid. She wasn't even sure if they liked each other.

He'd moved closer. Close enough that she could feel his breath against her lips. Close enough for her to register that his breathing had quickened.

Had she done that?

His other hand reached out, but it wasn't gentle like the brush of his fingers against her wrist. No, his hand at her waist was firm and sure as it tugged her closer. A whisper away from their bodies touching.

It was as if he was impatient—as if he couldn't wait around for her to make up her mind about what was going to happen.

And it was *that*—that little glimmer of familiar Gray, exasperated, focused, impatient, *imperfect*—that shoved all the other thoughts and doubts from her mind.

Right here, right now, all that mattered was that she wanted to kiss him. Needed to.

And incredibly, remarkably—and unquestionably—he wanted the same thing.

She looked straight into his eyes and he must have seen what she was thinking. Instantly there was no longer any gap between them at all.

The touch of lips against hers was firm. There was no caution in his kiss. But then, would she expect anything less from Gray?

His hand slid from her waist to the small of her back, although Lanie hardly needed any encouragement to move even closer. Both her hands snaked up and around his neck, and her fingers into his too long hair.

She wasn't sure who deepened the kiss but it didn't really matter. All she knew was the brush of his tongue against her lips and then the amazing sensation of their tongues touching and tangling.

She leant into him, enjoying how broad and solid and *tall* he felt, needing to get closer to all that strength and warmth. His hands traced random patterns at her waist and then moved upwards to the bare skin at her upper back. There, his touch made her shiver—and wish that she had more of his own skin to explore than just the nape of his neck.

Lanie didn't know how long they kissed or how many times they broke apart to kiss at some other wonderfully perfect angle. It was a confident, passionate kiss, giving them both the time to explore each other's lips and tongue—and to experiment with kisses both soft and hard. And everything in between.

It was like no other kiss Lanie had ever experienced.

She'd never felt quite so involved in a kiss, never felt so focussed on the touch of mouth and hands. It was as if her whole world had narrowed down to this kiss, to this moment, and absolutely nothing else mattered.

Gray had pulled his lips from hers and was kissing his way along her jaw. The luscious sensation made her tremble and hold on tight as otherwise she had serious concerns her legs were incapable of holding her upright.

'Lanie?' Gray murmured against her skin.

'Mmm-hmm?'

'We should probably head back to the resort. I'm not one hundred percent on Vietnamese law, but I'm pretty sure if we stay here we'll be arrested.'

The words were light and casual, but they were enough to snap Lanie's eyes open.

She froze. Immediately in her line of vision was that poor, forgotten cluster of lanterns—at first a blurry mass of colour but, as reality rapidly descended, soon refocussed into sharp relief. For a moment she watched as they swayed in the evening air and the rest of her surroundings also rushed back into her awareness. The buzz of the market. Music playing, somewhere in the distance. And the almost silent swish of a bicycle along the street.

Oh, God.

Her fingers were still tangled in Gray's hair, and she was still pressed chest-to-chest to his body. She felt a hot blush accelerate up her chest as she yanked her hands away, but before she could step back Gray's grip hardened at her waist.

'Lanie?'

Keeping her eyes on those lanterns, she aimed for a tone

that was hopefully breezy and matter-of-fact. 'Now, we can't go getting arrested, can we? Wouldn't be good PR for the resort.'

More brittle than breezy. But it would have to do.

'No,' Gray said. For an instant his grip tightened again—but then he let her go entirely. Taking his own step away.

She should be relieved. It frustrated her that she wasn't.

She risked looking straight at him and he caught her gaze.

He watched her with questions in his eyes—questions she definitely had no intention of answering.

So she filled the silence before he could. 'We'd better head back to the resort. Busy day tomorrow.'

Gray nodded—a slightly awkward movement. Then he fished his phone out of his shorts pocket and led the way from the relative seclusion of the dark to the multi-coloured brightness of the market.

Lanie kept her gaze straight ahead as she followed him, just putting one foot in front of the other, trying not to think about *anything*.

But her body—her hormones or something—was determined to keep reminding her how she *felt*, and it took an effort to push all that away. She didn't want to remember how she'd felt in his arms. How she'd enjoyed the romantic flutter of his fingers against the skin of her shoulder almost as much as the more earthy, more blatant way he'd claimed her lips.

She wasn't doing too well on that front.

As they stepped back onto the bridge a woman ran up beside her, a sea-blue lantern in her hand. Automatically Lanie took it and thanked her, but she didn't really want the lantern any more.

Which should be unsurprising, given that Gray had so adeptly brought to her attention tonight that she had no idea what she wanted.

Except for a short while, in the darkness just beyond a wall of hundreds of rainbow-coloured lanterns, she'd definitely wanted Grayson Manning.

CHAPTER TEN

HE SHOULD HAVE SAID something in Vietnam.

Gray knew it. And he kept on knowing it with each painfully awkward conversation with Lanie back in Perth.

After their kiss beside the Night Market they'd travelled back to the resort in total silence. He'd studied her as she'd stared out of the window, trying to figure out what to do or say.

At the time the issue had been that what he'd wanted to do and what he'd known he should say were very different things.

Even in the back seat of that car, with Quan only metres away, the temptation to reach out and touch Lanie had been almost impossible to resist.

When they'd arrived back at the resort there'd been a moment when they'd both stepped out of the car and Gray had been sure Lanie had swayed towards him. He'd been sure that whatever barriers she'd built since their kiss were just going to fall away.

And even though he'd known exactly how wrong it was for him to want that to happen he *had* wanted it.

But then she'd given a little shake of her head—like a reminder to herself, maybe—and walked away.

Thankfully, somehow he'd had the presence of mind not to follow her.

But even so his behaviour had shocked him.

He was her boss.

Even his dad and his too-quick-to-love heart had never had an affair at *work*.

And to think he'd been so smug about his relationship history when compared to his father's: dotted with mutually convenient temporary relationships, but never, ever anything hinting towards permanency.

He'd decided long ago that marriage was not for him. His career was his life's focus—he didn't need or want anything else. No distractions, no loss of control, and certainly no risk of losing what he'd spent his whole life working towards.

Besides, he had no doubt that he'd inherited his dad's propensity for divorce. All he had to do was look at his track record with his staff—it was clear he did not do long-term well.

But apparently he did think it was okay to kiss his personal assistant. In public, no less.

Gray realised he'd read the same e-mail three times and was still yet to comprehend any of it—so he pushed his chair away from his desk, spinning it around so he faced his window, and the view down to the magnificent Swan River.

He should have said something in Vietnam. Or on the plane home. Or when they'd arrived in Perth.

So many opportunities and yet here they were—almost forty-eight hours after their kiss and he'd done nothing.

Except maybe subconsciously hope that the whole issue would just go away.

Kind of the way his memories of their kiss had so successfully gone away?

Hardly.

The opposite had happened, in fact.

Lanie Smith.

She was not like anyone he'd ever met…

She intrigued him.

And she'd understood that stuff about his dad—stuff he hadn't told another soul.

When he'd kissed her it had felt as if they'd been building up towards it. As if he'd been waiting for that moment. Wanting that moment.

And then, when they *had* kissed…

He hadn't cared about where they were, who he was or who she was. He hadn't cared about Manning, or the investors, or his dad, or his dad's new wife—or anything.

He'd just cared about kissing Lanie. And then, later, he'd just cared about getting her back to the resort and to his villa as quickly as possible.

But that hadn't gone so well.

He needed to talk to her.

As if on cue, an instant message from Lanie popped up on his computer screen.

Raquel would like to organise a meeting later today.

This was good—one of the potential investors for the Hoi An resort.

Great. Can you come into my office to organise a time?

Of course that didn't really make any sense—this was definitely a task more efficiently sorted by instant messages. But, well…no time like the present and all that…

His office door swung open and Lanie stepped inside.

She wore a simple outfit—a knee-length slim-fitting charcoal skirt and a pale blue shirt. She looked tall and elegant, with the shirt skimming her curves and her legs appearing to go on for ever. Having seen her in her swimsuit, he now knew they did. She also looked neat and professional, and the gaze she had trained in his direction—as if she was making herself look him dead in the eyes—was equally so.

It also revealed nothing.

She had a tablet in her hand, and she turned its screen to face him as she walked to his desk.

'You've got a few meetings already in your calendar today, but I think you can safely move this one.' She zoomed in on the appointment. 'Or otherwise—'

'Lanie,' he interrupted.

She watched him calmly. 'Yes? Do you have another suggestion?'

'I don't want to talk about the meeting,' he said.

'What would you like to talk about?' she said.

Again, very calmly. Although as he watched she shifted her weight awkwardly from foot to foot.

'I'll give you one guess,' he said.

Her eyes narrowed. 'I have no idea what you're referring to.'

'Don't play dumb. We both know what I mean.'

'And we've *both* been playing dumb very successfully, I thought,' she replied. Her attention flipped back to the tablet screen. 'So—'

This time Gray stood up, and Lanie went silent as he stepped around to her side of the desk.

'We need to talk about this.' He followed her lead and met her gaze—as if it really wasn't all that hard to be having this conversation. And as if his brain wasn't unhelpfully supplying unlimited memories of exactly how good Lanie had looked with her hair slicked back in the middle of the ocean.

Ha.

'Look, I'm not going to launch some sexual harassment suit, or anything, if that's what you're worried about. It was a mutual thing.'

The idea hadn't even occurred to him—although of course it should have.

What was wrong with him?

'No, that's not it. I just wanted to—' He searched for the right words. 'Clear the air.'

Well, that was lame.

'There's no need,' Lanie said. 'Don't stress. I haven't picked out a wedding dress or anything—I know it was a one-off, random thing. Two people travelling together, an exotic location...' She shrugged. 'It was a mistake. I get it. I know you'd never be interested in me in that way...*blah, blah, blah*...and there's the whole you being my boss issue...'

Her gaze had shifted now, to a spot just over his shoulder.

His instinct was to correct her. What did she mean she knew he'd never be interested *'in her that way'?*

She said it with such certainty—as if she truly believed that he would have kissed any random work colleague he'd been with that night.

The opposite was true.

'Lanie—' he began, then made himself stop.

What was he going to say? That in fact, *yes*, of *course* he was interested in her in *that* way?

Was he really? She was nothing like the women he usually dated. She didn't look like them, and she certainly didn't act like them.

And besides—what would be the point? He couldn't afford a distraction right now.

He remembered how she'd looked in the market, when he'd questioned her about why she was working for him and what she really wanted.

Her pain and frustration had been crystal-clear—and he hadn't believed her for a second when she'd spoken of downgrading her dreams. As if she'd accepted that fate.

She hadn't. She was still processing the death of her dream.

She didn't need a guy like him to come along and hurt her some more.

So, after far too long, he didn't say anything at all.

'Good!' Lanie said, all *faux*-cheerfully. 'Glad that's sorted. Now—can we work out this meeting?'

'So!' Teagan said over the top of her hot chocolate. 'How was Vietnam?'

'Beautiful,' Lanie said with a smile. 'Fantastic beaches, and Hoi An town is amazing. I'd love to go back one day.'

There. Well-rehearsed and executed, Lanie thought.

A waiter placed an oversized slice of carrot cake between them. They'd met at a café near Teagan's place in Claremont, just beside one of the area's trendy shopping districts. Outside, people flowed past in a steady stream, expensive-looking shopping bags swinging from their fingertips.

'And how was your prickly boss? I can't imagine he'd be much fun to travel with.'

'Actually,' Lanie said, 'he wasn't so bad.'

That wasn't quite to script. She'd intended to say he'd been as difficult as usual—and as he had, in fact, provided a few decent grumpy-Gray anecdotes she even had sufficient material to back that up.

She'd figured it couldn't hurt—Teagan didn't know Gray. What harm would it do to perpetuate the idea that he was the boss from hell?

'Really?' Teagan said, looking disappointed. 'Damn. I was imagining you wearing one of those pointy hats, cycling around Vietnam searching for the perfect triple shot latte or something else equally unreasonable.'

'That's very specific,' Lanie said, and Teagan grinned. 'But, no. Honestly, he's not so bad.'

Teagan's eyes widened instantly. 'Pardon me? Is this the same guy?'

Lanie knew she should stop the conversation, but just couldn't do it. 'I don't know. He was almost *nice* while we were away. Seemed to want to get to know me better.'

He'd been more than nice, actually.

'You mean like a real-life *normal* person?' Teagan said with a grin. 'Wow. Amazing.'

And then the conversation turned to the famous Hoi An tailors, and Gray—at least from Teagan's point of view—was forgotten.

Unfortunately for Lanie it wasn't so easy to move on.

Part of her—a *huge* part of her, actually—wanted to blurt

it all out. She wanted to walk Teagan through her weekend blow-by-blow, so that together they could analyse what on earth had actually happened.

It was what she and Teagan normally did. In fact they'd just deconstructed her friend's latest date.

It didn't feel right not to tell her—but she just couldn't do it. It was hard to tell with Teagan. She'd respond one of two ways: either she'd be really concerned—both about Lanie and Lanie's job—or she'd go right to the other end of the spectrum and tell her to go for it.

And, given her conversation with Gray today, neither scenario was relevant.

It was—as she'd said—sorted. Over. There was nothing to analyse: quite simply it had been a one-off that was never to be repeated.

A mistake.

'Sienna was in *Lipstick* magazine this week—did you see?' Teagan asked.

Lanie nodded. 'With that rower in Paris, wasn't she? She looked really happy.'

She'd looked beautiful, in fact, with her new boyfriend in posed photographs taken all over the French countryside. Blissfully happy in a vintage convertible. Effortlessly gorgeous on a picnic blanket beside a picture-book lake.

'When does she come home?'

Lanie did the maths in her head. 'In a few weeks. She's meeting Mum in Dubai and they're flying home together.'

Teagan pulled a face. 'So you get them both at once? Lucky you.'

She had to laugh. 'It won't be so bad.'

'Is that what you're telling yourself?'

'It helps,' she said, grinning. 'And I can't move out, so I don't exactly have a choice.'

'Why not?'

Lanie swirled the remnants of her cappuccino in the base

of her coffee cup. 'I'm pretty sure I'm going to go back to uni. Finish that degree.'

'Really?' Teagan all but clapped her hands with enthusiasm. 'That's wonderful!'

She raised an eyebrow. 'Am I really in that much of a rut?'

'Yes,' Teagan said seriously, then clapped her hand over her mouth. 'Well, you know what I mean. This current job is okay, but it doesn't really *fit* you, you know?'

'But it's a similar job to yours.'

Teagan waved her hands dismissively. 'My temping jobs are about raising cash for my Grand Adventure.'

Teagan always referenced her planned year-long trip around the world as if it were capitalised.

'They're just a means to an end.'

'But why can't *I* have that?' Lanie asked. 'Why does everyone—' She stopped, correcting herself. Now was not the time to think about Gray again. 'Why are *you* so sure I should be doing something else?'

'Because you're the most driven, most focussed, most determined person I know. Do you think an average person would've kept on swimming, kept on believing, when their baby sister came through and did it all so easily? That takes guts, Lanie.'

'Or stupidity.'

Teagan glared at her.

But, honestly, sometimes Lanie did wonder.

The next morning Lanie went for a swim.

It was still colder than it had been in Vietnam, so she wore her wetsuit. The truly dedicated ocean swimmers simply wore their bathers, but while Lanie admired their dedication she wasn't about to give it a go.

Stroke, stroke, stroke, *breathe*. Stroke, stroke, stroke, *breathe*.

Just as she had in the South China Sea, she let her mind drift.

Should she go back to uni? Or continue to work full-time? Maybe even finally make use of the deposit she'd been so carefully accumulating and get her own place?

Was *any* of that what she wanted?

Gray's question had echoed within her skull all week. *'What do you want, Lanie?'*

Now she let herself acknowledge her answer to that question: she didn't know.

And that was terrifying.

Today, certainly, she didn't have an answer. So instead she just did what she knew: she swam.

Stroke, stroke, stroke, *breathe*. Stroke, stroke, stroke, *breathe*.

She lost track of the number of laps she'd done along the beach—she just swam until her shoulders ached and her legs were no longer capable of kicking.

Knee-deep in the shallows as she headed for the shore, a familiar splash of red came barrelling towards her.

'Luther!'

The dog leapt about excitedly in the water, running up close to Lanie and then running away back to the shore, as if to show her the way to go.

Unfortunately it was Gray who stood on the sand and who Luther kept returning to.

So her original plan to ignore Gray should she see him down here—after all, it wasn't as if he'd notice her—was not exactly going to work.

'Hi,' she said, coming to a stop in front of him. She tugged her goggles off over her swim-cap and swung them absently against her wet-suited thigh.

'Hey,' he said.

He was looking straight at her—right into her eyes.

A part of her—a big part—was horribly aware that she wore no make-up, that she definitely had the imprint of her goggles still encircling her eyes and that *no one* looked good in a swim-cap. Meanwhile Gray, with his hair ruffled all over the place by a swift breeze, and in running shorts and a T-shirt soaked with sweat, still managed to look gorgeous.

It was incredibly annoying, and maybe that was the reason for the sharpness in her tone. 'So you've bothered to notice me today?'

Oh, no.

It was supposed to be a teasing joke, but it so, *so* wasn't. She'd sounded hurt. Upset. Not at all like a woman who'd completely moved on.

'I don't know how I ever didn't notice you before,' he said.

His words were low and…intimate.

The way they immediately made her feel—the way they made her body react—didn't help her mood. 'Yes,' she agreed. 'I am a bit of a giant woman, aren't I? Difficult to miss.'

She pivoted on her heel, spotting her towel a few metres to the left of Gray.

'That isn't what I meant at all,' he said, following her. 'And you know it.'

She snatched up her towel and then realised this was generally the point when she'd unzip the top half of her wetsuit. Briefly she considered not doing so—but then, what did she care what Gray thought?

As casually as she could she unzipped her top, peeling it down to her waist. She'd worn her new violet bikini today, and strongly wished she hadn't.

She didn't bother responding to his last comment. She didn't fully understand her frustration—in fact she had no idea why she was standing here so wound up with tension.

Why was she angry at Gray?

She glanced at Gray, meaning to say something—something about not being at her best this early in the morning, maybe—when the way he was looking at her stole the words from her throat.

He was most definitely checking her out. And she was almost one hundred percent certain that he liked what he saw. The intensity of his attention—of his *appreciation*—was like a physical touch against her skin, warm and tingling. It skimmed across her from her hips, where the wetsuit hung low, to the indent of her waist and upwards, over the small-ish curves of her breasts.

And finally to her face.

His gaze locked with hers, and she saw that he knew that *she* knew what he'd been doing.

He shrugged without even the hint of an apology. 'I have no idea how I ever didn't notice you, Lanie Smith.'

Then he turned and with Luther trotting obediently beside him walked away.

'See you at work,' he called out, and the words were whipped away by the breeze.

CHAPTER ELEVEN

THE NEXT MORNING, when Gray ran with Luther along North Cottesloe beach, Lanie was there again.

As he ran he'd occasionally search for her in the water—looking for the rhythmic splash of her kicks and the elegant way her arms sliced through the water.

When she emerged from the ocean Luther spotted her immediately and sprinted across the sand and through the water to get to her as quickly as possible. Gray couldn't have stopped him, anyway—but he didn't even try. Instead he followed in Luther's footsteps, meeting Lanie just as she stepped across the line where the sand switched abruptly from soaked and grey to almost blindingly pristine dry and white.

'Hey,' he said.

Gray wasn't sure what to expect. Yesterday at work she'd done her ultra-professional thing and it had been as if they were seeing each other for the first time that day.

Definitely not as if he'd all but imprinted the image of Lanie in that amazing bikini onto his brain.

'Hi,' Lanie said eventually—quite softly, as if she wasn't really sure talking to him was that good an idea.

He knew how she felt.

'I received an e-mail late last night from Raquel,' he said. 'She wants one of the three-bedroom villas.'

He'd planned to tell her at work, not here, but the words had burst out.

Lanie's face broke into a wide, genuine smile. 'That's fantastic!'

'Yeah,' he said as they walked to her towel. 'A big relief, too.'

He hadn't understood how much until right this moment. And Lanie got that too. She knew how important this deal was to him, and pleasure in his success was reflected in her expression.

After Lanie had stripped out of her wetsuit—she wore her one-piece bathers today, Gray noted with some disappointment—she towelled off and pulled on a tracksuit. Together they walked up the beach to the street. Gray had Luther sit while he reattached his lead to the dog's collar and he saw Lanie wave to someone. He followed her gaze to the tired-looking beach café—empty this early in the morning—and the man with the shock of white hair who was waving back to Lanie as he wiped down a table.

'Bob's my biggest fan,' Lanie said, then grinned. 'Quite possibly my only fan, actually.'

And then, together, they walked up the road, talking about the new deal—until Lanie turned up her street and Gray and Luther kept on walking along the parade.

'See you at work,' Lanie said.

But at work the beach was never mentioned.

'My dad's new wife dropped by last night,' Gray said as they walked along the beach the next day.

Lanie hadn't been surprised to see Gray waiting for her on the shore when she'd emerged from the ocean. She didn't understand why he was, but she did know seeing him watching her walk through the waves made her smile. And for now that would have to do, because she'd discovered that thinking about Gray—about any of this—was far too confusing. She didn't understand it, and certainly didn't understand Gray.

Today their conversation had been about not much—a bit

about work, but mostly nothing too important or serious—and they'd both gradually relaxed. But Gray's tone had shifted at the mention of his father.

'New wife?'

Gray nodded. 'Number seven.'

'Seven! Do you have any brothers or sisters?'

He shook his head. 'No, I'm the only one—the result of marriage number two. It was the longest my father remained married—almost three years, actually.'

'Are you close to your mum?' Lanie asked.

'We're in touch occasionally, but we're not close. My dad was really my primary carer as I grew up. He was great—very hands-on—and he'd often drag me with him to work rather than hiring a nanny or sending me to childcare. Mum went back to Sydney, where she's from, after they split, although I saw her on school holidays.'

'When you were—what? Three?' Lanie asked, incredulous.

'Two,' Gray confirmed. 'As I said, we're not close.'

Lanie nodded, but was unable to imagine a mother walking away from a child that young. For all her own mother's flaws, Lanie knew her mum loved her.

But then she guessed her father had done exactly the same thing just a few years later.

'My dad worked away,' Lanie said. 'And then left for good when I was eleven. He didn't even bother to stay in touch.'

Gray slowed down his pace just a little as he turned to her. 'So you don't see him at all?'

'Not once since he left.'

The words were matter-of-fact, but it irritated Lanie that she still felt a faint kick in the guts as she spoke. Her dad wasn't worth worrying about, and certainly not worthy of any remnants of hurt and regret.

'That sucks.'

Lanie shrugged. 'Hey, at least he gave me these shoulders,'

she said, with a grin that she only had to force a little. 'So, the new wife came over…?'

'Yeah.' Gray rubbed his forehead. 'I don't get it. It happens every time. These women inexplicably feel the need to *connect* with me. To *know* me. When I know it's a total waste of time. This one will be gone in a year—guaranteed.'

Lanie snorted with laughter. 'Wow. I can't see at *all* why this poor woman is feeling insecure around you.'

Gray looked so surprised at her comment Lanie laughed some more. 'Oh, come on. I can just imagine how you'd be around her. Probably like you were with me at first.'

And how he still was, at times. Not down here at the beach but at work, where he got so caught up in what he was doing that her presence seemed to cease to register altogether.

He opened his mouth as if he was going to protest, but then stopped. 'Possibly,' he finally conceded.

Ahead of them Luther had found a friend—a small black poodle—and together they took turns chasing each other into the water.

'But what if this one—wife number seven—is, in fact, *the one*?' Lanie asked. 'Isn't it worth getting to know her just in case?'

Now Gray laughed. 'She's barely ten years older than me. It's not going to last. My dad's one flaw is his inability to be sensible around women. For such a successful, accomplished, intelligent guy, his stubborn faith in love is bizarre. In that way I'm nothing like him.'

Lanie smiled. 'I never would've guessed.'

The Manning office gossip had confirmed what Lanie had already guessed: Gray's previous relationships had been both short-lived and superficial. Since his father had retired the consensus was that he'd been seeing no one at all, so complete was his focus on work.

'I'm not sure I agree that being a success and believing in love are mutually exclusive things,' Lanie pointed out.

'Maybe they aren't for some people,' he said. 'But my dad has lost millions with each of his marriages. And yet he keeps going back for more.'

Lanie had never heard Gray criticise his father, but his scorn for his dad's romantic history was obvious.

'And has that caused him financial difficulty?'

'With his early marriages, yes—although he argues now that it was what spurred him on to diversify the business, to take risks. Because he needed the money.'

'So he's a risk-taker in life *and* in love?' Lanie said.

'Yeah.' Gray didn't sound so happy about it.

'I think that's nice.'

They'd almost reached Luther, who was busily digging a hole now his poodle friend had left with his owner.

'Really?' Gray said. 'You don't strike me as such a romantic.'

Lanie wasn't sure if she should be offended by that. 'I like the idea of love. Of marriage and a happy-ever-after.' She paused, trying to think how to phrase this. 'But I guess more in an abstract way. Something for other people to do, not me.'

'And why not you?'

Lanie laughed. 'My longest ever relationship was two months,' she said. 'I'm not much good at them.'

She said it lightly, although Gray's gaze still sharpened as he looked at her.

'I don't know, Lanie, I—'

Gray's words were cut off by a loud yelp.

Luther.

The dog was holding his paw in the air.

Instantly, they both broke into a run.

Gray dropped to his knees in the sand, reaching out gently to inspect Luther's paw. Immediately blood splashed onto Gray's arm—blood that hadn't been obvious against Luther's dark coat.

Lanie spotted the culprit—the dog had managed to dig up

a small pile of broken bottles that some thoughtless person had long ago buried.

'He's got shards stuck all over him,' Gray said, worry heavy in his voice.

'Take him to a vet,' Lanie said. 'I'll clean this up so other dogs don't do the same thing. And I'll cancel your meetings for today.'

Gray just nodded as he hoisted Luther up into his arms, his attention entirely on his dog.

Lanie watched as he ran up to the street, faster than she'd ever seen him run before despite the heavy weight he was carrying.

Then she laid out her towel and started piling it up with glass, piece by piece.

By the time Lanie drove up to Gray's front door she knew she'd made a mistake.

She'd questioned her decision to drop by on her way home from work more than once. Firstly when she'd gone shopping in her lunch break for a large rawhide bone for Luther.

At the time she'd figured it could wait—she would simply give the treat to Gray at work tomorrow. But then she wouldn't know how Luther was.

In which case calling him should have seemed the obvious option. Except she could just imagine how that phone call would go. Odds were she'd call at a particularly inconvenient time, Gray would be all distracted, and she'd be lucky to get a handful of words out of him.

So she'd told herself dropping by on the way home from work—especially as it was kind of on her way—seemed reasonable.

Until she'd actually been in her car on the way here.

Was she breaking the rules? Did they even *have* rules around their daily beach meetings?

She had no idea.

She glanced at the bone on her passenger seat, complete with a big red bow, and pulled herself together.

She was worried about Luther and had brought him a present. That was it. No more, no less. If Gray thought that was horribly inappropriate and it meant the end of whatever it was they were doing at the beach then so be it.

Maybe the beach thing was over now, anyway.

It was never going to last, their semi-friendship. Kind of like that one-off kiss. She should have known it was temporary right from the start.

Right. So. Yes. She was going to go to Gray's house and give Luther his bone.

She'd laughed at the analysis that had required her to get to that point at the time.

Now—at Gray's front door—her hesitation didn't seem so ridiculous after all.

This was a mistake. She shouldn't be here. Gray wouldn't want her here.

She knelt down in her slim-fitting trousers to leave the bone at the front door.

Maybe she'd send Gray a text to let him know she'd left it. Or ring the doorbell and then run away like some eleven-year-old playing a prank.

That idea—and the image of her running down Marine Parade in her heels—made her giggle. She was still giggling when the door swung open.

'Lanie?'

She looked up from where she was crouching on his doorstep—up long legs clad in faded jeans to his soft, ancient-looking T-shirt—to his bemused expression.

She shot to her feet. 'Oh!' she said. Then thrust out the bone she still held in his direction. 'I bought Luther a bone.'

'Thanks,' Gray said, and his lips kept quirking upwards, as if he was trying not to smile. 'Nice bow.'

'I thought so,' she said. 'Anyway, I didn't want to disturb you, so I'll just get going…'

'Do you want to see Luther?'

Lanie knew it was far from wise to stay any longer, and yet she found herself nodding enthusiastically. 'Yes, please. How is he?'

Gray held the door open for her, then followed her inside. 'He's okay. He needed some stitches, so he's a bit dopey from the anaesthetic, but he'll be as good as new in a few weeks' time.'

'That's excellent.'

Luther was curled up on a big cushion on the floor in Gray's lounge room. The huge windows showcased the rapidly setting sun and also provided an unobstructed view of the front porch. With the window's dark tinting on the outside she'd had no idea she was being watched. No wonder he'd been hiding a laugh—how long had she been dithering out there?

'Why didn't you knock?' he asked.

'I didn't want to bother you.'

'What if I don't mind being bothered?'

Lanie laughed. 'You hate being bothered.'

He shrugged. 'For you I'll make an exception.'

Suddenly uncomfortable, Lanie knelt down in front of Luther and scratched behind his long, floppy ears. He wore a large plastic cone to stop him licking his wounds, and looked most unhappy about the situation. 'Hey, buddy,' she said, low and soothing. 'You doing okay?'

Luther looked up at her with his gorgeous chocolate eyes and out of nowhere, Lanie felt her throat tighten.

What was she upset about? Luther, thank goodness, was going to be okay.

She stood up, walking briskly over to the kitchen to put some space between herself and Gray. 'Do you mind if I grab some water?' she asked.

Gray followed her—which wasn't part of the plan. So she moved to the opposite side of the bench as he found her a glass, needing that large slab of granite between them.

'I should've called you,' Gray said as he pushed her water across the counter top. 'Told you how he was.' He nodded in Luther's direction.

'No,' Lanie said, 'of course you shouldn't. You had Luther to worry about.'

He shook his head. 'I should've called you,' he repeated. 'I'm sorry.'

Lanie wrapped her fingers around the frosty glass. 'Okay,' she said. 'I'm glad you didn't come into work, though. I'm sure Luther appreciated it.'

Gray tilted his head back a little, as if he was suddenly intensely fascinated by his ceiling. He gave a short bark of laughter.

'That wasn't entirely why I didn't come in.' His gaze dropped to meet hers and he leant forward, gripping the edge of the granite with both hands. 'I didn't come in because I received *two* phone calls this morning while I was at the vet. Two more of the Hoi An potentials.' A pause. 'They're out.' He managed a humourless grin. 'Great timing, too.'

'Oh, Gray,' Lanie said, resisting the urge to go to him and…and *what,* exactly? She stayed put. 'I'm really surprised.'

'Me too,' he said. 'After Raquel signed up I thought I had it in the bag. That all that stuff we talked about in Vietnam really didn't matter—that nothing actually had changed since my dad retired.' He laughed again. 'That it was all in my head. Guess not.'

'It probably has nothing to do with you,' Lanie said. 'The investment just wasn't right for them.'

'What I do, Lanie, is target the right investors with the right projects at the right time. Those investors all had money to spend, and I'd hand-selected them. If the product was wrong for them that's *my* fault. If the weekend sales pitch was wrong for them, that's my fault too.' He walked to the fridge and grabbed a long-necked bottle of beer. Lanie watched as he twisted off the top and then just left the beer on the counter, as if he'd already changed his mind. 'So I stayed home this afternoon to mope with Luther.' He did that ugly grin again. 'Real professional of me.'

'I think you're being too tough on yourself,' Lanie said. 'I'm sure no one has a one hundred percent strike rate with this type of thing—not even your dad. You did your best. That's all you can do.'

His gaze jerked up to tangle with hers. Instantly she knew where this was going and took a step backwards before she'd even realised what she was doing.

'*Really,* Lanie? You think that doing your best is all that matters? I find that hard to believe.'

There was no point pretending she didn't understand what he meant.

Very deliberately, Lanie stepped forward again. 'I *did* do the best I could. I trained the hardest I could. I swam the best I could—my best time *ever* in the selection trials. I'm proud of what I achieved. That *is* all that matters.'

'You're right,' Gray said. 'Of course you're right. You should be incredibly proud of what you achieved—you *are* a champion. But I don't think you really believe that, do you?'

Lanie stared at her untouched water glass. 'I don't really think this is any of your business.'

'Why not?'

Her head jerked up. 'Because you're my boss and I'm your employee. This is all a bit personal, don't you think?'

All Lanie's sensible plans to remain on her side of the counter were ruined as Gray strode over to her. She crossed her arms, not about to back down.

'Is that all we are, Lanie?'

She nodded, very stiffly. 'Haven't we already covered this?'

'What are we doing at the beach each morning?'

Lanie shrugged. 'I swim. You run. We happen to do it at the same time.'

'Come on. That's crap and you know it. Why are you being so stubborn about this?'

Her eyes narrowed. 'I should get going.' She went to step around Gray. 'Bye, Luther,' she said.

But Gray grabbed her hand as she brushed past. 'Wait.'

She was right next to him and she twisted around to meet his gaze. 'Please don't touch me.'

He didn't loosen his grip one iota. But then she knew if she really wanted to pull away, she could. But she didn't.

She couldn't.

'Why can't I touch you?' Gray said, a dangerous glint to his slate-grey eyes. 'Because you can't concentrate? Why *is* that?'

Lanie glared at him. 'You know perfectly well what it is. You probably have women collapsing at your feet all the time. Don't act like you don't know the effect you have on women. You know *exactly* what you're doing.'

He took a step closer to her. Too close. But she felt frozen in place, incapable of doing anything but *looking* at him.

'Yes, I know what I'm doing,' Gray said, all soft and low. 'I can't speak for other women, but I have a pretty good idea what I do to *you*.'

Her body already felt hot, confused. Now an all-over mortified blush was added to the mix. Why did she have to be so transparent?

Finally her ability to use her limbs returned and she tugged her hand from his grip, taking a handful of steps away before turning to face him. 'What are you trying to prove? Just exactly how smug and arrogant you are?'

He walked towards her. Slow, deliberate steps.

'Has it ever occurred to you, Lanie Smith, that you have the same effect on me?'

All she could do was stare at him.

He took another step. Close enough to touch.

'I—' she began—but she really had no idea what to say. Her instinct was to deny—to shake her head and tell him that he was wrong, that this was unfair, that he didn't really mean that.

But would she actually believe what she was saying?

Did she really believe that incredible kiss at the Night Market had really been so one-sided? That their daily meetings at the beach were solely between work colleagues—or at a stretch, friends?

Or was it more that she hadn't wanted to acknowledge what was going on? That she didn't want to allow herself to consider—or hope—it was something more?

Because she knew she couldn't deal with another *no* right now. Another rejection. Another failure.

'What are we doing?' she managed eventually. 'What *is* this?'

Gray's lips quirked upwards. 'I have absolutely no idea. But right now I'd really like to kiss you.'

Well, when he put it like that...

What to do seemed obvious—the only thing possible. She reached for him blindly, her hand landing on his chest. Instantly his arms wrapped around her, pulling her close while he turned her, lifted her, and the next thing she knew she was sitting on the counter-top, Gray standing between her legs, her face cradled between his hands.

She'd never felt so delicate, so light—so sexy.

Then his mouth touched hers.

And just like at the Night Market suddenly it was as if this kiss was her whole world.

But this time there was no prelude, no preliminaries—it was immediately and completely desperate. He tasted delicious, fresh and clean, and he kissed her as if he'd been thinking about doing nothing else for weeks.

It was overwhelming—but also unbelievably good. With each and every kiss she felt her doubts flutter away.

That Gray was kissing *her*, that he wanted *her*, was obvious in every touch, every breath. His hands slid from her face to her waist, doing electric, shivery things to her insides as his hands moved upwards.

She had to get closer to him, had to feel his skin, and she tugged him closer, pushing his T-shirt up in messy handfuls of cotton.

His skin was hot beneath her palms—hot and firm and lean. He was kissing his way up her jaw to her throat and she heard his sharp intake of breath when she ran her fingernails along his spine. She gave a little laugh of surprise and felt his lips form a smile against her skin.

'Told you,' he said.

And she laughed again, before his hands, his mouth, just *him* swiftly converted it to a sigh. Then he was kissing her mouth again. And from then on that kiss—this night—was all that mattered.

CHAPTER TWELVE

'Tell me about your swimming.'

Lanie turned on her side to face Gray in bed. He'd propped his head on his hand and his gaze traced over her shape beneath the bedsheet. Said sheet had dipped quite low on his side of the bed, and Lanie found herself distracted by how lovely all that naked skin looked in the soft light of Gray's bedside lamp.

She cleared her throat. 'Um…*that's* what you want to talk about right now?'

He grinned. 'It's not every night I have a swimming champion in my bed.'

'Former swimmer.'

'Oh, yeah,' he said, looking thoughtful. 'Good point. Come to think of it, I've had *many* former world-class athletes. It's easy to lose track with all those women collapsing at my feet.'

She shoved him in the chest, but ruined the effect by giggling.

'Hey—*your* words,' he said, then reached out to tug her on top of him as he rolled onto his back, so Lanie lay half on top of him.

She almost said something about her being far too heavy—but she stopped herself. Gray wouldn't listen. And besides, for once in her life she actually didn't feel all that big. In fact, she didn't think she'd ever felt more feminine. More pretty.

'So?' he prompted.

'What do you want to know?'

'How about you tell me what it's like to represent Australia.'

Lanie closed her eyes for a moment, thinking. It took a mental shift to refocus on her past successes. They seemed a lifetime ago.

'It's such a cliché,' she said. 'But, honestly, just being there was incredible. I wasn't expected to make the team—even six weeks before the trials I never thought I had a chance. I'd been unwell earlier in the year—a bad case of the flu—so even to make the team as a relay swimmer was a huge achievement. Then when I got there…'

She spoke for longer than she'd intended. Told him about her sense of anticipation before the relay heats, how the noise of the crowd had somehow drifted away as she'd stood on the blocks, waiting for the split second the previous swimmer touched the wall. How the whole meet had seemed surreal—even the weeks and months after.

Even now it felt as if that experience had happened to somebody else.

'It's an amazing thing you achieved—you do know that, right?'

Lanie caught Gray's gaze as he studied her face. 'Yeah,' she said honestly. 'I do know. No matter what else happens in my life, I'll always have that.'

'But you really wanted more.'

She blinked, surprised. 'Of course. At one point I had a chance of swimming in the women's hundred metres as well as the relay. I had a really good year. But then a couple of the younger girls caught up with me.' Lanie managed a casual laugh. 'As you mentioned once, I'm not all that young for a swimmer.'

'You're not old, either. Twenty-six, right?'

'Good internet searching,' she teased.

'Plenty of time for a new dream, then.'

Instantly Lanie went tense and rolled away from Gray to sit on the edge of the bed, her back to him. Her eyes scanned the room, trying to locate her clothing.

'Why do you do that?' he asked. 'Why can't you answer that question?'

'Why do you keep on asking it?'

Her shirt was just within arm's reach and she snatched it up, pulling it on over her shoulders in an awkward movement.

'Because the drive that got you so far doesn't just go away. No one trains that hard for so long without being a little bit obsessed.'

He paused. He wasn't telling her anything she didn't already know.

'I love my career,' Gray continued, 'and I love Manning even now, even when it isn't going as well as I'd like. I *need* it. I need that focus. It's different, but still I guess it's an obsession. I can't imagine not having it.'

It was on the tip of her tongue to argue. To tell him he was wrong, that it *was* completely different.

But maybe it wasn't. It seemed ridiculous that she and Gray could be similar in any way at all, but was it possible?

Lanie wasn't entirely convinced. Besides, he wasn't the first person to ask what she was going to do now. To want to know how she'd fill this new void in her life.

But he was the first person to persist when she didn't answer. The first person who seemed to *need* to know—as if it was incomprehensible to him that she could exist without a goal. Without a dream.

Because he knew that *he* couldn't.

So maybe they weren't so different after all.

With a sigh, she stilled her hands, her shirt still half unbuttoned. She twisted around to face Gray and pulled her knees back onto the mattress.

'I told a friend the other day that I was going to go back to uni. Finish a degree I started a few years ago.'

Gray nodded.

Lanie chewed on her bottom lip, knowing she could just leave it at that. She'd answered the question and now watching Gray watching her, she knew this time he wasn't going to push.

But he knew in a way Teagan hadn't that she wasn't all that sure going back to uni was the answer. It was clear in the way he looked at her. In the still lingering questions in his eyes.

'The thing is,' she said eventually, 'I don't know if that degree is what I really want. If it will lead me anywhere near where I want to go. Wherever that is.' There was a long, long pause. 'I don't know what I want at all.'

Her throat felt tight and she blinked away the prickling in her eyes as she crawled across the bed to Gray. He met her halfway and drew her into his arms.

Then she kissed him—because she desperately wanted to, and also because she didn't want him to see her cry.

The next day was Saturday, so they had breakfast at Bob's Café.

They didn't swim, or run, as Luther wasn't really up to either. Instead he curled up at Gray's feet, banging his cone-shaped collar on their chair-legs whenever he moved. It was warm, and they weren't alone in pretending it was already summer: the café was packed, as was the beach below them.

Bob came over with a menu, handing it to Lanie.

'Taking the weekend off?' he asked her.

She nodded, but Gray could see her smile was a little forced.

'I'll be back in the water on Monday,' she said.

'Good, good…' the old man muttered, then wandered away to take an order from another table.

Lanie leant back in her chair and propped the menu against the edge of the table. Her sunglasses-covered eyes were looking at Gray, and not at what they were going to have for breakfast.

'He doesn't give up,' she said. 'I don't get it.'

'Bob?' he prompted.

She nodded vigorously. 'First he was on about me swimming, and now that I am he's checking up on me. It's bizarre—like he's convinced I'm going to make some amazing swimming comeback or something.'

'Is that why he's asking?'

Lanie shrugged. 'Why else would he?'

Gray didn't know, but the man's persistence bothered him. Lanie wasn't going to swim competitively again. She'd made that clear. She certainly didn't need someone making her feel guilty about that, however well meaning.

'Do you mind if I ask?'

'Knock yourself out.'

A few minutes later Bob returned to take their orders.

'Lanie's retired,' Gray said, which wasn't exactly what he'd meant to say. There was an edge to his tone he also hadn't intended—but then, he'd never been known for his tactfulness.

The older man appeared unmoved. 'Yes, I'm aware of that.'

Lanie leant forward. 'And I'm not planning on competing again. When I swim now I'm not training. I'm just swimming.'

Bob turned to her. 'I know that too. So, what can I get you today?'

Lanie gave a little huff of frustration. 'Then why do you keep asking me about my swimming?'

For the first time Bob seemed to realise that Lanie was unhappy. There was a spare chair at their small table, and he pulled it out to sit down.

'It's simple, really, Lanie—you're a swimmer. A beautiful swimmer. You should swim. You're unhappy when you don't. I've seen you swim on TV before—I've seen the fire in your eyes and the joy you take to the pool. When you quit you were miserable.'

'I was miserable because I didn't make the team,' she clarified.

Bob shrugged. 'Possibly. But you're happier now you're swimming again.' He stood up again. 'Now, what can I get you?'

They ordered, and Gray studied Lanie as she sipped her coffee.

'That was kind of weird,' she said. 'But kind of nice.'

'Anyone who's seen you swim can see where he's coming from. You're something else in the water.'

A natural. His ocean nymph.

Gray smiled at such an uncharacteristically romantic idea. *Look what Lanie did to him.*

'Do you feel like a swim?'

Lanie raised an eyebrow. 'What? Now? It must be almost midnight. And,' she added, 'it's not exactly warm.'

The weather's premature attempt at summer had disappeared along with the setting sun. After breakfast they'd walked leisurely along the beach with Luther, enjoying the warmth and the salty breeze. Later they'd gone out to pick up Thai food for dinner, and by then it had been cool enough for Gray to wrap an arm over Lanie's shoulders as they'd returned to his car.

The action had surprised her—yet it had also felt somehow natural and almost normal.

Kind of like the entire weekend.

Now they sat together on one of Gray's soft leather sofas. Lanie had her feet curled up beneath her and a half-finished glass of wine in her hand. Gray was sprawled out beside her, his feet propped up on an ottoman. Beneath the bridge of his legs lay Luther, happily asleep and snoring softly.

'Why not? My pool's heated.'

Lanie grinned. '*Ooh,* fancy.'

'Only the best for Luther.'

She looked down at the slumbering dog. 'I don't think he's up for a swim.'

'No,' Gray agreed. 'And I can't say *he's* my preferred swimming companion tonight.'

His gaze caught hers and held—and its heat made Lanie's skin go hot, and somewhere low in her belly became liquid.

Lanie wondered if at some point she would get used to this. To her instant, visceral reaction to Gray.

Then he smiled at her.

A slow, sexy, smile.

No, she decided. She wouldn't—she couldn't.

Everything about Gray—the way he looked at her, the way he touched her, the sound of his voice—was almost too much. She'd never get used to it.

At the back of her mind a little voice niggled, attempting to remind her that she wouldn't get the chance to *get used* to Gray, anyway.

Lanie didn't know what this weekend was, but she did know that right now she couldn't think beyond it. And Gray certainly wasn't. They had tonight and tomorrow. That was it.

'I didn't bring my bathers,' Lanie said.

Another smile. 'I don't think that'll be a problem.'

The pool was deliciously warm.

Lanie swam its length under water, heading towards Gray's board-shorts-clad legs in the shallow end.

She surfaced beside him, standing. Her upper body cleared the water and her skin goosepimpled where it was exposed to the cool night air.

It was dark in Gray's garden, the only light coming from tiny uplights that glowed amongst the decking that surrounded the pool.

'You do realise you are very nearly naked in that get-up?' Gray asked. His gaze roamed over her—slowly enough to make her skin tingle.

Lanie glanced down at her underwear. She'd stopped at home earlier that day, so she was wearing her absolutely best lingerie—pale pink satin edged with white lace. Unfortunately at the time it hadn't occurred to her to grab her bathers, and underwear wasn't that great a substitute. As she'd expected, her bra clung to her like a second skin—and she didn't want to even *think* what the chlorine was doing to it.

'But I'm not naked,' Lanie said primly. 'I really do feel modesty is *quite* underrated these days.'

Gray's mouth curved upwards. 'Or,' he said, 'you're just chicken.'

Lanie sniffed deliberately. 'Well, I think I deserve a little more respect for showing some decorum—'

Her words ended on a shriek as Gray launched himself at her and they both ended up underwater. By the time they resurfaced Lanie was *sans* bra, and Gray held it aloft triumphantly.

Lanie couldn't help but grin back—especially as she realised it didn't bother her at all to be topless in front of Gray. How strange… Only minutes ago she'd almost lost her nerve while undressing beside the pool, but now—unexpectedly— it was okay.

Quite possibly Gray's *very* admiring gaze had something to do with it.

'You are gorgeous, Lanie Smith,' he said, soft and low.

Suddenly uncomfortable again, she automatically moved her arms to cover herself.

Gray's eyes narrowed. 'Don't,' he said.

'Gray, I'm not gorgeous—'

'Want to race?' he interrupted.

'What?'

'To the other end and back? Ready?' He didn't wait for her to reply. 'Go!'

He was off in a huge splash of water before she'd had a chance to register what was going on.

And because it was so ingrained in her she found herself swimming after him as fast as she could.

But even with a championship-quality tumble turn he still beat her back to the wall.

'I knew it!' he crowed, tongue firmly in cheek. 'That was just a lucky race in Vietnam.'

'How about we go again?' Lanie asked. 'This time both starting at the same time.'

Gray shrugged. 'I'd love to, but…'

'But?'

He grinned. 'This way we finish with me winning.'

Lanie laughed out loud.

But her laughter faded away to nothing when Gray stepped closer. He reached out to tuck a stray strand of soaked hair behind her ear.

'I like your hair like this,' he said.

'Wet, messy and knotty?' Lanie asked in disbelief. She reached up, patting at her hair ineffectually.

Gray's hand moved to still hers. 'Slicked back like this, so I can see your face properly.' He moved his hand from hers to trail a fingertip along her cheekbone, then down along her jaw. 'You have a lovely face.'

She shook her head unthinkingly and Gray's fingers slipped beneath her chin to still the movement. He tipped her chin upwards, so she was forced to meet his steely gaze.

'Let me say nice things to you, Lanie.'

She looked away, looked everywhere but at Gray—at the plants around the pool, the water surrounding them, then up at the moon.

But Gray still held her gently in place, and now he leant forward, his breath warm against the damp skin beneath her ear.

'I'm not making this stuff up, Lanie. I mean it.'

His words and his proximity made her shiver.

But not quite believe him.

And he knew. He sighed loudly in frustration. 'I'm not in the habit of lying.'

Lanie took a step backwards. 'You barely knew I existed until recently. Can you see how that might leave me a little unconvinced of your compliments now? From invisible to *lovely* or *gorgeous* is quite a jump.'

She could just process the idea that he was attracted to her, but the concept that she was anything approaching beautiful was a step too far.

'Lanie, I—'

She ignored him. 'You didn't even notice—'

She stopped, not liking the vulnerability in her tone.

'Notice what?'

She attempted a smile. 'My make-over. You know—new outfits, new hair, new make-up?'

Gray's forehead furrowed as he considered her words.

Suddenly Lanie wished she'd done as her mother had always taught her and simply thanked Gray for his compliment. She didn't even know what she was trying to achieve—did she actually want Gray to *agree* that, in fact, she wasn't even close to beautiful?

Really, there were far worse things to deal with than a man like Gray insisting on pretending she was something she wasn't.

'The day I asked you to come with me to Vietnam,' Gray said.

'Pardon me?'

His look was typical frustrated Grayson Manning. 'That was the first day you came to work after your make-over, or whatever. It was, wasn't it?'

Lanie nodded mutely.

'I thought so. Your hair was different. It reminded me of the day you tied it back for the first time. I remember I liked it.'

Another silent, incredulous nod.

He stepped forward, closing the gap between them again. He reached out, sliding a hand onto her hip beneath the water. Somehow she'd managed to forget her near naked state, but Gray's touch was an instant reminder. And now she didn't feel awkward or shy. Instead the soft breeze against her skin felt…amazing.

So did she.

'Why did you do it?' he asked softly. 'The make-over?'

'I was sick of being invisible,' Lanie said. 'And not just to you,' she added, only for the first time acknowledging that. 'But also in general. I've spent my whole life in my little sister's shadow.'

'You're not invisible, Lanie. I didn't pay as much attention as I should have, but I did notice you. Everything's been about Manning for me these past few months. It's all I think about it. It's all I do.' He paused, as if he'd just realised something surprising. 'Until now,' he said. 'Actually, ever since you argued with me about Vietnam.'

'Not agreeing with you instantly is *not* arguing,' she pointed out.

He shrugged his shoulders dismissively, but smiled. 'Since then, I can assure you, you've been far, far from invisible.'

His hand at her hip pulled her closer, then closer still, so she was pressed up against him, skin to skin.

She tilted her head upwards so their lips were only centimetres apart—but Gray didn't close that small gap.

'You're gorgeous, Lanie.'

He waited, her gaze caught in his.

'Thank you,' she said.

Then—finally—he kissed her.

* * *

They needed to talk about what was going to happen tomorrow at work.

Lanie knew that.

But she couldn't quite do it.

Of course neither of them had spoken about what was going on. Or about what was going to happen next.

All they had was this remarkable electric connection between them—but then, that was just physical attraction. Chemicals.

It didn't mean Gray wanted anything more from her than this weekend.

It didn't mean that *she* wanted anything more.

Did she?

They sat together on the balcony adjacent to Gray's bedroom. Dinner—a platter of cheeses and antipasto they'd thrown together—was on a small table, but they'd both stopped eating a while ago.

The sun was well on its way to dipping beneath the Indian Ocean's horizon. It was deep and red as it sank lower amongst the clouds it streaked in purples, oranges and gold.

Once the sun disappeared, *then* she'd talk to Gray.

But say what, exactly?

She had no idea.

Beneath them a cream-coloured, clearly extremely expensive sedan, turned into Gray's driveway.

Gray swore, and she raised an eyebrow in his direction.

'My dad,' he said in explanation, pulling himself to his feet.

And then, without another word, he walked back into his room. Moments later she could hear the thud of his feet on the stairs.

Lanie watched as a tall man—she would have instantly identified him as Gray's father anyway—opened the passenger side door for a delicate woman. She wore a polka-dot sundress, stacked platform heels and huge, oversized Hollywood sunglasses.

She looked exactly like the type of woman she'd expect *Gray* to date. Perfect, straight from the pages of a magazine—kind of the way Sienna was dressed in that Paris photoshoot, in fact.

Lanie looked down at herself. She'd only gone home briefly to grab some clothes, but her wardrobe didn't have anything like that woman's dress inside it regardless. She wore faded jeans, leather sandals and a loose camisole top. Very casual, very relaxed.

She'd felt good in what she was wearing. Thanks to Gray she'd felt good about everything she'd been wearing—or not—all weekend. Until about two minutes ago.

The front garden was now empty, and Lanie could hear the murmur of voices in the kitchen, followed by footsteps ascending the stairs.

'Lanie?'

Gray was standing at the doorway to his room and Lanie stood, stepping through the billowy curtains onto the thick carpet.

'My dad and his wife have surprised me with a homemade dinner.'

Gray sounded several notches below thrilled.

'Okay...'

And?

Lanie wished fervently that she'd got her act together earlier, or even that the sun had set faster. Then she would know what was going on—she'd know if Gray expected her to stay or if he wanted her to disappear into the distance.

As it was, she just felt terribly awkward. As if it was somehow her fault for being here.

She explored Gray's expression for some hint of what he was thinking.

But it was difficult. He wasn't even looking at her. Instead, he was looking past her—at the setting sun, maybe, or quite possibly at nothing at all.

Definitely not at *her*.

Lanie stiffened her shoulders. It had been so long since Gray had looked at her like this—or rather *not* looked at her, she'd forgotten how much it hurt. Or at least she'd thought she'd forgotten.

But just like that—just one dismissive glance—and she remembered. She remembered that first morning at the beach, when she'd felt invisible.

Last night he'd told her she was far from invisible.

Beautiful words she'd so pathetically wanted to hear.

But his glance now told her that was all they were—beautiful, *meaningless* words.

'Do you want to stay for dinner?' he asked.

She should have been pleased, but she wasn't. There was no question now about what Gray wanted her to do. And it *wasn't* to sit down for a cosy dinner with his family.

The simplest thing, probably the smartest, would have been to come up with some excuse for why she needed to go. Easier for her—she could pretend to be a breezy, fancy-free woman who had incredible weekend flings without a care in the world—and much, much easier for him. But she just couldn't.

'Do you want me to stay?'

She needed to hear him say it. She needed the answer to the question she should have asked hours ago: *What's going to happen tomorrow?*

Gray's gaze flicked to hers and held, and for once she wished he'd kept on looking out of the window. Because seeing him looking at her—truly looking at her when he spoke—meant she already knew the answer. And, stupidly, when she'd asked it she'd still held the smallest smidgen of useless hope.

'It's probably better if you go,' he said.

Lanie nodded.

There—she had her answer.

Tomorrow, nothing was going to happen. Because whatever they'd had, it was over.

She followed Gray out of the house, past the curious glances of Gray's father and his beautiful, perfect wife and out through the front door.

He didn't walk her to her car. He barely looked at her.

She was—once again—utterly and completely invisible.

He muttered something about work, but Lanie could barely hear a thing past the furious mix of anger and humiliation that powered through her veins.

Lanie considered skipping her morning swim the next day.

In fact lying in bed for as long as possible had very significant appeal.

But a mixture of things—Bob's words, partly, but mostly her own need to feel the drag of the ocean against her skin—hauled her from her bed. Earlier than normal, though. With luck, she'd be long gone before Gray made his way down to the beach. If he came down at all.

She didn't wear a wetsuit. The perfect almost-summery weather had persisted, although it was still far from warm this early in the morning. She thought maybe the full brunt of the cool water would help knock some sense into her.

Or something, anyway.

Stroke, stroke, *breathe*. Stroke, stroke, *breathe*.

It was her racing breathing pattern, and her stroke rate was well up. This wasn't a leisurely swim while she let her mind drift. She was powering through the water, slicing through it as fast as she could.

Every muscle in her body ached. She hadn't warmed up properly. She hadn't intended to swim like this—to swim this fast.

But she couldn't help herself. She needed to do this.

Needed to remind herself of the speed she was capable of. Of her power.

This she could control. She couldn't control the outcome of the team selection trials. She couldn't control the contrast between her sister's success and her own. She couldn't control whether Gray wanted more from her than a weekend. And it seemed she certainly couldn't control how she felt about that.

But she *could* control her body. She could harness the height and the strength she'd been born with, the years of training and perfecting her technique. She could swim, and swim brilliantly.

Her arms tangled in something and she came to an abrupt halt. She gasped, treading water, as she took a moment to register exactly what she'd swum into.

Seaweed—browny-green and curling. She pulled it from her arm, then rotated on the spot to look back towards North Cottesloe beach.

She was breathing heavily. She was far from race-fit and her body wasn't used to such punishment.

But, strangely she quite liked the ache in her lungs, the way her chest was heaving and the way her legs felt heavy as they moved in the water.

She felt alive. Wide awake. Not in that fog of hurt and anger she'd been existing in since she'd driven away from Gray's house last night.

She'd been so, *so* stupid.

As if Gray had *ever* suggested he wanted anything more from her than an opportunity for them both to explore the unexpected electricity between them.

He hadn't promised her anything. He hadn't even implied.

And yet she'd relaxed into his world with him over the weekend—she'd relaxed around *him*. She'd let down the walls that she'd so carefully built—walls intended to keep her from hurt just like this.

She was angry with him for the way he'd treated her last

night. But mostly she was angry at herself. She should never have allowed herself to be in that situation. It should never have happened.

She swam back to the shore much more slowly, taking her time and keeping her head above water as she swam leisurely breaststrokes. It seemed Bob was onto something, although today she couldn't say that swimming was making her happy.

But it helped.

CHAPTER THIRTEEN

JUST BEFORE NINE A.M., Lanie strode into his office.

He'd been there for hours, arriving even before sunrise. His theory had been that the familiarity of work would be a good distraction.

The fact he even needed a distraction bothered him. His time with Lanie was never going to be anything long-term, let alone permanent. He'd always known that, and he assumed Lanie had too.

He hadn't really planned on it being *quite* so short, but really it was for the best.

His father's raised eyebrows and blunt questions after Lanie had left only underlined that.

'Who is she?'

'A work colleague?'

'Not a girlfriend?'

'No.'

'You're sure?'

'Absolutely.'

At the time he'd answered his father's questions honestly.

She wasn't his girlfriend. But later he'd felt uncomfortable, as if he'd lied.

Which was just stupid.

Now he just needed to apologise to Lanie for the awkwardness of last night and for causing her rushed exit—and that would be that.

But he didn't really believe that. He had a pretty good idea what was going to happen. The odd thing was, he wasn't happy about it.

Lanie came right up to his desk. Onto it she dropped a brilliant white envelope, his name neatly typed on its front.

'My letter of resignation,' she said.

Yes, exactly as he'd expected.

'You don't have to do that.'

She laughed. 'Ah, I think I do, Gray. You made that pretty clear last night.'

He pushed his chair back and came around to her side of the desk. He could see her considering and then resisting an impulse to back away. She stood her ground, of course—it was what she did.

He could count on one hand the other people who stood up to him, but he liked it that she did. Really, *really* liked it.

She'd forced him to see her properly, to really notice her—and to want to understand her.

Over the weekend he'd begun to think that maybe he did.

Which was fanciful. A weekend plus a handful of walks along the beach was nothing. It was as silly a romantic notion as his imagining of Lanie as an ocean nymph.

That should have been the red flag—the flashing stop sign he'd needed. At the time he'd ignored the warnings. It had been his dad arriving with his head still in the sparkling, naïve clouds about Wife Number Seven that had finally galvanised him.

He wasn't about to get caught up in the moment the way his father was so apt to do. To extrapolate a simple weekend of fun into something much, much more. No way.

Especially now. Manning couldn't afford the risk.

'I mean it. Although of course I understand if you want to move on. But you're welcome to stay. I'm sure we can retain our professional relationship.'

Lanie snorted with laughter.

'Professional like how we kissed in Vietnam? Or, even better, how we spent most of the weekend naked in your bed? Yeah, that was *super*-professional.'

She was trying to brazen it out, but he didn't miss the pink hint to her cheeks.

He didn't know why he was trying to argue with her. She was right. Their working together was not a smart idea. Standing this close to her only made that reality more clear.

Despite how inappropriate it was to be thinking it right this second, all he wanted to do was reach out and touch her. To drag her into his arms and carry on as if yesterday evening had never happened. To take them back to those moments as she'd watched the sun set over the Indian Ocean and all he'd been watching was her.

'I believe my contract requires two weeks' notice,' she said, when he remained silent. 'I'll honour that, of course. I'm sure the agency will be able to find a suitable replacement in that time.'

Gray just nodded.

He tried to hold her gaze, tried to interpret what she was thinking. Usually it was easy—she had such a direct way of looking at him. Direct and open, as if all her thoughts and feelings were on display.

But this morning it was different. She wasn't looking straight at him. She was looking at a spot on his shirt, or over his shoulder. Not at him.

She turned on her heel to walk away, but he reached out, touched her arm.

Just enough to stop her rapid exit—then his hand fell away.

'I apologise for last night,' he said. 'I was very rude. I—'

'Don't worry about it,' she said with a dismissive wave of her hand. 'It's fine.' She laughed. 'I don't think our weekend was really an appropriate prelude to dinner with the in-laws, do you?'

She made their weekend sound...like what?

He couldn't argue with her. She made it sound exactly as it was—a bit of fun. A fling. A weekend. Nothing more.

'You've got nothing to apologise for, Gray. We both knew what we were getting into, and it was fun while it lasted. But I think we can both agree it's for the best that it's over. You're not interested in anything long-term. And I...' There was a long, long pause. She swallowed. 'We both know that my life is messy right now. I need to sort myself out, figure out where my life is taking me now I don't have a medal to reach for. You've actually helped me realise that. And you're right— this job is *not* where I should be. Especially now.'

He didn't want to believe her. She'd been upset last night. Angry.

As if he'd hurt her. But she spoke today as if she'd wanted nothing more than he had.

As if she agreed that it was for the best it was over almost before it started.

Did she mean it?

He gave himself a mental shake. Of course she did. And if she didn't what was he going to do? Would anything about the situation change?

Of course not. He knew he'd done the right thing. He should be glad that she agreed—that in fact he hadn't hurt her feelings the way he'd feared.

What sort of person would he be if he wasn't?

'You don't have to give notice,' Gray said. 'Actually, if you'd prefer, you can finish immediately.'

Lanie blinked and her mouth dropped open. 'But you have meetings all day, and I'm only halfway through that report—'

'I'll manage,' he said, cutting her off. 'Really. And I'll pay out your notice period, too, to give you a chance to find another job.'

She bristled. 'If I'm not working for you, you're not paying me.'

He shrugged. 'Then it's up to you.'

She chewed on her bottom lip.

'Okay. I'll finish up what I'm working on. It should only take a few hours.'

Then she nodded sharply, as if to confirm her decision, before finally walking out of his office.

After lunch Gray had a meeting across the city that ran well over time. By the time he returned Lanie was gone, her desk completely spotless.

It was for the best.

Teagan had arrived with a very large box of chocolates.

She thrust them at Lanie as she opened the door. 'I have no idea what this is about, but I thought calories and soft centres might help.'

'I'm sorry to worry you,' Lanie said. 'Honestly, it's not that big a deal…'

Her friend held up her phone to Lanie as they walked into the lounge room, her text message clearly displayed.

'Ahem…' she said, '"*Call me, please. I need to talk to you.*" And no smiley face. So I knew it was serious.'

'I sent it at a low point of my day,' Lanie said. Just after she'd resigned. 'It was possibly over-dramatic.'

Teagan studied her sceptically. 'Right. Because you're *so* inclined towards hysterics.'

Lanie located a bottle-opener and went to work uncorking the Cabernet Sauvignon she'd picked up on the way home. When Teagan had called she'd asked her to come over after work instead. At the time she'd thought it would be easier than explaining the past few weeks over the phone. But now she had a sneaky suspicion she'd just been delaying talking about Gray.

But she did need to talk. She figured she'd just get it all out and then it would really be done. Over.

Although that was what she'd thought resigning would achieve.

Right in the middle of pouring the wine, Lanie found she couldn't wait any longer.

'I slept with Grayson Manning,' she said.

Teagan dropped the box of chocolates on the floor.

Most of the bottle of wine later, Lanie lay stretched out on her mother's overstuffed sofa, swirling the last of the wine in her glass. Across from her Teagan was sprawled in an armchair, her long legs overhanging the arm and swinging rhythmically to the sounds of late-night radio and the hits of a decade ago.

'You know,' Teagan said, 'I think this is a good thing.'

'How, exactly?'

Her friend turned her head on the chair's arm to look at her. 'I thought you needed to go out and have some fun. And I like that you finally did something even vaguely less than sensible.'

Lanie rolled her eyes. 'I slept with my boss, then quit my job without any other source of income.'

'See?' Teagan said. 'That's so unlike you. I like it.'

Lanie had to laugh.

'It's addictive, you know,' Teagan said. 'Doing impulsive things. Living your life in the moment.' She studied Lanie as if pondering something. 'It's a real pity you didn't get more than a weekend with this guy. Stretch the fun out a bit longer, you know?'

Lanie had told Teagan everything—almost.

She'd described the Night Market, their walks along the beach, that kiss on top of his kitchen bench…

But what she hadn't spoken about was the details. Their conversations. The sense she'd gotten sometimes that she was seeing a part of Grayson Manning that others didn't get to see—when he talked to her about his doubts, his father, or even his unusual view of relationships. And along with that came the knowledge that she had shared more with Gray then she'd shared with anyone—even Teagan.

He knew how to slide beneath her defences. He seemed to understand her. To *get* her. To push her buttons.

And she was different around him. It was ironic—the man who'd once made her feel invisible had triggered a...a quiet confidence, maybe. Definitely an edge. Gray's behaviour had pushed her to stand up for herself, to say what she was thinking.

To do what she wanted.

And where had that got her?

To her mum's lounge room, with a demolished box of chocolates and too much wine for a week night.

Gray sank back into his office chair. He didn't relax into it because he certainly wasn't relaxed. He more collapsed, actually.

Because that phone call had just made it official. He'd sold one villa—to Raquel—and that was it. The other investors were out.

Logically, he knew this wasn't a big deal. He'd had projects before that had been more of a slow burn. Others had sold in weeks, snapped up immediately. But then, this was something different for Manning. A new venture. He should expect progress to be slow. A delay was not a disaster. Yes, he had more capital than he'd like tied up in the resort. But they *would* sell. He did truly believe that. He needed to trust his instincts, to believe this development had been a savvy business decision. He'd entered a growing market at the right time. He would make money on this.

He did believe that.

But looking at the situation logically didn't make it any less frustrating. It didn't stop him from really, really needing some caffeine.

He leant forward again, lifting his hands above the keyboard to type out an instant message—but then paused. His new assistant was good. Über-efficient.

But really he was perfectly capable of getting his own coffee.

Besides, maybe a walk would do him good.

Was it the new venture? Or him?

Or, even better, a run.

It was mid-afternoon, so he hadn't really expected to see Lanie at the beach.

Still, he found himself scanning the waves for her, for that familiar way her body cut through the water.

She wasn't there, of course.

He ran hard, his feet leaving deep imprints in the wet sand as he propelled himself through the shallows.

He wanted to tell Lanie about what had happened today.

As he'd driven home he'd considered calling his dad instead.

But what was the point?

Gray already knew exactly what he'd tell him—and it would be no different to what he was already telling himself.

He just needed to carry on as he always had. To ride this wave and not let his frustration impact on the way he did business. Maybe it had in Vietnam, and the fact he'd allowed that possibility was infuriating. It couldn't and wouldn't happen again.

He hadn't changed. Manning hadn't changed. Eventually everyone would realise that.

He just wished they'd hurry up.

So, while his dad would understand, would be reassuring and say all the right things, going to him would feel as if he was doing exactly what many people seemed to think he'd always done: running to his dad for help. He hadn't done that and he wasn't going to start now. Gray *was* Manning now. On his decisions, his ideas, the company's success or failure rested.

So, no, he wasn't about to go running to his father. But he *did* want Lanie.

Not for business advice, or to tell him it was going to be okay—or anything meaningless like that. He wanted her because she understood this. She understood what it felt like to want something so badly and to be ultimately the only one in charge of your fate. When it came down to it, it had been just Lanie alone in that swim-lane. And it was Gray alone at Manning.

Gray's run slowed right down to a jog, then to a walk as he took big, heaving, breaths.

He looked out onto the ocean—out to the distance from shore where Lanie usually swam.

This beach was a world away from any aquadic stadium.

The kind of stadium she'd never return to.

For the first time the reality of that hit Gray.

All along he'd compared Lanie to himself. He'd sensed her passion, her drive to achieve. And he'd pushed her, unable to comprehend that a woman like her could be satisfied working for him. Could be satisfied without a new dream to chase.

But that was the thing. It was not possible to compare their dreams.

Here he was, furious with himself for a less than successful business transaction.

But he had another chance. Tomorrow. Next year. Next decade.

If he was stupid enough to lose everything, even to lose Manning, he could always start again.

There was no deadline on his dreams as long as he believed in them.

But Lanie…she didn't get another chance. She didn't get to go back and try again. To take a different tack, to review her training routine, to wring some non-existent bit of extra speed out of a body he was sure she'd honed to perfection.

She'd done everything right—her absolute best—and it hadn't been good enough.

She had to live with that. She had no other option.

And he'd been ignorant enough to push her. To question her. To think he was somehow helping by pointing out that she needed something new to strive for.

As if he had a Plan B for *his* dream. Manning was it. It was everything.

All he had.

His breathing had slowed to normal.

He should go home, have a shower. Maybe go back to work, or at least log into his e-mails from home.

He had lots of work to do. New projects to focus on. New investors to target.

But for once none of that excited him.

All he could think of was Lanie, swimming alone.

Lanie's mouth dropped open when she opened her front door.

'What are you doing here?'

A few weeks ago Gray had watched Lanie fidget outside his house as she over-thought how to leave her present for Luther.

Tonight Gray had done exactly the same thing. He still didn't know if this was a good idea—but it was too late now.

'I'm sorry,' he said.

Lanie raised her eyebrows. 'I know. You said so in your office. And, just like I said then, you have nothing to apologise for. I knew—'

'Of course I do,' he said. 'And you know it. I'm sorry for being such a bastard that night—because I was—but that isn't why I'm here.'

She crossed her arms and just looked at him, waiting.

'Can I come in?'

She shook her head. 'No.'

He took a deep breath, trying to organise his thoughts.

'I didn't get it,' he said. 'Actually, I *can't* get it. It's impossible for me to get it. And I'm sorry that I assumed I did.'

Lanie looked at him blankly. 'Pardon me?'

'Your swimming,' he said. Instantly Lanie tensed before his eyes. 'How you're feeling. What you should be doing now. I don't have a clue, and it wasn't my place to push you. To question you. I had no right, and I'm sorry.'

Her gaze had dropped to the wooden porch they were standing upon, but slowly she lifted her eyes until she met his.

'You weren't so wrong,' she said. 'You didn't ask me anything I wasn't asking myself.'

'That doesn't make it okay,' he said. 'You're strong enough to find your own new path.'

'I am,' she said with a slight smile. 'But you probably did speed things up a little. That's not a bad thing.'

There was a long pause. This was probably the point when he should leave, but he didn't.

'I miss the beach,' he said.

He didn't need to elaborate. She knew what he meant. Not the beach itself, but the two of them together there. Walking, talking. Laughing.

He could see her wavering, ready to deny him. Her eyes had narrowed and she'd taken a step forward, as if she was going to push him away physically as well as verbally.

But then, it was as if she deflated before his eyes.

'Me too,' she said. Then her gaze sharpened and she pasted on a plastic smile. 'But, hey, it was kind of fun while it lasted, right?'

'Does it have to end?' he said.

Her lips firmed into a thin line.

'You seriously want someone to walk with at the beach each morning?'

She was deliberately taking him literally, not making this easy for him at all.

But, really, could he blame her?

'I don't know what I want,' he said. 'I just know that I've wanted to tell you things—serious things, stupid things—I don't know how many times in the past weeks.'

Something softened in her gaze, but it was subtle, barely perceptible.

'And I know that I've wanted to touch you. To hold you. To kiss you. A hundred times more often.'

He was doing it again—tapping into this previously undiscovered romantic streak. It bothered him, made him uncomfortable—but not enough for him to wish back the words.

'What are you saying?' she asked. 'That you want more than a weekend together?'

'Yeah,' he said. 'More than a weekend.'

'And…'

'That's it,' he said honestly. 'That's as far as I've got.'

He knew it wasn't much, but it was all he had right now.

Her arms had dropped to her sides and she took a step forward. Then she seemed to think better of it.

'So you're saying we should live in the moment? Keep on doing this together for as long as it lasts?'

He nodded.

'That's pretty vague, you know.'

He did.

But then she took another step forward and reached out, touching his hand. He watched as she traced her fingers upwards, along his arm, up his bicep to his shoulder, then, finally curled them behind his neck.

She was close to him now. So close he could barely think.

She stood on tiptoes, her breath warm against his cheek.

'Okay,' she said, incredibly softly.

And he knew instinctively that even Lanie hadn't been sure what she was going to say right up until that moment.

That was how fleeting this was—whatever it was they had.

It wasn't a good idea. They both knew that.

But kissing her now, beneath the light of her front porch,

was the best idea he'd had in weeks. As was picking her up in her arms, despite her immediate half-hearted protest that she was far too heavy, and carrying her inside.

CHAPTER FOURTEEN

SOFT CONVERSATION DRIFTED into Lanie's subconscious.

Voices—women's voices.

She rolled over in her narrow bed and in her half-asleep state found that odd.

A few hours ago she'd definitely not been able to roll over so easily. Instead she'd been rather pleasantly squished up beside Gray.

But clearly he was no longer in her bed.

Lanie's eyes blinked open.

It was still dark in the room—not even a pre-dawn darkness, but proper, middle-of-the-night black.

She reached out blindly with one hand to turn on her bedside lamp, then flopped back against her pillow. In the corner of the ceiling hung the ocean-blue lantern she'd had made in Hoi An and she stared at it sleepily, thinking.

So Gray hadn't stayed the night.

Maybe that was how this new 'living in the moment' thing was going to work.

Lanie didn't know how she felt about that. She didn't know how she felt about the whole thing, actually.

But—no. Wait.

That was Gray's voice she heard. In the kitchen.

Lanie sat up, suddenly wide awake.

That *was* Gray's voice in the kitchen. Talking to her mum. And her sister.

Oh, no...

She leapt to her feet, fumbling about for a shirt to pull on. Moments later she was all but running down the hallway.

And there, in the kitchen, was Gray—in boxer shorts only, a hip propped against the benchtop. Across from him, perched on barstools, were Sienna and Lanie's mother. A small mountain of luggage sat waiting in the lounge room beyond.

'I didn't realise you were back today,' Lanie managed. She'd been sure it was tomorrow—although, to be honest, she hadn't paid too much attention. With an early-morning arrival, she'd just assumed she'd wake up one day this week with Sienna and her mum home again.

And of course that day was today—the night Gray was here.

She should have been more careful—but then, last night had hardly been planned.

'We guessed that,' Sienna was saying, with a very pointed look in Gray's direction.

'I thought someone was breaking in,' Gray explained, 'and then realised that was unlikely with their own key.'

Sienna laughed prettily, tossing her blond hair over her shoulders. For a woman who had just been on a plane for twenty-four hours or more, she looked remarkably well rested. And as beautiful as always.

Grey smiled back—men always did around Sienna—but then excused himself to get dressed.

The instant he'd left the room the questions started.

'Lanie, surely you aren't…?'

'Is he your *boyfriend*?'

'Who *is* he?'

Their surprise, shock and disbelief were obvious. And seriously unflattering.

'He's a friend,' she said quickly as Gray returned to the room. Now fully dressed, in jeans and a T-shirt, he was no less attractive than the boxer-shorted Gray.

To keep herself busy Lanie started to fuss around the kitchen making tea, while Gray answered Sandra and Sienna's questions.

He was doing well, really, given he clearly didn't want to be there. Lanie didn't want him to be here, either—this reality of Gray, her mum and her sister together was not one Lanie had ever expected to experience.

Gray said little. He didn't need to. The two other women filled all the spare conversation space and more. Lanie remained off to the side, watching them as she sipped at tea she didn't really want. Sienna was in her usual fine, flirtatious form—that was just who she was. Lanie knew it wasn't anything more than that, but still it irritated her.

And then Sienna brought out her medals.

As they were fished out of her sister's handbag and placed carefully in their boxes on the counter, Gray took a step towards Lanie, but she shook her head subtly. *No.*

Before she removed the lids Sienna's hand stilled and she met Lanie's gaze.

Lanie saw concern there. Hesitation.

But she also saw a mixture of excitement and pride—as if her little sister couldn't wait to show them to her. As if she was desperate for the praise of her big sister.

Lanie had never considered flying to London to watch Sienna swim. At the time she just *couldn't.* And she hadn't regretted it—until now.

Now she wished she'd been there to see these medals the day Sienna had won them.

Lanie smiled—a small smile that became broader when Sienna let out a breath she must have been holding.

Immediately Sienna reached for the boxes, and soon the medals were shining brilliantly beneath the kitchen's downlights.

They were beautiful, and far bigger than Lanie expected. She couldn't help but walk over, reach out and lift one from its padded bed. She weighed it in her hands and ran her thumb over the embossed surface.

Sienna was watching her with a worried expression. So was her mother—and Gray.

But there was no need.

That these medals were Sienna's—the result of *her* work, and *her* dreams and *her* achievements—was clear.

These medals weren't about Lanie. Not about her disappointment, or about what would have, might have…could never have been.

With a medal still in her hand, she went to Sienna, wrapped her arms around her and held her tight.

'I'm so proud of you,' she whispered.

And it was as simple as that. It was all that mattered.

Lanie walked Gray to his car. It was about two in the morning, but the idea of Gray returning to her tiny bed now her mother and sister were home seemed ludicrous.

It was perfectly still—still enough that Lanie could just hear the sounds of the ocean at the end of the road. She'd pulled on a pair of jeans, but now wrapped her arms around her body against the cool edge in the salty air.

'You okay?' Gray asked.

Lanie smiled. 'Yeah,' she said. 'I am.'

Gray reached for her, but she made herself step away.

'Lanie?'

She shook her head. 'I don't think it's a good idea,' she said. 'This. Us. Whatever it is.'

She had to push the words past her lips.

'Why not?'

Her gaze flipped up to the streetlight a few metres away. Its brightness made her blink as she stared at it.

'I think I've spent enough time in the past few months focussing on the wrong things. On my failures, my disappointments.'

'You're no failure, Lanie,' Gray said, his tone definite. 'Don't say that.'

'I know,' she said with a smile. 'I'm getting that now.' And Gray had played a big part in that—more than he'd ever know. 'I *did* fall short of my goals, and that hurts. A lot. But I need to move on.'

He nodded, letting her explain.

'The thing is, Gray, I don't think I can handle another failure right now. At least I can't handle one that's guaranteed. I need to believe in myself again.' She swallowed. 'So I can't do this with you. It's not going to work. We both know that.'

'But what do you want from this?' he asked. 'How can you be so sure it's going to fail?'

She laughed, but sadly. 'Of course it's going to fail. You can't even articulate what you want—neither of us can. But I know what you *don't* want. You don't want love, and you don't want for ever.'

She gave him a second—a moment to contradict her—but he remained silent.

She bit her lip, angry that her throat felt tight.

'That's what you want, Lanie? Love?'

Stupidly, she hadn't really considered the word in relation to herself. She'd just known that Gray didn't want it and had focussed on that.

But of course it was what she wanted. She turned her gaze back to him, looking him straight in the eye.

She had an awful feeling that love was something she already felt.

Could he see that in her gaze? She thought so, because his eyes drifted away.

'I think I get it now,' she said. 'That dismissive thing you do. I thought you were rude, or arrogant, but it isn't that, is it? You want to keep your distance from people. If you don't engage they can't get too close. Then there's no risk of any type of distraction—from Manning, and from your goals.'

He looked at her now, his gaze hard. 'You don't know what you're talking about.'

'I think I do, actually,' she said. 'I think for years I've been doing the same thing. My life was all about swimming—training, competing, day after day. There was no space left for anything else, and I didn't want anything else. But,' she said, with a smile, 'the good thing is that *now* I do have space. I have space for new dreams, new goals, new experiences, new relationships—and, I guess, for love.'

She'd only realised this as she'd been speaking. For the first time in months it was as if a whole new world was opening up before her—full of opportunities far beyond her swimming career.

Adrenalin pumped through her veins. Excitement.

Sienna's medals had been the catalyst, but this had started long before. Maybe that day she'd first stood up to Gray. Or when she'd finally believed in the way his body responded to hers. New emotions. New reactions.

Gray was shaking his head. 'You're wrong, you know. My whole career is about building relationships.'

'*Working* relationships, Gray. Not real ones.'

He laughed. 'Like my dad's marriages? Right. Or my mum's relationship with me? Or yours with your father, even? If that's what real relationships are, I don't want a part of one.'

Which was it, exactly.

Her gaze lifted to that streetlight again. She was discovering that right at this moment she was more like Gray than she'd realised. She couldn't look at him. Not now.

'Goodbye, Gray. This was fun while it lasted.'

He opened his mouth as if he was going to say something. But then he didn't.

Instead he looked at her—*really* looked at her—in a way that made Lanie wish she could take back everything she'd said. That made her want to throw herself at him and hold him and kiss him, take whatever it was he *could* offer for as long or as little time as he could.

There was passion and connection and maybe even something else in Gray's gaze.

But it wasn't enough.

She needed more now. A lot more.

And Gray wasn't capable of giving her what she needed. Or at least he didn't believe he was—and that was exactly the same thing.

He'd not contradicted her. He'd not even said he was willing to give it a try.

He was letting her end this and he was going to walk away.

That told her everything she needed to know.

So she let him.

One month later

It was a Friday night in an inner city pub, and Gray had met his dad for a drink. It was a celebration of sorts—three months since Gordon's retirement.

Gray couldn't say that everything at Manning, or his relationships with his clients and investors, was one hundred percent back to normal. But it was a heck of a lot closer than a month ago.

Nearly everyone was relaxing into the change, and Gray could sense a gradual return to the trust in him he'd once taken for granted.

And he thought *he* had relaxed into the change too. For a long time he'd had no idea he'd even needed to —nor even acknowledged that Gordon's retirement was a major change for him. Not just the people he worked with.

It had been Lanie who'd made him figure that out. Lanie swimming alone in the ocean, working her way through the biggest change in her life with so much dignity—and also moments of weakness.

Those moments were okay, though. Necessary, even.

So he too was allowing himself to be less than perfect. To adjust. To—as Lanie had told him—accept that he could do no more than his best.

It was all he and she could ever do. And that was okay.

It appeared to be working, too. This week he'd sold one of the Hoi An villas.

'It's over. With Tasha,' Gordon said out of the blue.

'I'm sorry to hear that,' Gray said, taking a sip of his beer.

'But not surprised?'

Gray shrugged. 'No.'

Normally that was as far as his conversations with his father went in relation to his divorces.

'What happened?' he asked, surprising himself.

Gordon raised his eyebrows, but answered the question. 'It wasn't working,' he said. 'It didn't turn out as either of us had expected.'

'And what *did* you expect?'

His father smiled. 'The perfect marriage, maybe?'

'What's that?'

Now a laugh. 'Maybe that's the problem. I don't know. Not what I keep on getting, anyway.'

'So why keep on trying?'

Gordon put down his beer glass as he studied Gray. 'I don't know. Each time it seems like a good idea. The best idea, even.'

'It's a good thing you're better at learning from your mistakes in other areas of your life,' Gray pointed out.

'Ah,' Gordon said. 'That's the thing, Gray. I married seven very different women. Given I didn't marry any of them twice, you could say I *did* learn.'

Gray laughed.

Their conversation shifted to more familiar territory—business, mostly. But Gray found himself studying his father and trying to understand how he was feeling.

Because surely—given he'd just separated from a woman he'd supposedly loved—there should be some evidence of… he didn't know… Hurt? Anger? Sadness?

He'd never been able to relate before. When his father had announced his separations—the ones Gray could remember, anyway—he'd paid little attention. As his dad said, Gray had always expected the demise of each relationship. It had never been a surprise.

He'd felt a little smug, actually, that once again he'd been proved right.

But this time he felt ashamed of his previous behaviour. His father must be devastated to have lost such a connection with another person. To have lost that spark, that magic, a person to share your day with. To laugh with. To share *everything* with.

And yet as his father related some golfing anecdote Gray didn't see any of that. No sadness. No regret. Nothing.

'Did you love her?' he asked, interrupting his father.

The older man's eyes widened. 'I thought I did,' he said, after a long moment. 'But no. I didn't. If I had, I don't think I'd feel so relieved that it's over.'

Yes, that was it. *Relief.* That was his dad's overriding emotion. As it had been in every divorce that Gray could remember.

Relief. Wasn't that what he should be feeling when it came to Lanie?

She'd done the right thing by ending it. She'd been absolutely right. Their relationship hadn't been going anywhere.

And, more importantly, she *did* deserve more than that. A lot more than that.

She deserved everything she'd spoken about that night—to live her life beyond her swimming career and to fill it with experiences, and joy, and definitely with love.

In which case, why was he thinking about her now?

Now, weeks later—weeks since he'd seen her, given he'd

changed his daily running track. He'd figured it wouldn't be fair to Lanie to share her beach.

Or fair to him…

He went to take another long drink of his beer—only to realise his glass was empty.

He had no idea what his father was saying, but he nodded occasionally as he tried to pull his own thoughts together.

He did know one thing: he *wasn't* relieved that things had ended with Lanie.

Lanie sighed as she unknotted her apron and hung it on a hook in the café's small office.

Bob grinned as he looked up from counting the day's takings. 'You'll get used to it.'

She smiled back. 'Honestly, you'd think after all my years of swimming I'd be fit enough to run about all day.'

'Maybe that should be your plan when you reopen the place—an underwater café. Then you could swim the orders out to customers.'

Lanie tilted her head, as if giving the idea serious consideration. 'You know, you could be onto something.'

Five minutes later, with her bag swung over her shoulder, she headed for the beach. The little café shut each day at five p.m.—something she *did* plan to change when her purchase of the café was finalised—and at this time of year there were still hours of daylight remaining.

The sand was only sparsely dotted with people—a few sunbathers, a handful of dogs, and some kids splashing about in the shallows. The afternoon sea breeze had kicked in, and it urged small white-tipped waves from the ocean. One hopeful surfer bobbed just behind the waves, and far, far beyond him a lone container ship was silhouetted against the sky.

Lanie dumped her bag, quickly tugged her cotton dress off over her bathers, then pulled her swim-cap on over her hair. Lacing her fingers behind her back, she stretched her shoulders and chest slowly, then moved through the remainder of her stretching routine. She finished by sitting on her towel, her fingers wrapped around her feet as she pulled them gently towards herself to stretch the muscles of her hips and legs.

Now was normally the point when she leapt to her feet—ready and raring to go, to feel the shocking coolness of the ocean against her skin, and then minutes later the satisfying burn in her lungs.

But today she paused.

The sun was still high in the sky, and it made her squint as she stared out to the horizon.

She should be feeling good. Fantastic, even.

The moment Bob had told her he was retiring and selling his business she'd known taking over the café and his lease on the building was the right thing for her to do. It had taken every cent of her savings, plus a substantial loan, but she figured her own home could wait, and for now she was living in the two tiny rooms at the back of the café.

Lanie now knew she couldn't work for anyone but herself—and not just because of her experience working with Gray. She needed to feel in complete control of this next phase of her life—good or bad, *she* was in charge of what happened next. That meant a lot to her.

But this was going to be good. She truly believed it—especially when she was down here at the beach.

This place reassured her.

Here she was in her element. The ocean didn't think she was tall or awkward—in fact amongst the waves she felt alive, strong, powerful. Elegant in a way she'd never felt in a fifty-metre pool. There she'd compared herself to others—to the girls on the blocks either side of her, to her sister.

Someone was always faster, prettier, or more talented.

But here in the ocean she let go of all that. She stopped judging herself. Stopped judging others.

It was impossible not to—out there it was just her in the water. No stopwatches, no competitors, no finish line.

In the water sometimes she even felt beautiful.

She never had before—except, of course, with Gray.

She shook her legs as if to chase the memories of Gray away.

There was absolutely no point thinking of him, although knowing that didn't really stop it happening. Especially when she swam.

Lanie clambered to her feet and slid her goggles over her eyes.

Stroke, stroke, stroke, *breathe*.

The sun was about to start moving towards the horizon as Lanie swam towards the shore. She pulled her cap and goggles off and held them in one hand as she dived beneath the surface, finger-combing her tangled hair away from her face.

Moments later a splash a few metres to her left grabbed her attention. A tennis ball, bright yellow, bobbed beside her.

Its owner made himself apparent almost immediately, leaping through the water until his paws didn't reach the bottom, then thrashing about enthusiastically as he paddled to the ball.

Luther.

True to form, the dog ignored her entirely, his focus exclusively on his prized possession. He snatched the ball up into his mouth, then swiftly made his way back to the sand—only to drop the ball as soon as he got there, then look back at Lanie, his body tense with anticipation.

'I can't throw it from out here, mate.'

A male voice—Gray's voice—immediately to her right.

As if the dog understood he happily trotted a few metres up the beach, then dropped to his stomach, the ball between his paws. Waiting patiently.

Of course Gray was here, if Luther was. But still, having him so close was unexpected and disconcerting. Or at least that was the reason she gave for the way her tummy immediately lightened at the familiar sound of his voice.

She'd been swimming back, but now the water was shallow enough to stand, so she did as she turned to face Gray. He was standing in the water too, his hair slicked back and his bare chest gleaming in the sun.

'Hey,' he said.

'Hi.'

For long minutes they just stood there. Lanie didn't know what to do or to say.

'Bob told me you bought his café,' Gray said eventually.

She nodded. 'Yeah. He's spent the past month teaching me everything he knows, and then he's leaving me to it.'

'You'll do great.'

'That's the plan.'

The terribly awkward conversation segued into an even more awkward silence. Lanie realised she was still splashing her cap and goggles about in the water, so she made her hands go still.

'I'm glad you came back to the beach. Luther loves it here. I hope you weren't avoiding it because of me,' she said. Her gaze drifted to the shore and she wished herself back at her towel. Or at home. Anywhere but here.

Because it had been bad enough thinking about Gray over the past few weeks. Standing metres away from him was impossible.

'Of course I was avoiding it because of you.'

Her attention snapped back to Gray. 'Oh,' she said. 'You shouldn't.'

'Why not?'

She attempted a blasé laugh. 'I'd hate for one simple weekend to ruin North Cottesloe beach for you for ever. Seems a bit dramatic, don't you think?'

'But that was the problem, wasn't it, Lanie? It was more than just a weekend.'

Lanie's realised she was gripping her goggles so hard that they were digging into her palms.

'You didn't seem to think so,' she said, then immediately wished the words back.

She needed to end this conversation now. It was pointless. They'd covered all this before. And it hurt just as much the second time around.

'What if I was wrong?'

She made herself meet his gaze, trying to ignore the pathetic butterflies of hope that swirled around her stomach. 'Were you?'

He nodded. 'I used to think that love was a weakness. A possible chink in my armour. A risk—a complication that I didn't need and that could distract me and shift my focus from what was really important.'

'Which is Manning,' she said.

He shook his head. 'No. It's part of it—but now I know it's not everything. It's not even close to everything I need in my life. My dad knows that too. That's why he keeps searching for love. He definitely doesn't always make the right decisions, but I can no longer deride him for trying. We've been talking a lot, and I think once he was in love. He keeps searching for that feeling again.'

Gray had stepped closer—or maybe the waves had pushed them closer together.

His gaze was still locked with hers, and he was now near enough that she could see the intensity in his eyes. And she could certainly feel it. Right now she had no doubt she was all he was seeing.

Maybe right now she was all that mattered.

It was an overwhelming sensation. But it drew her towards him like a magnet.

Another step through the lapping waves. So that if she reached out she could touch him.

'I don't want to be like him,' Gray said. 'I don't want to spend the rest of my life searching for something I once had.'

'Or getting married seven times?'

He laughed out loud. 'I can't see that happening.'

No, but Lanie could too easily imagine Gray shutting himself off from the world, keeping his distance in the guise of arrogance.

Gray took that last final step. The step that made her tilt her chin up to look at him and made each deep breath she took bring their bodies dangerously close together.

'I love you, Lanie,' he said.

After everything, it seemed almost too simple. Too basic and straightforward when everything about their relationship had been complicated and confusing.

But it was far from simple.

Could she do this? Could she risk herself again? Could she risk the all too familiar pain of rejection and failure?

The possibility scared her. Terrified her, even.

But as she looked up into Gray's eyes she didn't see any doubts.

And when she searched inside herself she couldn't find any either.

She wouldn't take back a moment of her swimming career, even though it hadn't ended the way she'd dreamed.

Besides, this was love—not sport.

Sure, there were risks, and no guarantees.

But their love wasn't dependent on others. On injury, or illness, or team selection policy.

It was just her and Gray.

'I love you, too,' she said softly, just loud enough to be heard over the gentle splash of the ocean.

Then she was in his arms and kissing him, with the taste of salt water on her lips and the bite of the sun warm against their damp skin.

On the beach, Luther barked—loudly.

It took a while, but eventually they broke apart.

'I think he wants someone to throw his ball,' Lanie said, smiling.

And, hand in hand, they walked back to the shore, together.

* * * * *

PROMOTED
TO WIFE?

PAULA ROE

For my parents.
Your love and support have
helped me follow my dreams.

One

"You did *what?*"

Emily Reynolds yanked the phone from her ear and winced before readjusting it back under her chin. "I kissed my boss."

"Wait. Back up," her older sister AJ demanded on the other end. "You kissed Zac Prescott."

"Yep."

"The guy God built just to make a woman whimper with joy."

"The same."

"And you, my little sister who hates surprises and runs the man's company with clockwork efficiency?"

"No need to rub it in—I *know* I'm the dumbest female on the planet." Holed up in her apartment on her comfy two-seater, dressed in her bathrobe and with ankles crossed on the coffee table, it was easy to believe that last week had been just a figment of Emily's overactive imagination. But the telltale warmth on her skin gave her true thoughts away every time.

"Emmy, you are the *luckiest* female on the planet! Was it good?"

"Have you not been listening? He's my boss. I finally had a strong, respectful work relationship going and then I go and do something stupid. Talk about déjà vu."

"What do you mean 'had'?" Emily heard a loud bang down the line: AJ had slammed a door closed. "Details."

Emily groaned, tugging off the towel turban that held her freshly washed hair. "I've been on leave for the past week. On Thursday night he called me from the office, blind drunk. I drove him home, got him in the front door, we stumbled…and it sort of happened."

"Ah, the old 'stumble and kiss' routine."

Emily scowled at her distorted reflection in the dark TV screen. Zac being drunk didn't excuse her behavior: that she'd been secretly lusting after a completely-off-limits guy this past year only compounded her stupidity.

"It's not funny. I panicked, shut myself in at home and spent the weekend thinking."

"That's dangerous. And…?"

"And then I quit. This morning. By e-mail."

"Oh, Em! The drunken kiss aside, why?"

"You know why." She ran a hand through her still-damp hair, twisting the ends around her fingers. "I can't go through another misconduct accusation again."

"But Zac isn't like that—that other jerk lied!"

Emily sighed, self-anger congealing into a lumpy mess that sat heavily in her belly. She'd thought talent and dedication got you ahead in the corporate world, not how blond your hair was or how short your skirts were. She'd always dressed professionally, always worked hard for her temping jobs, believing that one day an employer would recognize and reward her business skills.

And four years ago they had, but not in the way she'd assumed. The permanent position at one of Perth's top accountancy firms had come with strings, as she'd found out at the office Christmas party six months later. The first time she'd put on a miniskirt and a nice top, a managing director had groped her on the balcony.

Emily shuddered. She'd been twenty-two, humiliated and alone in the world. No family, no home, nothing—until some uncle she'd never known had died and left his Gold Coast apartment to her. So she'd moved clear across the country to Queensland and started over with barely healed wounds and a brand-new hard-ass attitude. She'd scraped back her hair, donned her glasses and shoved herself into monochrome business suits and sensible shoes in order to play the part of a serious professional. And it had paid off when she'd landed the job as Zac Prescott's personal assistant two years ago.

"Maybe it isn't as bad as you think," AJ was saying now.

"No, it's worse." Emily sighed. "I've had it with men."

AJ spluttered on whatever she'd been drinking. "So after a bunch of idiot boyfriends, a false misconduct threat and a loser ex-husband, you're gay now?"

"No." Emily stifled a laugh. "I meant I've had it with getting emotionally sucked into their games, their baggage, their whole mess-with-your-head thing."

"Ah! You're finally coming over to the Dark Side?"

Emily did laugh then. "At least the Dark Side has sex without commitment."

"But that's *me*. You're Angel to my Spike. You're the hyper-organized good girl with the strong moral compass, the one looking for Mr. Right."

"Yeah, and look where that's gotten me." Emily tilted her ear to the narrow hallway. "Someone's at the door."

"Damn. I told that stripper-gram *after* seven."

"Ha, ha. Look, I'll see you tonight. Eight-thirty at Jupiters, right?"

"Yep. And I expect to hear more details then. Happy twenty-sixth birthday, Em."

Some birthday. Emily clicked off the phone, then scowled as the thumping on her screen door became ever more impatient. "All right, I'm coming!"

Probably her grumpy old postie complaining about her missing letterbox again.

She grabbed an elastic from the bookcase as she passed, pulled her hair back, then secured it low on her neck. It wasn't just men who were the problem—she was. After two years of organizing the minutiae of Zac Prescott's life, after working twelve-hour days and scrimping each dollar, she finally had enough to start her own business. Her week off was supposed to pave the way for her resignation, to ease Zac into it. Instead she'd ended up as his personal on-call service.

Pound, pound, pound.

"Dammit, George." She grabbed the door handle and yanked it open. "Can you stop with the— Oh."

"What the hell is this?" Zac Prescott stood on her stoop, all angry male, a piece of paper crumpled in his clenched fist.

She took a cautious step back. Zac wasn't a yeller. The one and only time she'd seen him lose it was during a call from his father, close to a year ago.

"It's my resignation," she replied calmly.

Zac's olive-green eyes narrowed. "Why?"

What was the collective noun for a group of butterflies? A swarm? Whatever it was, they were doing a number on her insides. Zac Prescott was dressed in sharply creased dark gray pants, a pristine white long-sleeved shirt and a silk tie with blue-green swirls that she'd given him last Christmas. He cut an impressive figure, but it was the face that got her: a beautiful, rugged package that was the result of a dark, brooding father and a blond-haired, green-eyed Swedish mother. The elegant, almost artistic compilation of all-male angles and tanned clean-shaven skin tightened her insides and sent hot sexual awareness pounding through her veins.

She blinked, forcing the delicious ache aside. "Because I quit."

"You can't quit." He surged forward, and Emily had no choice but to give way. His broad body invaded her space, his larger-than-life presence sucking away the very air in her small one-bedroom apartment. It was overwhelming—he was overwhelming.

She took a measured breath, and his distinctive, fresh-yet-sinful scent teased her nostrils, filling her senses, making her head spin with delicious memories. She bit off the hitch in her throat and gently closed the door.

He'd paused in the middle of her lounge room, a clear contrast to her humble collection of neatly arranged possessions. She crossed her arms as Zac's gaze raked over her, taking in her makeup-free, damp-haired presence.

You're practically naked. Heat pooled as she drew the ties of her threadbare robe more securely around her waist. That intense focus was narrowed right in on her. He had a way of staring as if he was picking through all her secrets yet revealing none of his. A complete contrast to Thursday night, when he'd been unguarded, almost vulnerable. It had dragged her in quicker than Southport's killer rip tide.

"You can't quit," he stated again, that dark frown still creasing his perfect face.

She blinked. "Why not?"

"Well, for one, your temp—Amber?—sucks."

"It's Ebony. She came from Marketing as a favor to me."

"She's stuffed up the filing system."

"I see." With a keen eye, she watched him massage his neck. Two years of close personal contact had taught her a headache was brewing in that brilliant head of his. For one second she felt sorry for him.

"And she puts sugar in my coffee."

Oh, boy. I've spoiled him. "And let me guess…she doesn't remind you to eat?"

Zac scowled, still rubbing his neck. "And her God-awful perfume gives me a headache. It isn't funny. Everything's gone to hell this past week. I need you back."

Oh, Lordy. Her bones melted like ice cream in summer, her body held up only by sheer will. She wanted to groan aloud but instead took an unsteady gulp. "You need me?" she repeated faintly.

His nod was brief and spare. "For some insane reason, Victor Prescott is about to name me as his successor."

"Your father? What…to VP Tech?"

"Yep."

Whoa. Stunned, Emily felt her jaw sag. Zac never talked about his past, including his family: it was as if he'd emerged onto the Gold Coast's construction scene fully assembled and commanding a million-plus annual turnover. Sure, she knew his father was the iron-fisted CEO of a billion-dollar software company, but that was about it. Zac didn't pay her to gossip with his employees.

"That's why you were…" She paused delicately but he brushed away her hesitation with an imperious wave of his hand.

"Drunk in my office, yes. Not a good impression for the cleaning staff."

Her boss never drank at work. And that was why he'd called her, his loyal assistant, to get him home. *Great.*

"Zac," she sighed. "I spent two years being the best damn assistant you ever had. I organized your work and personal life without comment, without complaint. I soothed clients, I arranged last-minute meetings, business trips and dates. I worked overtime and weekends more times than I can count—"

"I didn't realize you hated your job so much," he interjected stiffly.

"I don't! *I didn't.* It's…it's just time for a change."

"And helping me sort out this mess with VP Tech isn't enough of a change?"

"No…yes. I just—I'm leaving, okay?"

Silence fell for a moment, thick and palpable, until Zac said slowly, "So tell me who's lured away my assistant—the best damn one I've ever had—" his mouth tweaked "—when I need her the most?"

There was that word again. *Need.*

Crazy fantasies suddenly flooded her brain, ones that involved more than a stolen kiss. Like being touched all over by those incredibly masculine, long-fingered hands…

She blinked and smoothed back a nonexistent lock of hair, waiting for him to mention That Night. But as time ticked by, all he did was glare at her. That's when it finally hit.

He didn't remember.

Emily felt the flush start low, then gradually spread up her neck. It finally settled on her cheeks, twin burning indications of her foolishness. While her mind had played out that kiss over and over all weekend like a CD on repeat, apparently Zac hadn't lost a second's thought about it.

Well, what do you expect when this VP Tech thing's just dropped in his lap?

"Are you going to say something?" he said now, crossing his arms.

She sighed. "I can train someone else."

"I don't want anyone else." He shifted his weight, one hand going to the base of his neck again. Emily watched in fascination as he absently massaged, his triceps in mouthwatering relief against the straining shirt. "Of course I'll give you a pay rise."

"But I don't understand why you'd get... I mean—" She stopped.

"Why do I suddenly get handed a software company? Or what happened to my stepbrother, who's been the undisputed heir apparent?" His gaze turned wily as it swept her flushed face. "Have I piqued your curiosity?"

"No," she lied.

He gave her one of those casual grins, one that never failed to flip her stomach. "You sure? It's a mess. We'll have to arrange meetings, reschedule my appointments. You know you're itching to sort it out."

"I'm the last person motivated by morbid curiosity and office gossip."

"No," he said, his eyes running over her again in unhurried deliberation. "That's true. So think of it as a promotion—I'm prepared to double whatever offer you've got lined up."

"Money isn't the point." She turned on her heel and walked over to her couch, desperately needing space to clear her head. "Zac, you're a workaholic," she said, picking up her discarded towel, then flicking a glance over her shoulder. His expression had turned cautious. "And that's not a bad thing, it's just... you expect me to be one, too. I want to be in control of my destiny—be my own boss and make my own decisions." She lifted her chin defiantly. "I'm going to university to get my small-business degree. I'm starting my own company."

"Doing what?"

"Personal organization. You know, time management, life coaching, getting clients on track with—" At his ambiguous silence, she scowled. "You know, just forget it. I've already signed and paid for the first semester. In lieu of two weeks I won't take my last paycheck."

In all her years working with Zac Prescott, she'd been the consummate professional, beyond gossip, beyond reproach. She'd never returned his light banter or gotten beyond the standard noncommittal answer to his "how was your weekend?" inquiries. Like the rest of his thirty-strong office staff, she suspected he saw her as a solitary career woman of average height and weight, someone who'd blend into a crowd, someone definitely not eligible for the "I've dated Zac Prescott" club. Which made Thursday's kiss all the more humiliating, because apparently it was forgettable. Just like her.

Even though she'd made her bed, lying in it was distinctly uncomfortable.

He frowned as she stood there, the towel damp and heavy in her hand. She'd never deliberately defied him…until now. It was fascinating the way his jaw clenched beneath that warm, smoothly shaven skin. *And you know exactly how warm it is. And how smooth. And how it smells—like stealing forbidden kisses in an orange grove, exciting, fresh, exhilarating…*

Mortified, she quickly busied herself with collecting last night's take-out containers from the coffee table as her treacherous heart began to speed up.

He followed her into the kitchen.

"Listen. If you're hell-bent on going, I can't stop you. But it's only October. You've got nearly five months before the term starts, so why not work for me until then? Help me sort out this stupid stunt of my father's."

"I don't—" She abruptly turned from the sink, but he was there, a huge wall of wonderful-smelling, rock-hard muscle. She just managed to stop herself from smashing headfirst into that broad chest. Before her body could start its annoying little joyful hum, she took another step back. The movement was not lost on him, judging by the way his brow creased.

"Are you annoyed because I dragged you from your vacation on Thursday night?"

In incredulous silence she stared at him, eyes wide, until irritation began to bubble up inside. "You think my change of career direction—one I'd been planning for many months now—was precipitated by your demand that I drive you home? Without thanks, I might add?"

"Guess not," he muttered. Then, stiffly, "Thank you. For driving me home."

"You're welcome."

His gaze fixed on hers, holding it for seconds longer than necessary before he glanced away and shoved his hands in his trouser pockets. If she'd expected something, anything to indicate their prior carnal knowledge, then she was disappointed. Firm lines bracketed his mouth, and she watched irritation surge across his expression before he tamped a lid on it.

I was right—he doesn't remember.

"I don't normally drink in the office," he said suddenly.

"I know."

"Yeah." He returned to his scrutiny, making her insides squirm. "You do."

The warm morning sunlight coming through her tiny kitchen window seemed to thicken then, wrapping around her body and creating an uncomfortable ache low in her belly. As she glanced at his mouth, the night came flooding back in all its illicit glory. She'd spied the half bottle of tequila on his desk, seen the belligerent gleam in his eyes, even in the darkened light of his office.

"I need to get dressed," she blurted out now. Automatically his eyes flicked over her state of non-dress, which only made her breath catch. "And you need to go."

"Are you going to think about my offer?"

"Will you go if I promise to think about it?"

"Only if you'll actually think about it," he said. "We both win here. I get you for another five months and you get a massive incentive. Win-win."

"I promise I'll think about it."

As she followed him down her hall, watched as he opened the door, then crossed the threshold, she knew she wouldn't—couldn't—go back to work for Zac. Not after that kiss. She didn't need more chaos, not when she'd spent her whole childhood fighting for order.

He paused on the peeling deck before turning back to her with a thoughtful expression. "How did my car get from the office to my house?"

Her mouth involuntarily twitched. "That's one mighty nice vehicle."

"I let you drive my Porsche?"

"Sure." She couldn't completely hide the smug smile. "You were quite drunk."

He rubbed his chin with a dark scowl. "And you got me into the house without help."

"Yep." Her arm had been around his waist, his delicious warmth distracting her as she'd steered him through his front door. And then...

Anyone could've made the mistake. He'd stumbled, she'd only just managed to retain her balance, they'd turned at the same time. And their lips had met. And met. And kept on meeting, until Emily had managed to wrench free and escape.

A stupid lapse in judgment that had paradoxically brought clarity to her life plans.

With a sigh, she tightened the belt on her robe. "Goodbye, Zac. I'll let you know what I decide."

Like never kiss your boss, then believe everything will be normal. Been there, done that, been trying to burn it from my mind ever since.

Zac barely heard the soft click of the door behind him, too caught up in his frustration to notice. Past the wooden railing, down the rolling grassy slope of the apartment block perched high on Currumbin's Duringan Street, the long waveless estuary locals called The Alley glittered in the early morning sun, a tempting sight for those inclined to call in sick and spend the day lazing on its sandy banks.

Not Emily. She was an employer's dream: always prompt, superefficient and highly intelligent. She knew what he needed before he needed it. She knew how he had his coffee, she reminded him to eat, she always came in under deadline.

And she was an amazing kisser.

The stairs creaked beneath his feet, an aural protest to echo his own irritation. He wasn't confident Emily would return, which meant he had to think up a Plan B.

Emily blinked a lot when she was uncomfortable. It was like a nervous tic, those thick, impossibly long lashes fluttering away over navy-blue eyes obscured by glasses. He'd noticed it the first time he'd casually asked about her weekend. Intrigued and amused, he'd been compelled to test his theory. The confirmation had come when they'd finally negotiated a major contract and he'd struck up some friendly banter to relieve the tension.

She'd also blinked like that after he'd kissed her.

He paused on the path, the cheerful mid-spring warmth doing nothing to ease the headache sluggishly throbbing away. Damn, how many prompts did he need to give a woman? But she'd steadfastly refused to acknowledge that kiss.

A kiss that had rocked his world in more ways than one.

It had, just for one moment, taken his mind off this entire VP Tech fiasco and all the lingering anger it dredged up. Just one moment, and yet long enough for a powerful need to arrest his brain, rush into his groin and conjure up all sorts of delicious, slick images of Emily in his bed.

She wasn't only the best damn assistant he'd ever had: she'd somehow managed to pique his interest to the point that focusing on work had become a major effort these last few months.

And for the first time in months, he wanted. Wanted with an unrelenting intensity.

He scanned the watery view, automatically picking out a handful of his company's early designs on the opposite bank, lingering on the smooth clean lines of those multimillion dollar homes with a deep flush of pride. Once-average homes that he'd single-handedly redesigned, rebuilt and flipped for a profit. And even now, with full-time staff and a corporate development department, he still designed. Yes, he could now afford to pick and choose his clientele, but those original projects were still a humble reminder of how far he'd come.

His days were perfectly streamlined. He enjoyed his work, the women he dated and his life in general. He had peace—unlike the years that had come before, years of constant emotional upheaval, of stress and migraines, sleepless nights and endless, conflict-filled days.

He'd worked like a demon for his new life. If his father had taught him one thing, it was that nothing worth having ever came easy.

Especially when it came to pursuing a woman.

He'd persuade Emily to return and then take the time to find out if his fuzzy memories were correct, that she'd been an eager and willing participant in that kiss.

He glanced back up to her apartment door, to the closed blinds across her living room window.

Waddyaknow. The same day his life had taken a crazy turn, he'd finally gotten an answer to months of idle speculation about what lay under Emily's severe business suits. She'd fronted up at his office without her trademark glasses, dressed in a baggy T-shirt and ratty Ugg boots, a worn denim skirt cupping a perfectly delicious curvy butt.

His assistant hid a smoking body. Why?

If he closed his eyes, he could still feel the imprint from those luscious breasts as she'd walked him into his house. *Oh, yeah.* She'd been into that kiss even if it hadn't lasted for more than three nanoseconds.

Deep in the fantasy, the stranger was almost upon him before he clicked.

The man was built like a brick outhouse: a bouncer's massive body crammed into a sleek suit, all restrained menace beneath the sheen of barely there respectability. It wasn't just the man's overwhelming physical presence that set off warning bells as he passed Zac on the narrow garden path, giving him a bare nod. It was the focused, almost mean aura in that smooth coffee-colored face, the way those shrewd eyes skimmed over Zac before returning to his purpose.

Zac had seen that look before. Hell, he'd faced it down too many times in his line of work. Unfortunately, the construction industry brought with it a certain type of thug who thought they could bribe and terrorize their competitors.

Zac slowly turned, watching the man take the stairs, then continue on.

Emily's apartment was the only one at the end of level two.

Swiftly, Zac backtracked, the wooden balcony above providing cover just as he heard Emily's door open.

He glanced up through the wooden slats. She'd left the security screen locked. Smart girl.

"You Mrs. Catalano?" the big dude said.

"It's actually Miss Reynolds."

Zac frowned. Since when the hell had she been *married?* But then, there were a thousand things he didn't know about her, though not from his lack of gentle probing.

"But Jimmy Catalano's wife, right? Daughter of Charlene and Pete, younger sister to Angelina?"

There was a pause where Zac thought he'd heard Emily drag in a shocked breath. "What's this about?"

"Jimmy owes my boss money."

"Who's your boss?"

"Let's just call him…Joe."

When Emily finally replied, it was with the same tenor and firmness she used when dealing with his most demanding clients. "I'm sorry, but Jimmy died seven months ago."

Zac swallowed his surprise. His assistant was hiding more than killer curves behind that superefficient persona.

"I heard," Big Dude was saying. "And I'm sorry for your loss." His tone implied anything but. "Joe is a compassionate businessman. He gave you longer than most to come to terms with your grief. Now he wants his money."

"What money?"

Zac angled for a better view and caught the movement of Emily's door closing. The Big Dude's slap on the screen rang out, startling her and jerking Zac to attention. A surge of fury propelled him forward, but at the last minute, caution prevailed. In tense silence, he waited.

"You were Jimmy's guarantor, which means his debt is now yours," the man continued roughly, losing patience.

"I didn't sign anything."

There was a rustle of papers. "That's your signature, right?"

"It looks like mine. But I didn't—"

Big Dude sighed, as if her denial disappointed him. "You got fourteen days to pay."

Emily paused, then said firmly, "Then I'll see you in court."

The man's sudden laughter, deep and menacing, sent a chill rippling through Zac's skin. "A wife of a guy like Jimmy knows the drill—no cops, no solicitors. My boss doesn't waste money dealing with the courts. Geddit?" He let that ambiguous threat settle before there was a rustle of cheap material. "Here's my card." A snick of paper and a groan of mesh: he'd shoved his card in her screen door. "Let me know when you have the money." He paused, his voice suddenly softer, more ominous. "Your sister is a nice-lookin' girl. She's what…thirty or so? And just got a brand-new car, too—"

"You stay away from my family."

The panic threaded beneath Emily's granite words stabbed straight into Zac's heart. His hands tightened into fists.

"Hey, I was just making an observation." The man's hands went up in mock defense. "You know, *you* could always pay off the debt in other ways…"

The vicious slam of Emily's front door, followed by the click of the lock, was the final straw. As the man's chuckle floated down the stairs, white-hot fury seethed up, choking off Zac's breath, taking with it common sense and self-preservation.

He straightened, pulling his shoulders back, then gently rolling his neck to work out the kinks. Then he stepped into the path and barred the way.

The man strolled down the stairs, a smug smile still on his

face. When he spotted Zac, his expression flashed into menacing caution.

"Hey, mate," Zac said casually, forcing his fists to slowly unclench. "You got a minute?"

Two

Residual annoyance punctuated Emily's stride as she stalked into the foyer of the office building on Thursday morning. On Monday night, after a few drinks and a deep discussion that became way too serious for a birthday celebration, AJ had confirmed Emily's doomed realization.

She had to go back to work. The cops could do nothing about a vague verbal threat without proof, and a complaint would no doubt piss off this "Joe," which was something she so didn't want to do. His intimidating thug had done more than rattle her: he had forced memories of her former life to the surface where they'd sat, alternately irritating then panicking her until the early hours of the morning.

You could always pay off the debt in other ways.

The thug's rough suggestion still made her skin crawl. Jimmy had voiced that disgusting thought once, and only once, which had been her impetus to walk out. She'd rather pay up and defer her course than settle her ex-husband's debts on her back.

If you weren't dead, Jimmy, I could just kill you.

The security guard held up a hand, scrutinized the ID card around her neck, then waved her on through.

Her face burned as she reached the elevators. How many times had she walked through that reception area and been stopped by the same guard as if he'd never seen her before in his life? For the other pretty things in the building he smiled, nodded and barely glanced at their identification. For her, she was no one worth remembering.

The elevators pinged open and she got inside, cramming in with the other workers.

Every instinct rebelled against handing over her hard-earned cash, but being married to a professional deadbeat had revealed a dark underside to Jimmy's seemingly carefree life. Through all the lying and the cheating, she'd never forgotten one important fact—debt collectors were deadly serious about their money.

Money was replaceable. Her and AJ's well-being were not.

So last night, through alternating tears of frustration and anger, she'd worked out her course refund, then rung The Thug—aka Louie Mayer—to negotiate an extension on the due date. After he'd laughed himself into a coughing fit, he'd finally got out, "Sure. I'm a sucker for a chick with a great pair of tits. I'll talk to Joe. Call me on Monday, blondie."

Humiliation burned as she finally got off on the twentieth floor. Her credit rating was shot thanks to Jimmy, which left selling her apartment—out of the question—or stealing or gambling. *Irony, thy name is Jimmy Catalano.*

Muttering under her breath, she swooshed open the pristine glass doors that proclaimed Valhalla Property Development in elegant gold script.

She went through the motions of stashing her bag, then turning on the computer before tackling the mess the temp had left on her desk.

"Ah, great. You're here."

She whipped around, her eyes landing on Zac framed in his doorway. Seeing him there, dressed in his signature business shirt, pants and precisely knotted tie, something strange happened.

Her mind emptied. As her heart upped tempo, breath catching, her skin began to tingle. The sensation was not unlike an intimate breath swooping over her flesh, goose-bumping her entire body into a sensitive bundle of nerves.

She offered a thousand colorful reprimands to her self-control, even as she felt her nipples stiffen beneath her blue silk shirt.

"Everything okay?"

If you could call wanting to see your boss naked *okay*. "Just peachy." She forced out a tight smile.

"Then let's get started," he said, clearly oblivious to her state. "Come on in."

Emily swallowed and picked up her notepad.

After she sat and Zac relaxed into his plush leather chair with graceful ease, his green gaze swept over her from head to toe. Nothing new—Zac always studied people with a silent intensity that flustered or flattered, depending on the recipient. It hadn't bothered her before. But now...

She felt the sudden overwhelming urge to squirm, to fiddle with her hair, straighten her collar and do a thousand other self-conscious girly things she'd thought she was immune to.

She followed his eyes as they lingered seconds longer on her hair, her mouth. Blood zinged through her veins, sending twin shots of panic and excitement to every dormant inch of her body.

She was reacting like any red-blooded female under the gaze of a charismatic, attractive man. And that scared the hell out of her.

"You wear contact lenses."

The question threw her and she answered unthinkingly. "Yes."

"But not to work."

She flicked the edges of her notepad under her thumb, over and over. "No."

"Why not?"

"I like glasses." She paused, then deflected calmly. "So what do you need me to do regarding VP Tech?"

He leaned back in his chair, his expression almost teasing. "You know, you look much better without them."

"Thank you. I assume you'll want to issue a press release about your new acquisition—"

"Did you get your blue eyes from your father?"

"My mother." She pushed her glasses back up the bridge of her nose, floundering at his intense interest. Zac had a virtual buffet of women to choose from thanks to his gorgeous looks, masculine command and charm. Charm that she'd come to realize was completely unaffected, as effortless as creating his award-winning designs. He was a man who appreciated and loved women, a natural flirt. So why the hell was he flirting with her and why…?

Oh, no. She quickly turned the page of her notebook, desperate to focus somewhere else. The kiss. What else could it be?

Hot mortification flooded her cheeks and she crossed her legs, demurely straightening the long black skirt over her knee. But when she shot him a glance from under the lowered lashes, his eyes remained locked on her warm face. His mouth curved into a small, teasing grin, and for one second she felt a desperate desire to kiss that mouth.

She cleared her throat. "Back to VP Tech…"

Zac leaned forward, his elbows on the desk, hands clasped. "I'm not taking my father's company."

"Sorry?" She blinked. "I thought you said—"

"I have Valhalla. This is obviously a stunt, not a genuine offer. We haven't really spoken in years, and I know nothing about the software industry."

"Oh. So why…?"

"I don't know. But Victor got my attention by threatening a press release unless I discussed it face-to-face." The muscle in his jaw clenched, a rare burst of anger quickly reined in. "We'll leave for Sydney early tomorrow, meet with my father and brother, then concentrate on the Point One project. We'll fly home Sunday morning."

Emily nodded as she noted down the times, but inside a hard lump of apprehension began to form. Zac and close quarters did not mix, not when she had a dozen other worries on her plate. She needed her inner strength, and fighting with this overwhelming urge to get intimate with her boss took too much of it.

She rose to her feet, determined to focus on her job. "I'll make the arrangements."

"Thanks."

When Zac's attention returned to the papers on his desk, an odd feeling of disappointment swept her. What did she expect, the man to throw himself at her feet with slavish thanks? *A simple "it's good to have you back" wouldn't go amiss...*

"Oh, before you go..."

She turned, flushed with faint hope.

"Those debts your ex-husband owed? You don't need to worry about it. I paid them off."

She stilled.

Zac's brows shot up in quizzical expectance, but she could barely choke out the words.

"You did *what?*"

"I paid off the debts. So you can—"

"You didn't. Please tell me this is a joke."

He frowned, clearly not anticipating this reaction. "I don't joke when it comes to money. I paid it in full Monday night."

Her insides crashed to the bottom of her sensibly shoed feet. "What the hell were you thinking? I've already—" She turned away, tunneling a hand through her hair, destroying the neat coiffure in the process. "I got scammed. Again."

"What are you talking about?"

She whirled back, hot anger pulsing low in her throat, choking her breath. Jimmy's betrayal, the thug's visit and now Zac's revelation welled up, pounding against her walls of restraint. She could practically feel her self-control slipping from the tight knots she'd bound them in.

"I've already deferred my course," she said tightly. "I'm picking up the refund check this afternoon... I even got an extension on the due date..." *And Mayer had known and was going to take my money anyway.* Her head felt like it was going to explode. Not since she'd been ten years old had she felt so insignificant, so powerless. First her deadbeat parents, then Jimmy, now Zac—

Zac studied his conservatively dressed assistant with mounting confusion. He could see the tension winding her up, from the pulled-back shoulders, down the painfully rigid spine, to the white-knuckled grip on her notepad.

She finally spoke in a cool, clipped voice he knew all too well. "You didn't need to do that."

"It was nothing—"

"Don't." Her eyes slashed at him behind those protective rims. "Don't you *dare* tell me it was nothing. I know how much Jimmy owed." She took a breath then said, "So. That means you have me, guaranteed, until I can pay you back."

Zac frowned. "That's not why I did it."

Her look was riddled with skepticism. "I see. So why did you do it?"

"Because you were in trouble. Because I could."

"And it works out great for you, right?"

Zac stared at her. "You're out of line, Emily."

"And so are you," she shot back before clamping her mouth shut, but not before he caught a glimpse of her barely hidden disgust.

Disgust. At *him*. Irritated now, he scowled.

Pride. That was the last thing on his mind when he'd stopped Louie Mayer on Monday morning. Admittedly, he had intended to deck the guy—hell, he *still* wanted to. But instead he'd slapped down a bundle of notes for Gold Coast's number-one bookie in some noisy nightclub later that night. And throughout the entire adventure, Emily's pride hadn't entered into the equation. He'd never even entertained the thought that she could take his gesture the wrong way.

But she had, judging by that subzero glare boring into him.

So much for his impulsive good deed. He couldn't ask her out now, not when she was all fired up like this. The implications, her misinterpretation…man, it was an invitation to disaster.

Dammit all.

He gathered up his frustration, forcing it into the backseat. "Look, this is simple. It's not about enslavement or blackmail or anything else. You didn't have the money. I did. You were threatened— Don't deny it," he added as her mouth opened. "Or would you rather owe some criminal than me?"

Her mouth snapped closed and he could see her throat working, swallowing hard. Her composure cracked a little. "No…"

"So there you have it. At least I won't threaten your family when you don't pay up."

Her chin shot up, a defiant gesture that would have made him smile if he weren't so annoyed with himself. "Oh, I intend to pay."

"I know you will." He nodded firmly. "You're Emily Reynolds."

"What's that supposed to mean?"

This time he did smile. *Well, well.* He'd finally managed to dig under her professional armor. There could be hope for him yet. "Over the last two years, you've shown yourself to be highly efficient, reliable and completely professional."

At her embarrassed confusion, he paused. He'd been generous with her workplace performance reviews, hadn't he? Given praise where it was due? Yet her obvious discomfort at his summary niggled at him. "Which is why," he continued carefully, "You're going to be my event manager for the Point One complex."

"The new executive apartments in Sydney?"

"Yes. No relocation necessary—you can do it all from the office via videoconferencing. And it's more pay, a bigger challenge," he reminded her.

"But—"

"You're not up to it?"

"No. Yes!" She took a quick breath. "But we normally use Premier Events."

"I'm looking to start a new in-house department, and you know our staff and our contractors. You should talk with Jenna in Accounts about a budget and get together a list of suitable people you want on your team. When we're down in Sydney—"

The phone on Zac's desk rang. He glanced at the display, frowned, then picked it up.

Emily knew the caller had to be family the instant he spoke. No one else could tense up his shoulders, flatten his mouth and bring such a wary expression to his eyes. But as she made to leave, he halted her with a sharp gesture.

She stood there, an unwilling eavesdropper, until he finally clicked off the call, his green eyes bearing residual irritation as they refocused on her.

"As I was saying, we'll inspect the Point One site and meet the people I've been dealing with. Pack for the weekend."

Finally dismissed, she nodded before turning on her heel and walking out the door. A weekend with Zac Prescott. She swallowed the swell of unbidden excitement with a forceful gulp.

How could she focus on the incredible opportunity he'd just given her when her heart hammered crazily in her chest? Sure, she'd have to work like a dog up to and including the launch, but that wasn't it. This wild, breath-stealing excitement was about more than just a job promotion.

She didn't want to want Zac…damn, she refused to want a man who blithely made decisions about her life without even asking her. A man who didn't want her the way she wanted him to want her.

And yet he'd kissed her. Flirted, even. Didn't that tell her something?

She tossed the notebook on her desk. Zac had crossed the line, invading her private life—a shameful, personal part of it—without invitation. Embarrassment and anger flared up, replacing the fleeting desire. She'd been forced to grow up too early, the responsible one in their fractured family, until she'd been fostered out at ten years old. Relying only on herself had become a way of life. She didn't need saving.

Not even if her personal white knight was Zac Prescott.

Three

As befitted his top-end income bracket, Zac traveled in style all the way, from the flights and airport car service to the accommodations. Normally Emily took secret delight in their business trips, in the unfamiliar luxury she could wallow in, albeit briefly. Outwardly she was perfectly composed, but inside her stomach jittered with glee each time, just like a kid on her first plane trip.

But this time was different—*she* was different. She was acutely conscious of every inch separating them on the flight south, of each small movement as he shifted his arm on the rest, when he brushed away that lock of hair while bent forward, concentrating on work. The way he took her overnight bag with a smile, shouldering it as they made their way to their waiting car. Even their "adjoining room" status at Sydney's five-star Park Hyatt on Circular Quay took on new meaning.

When they both got into the elevator and he pressed the top-floor button, she felt his interest, his eyes lingering for seconds too long.

"New suit?"

Startled, she darted him a glance. "No."

"Shoes?"

"No."

He paused then said, "There's something different about you."

"Maybe it's my absence of rose-colored glasses."

She hadn't meant to make him laugh. And in this luxurious harborside hotel, with the cloud of serious circumstances hovering in the background, it was a relief to see his normally animated face crease into humor.

"Does this mean," he said with a quirk of an eyebrow, "you've forgiven me for butting into your life and paying off your debt?"

"No."

"Even though I've handed you my highly-sought-after Point One account?"

Her eyes narrowed. "Is that why—"

"No." The truth lay in his direct gaze. "They're two unrelated issues. You can do this job without worrying about you or your sister's safety."

Man, why'd he have to put it like that? She pressed her lips together and stared at the ascending floors. Her objections were beginning to make her sound like an ingrate, and he knew it.

He returned his attention to the numbers, hands in his pockets. He was still smiling when they got off on their floor and he indicated she lead the way. They paused at their respective doors, Emily making a big deal of digging the keycard from her pocket.

"I'll see you in an hour," he said as she finally shoved the door open.

She nodded like she had a thousand times before, knowing he'd be knocking on her door a minute to the hour, ready to throw himself into work. But when she stumbled into the familiar surroundings of her premier suite, pulled in her bag and closed the door, heavy tension came crashing down, forcing her over to the cream couch. With a groan, she collapsed into it.

Acute and painful awareness. That's what it was. He moved

and she flinched. He spoke and she felt a burst of desire spike her heart rate. And when he inadvertently touched her, she had to bite her tongue to swallow a frustrated groan.

You have got to get a grip.

Toeing off her shoes, she shoved her glasses up and rubbed her eyes. Work. This was work. She'd had no trouble focusing on it before. And now it was more important than ever. Zac had enough confidence in her to oversee the launch of Point One instead of outsourcing to a more highly qualified event-planning company. Whatever his motives for paying off Jimmy's debt, he wouldn't jeopardize his company or his reputation in order to do it.

Which meant she owed it to him to do her job.

Emily sensed Zac's mood change the moment they walked through VP Tech's huge glass doors in affluent North Sydney. They cut a silent path through the hushed foyer, all polished marble floor, chrome-and-leather fittings and subtle lighting. His posture signaled an impending battle even though his expression gave nothing away. Yet no matter how tense she knew he was, he still spared a smile and a greeting for the front-desk secretary and security man as they passed. Emily noted their surprised glances before his pace increased and she almost had to run to catch up with him. His haste, his irritation, all spoke volumes.

Do it quickly, then run. Don't get caught.

The words were so clear her mother could've been standing right there, slurring in her ear, her eyes glassy with drugs and bourbon. With an inward gasp Emily pulled up short, just in time to avoid Zac's broad back as he stopped at the elevator bay.

She was nervous for him, and that sent her heart into a jarring rhythm. Even as she covered up with efficient aplomb, readjusting her jacket over her hips and shoving her glasses back up her nose, she needn't have bothered. Zac was staring at the ascending elevator numbers with single-minded concentration, a frown creasing his brow.

They rode up forty floors in silence, and when the doors slid open onto what was obviously the executive level, an imposing man stood awaiting them.

Zac's expression abruptly shut down.

Cal Prescott was the taller and broader of the two, with dark, lush features that spoke of a Mediterranean heritage. In comparison, Zac's face was more angular, more aristocratic, and coupled with his lean frame and tanned Nordic skin, the differences were a sharp and distinct contrast. Stepbrothers, so different in appearance, yet sharing an innate air of authority and confidence.

"Cal." Zac finally offered his hand, which Cal took firmly. Then suddenly Cal enveloped him in a hug.

Emily watched them closely. When Zac finally extricated himself, awkwardness was etched as clearly as permanent marker over his entire body.

He took a step back and cleared his throat. "This is Emily Reynolds, my assistant."

Cal smiled, thrust out his hand and said, "A pleasure, Emily."

Emily could name only a handful of Zac's clients who gave her the courtesy of a handshake. Having Cal Prescott, heir to the VP Tech fortune and Mr. One-Click himself, pay her the subtle respect threw her. And judging by the look on Zac's face as their eyes met, it threw him, too.

Without missing a beat she recovered, returning the shake with a nod. "Same here, Mr. Prescott."

"Well, let's go into the conference room." Cal clapped a hand on Zac's shoulder. "Victor's on his way up."

"We're not staying."

Cal paused, hand dropping. "Why not?"

"Because I have a business to run and frankly, threatening me with press coverage to get me here was childish. Whatever game Victor's cooked up, I'm not playing."

"Victor threatened you?"

"Via voice mail."

"Great. Typical Victor," Cal snorted. "Well, come in and

you can tell him yourself." And he swept open the conference doors.

After Zac finally sat at the long boardroom table, eerie déjà vu crept over his skin with dark foreboding. Cal's odd welcome aside, nothing had changed in this place. Yet *he'd* changed. The years he'd spent carving out his own niche, finally free from Victor Prescott's suffocating influence, had given him new life and opened his eyes to new possibilities, new horizons.

It had made him who he was.

"So how've you been, Zac?"

His older brother sat opposite, the innocent question coated in loaded expectation. Zac studied him carefully. Cal had been his one and only regret when he'd walked out. He'd suspected his defection would cost him Cal's respect, but he still hadn't been prepared for the man's total ostracism.

So when Cal's immaculate yet impersonal wedding invitation had arrived in August, he'd been thrown for a loop, those old wounds threatening the peace he'd worked so hard to create. He'd declined the invite but still that perfidious Prescott blade managed to draw blood.

"Business is great," Zac finally said. "Buyers are flocking to the Gold Coast, thanks to Sydney's outrageous land tax."

"And yet I hear you've got a new property venture down here."

He nodded. "Apartment blocks in Potts Point."

When Cal's gaze landed on Emily, she returned it with a polite smile before opening her notebook, ready to take notes.

Her familiar cool professionalism was like a shot of Valium in the arm.

"Where are you staying?" Cal asked.

"The Park Hyatt on the Quay."

"Nice." Silence fell, and awkward seconds stretched by until Cal finally said, "Are you free on March the fifteenth?"

"Why?"

"Because I'm getting married. Attempt number two," he added with a self-deprecating smile.

"What happened to—?" Zac clamped his mouth shut. He didn't need to know.

"You didn't see the write-up in the papers?" At Zac's curt head shake, Cal looked oddly irked. "Ava fainted, got taken to hospital. We're putting it off until after the baby's born in January."

The automatic refusal fizzled on the tip of Zac's tongue, his hesitation furrowing Cal's brow.

"Congratulations, Mr. Prescott," Emily automatically responded, her fingers flicking through her schedule book. "Zac, you have a meeting on the thirteenth—" to her credit, when she looked up and caught his expression she didn't even stumble "—but that's not confirmed," she added diplomatically.

"You're going to turn me down *again?*" Cal said in disbelief.

What the hell was going on? Cal's thunderous silence over the years had screamed everything words couldn't. And now in the space of a few months, he'd not only called twice but was inviting him to his wedding again?

Then Victor strode in and all conversation ground to a halt.

Like all great businessmen, Victor Prescott commanded the room by his mere presence. "Reputation, authority, attitude and entitlement—make like you have them and people will give you respect," he'd always said. Zac swallowed heavily. He couldn't remember a time when Victor's little decree of wisdom hadn't been on the tail end of every life lesson, every business deal he'd made.

The sour pill of irony was that he'd called upon it more times than he cared to remember these last three years.

Yes, he was free of all that tension and conflict. Yes, he knew who he truly was. But that didn't stop the suffocating expectation from surging up to tighten his chest and quicken his breath.

"Dad," he said now, forcing his voice into neutrality.

"Zac." Victor made a point of leaning over the table and offering his hand. Zac returned the handshake, then sat back down.

"Look, I have a meeting this afternoon," Zac said without

preamble. "So I'll make this quick. You've got me here. What do you want?"

Victor paused, his eyes going from Zac then to Cal, who gave him a faint nod.

"I told you—as soon as you sign the papers, you'll be VP Tech's new CEO. Of course, you'd start as cochair on the board," Victor said, ignoring Zac's scowl. "Then, after six months' probation, getting to know the business, our products and clients, you'll take on the position of CEO. That means you'd—"

"Hang on," Zac lifted an impatient hand, then glared at Cal. "You actually meant what you said last Thursday?"

At Cal's nod, Zac speared Victor with his gaze. "You're CEO. Where are you going?"

"It's time I took a step back."

No way. "You're retiring?"

"Sort of."

"Victor…" Cal began, but paused as Victor stared back. Something passed between the two men, then Victor finally let out an aggrieved sigh.

"I had an operation a few months ago. I'm fine now," Victor shrugged off Zac's look, "but the doctors advised I should cut back on my hours."

"I see." Zac looked to a suspiciously silent Cal. "And what about you?"

"Cal has a family to think of," Victor said coolly. "He doesn't need the pressure or stress."

And I bet that just pisses you off. "And I do?"

"Zac," Cal began, but his younger brother's glare silenced him.

"After all those years," Zac said, "those brutal hours working yourself half to death, you're passing up the top job?"

The look on Cal's face was unreadable. "As Victor said, I have a family now."

This was unbelievable. "So you both thought I'd fall over myself to step into the breach? That I'd embrace this opportunity to return to the Prescott fold?"

He couldn't—wouldn't—hide the sneer in his voice. Latent

anger bubbled up, burning his throat. Once he'd desperately needed his father's approval, but Victor's lies and manipulation had pushed him over the line. Way, way over the line.

Zac had walked away from it all without a drop of guilt.

I can't go back to that.

He rose swiftly, back rigid. "No. Find someone else."

"Zac!" Victor rose too, preventing his escape with one swift step forward. "At least think about it. You owe it to—"

"Don't. Say. Another. Word," Zac ground out as the past swirled his vision, shrouding it in a patchwork of shadow and bright, painful light.

"You're a Prescott whether you like it or not," Cal said calmly behind him. "It's part of who you are. So is this company."

Zac spun back, a dozen furious comebacks tangling his tongue before he chewed them down. "That was your dream, Cal. I never wanted it. And I'm sure as hell not going to be *guilted* into it."

And then he stalked out the door, Emily close behind.

As the elevator glided down, Emily chanced a glance at Zac. She'd known this meeting was the last thing he'd wanted, but the struggle now etched on his face spoke of so much more.

He took a deep breath, then another. If that was her, she'd be a quivering mess on the floor. Not Zac—he dealt with conflict, breathed it out and then moved on. He didn't let things get to him, which was why he was so perfectly comfortable in his own skin.

It was a quality that fascinated as much as it attracted.

As the doors slid open, Zac surged forward, long strides devouring the corridor. Yet as they made their way toward the exit, he gradually began to ease up. First, his rigid back and tense shoulders loosened an inch. Then, that furious march turned into his familiar rolling gait. When he nodded goodbye to the front desk, his jaw had relaxed. Finally, as the doors swooshed open and they stepped out onto sun-filled Berry Street, whatever lingering traces that remained had fallen away.

"We're meeting with the Point One team in an hour," she reminded him.

"Good." He glanced at his watch, then at his mobile as it started to ring. He pocketed it. "Let's get going."

"Zac! Wait up."

They both turned as Cal emerged from the glass doors, breaking into a jog to catch up. "I need to talk to you."

Emily glanced at Zac. He gave her a quick nod, his expression stiffly cautious. "I won't be a minute."

Zac waited until Emily had reached their car parked a few spaces down before he turned back to Cal. "I thought I made myself clear upstairs."

Cal pocketed his hands and shifted his weight. "Very. And I don't blame you." His surprise must've shown, because Cal let out a small laugh. "You don't think I know how Victor operates? Do you have any idea of the crap he's been dealing out these past few months?"

"Yeah, thanks for including me."

"Don't be a smartarse. Whatever Victor's faults—and we know he has many—he's had a rough time. He—"

"I don't want to know, Cal. I left all this behind, in case you've forgotten."

"Yes, you did."

Irritation flared at Cal's subtle jab. "What's that supposed to mean?"

"You left—not once but twice. The first time I get—you were eighteen, you'd scored a place at that university in Sweden. You needed to do stuff for yourself, to stand on your own feet. But the second time, after you'd graduated, you were home one week, gone the next. No calls, no e-mails. What the hell do you think *I'd* think?"

Zac scowled. "Would it have changed anything? You were on Victor's side, you always were—"

Cal's foul curse snapped Zac's brow up. "You're my brother, Zac. You owed me an explanation."

"Victor thought I owed him, too, and look how that turned out." Cloying memories wound their way around his chest, choking his lungs. "And hey, if we're laying the blame here, why didn't you pick up the bloody phone before now and call *me?*" He snapped his head back to the car, refusing to feel guilty about the fleeting remorse twisting Cal's face. "I've got to go."

"Zac…"

He turned and marched off toward the car, toward Emily, and away from the gut-wrenching emotions of his past.

Four

Seven. That's how many times Zac checked his phone, then ignored the call. Throughout their two-hour meeting with the Point One Sydney team in the hotel's private meeting room, Zac's attention had been distracted by that phone, which was so unlike him.

"Are you okay?" she asked casually when the meeting finally broke up and she began gathering up the files.

"Huh? Yeah. Fine." He firmly stuck his phone back in his pocket. "Do you have any questions so far?"

"Not yet. Thanks," she added when Zac relieved her of the document bag, hefting the long strap onto his shoulder. "We have our site inspection at four—shall I order lunch up?"

He nodded absently, his mind a thousand miles away, and Emily wondered if his thoughts were on the business at hand or still stuck back at VP Tech.

When she returned to her suite, his mood had rubbed off, dimming the enjoyment of room service, distracting her thoughts as she went over the paperwork again.

Finally, at three o'clock, she gave up. As she leaned back in the couch, pulled the band from her hair, then smoothly retied it, a sudden thought occurred.

The laptop glowed back at her. *I could just…*

No. She slammed the computer closed and crossed her arms. Zac had never discussed his family, which meant that part of his life was off-limits. She wasn't about to violate that trust now by trawling through the Internet in search of salacious—and probably highly inaccurate—details.

Yet thanks to this morning, her curiosity had begun to grow.

She'd never seen Zac so wound up, barely able to keep a lid on his simmering anger, which meant something major had happened. Something big enough to make him walk away from his family.

She rose, suddenly restless, and stalked over to the huge sliding doors that led onto the balcony. The tinted glass warmed her palms, a familiar sensation that brought to mind another time, another place. Another kind of heat.

With her forehead resting on the smooth window, she allowed herself a brief moment of indulgence, a moment to recall Zac's mouth, his scent. His ability to make her forget everything in her past and just be. With him.

Finally, she straightened, dragging a long breath in. *Enough.* She'd been appalled at the thought of Zac digging around in *her* life. Getting involved in his family problems was unprofessional. It had nothing to do with her.

Nothing.

When they reconvened in the foyer at three-thirty, she was relieved to see Zac back to his normal self. Yet even as they talked work during the entire drive to Potts Point, Emily still found herself thinking increasingly unprofessional thoughts during the lulls.

She was worried about him. This thing with the Prescotts had gotten under his skin, affecting him in a way she'd never seen before. The most difficult of clients hadn't elicited even half the reaction he'd given this.

"We're here."

As Zac pulled up into a space, Emily's gaze automatically went to the window.

Building plastic and chipboard covered the ground floor. Leaning forward, her gaze went up…and up, and up. From what she'd read, the complex was twenty-five stories high, twenty levels of private apartments, a fourth-level gym and indoor pool, a laundry level, three more for businesses, and a ground floor restaurant, coffee shop and café.

And Zac had put his faith in her to launch this to the Sydney public.

"Coming?" Zac was on the sidewalk, peering steadily in at her.

"It'll be full-on getting it all ready by December." She scrambled out, barely faltering as he rounded the car to take her bag.

"Yep."

"Long hours, late nights…" She smoothed her jacket then retrieved her bag from him.

He nodded. "For a while, yes."

Irritation threaded her blood, her partly demolished wall teetering as one brick reappeared with a solid thunk. "I've drafted a preliminary list of requirements—staff, budget…"

"Sure. E-mail me when it's finalized." He swept one arm toward the service entrance. "They're meeting us in the penthouse suite."

Emily straightened her shoulders and nodded. She'd said yes to this job, had given her word. It wouldn't be forever. Even if she couldn't get into Queensland University by second term, she'd still end up repaying Zac by then.

You can do this. You've honed professional *to a fine art. You're an expert at focusing on work.*

And she would *not* stress about Zac Prescott.

As the Sydney team made their way through the freshly painted top-floor penthouse apartment, Emily studied them again, filing away their names and positions for future reference. The structural engineer, the acoustic consultant, the fit-out specialist. But it was Sattler Design, Sydney's leading brother-and-sister interior design duo, that captured her attention. Steve and Trish Sattler were walking, talking ex-cover models—Steve with rangy good looks and artfully messy hair that only added to his urban sophistication. He was a perfect foil for Trish, with her long, glossy mahogany mane and big brown eyes that frequently focused on Zac with entirely too much interest.

Zac, to his credit, didn't pick up on that, instead conducting himself as professionally as always. She had to give him points for that, if not for the way he didn't entirely discourage Trish's overly friendly body language.

Her boss was unlike any man she'd met: trustworthy, honorable, loyal. She actually liked him, which was saying something. He couldn't help it if all those attributes oozed a "come here" aura that attracted women of all ages.

She glanced up from the schematics just in time to catch Trish's look. She was studying Zac's profile with almost lustful relish, a small smile hovering on her lips. When she caught Emily looking, she merely raised one eyebrow, giving her a woman-to-woman smile. Without acknowledging it, Emily returned to the plans.

Point proven right there. Another ex-girlfriend-in-training. She fielded a handful of those calls each week.

From the twenty-fifth floor they went systematically down, addressing outstanding issues until they ended up in the plastic-covered foyer of a soon-to-be authentic Balinese restaurant.

Meeting over, Emily shook everyone's hand with a smile and a nod. From the corner of her vision she watched Trish approach Zac.

"I just wanted to thank you for this wonderful opportunity, Mr. Prescott," she began, a wide smile on her perfectly made-up mouth.

"Zac, please."

"Zac." She practically purred out his name. Emily narrowed her eyes as she checked her phone messages.

"Sattler Design's reputation precedes you, Miss Sattler."

"Trish, please."

Trish, please, Emily mentally mimicked, scrolling through her calls with single-minded intent.

"Are you free for dinner? Steve has another client, but I thought you and I could discuss the finer points of our brief, to get a firm handle on what you really need."

Oh, please. Emily nearly rolled her eyes at the double entendre but noted that Zac had pulled out his phone again.

"No, I think everything's looking pretty good at this stage. Emily?"

"Sorry?" Emily blinked innocently as both sets of eyes fell on her.

"Do you have any issues you need to raise with Trish?"

Yes. You're only one in a long line. She smiled and shook her head. "Not right now. But I'm sure we'll be talking later."

She watched Zac shake hands, thanking them for coming. The look on Trish's face didn't crack, but Emily knew the woman was reconnoitering, already working out another way to achieve her goal. It was a familiar dance, one that had begun as an amusing weekly anecdote she related to her sister. But now it had slipped from amusing to tiresome. Especially since…

She pulled herself up short with a frown.

Especially since you kissed him?

Yes.

He was talking to her and she was nodding, giving the outward appearance of actually listening. But inside her heart pounded, her blood racing at breakneck speed while her brain buzzed annoyingly.

Okay. So this is just a physical thing. You've been celibate for close to two years. Of course you're reacting to the first man who's shown any interest in you since…Jimmy.

Ooh. Bad comparison.

"Emily? You okay?"

A hand on her shoulder stopped her thoughts. She blinked up at Zac, at the concern in his eyes. Expressive olive eyes designed to make short work of a woman's will.

A pulse of irritation spread through her belly and she quickly jerked her jacket back into place. The stiff collar suddenly chafed.

"Just thinking about Point One. It's…different from your usual."

"There are only so many mansions you can build before you need a bigger challenge," he answered with a smile, pulling open the glass doors for her.

"True. A challenge is good."

He slid in the car after her, clipping on his seatbelt. "You up for it, Emily?"

His eyes mesmerized her, part amusement, part determination. Suddenly the air in the car got way too warm.

"Yes." Her voice came out way too breathy. Her cheeks heated as his lips spread into a grin, and she quickly coughed, warmth swamping her limbs. "Yes," she added more firmly. "I am."

"Great." With that devilish smile still in place, he shoved on his sunglasses and started the car.

Five

"Dinner at six downstairs." The note had been pushed under her door, signed with a large "Z" at the bottom.

She'd planned on eating alone in her room, going over the files and refining her action plan, not sharing an intimate meal with Zac. *No, not intimate.* A working dinner. They'd talk business like they had a hundred times before. There'd be schedule discussions, costings, launch ideas. There would be no hand-holding, no seductive looks, no footsie under the table.

Just work.

Ignoring that tiny swoop of disappointment, she walked firmly into the dining room at two minutes to six, shoulders back, eyes straight ahead.

The Harbour Kitchen & Bar was prime waterfront dining, with floor-to-ceiling folding glass doors and an open-plan kitchen so the diners could watch their meals being prepared by the chef. Its clean lines and quiet elegance sent a shot of confidence and calm into her bones.

But when Zac spotted her from the window table he'd secured and smiled, her body tensed up.

He pulled out her chair, seated her with effortless aplomb. She murmured her thanks as her heart thumped, making her skin twitch uncomfortably under her suit.

"Still in your work clothes?" He asked, reseating himself.

"Yes." *I'd rather be out of them. With you.* She swallowed quickly, glancing from his broad, jacketless shoulders to the spectacular harbor view outside. That one brief summary was enough for her to note his loosened collar with tie still in place.

"Great view," she murmured as the sun's low golden beams spread wide across the sparkling water, dousing the Opera House's white sails in a similar glow.

"Always is." From the corner of her eye she saw his gaze barely leave her before he picked up the menu.

Discomforted, Emily did the same, noting over the stiff gilt-paper the way his shirt cuffs skimmed perfectly tanned hands, hands that bore the scars of hard labor yet still looked clean and touchable.

She'd always liked a pair of strong hands.

Aaaaand…she was staring. Great.

She hauled her gaze up to his face before quickly glancing away. Well, *that* was such a tempting distraction she refused to look any more than absolutely necessary.

"I never knew you'd been married."

That dragged her attention back. "It's not something I talk about."

"So what *do* you talk about?" He casually unfolded his menu as she frowned. "Come on, Emily. You know practically everything about me, especially after today."

"That's not true."

"Well, what do you want to know?"

Oh, do not go there. "I know enough." She tipped her menu up, but Zac was having none of it. With one finger he gently lowered the barrier, forcing her to look at him.

"You organize me, feed me, ensure I have what I need, when I need it. You're also privy to the inner workings of my private life and now, my family. You're my work wife."

"Your what?"

He grinned at her alarm. "My work wife—a work-based partnership between a man and a woman. You haven't heard that expression before?" She shook her head and fixated on restraightening her perfectly straight cutlery as he continued. "I'd thought that, after working together for so long, I was a friend of sorts. Someone you can trust."

Her head snapped up. "Someone who took charge of my life and paid off my debts without asking?"

Was that a flash of hurt flickering behind his eyes? Contrite, she bit the inside of her bottom lip, embarrassment flooding her cheeks. "I'm sorry. That was rude."

The corner of his mouth tugged up. "I guess I deserved it. For not asking you first."

Zac watched her war with that, the struggle from his apology showing in those dark blue eyes, in her luscious mouth now thin and firm.

Man, it was like getting blood from a stone! He tried a different tack. "I overstepped, and I apologize."

"Okay."

He studied her, trying to get a handle on that closed expression. "Friends?"

As he watched, her lashes began to blink out a rapid beat. "Okay," she repeated, her voice soft and low, before she quickly took a sip of water.

Zac rested his arms on the table, locking his fingers thoughtfully as the waiter approached.

After they'd ordered, he watched her straighten the cutlery—again—then reposition her water glass.

He'd seen her glide through countless business meals, unruffled and professional. But now…things had changed. He'd changed them by violating her privacy, crossing the line by, oh, about a thousand miles.

Yet the inexplicable urge to dig deeper, to find out who Emily Reynolds really was beneath that unflappable facade, urged him on.

"It must've been tough being married to someone like—"

"Zac." She breathed out his name, almost as if it pained her. "Please don't."

"Don't what? Express sympathy? Regret that your ex hurt you? Sometimes," he added slowly, "the ones closest to us can do the most damage."

He fully expected her to shut down then and there, but instead her eyes filled with something...*almost vulnerable*. Then she glanced away. "Yeah."

Interesting.

She flipped her glass over. "I think I'll have that wine now."

Zac poured the golden liquid as she switched the topic to the Point One project. He knew she was doing it to gain control, to lead their conversation into nonpersonal waters. So he let her, until they'd finished their main meals and the wine was all gone. Then the dessert arrived.

"Thank you." She beamed up at the waiter as he placed a berry-topped baked cheesecake in front of her. When she picked up her fork, her lips curving in delight, Zac's heart rate began to pick up.

"You like cheesecake?"

"Love it. That little French patisserie across the street from Valhalla does an amazing one." She rolled her eyes. "Chocolate fudge. To die for."

Then she slid a small forkful of cake between her lips and his brain shorted.

"How..." It took all his willpower not to groan. "How did you meet him?"

"Who?" she mumbled past her mouthful.

"Your ex."

Her fork clinked down on the plate. She spent a few seconds swallowing before clearing her throat.

Zac sighed. "Look, I don't want you to think my money came with conditions. But I'd like to know. If you want to tell me. Apart from your sister, I'm guessing you don't confide in a lot of people."

The look on her face told him her internal war went beyond

the standard issues. When she finally replied, her words were deliberately measured. Cautious.

"My story isn't that interesting. I was twenty-three, young and stupid and in love, or so I thought. Jimmy turned out to be a liar and a cheat and then he died."

"I can't imagine you ever being stupid."

Her short laugh surprised him. "Oh, you'd be surprised."

They both sat in silence, eyes locked, until the seconds lengthened. And in those seconds, he sensed a tiny chink in her armor—nothing groundbreaking or defining, but something definitely positive, however small.

It sparked a glimmer of quiet confidence.

She finally broke eye contact to stare at her plate. "He drowned. For a surfer that's kind of ironic, don't you think?"

"I'm sorry."

Her expression hardened as she reached for her water. "Don't be. I just wish he was alive so I could kick his sorry, freeloading ass."

Zac waited as she downed the dregs of her glass.

"You really want to know," she finally said, her eyes glinting in challenge.

"Yes."

Her brow rose. "Fine. I met Jimmy three years ago at a Brisbane nightclub where he was singing in a band. He fancied himself a rock god—he got heaps of mileage off that cool 'struggling musician' chestnut. The kicker was, he was pretty good. But he lacked discipline and motivation, and the band finally dumped him out after one too many no-shows."

Zac just nodded, unwilling to break the moment.

"The last time I heard from him was when he signed the divorce papers, over a year ago. Now I know why. He was too busy working out ways to steal my money." She paused at the look on Zac's face. "What?"

"I was just thinking—" He hesitated, then went on tactfully. "I don't see it—you the nightclub type, marrying a musician."

Her eyes turned stormy. "Because I'm so organized and straitlaced?"

"You like order," he clarified. "But yeah, it does seem out of character."

Emily's heart twisted a little. Her curt confession hadn't satisfied his curiosity as she'd hoped. Her chin went up. "Maybe that was my little rebellion," she added, staring at her wine glass. "Emily the rebel, that's me. Or maybe I just—" *Wanted to be loved.* She bit off that last bit, mortified. She'd thought herself in love with Jimmy. No, that was wrong. She'd hoped. Desperately wished. Just like with all the others.

"What?" Zac asked.

"Nothing."

"Maybe…you just wanted to let your hair down for a change."

She scowled, a nerve well and truly touched. "You don't—"

"—know you?" His expression remained inscrutable. "I know you can't leave for the night until your desk is completely clear."

She waved that away. "You've seen my desk a thousand times a day."

"You deny yourself hot chips for a ham-and-salad sandwich."

"That's—"

"You love pink and blue but you wear black all the time. You're no-frills—you don't care for a lot of makeup or jewelry. Your hair is naturally blond, but you get highlights every two months." His gaze swept over her head, then across her face before coming to rest on her mouth. "You smell like ginger and a warm summer weekend." His voice became rough. "You taste like—"

"Stop!" She blinked. "How do you know what…" She paused blankly until her brain finally caught up. "You remember."

His smile curled with male knowledge. "So do you."

"But you—"

"I was being gentlemanly, waiting for you to say something. When you didn't, I thought it was one of those things that Must Not Be Mentioned Again."

She opened her mouth but her words jumbled together. With a swallow she tried again. "I didn't mean to…"

"I know."

"It was just…"

"I know."

"It won't—"

"Emily," he barked, a little too sharply. She clamped her mouth shut. "Enough with the apology."

The look on her face was so appealing, all flushed embarrassment, that Zac suddenly wondered what she'd do if he leaned in and kissed her.

"It wasn't even a kiss. More like a brief…" she glanced at his mouth, "brush of skin. A non-kiss."

That soft sigh she ended on hit Zac in all the right places. It revved up his blood, quickening his heartbeat into a familiar thud of arousal.

He gritted his teeth, battling for control. Yet when he thought he'd finally regained it, she had to go and chew on that full bottom lip. It wasn't a big thing, just a couple of perfect white teeth worrying the curve of her mouth for a brief second before she dipped her head and picked up her dessert fork. Yet his body jolted, her tiny reaction forever imprinted in his brain.

"Go on a date with me."

Her fork paused halfway up to her mouth. "What?"

What the hell are you doing?

He leaned in closer and unashamedly breathed in deep, drowning out that inner voice with her delicious scent. "Go. On. A. Date. With. Me."

A look of sudden horrified surprise bloomed before she smoothed out her expression.

"Very funny." She put her fork down and shoved the plate away.

"I'm not joking."

"Sure."

He frowned. "I'm not."

"Stop it, Zac. It's not funny."

"I'm not laughing." Man, her denial was beginning to nettle him.

She stared at her plate again, concentrating on edging it further to the side. "I'm sure there are a thousand other suitable women who would—"

"I'm asking *you*."

She glanced up, her brows dipping down behind those heavy-rimmed glasses, and he had the sudden urge to ease them off her face.

"Why me, when I'm…"

He smiled at her small self-directed gesture. "When you're trying so hard to hide behind bland suits and sensible shoes?"

When her face flushed pink and her gaze shot past his shoulder, he silently cursed.

"Because," he continued more gently, "despite your best efforts, I find myself attracted to you."

"Because of a non-kiss?"

And your sweet curvy a— You can't say that! "Yep."

Blinking quickly, she refused to meet his eyes as she removed her napkin from her lap. "We work together." She began to fold the cloth efficiently on the table.

"So?"

"It's not professional."

"Says who? I'm the boss."

"Exactly. People will talk." She finally looked at him, her eyes unsettled.

"At the risk of repeating myself—so?"

"I owe you money."

He leaned back in his chair and silently studied her as she went on.

"And you've just paid off my ex's gambling debts, given me a raise and—"

"How long have we worked together?"

"What kind of—"

"Close to two years, right?"

"Yes."

"And in that entire time have I given you any reason to believe I'd blackmail you—or anyone—in that way?"

She paused, those lashes fluttering at his growing irritation. "I didn't mean to insult you."

"Well, you have."

"Look, Zac," she took a breath and leaned forward. "This is coming out all wrong. I appreciate your offer, but—"

He scowled. "You *appreciate* my offer?"

"I mean, I'm flattered, naturally—"

"Really."

"No, really. Any woman would be thrilled to be asked out by you."

"But you're not."

She shook her head. "I am *so* not your type."

He leaned in, which made her pull back. "And what is my type?"

"Oh, tall. Leggy and gorgeous. Rich. Any one of your ex-girlfriends fit the bill." She paused then added, "Trish Sattler fits the bill."

Emily studied Zac's frowning face—a beautiful, angular, all-male face—from behind the security of her glasses. Seriousness rippled off him in waves, his focus squarely on her. It was a look that made movement impossible, that dissected and disarmed.

Oh, my Lord. Her heart skipped a beat. "You *are* serious," she finally managed.

"Deadly."

"You *do* know there's a betting pool going on in Payroll? Who your next bed partner's going to be?"

His hand went to his nape, ruffling the hair there. "Okaaaaay…?"

"And that doesn't bother you?"

He shrugged. "Not really. What's your point?"

Was she thrilled? How about terrified. Shocked. Tempted. All of the above. But…

"This is not good," she muttered to herself.

Zac sighed. "The money thing again?"

"How can that not be an issue?"

"It just isn't. That was something a friend would do. This—" he flicked a finger between them "—is something different entirely."

"I see." Now her skin was tingling in earnest. She glanced away.

"So? What do you think?"

"I think..." *I think you're crazy, actually having this conversation aloud.* With a deep breath, she dragged her eyes back to his. "Workplace affairs always change things—when it goes wrong, it will go *really* wrong."

"What makes you think it'll go wrong?"

"Because it always does."

He paused, giving her a strange look. "Speaking from experience?"

"No." But as she watched him quirk up a disbelieving eyebrow, she swallowed thickly.

She leaned back in her chair, her mind churning. Even through everything—the parents from hell, the sexist boss, the numerous failed relationships—she'd kept believing, had clung tooth and nail to optimism, to the chance that love was out there somewhere. Despite the six-year gap, she'd been the strong one, keeping her sister AJ afloat when they were kids. She'd refused to use her sexuality as a career jump. She'd started over in a new city.

Yet had all those setbacks managed to steal more than money, self-respect and trust from her?

Had she turned into one of those cynical, hard-assed man-hating females?

"I'm not like your ex, Emily."

She smoothed down the tablecloth once, twice. "No, you're not."

"So...?"

"So what happens if it's a disaster?"

His mouth quirked. "We're adults. *If* it's a disaster, then we spend a week or so in awkward silence, then go back to being work colleagues. We'd do our jobs, you'd pay me back that money, and you'd go back to school."

You are not actually giving this serious thought?

She abruptly rose. "I have to…go."

Zac got to his feet. "I'll walk you to your room."

"That's not necessary."

"It is."

"No."

As she glared at him, the corner of his mouth curved. "I don't believe it."

"What?"

"*You're* giving *me* that look."

"What look?"

"That don't-mess-with-me-mate look." She frowned, which only made him chuckle. "You give it to all our difficult clients. I call it the rottweiler look—because no one's going to get past you without some serious backup." His warm hand seared through her jacket as he guided her out the restaurant.

"Nice. Did you just call me a dog?"

His laughter rang out in the elegant foyer, turning a few heads. When they paused at the elevator bank she tilted her chin up, exasperated at his amusement.

"You did!"

"I said your attitude was *doglike*. Big difference."

The doors slid open and they got in, Zac pressing the button before settling into the corner, his elbows resting on the railing, taking her in with a lazy smile. Emily steadfastly kept her eyes on the ascending floors.

When they arrived at their floor, Emily surged out, desperate to escape the confinement of that tiny space.

When she finally got to her door, she dug in her jacket pocket for her keycard, painfully aware of Zac at her shoulder.

She swiped the card once, then twice. The light remained red.

With a soft mutter, she tried again.

Still red.

"Here, let me." He took the card from her fingers and swiped it.

Red. He tried again.

"Can't we just go through your room?" Emily said impatiently.

"We could, but—"

"Then let's do that."

He glanced at her, shrugged and pulled out his keycard.

The lock green-lighted them on the first attempt, an irony that wasn't lost on her. Then he shouldered the door open, sweeping his hand in to allow her entry first.

With back straight, eyes ahead, she entered his room, walking swiftly across the living area to the connecting door. She opened it, then tried hers.

"It's locked," she said with a frown.

"I know."

Why hadn't she thought of that? She turned, only to find Zac with arms crossed, studying her in silence.

"So why didn't you say something?"

"I tried, but you were hell-bent on running away from me."

She blinked. "I wasn't running away!"

"Right." He unfolded his arms, then, to her consternation, reached for her glasses.

"What are you doing?" Instinctively she grabbed his arm, but the unexpected heat of his skin jerked her back. It was all he needed to claim his prize.

He inspected her glasses, looking through the thick lenses before pulling out a handkerchief from his pocket.

"You're shortsighted."

"Yes." She frowned as he brought her glasses to his mouth then breathed thickly over one lens.

It felt like her entire insides tightened with unexpected delight.

He began to polish the glass, a mischievous smile tilting his lips as he watched her squint at him.

"You don't need to…" She broke off as his lips parted again, mouth opening in slow deliberation before his hot breath frosted the glass.

What would it feel like to have those lips, that mouth, that breath on her skin?

Even with Zac so horribly out of focus, she could still make out that grin that told her he knew exactly what she was thinking.

Her belly flipped, warmth flooding her limbs.

"You should really leave these off."

"I need them to see." She blinked for emphasis. "Everything's fuzzy otherwise."

He moved and suddenly Zac-in-soft-focus became Zac-in-sharp-definition. "This better?"

She leaned back, desperately trying to ignore the warm singing of blood coursing through her body. "Uh…no…"

Before she could say another word, he put a hand on her nape, pulled her forward and kissed her.

Surprise held her still for a heartbeat, until heat surged into her chest where it swirled and dipped in delicious expectation.

His warm mouth was firm and skillful. He kissed her like he'd been practicing this all his life, a kiss that told her he knew what he was doing, knew how to please a woman. A kiss that melted her bones and quickly turned her on in a thousand different ways.

Through the haze of swiftly building desire, she felt his body move, and suddenly he was pressed up against her, heat spilling out to infuse them both.

Years of sexual frustration surged up, scorching her from the inside out as their breath and lips merged. She let out a groan, knew he'd felt it when his mouth curved against hers…just before he gently eased his tongue inside.

Oh. Wow. Emily let out a shocked squeak, which quickly petered off into a breathy sigh. She was vaguely aware of him gently palming her cheek, his thumb caressing her jaw, but she was too caught up in the divine sensation of his mouth making love to hers.

The hard insistent throb of his manhood began to grow between them, solidifying the reality of their location. Gradually, like wading into consciousness from a deep dream, she became aware of Zac pulling back.

It was, she realized groggily, her eyes at half-mast and her mouth still puckered, the most delicious few minutes of her entire life.

"Emily."

Her eyes sprang open, looking directly into his olive ones, dark with desire and amusement.

She swallowed thickly as the heat rose in her face. "I...can't. I just can't."

"Emmm—"

She ducked her head and practically raced for the door, eyes downcast. Zac surged forward but was too late—the solid thunk in her wake felt like the full stop to his unspoken sentence.

"—ily." He finished softly to the closed door. With an aggravated sigh he shoved his hands on his hips, then raised his head heavenward and scrunched his eyes shut. *Damn.*

Six

He stood there for what felt like ages, reining in his body, forcing it to relax through gritted teeth.

Until the small tap.

He yanked the door open. She stood in the doorway, blinking and squinting. She'd undone her jacket, revealing a white shirt tucked into a skirt that inadvertently emphasized curvy hips and a defined waist.

"My key works but I need—" Zac gave her no time to finish the sentence, instead grabbing her arms and firmly pulling her inside, kicking the door shut with one foot. Then he pushed her up against the wall and kissed her.

She offered a tiny protest, one that abruptly snapped off when his lips collided with hers, her breath in his mouth, her scent everywhere. It teased and tormented, that innocent gingery-appley smell that made him want to rip her clothes off and bury himself inside her.

Instead he yanked her jacket down her shoulders, then pulled her shirt from her waistband, desperate to feel skin.

Yes. He groaned approvingly, closing his eyes to fully

appreciate her smooth torso as it arched forward, arms pinned behind her back by her jacket, skin silken heat beneath his palms. Beautiful. Just beautiful.

"This needs to come off," he muttered into her mouth, tugging at her shirt.

Her breathless agreement was all he needed to wrench those damn buttons apart and tug the shirt from her shoulders.

Emily finally managed to struggle free of her jacket, her eyes flying open as his hands continued their exploration. He overwhelmed her, filling her skin, her pores with hot desperate longing.

This. This was what she craved. What she needed. And when he bunched her skirt up around her waist before easing her legs apart with his knee, she groaned from sheer pleasure.

Pleasure that exploded into a thousand tiny sparks of need when his hand dove into her knickers and intimately cupped her curls.

She would've fallen if he wasn't pinning her to the wall with his mouth, his hands, his hard thigh. And when his fingers slid through her warm slickness, brushing over hot flesh to unerringly find her taut sensitive bud, she groaned, wrenching her mouth from his.

It was too much. Too hot. Too…

"Zac," she got out. "What are we doing?"

His other hand clasped her chin, dragging her face back to him.

"I'm touching you. Now take your hair down."

With shaky hands she did as he asked, pulling her hair free from the severe knot. The strands fell down her back and shoulders, across her face, and he reached up a finger to gently brush them from her eyes. Those all-seeing, all-knowing eyes were almost black with desire, his breath hot as it fanned over her cheek.

"Let go for me, Emily."

She seemed to have lost all ability to think. Each single heartbeat echoed, blood racing through her body like a wall of flames.

She managed to get out a small nod, then a sigh when Zac let out a rumble of triumph and covered her mouth with his.

Then his finger slid inside her and her world ground to a breath-stealing halt. When she thought she might pass out from pleasure, he swiftly took charge, setting up a steady stroking pace that quickly began to swell and grow.

Her entire body screamed with joy. He'd set her skin on fire, his fingers dipping inside before easing out to smooth over her engorged bud. Over and over, again and again, until she whimpered beneath his mouth, a ragged plea for relief tearing from her lips.

He suddenly shifted, bracing himself, pressing her hard against the wall. Then his tongue was in her mouth, echoing the erotic glide of his fingers deep inside her, and she couldn't hold back any longer.

Zac felt the exact moment she went crashing over the edge. He gritted his teeth, desperate to hold on to that thin thread of control so he didn't embarrass himself and follow her.

Her hot wetness as it flooded him, the sheer beauty of her face frozen in climactic joy, nearly did him in. With a racing heart and an almost unbearable throb in his groin, he held on, waiting until Emily stopped trembling, until her breathing regulated and he finally registered her hands on his shoulders, pushing him back.

"Emily?" He tried to meet her eyes, but they were averted to the floor, her face flushed in acute embarrassment.

"I came back for my glasses," she muttered.

In the wake of his stunned surprise, she pulled away, quickly refixing her clothing.

The air was warm and thick with that familiar musky scent of sex, the silence complete as he forced his body into some semblance of control.

Her clothes were rumpled, shirt hanging loose and buttons askew. Her mouth was still puffy from his kisses, her hairdo now falling in gentle waves around her shoulders.

She looked so damn delicious, like a lush, slightly debauched

angel made for love, that all he wanted to do was take her to bed
and worship her body all night.

But her expression barred him entry, her stormy eyes rife
with confusion. So, with careful deliberation, he pulled out her
glasses and placed them in her outstretched hand, folding her
fingers around them while he battled with the siren's call.

"Good night, Zac."

All he could do was nod, staring as she turned and practically
ran from his room.

The lock clicked into place just before he ground out a groan
full of pure frustration.

Emily sat on her darkened balcony, staring at the glittering
Sydney harbor lights spread before her.

What on earth had she just done?

Her breath faltered again for about the millionth time that
night, her thighs flush with excitement.

Zac had paid off her debt, given her this Sydney account and
offered his services as a lover. He was the textbook definition of
the answer to all her problems.

And now this. He'd been on her, inside her. Touching her in
the most intimate of places while she broke apart beneath his
hands and lips.

Things like this just didn't happen to her. Not ever.

*Men were for fun. No emotional entanglements, no re-
sponsibility.* Her declaration to AJ felt like a year ago, not just
a few days. The irony would have made her laugh if she weren't
so torn in a dozen different directions.

With a frown she pulled her tracksuit jacket tighter and studied
the sparkling waterline, her eyes tracing the Opera House's
illuminated curves against the black night before dropping down
to the table where her notepad and pen sat.

She was a big girl. Sure, the thought of facing Zac after tonight
made her squirm with embarrassment, but she'd gotten through
worse. And if his date offer was still on the table, she still had
to logically dissect it.

Since the age of fifteen, she'd made all her major life decisions after carefully listing the pros and cons. With one major exception. She clicked the pen button up then down. *Jimmy.* He'd been charming and confident, so persistent he'd thrown her for a loop.

Expensive shoes or a flashy car were impulse buys. Marrying Jimmy had been hers.

C'mon, babe. Live a little on the edge, huh?

She grimaced. Her ex's enthusiasm for all things spontaneous had chipped away at her caution, made her doubt everything she'd thought herself to be. He'd tried to change what she now realized was in her very bones.

So what was better—going into a relationship with improbable hopes of love, or with realistic expectations that it would just be for mutual pleasure?

Picking up the pen, she drew a line down the center of the page, wrote "Pros" in one column, then "Cons" in the other.

A few minutes later, she stared at her list.

Pros—one, she was single. Two, she needed a fling to erase the leftovers of Jimmy's betrayal. Three, Zac was a great lover. Four, if it crashed and burned, she was leaving in April. Probably.

Cons—one, he was her boss: it'd not only look bad if it got out at the office, but could she handle going through the stress of workplace gossip again?

No.

Two… She nibbled on the end of the pen. He had a bevy of gorgeous ex-girlfriends, ones she couldn't hope to compete with.

Sighing, she took a gulp of coffee from her steadily cooling cup, then scribbled "3" in the "Cons" column: *Leaving in April,* before sitting back in the chair and scrutinizing the list in silence.

You don't do impulsive. It isn't you, remember?

The irony of that statement warred inside as she recalled what had happened next door. It had been good. No, not good. Amazing. Mind-blowing.

And she wanted more.

Somewhere along the line she'd lost herself. Once upon a

time she'd liked dressing up and going dancing. But now she was always working. She had no friends to speak of, unless she counted AJ's. And a hot date when she looked like Miss Moneypenny every day? Right. She'd not only disguised her physical appearance but had become entirely wrapped up in playing the part, too.

And here Zac was, a tempting way to break free from that. Even if it was only temporary.

"Look, you're totally looking at this the wrong way," AJ reasoned when Emily called her sister a minute later. "Stop thinking of sex as one of your fairytale romance novels that ends in marriage."

Emily scowled. "What's wrong with—"

"You're both attracted to each other, you're both single, and you're not hurting anyone. Keep it a secret at work if you want—it'll add to the excitement. And Zac's a no-commitment guy, perfect for you right now. It'll be fun. A *lot* of fun. Which is something you're due for after…well…after the crap that was our childhood," AJ finished diplomatically.

Her uncomplicated, straight-talking sister always knew how to get to the heart of the matter.

Yet that thought didn't comfort her as she finally headed inside to her empty bed.

Saturday passed in a round of meetings that included a working lunch before Zac gave Emily the afternoon off while he met with a potential client.

Delighted at the unexpected windfall, she pulled on jeans and walking shoes and spent a few pleasant hours shopping along Pitt Street Mall before wandering through Skygarden, then the Queen Victoria Building.

When she finally made her way back to the hotel, she'd bought the latest Debbie Macomber novel, a frangipani-scented candle and a Swarovski crystal butterfly for AJ's growing collection.

Emily called for room service, then packed away the last of her clothes. She and Zac had spent the morning with other people, no time to exchange awkward glances or ruminate on what last night meant. If it meant anything at all. To her critical eye Zac had appeared exactly the same, commanding those meetings with his usual aura of professionalism, neither overtly or covertly avoiding her.

He was discreet.

As she went over her action plan for the Point One launch she devoured a club sandwich, then a decadent pistachio crème brûlée with biscotti. With the last bite she rose from the table, leaving the computer as she stretched out her back.

It was seven-thirty, and while she'd worked later countless times before, something inside urged her to call it a night.

So she did, closing the laptop with a decisive snap before grabbing her iPod and padding over to the balcony.

With a smile and a deep cleansing breath, she drew the heavy curtains apart to reveal the breathtaking harbor sunset, pausing for only a second before opening the doors and stepping outside.

Behind the hotel the blood-red sun hung heavy in the sky, bathing the Opera House in shards of amber and orange as Zac sat in cool, darkening silence.

As a teenager he'd studied the color, the form and play of shadow and light, across Elizabeth Bay a million times from his bedroom window. He'd sketched a bunch of those houses, an apartment or two, a uniquely styled building. Where were those sketches now?

Long gone, he suspected, recrossing his ankles on the low patio table and taking another sip of beer. At eighteen he'd traded in Australia for Sweden, refusing an automatic placing at Sydney's University of Technology to study architecture at Lund University. Victor had hit the roof then cut him off without a penny.

His hand tightened on his glass as familiar bitterness swooped in on black wings.

The man may have been a legend in business, but Zac knew the true Victor Prescott. A liar. A hypocrite. An unyielding, stubborn, unforgiving sonofa—

A small sound to his right had his hairs standing up, and when he glanced over, the entire world took that moment to pause.

A row of terra-cotta pots divided their shared balcony, and with light spearing from her suite, he could clearly make out Emily's figure a few feet away.

She leaned forward, hands crossed casually over the railing. The snug pink long-sleeved T-shirt accented her waist and generous hips, soft tracksuit sweats clinging to her rounded butt. His eyes traveled leisurely over those generous curves until they came to rest on her bare feet.

Then she shifted her weight and leaned into the balcony, treating him to a view of her beautiful bottom.

His mouth went dry. *That would fit perfectly in my hands...*

Memories of last night flashed past—her soft skin and warm limbs, her gentle sighs of pleasure teasing and taunting as his body stiffened.

Then she began to hum.

He blinked, surprised, as her head started to bob, then her shoulders swayed. Her humming became indistinguishable words, something about "party" and "starting tonight"...

She actually had a nice singing voice, kind of smoky and breathy. He grinned when he spotted the earphones, then finally recognized the song. He'd never pick his assistant as a closet Lionel Richie fan.

She suddenly turned, eyes closed, a small smile on her face as she began to dance.

Good God, she was absolutely luscious. Her hips swiveled, shoulders swayed. He choked out an appreciative groan. She made his blood race and his breath stutter. She filled him with a burning need to touch, to kiss, to taste. A dangerous need.

His drink sloshed over the rim of the glass as he abruptly dropped his feet to the floor with an audible thump.

And still she moved, her grin wide, mouthing the words as his vision began to glaze over.

Then his phone rang.

He grabbed it from the table, seizing a ragged breath as he jammed his finger on the off button. Too late.

Emily had yanked the earbuds out, her wide eyes skimming the shadows until they finally settled on him.

"Zac?"

Busted. He sighed. "Yeah?"

"Were you…" Her self-conscious hesitancy was so endearing that he couldn't help smiling. "Watching me?"

"Yep."

"Uhhhh…" She threaded, then unthreaded her fingers until she realized what she was doing and dragged her palms over her thighs.

"'Dancing On the Ceiling'?" he teased. "You like the eighties, huh?"

He fully expected her to turn tail in a haze of embarrassment. Instead she surprised him with a chin tilt and a nod. "It varies. Lionel Richie, Michael Jackson, Duran Duran. Some Prince. 'Baby I'm a Star' is great running music."

"You run?" He tried to stop his eyes from skimming down her legs. He failed.

"Most mornings."

He shifted in his chair and crossed an ankle over his knee. "I must admit I'm more of a commercial rock guy."

"Oh, you don't know what you're missing." She palmed her iPod, wrapping the ear buds around her hand. "One of my major year-twelve assignments was comparing the relevance of eighties music to the political and socioeconomic climate at the time."

She'd never cease to amaze him. "Wow, that's, uhh…"

She chuckled. "A challenge? I knew my music teacher had a thing for retro." Her eyes creased mischievously. "She gave me an excellent grade."

"Clever."

They grinned at each other, until Zac's phone once again shattered the moment.

"I'm…" She glanced back to her suite. "I should go and take a shower. You'd better get that."

He turned his phone off and stood, pinning her eyes with his. "It can wait."

He walked casually to the balcony. Even from this distance he could see caution warring behind her eyes, reminding him of a day long ago when he was living in Sweden. A cat had suddenly appeared around his apartment block, wary of the kindness of strangers. Yet beneath those almond eyes there had been an almost heartbreaking desperation for affection.

He'd eventually worn her down with a mixture of food, patience and space.

"Come here."

"Why?" she squeaked out.

His grin spread wider as he heard her breath catch nervously in her throat. *That makes two of us, sweetheart.* "So I can kiss you."

"Ahhh…."

Impatience propelled him over those terra-cotta pots before he finally managed to tamp on the brakes less than a foot away.

The breath rattling in Emily's throat threatened to choke her as Zac's hard body came into unhurried full-on contact with hers.

Shock hit first, and she instinctively recoiled. But as his arms snaked around her waist, heat quickly engulfed her. She felt like melting into him, all commanding, six-foot-two of hard muscle and hot skin. Muscle she wanted to touch and knead, skin she was aching to taste. A body she wanted to claim and to be claimed by.

Yet the blunt reality of having Zac up close and personal, his groin pressing hard into her belly, kept her frozen to the spot. Her back arched, hands clutching his arms, almost as if she'd changed her mind and decided to stop him.

Which was ridiculous. She didn't *want* to stop him.

Then his lips went to her neck, tasting her racing pulse, and all thought crumbled as need took over.

Hot, solid male. Heady, musky scent. Arms that wrapped around her, strong and protective. She registered it all, her body twitching with remembered delight.

She gulped and squeezed her eyes shut as his mouth drew soft kisses along the length of her neck.

Yes. Oh, yes. Emily let the pleasure of his mouth pull her under as his hands cupped her cheeks.

Beads of sweat pooled down the small of her back, her body singing with anticipation as his lips stroked, caressed, teased hers, before firmly pushing them apart to boldly explore her mouth. His small murmur of appreciation filled her with pleasure and she leaned in closer, desperate to feel him.

A sudden craving thundered through Zac's veins, making his groin swell, forcing his breath out. She tasted so good, felt even better. Her lush breasts pushed up against his chest, an erotic teaser of things to come. Chaos swirled behind his eyes as he continued to kiss her, running his hands over her arms, to her waist, then leisurely over the curves of her rounded butt. She moaned in his mouth, ending in a gasp as he roughly pulled her closer.

"Can you feel that?" He growled beneath her lips.

She got out a muffled affirmation, a kind of half sigh, half whimper that fired his blood even more.

Gradually he pulled back, taking in her languid, desire-filled eyes, her thoroughly kissed Cupid mouth. Images of her wearing nothing but that expression sent an urgent bolt of heat straight to his erection.

With a thick swallow, he said roughly, "Emily. Look at me."

She blinked, breath hitching, before reluctantly dragging her gaze to his. Those thickly lashed, wide blue eyes, shining with vulnerability and uncertainty sent a jolt of protectiveness into his heart.

"You can feel how hard I am but you can't meet my eyes?"

The corner of her lip dipped inward, those teeth worrying the swollen flesh. "Zac," she breathed out, her grip tense on his biceps. "I need to—"

He placed a finger over her lips. "Just one kiss. Then you can go."

With eyes at half-mast she sighed, her warm breath grazing over his skin, stoking the flames below. When her hands skimmed up his arms, goose bumps rose even as his skin heated. "Okay."

The surge of victory melted into desire as he claimed her mouth once more, her decadent curves pressing into his arousal.

They kissed for long minutes, until he felt her begin to pull away. Everything screamed in protest, his groin throbbing unbearably, but he let her go, his fingers loosely trailing down her arm as she turned away.

She didn't glance back. If she had, she would've seen the burning need on his face, need echoed in every rigid muscle as he stood there with only the mild November night as relief.

As her door slid closed, he muttered a dozen colorful curses under his breath before grabbing his empty glass and storming back inside.

It was only then that he realized someone was at his door. And given the energy with which the caller was thumping, they'd been there for some time.

He stalked to the door and grabbed the handle.

"Zac. It's Cal."

His hand stilled as he glanced through the peephole. "What do you want?"

"Victor was really sick, you know," came the muffled reply.

"What?"

Cal paused. "You're not answering my messages. Can we not talk through a door?"

With a muttered curse, Zac yanked the door open.

Cal's palms were up in a conciliatory gesture. "I didn't come here to start a fight."

"So what are you here for?"

"A truce. An olive branch. Whatever it takes."

Zac's hand dove into his hair, guilt, anger and a tiny, faint hope churning together to make a huge confused mess in his brain.

"So can I come in?" Cal asked after a moment.

Zac shrugged, turned and stalked over to the bar.

Cal closed the door behind him.

"I've got nothing to say. Everyone knows VP's yours."

Cal's expression was a mix of chagrin and apology. "Yeah, well, let's just say becoming the next Victor Prescott isn't what I want for the rest of my life." His expression softened then. "The baby's due in January and I'm getting married in March. I'd like to have an actual relationship with my wife and child."

The rest of that unspoken sentence lay between them, reluctantly bonding the two men for a long moment. As a boy, Zac couldn't remember a time when Victor hadn't been coming from or going to a meeting, the office, a business trip. Up until he was seven, when his mother had abruptly left, he'd grown up in an absent-father home, albeit a fantasy home filled with more toys, gadgets and electronics than a kid could wish for. He couldn't blame Cal for wanting a normal life.

Cal finally broke the silence. "We need to sort this VP mess out."

Zac eyed him carefully as he wrenched off the cap of a long-neck beer and tossed it in the sink. "I don't have a mess. You do."

"You're a Prescott. It's yours, too."

"You keep saying that like it means something to me."

"It should."

"Well it doesn't. I stopped being part of the family a long time ago."

"Oh, for God's sake, what the hell did he do to make you so damn cynical? To turn your back on everyone who—" With blazing eyes, Cal bit back the last words, hands on his hips, before averting his gaze with a derisive snort.

"Have you asked him?" Zac asked slowly.

"He won't talk. You won't talk." Cal glared. "No one will bloody talk."

"Cal…" What could he say? To Cal, Victor was a savior, marrying his mother and transporting them from a life of hardship and struggle to wealth and privilege. Cal worshipped Victor, and Victor had basked in the glow. Long ago, Zac had furiously resented that connection, the attention that should have rightfully been his. Cal had been determined to prove himself, the boy with the razor-sharp mind who dissected, then rebuilt computers for fun. Of course he and Victor had bonded over that. Then there was Zac: a quiet thinker, a lover of visual arts and drawing. While he'd been seething with teenage angst and rebelling against everyone and everything, Cal had developed what would eventually become One-Click, Australia's number-one software package.

Zac was an adult now, with an adult's understanding and perspective. It wasn't his place to destroy whatever bond Cal and Victor had, no matter how terrible a father Victor had been to his own flesh and blood.

"It's...in the past, Cal," he finally got out.

"Bull. It's still happening." Cal put his hands on his hips, a direct challenge. "It started ever since you took off overseas to study."

It had started long before that, but still... "I was eighteen. Nearly ten years ago."

"Yeah."

"Cal..." The thick warning was clear. "Don't push it. You won't like what you hear."

Cal's humorless laugh startled him. "Nothing Victor does surprises me anymore. He's stepping back from the company, donating to charity, talking about investing in small business. And this from a man who tried to marry me off instead of telling me the truth about his tumor."

Shock jolted Zac back a step. "What tumor?"

"Victor had a brain tumor," Cal said softly. "He actually died on the operating table. For a while there, we didn't know if he'd make it."

What the hell was he supposed to do with that? Past and present swirled into a dozen churning emotions, humbling him. "Why didn't anyone tell me?"

Cal's expression was astute. "Would you have taken my call?"

Would he have? A surge of guilt and cold, hard truth flooded Zac's conscience. Probably not. "Is he...?"

"He's fine now," Cal said firmly. "But you know what he's like—Victor manipulates, that's what he does. It doesn't mean the company should suffer for it."

Neither man spoke for a long while.

"Okay," Cal finally conceded. "You don't want to talk to me. After the last few years of silence, I don't blame you."

"Cal—"

"No, I get it. *I* wouldn't want to talk to me," he added with a twist to his mouth. "Can we just put that aside for now? I need your help. I might not want the top job, but that doesn't mean I want to see the company crash."

Guilt twisted inside. "So you're really giving it up."

"There's more to life than working."

"Jesus, don't let Victor catch you saying that."

Both men laughed, a welcome moment of levity.

"Look, mate." Zac began. "Me and Victor—" Cal shook his head, but Zac forged on. "It's a complicated, toxic relationship, you know that. I had to get away."

"And not one call. I know," Cal added at the look on Zac's face. "I didn't, either."

"Yeah." Zac reached into the minibar and pulled out another beer, offering it to Cal. "So we're both crappy brothers." He flicked his head to the sofa. "Want to sit?"

For one second, caution warred on his stepbrother's face. He'd put that there when he'd walked out all those years ago. That realization made Zac's jaw clench.

"If you want me to," Cal said.

Regret seeped into Zac's bones, the years they'd lost gaping wide. He'd done this, had driven cracks into their once-amiable relationship so that Cal no longer trusted him.

That was wrong.

"Please," he said gruffly. "Sit."

They drank too much, stayed up too late and, Zac thought fuzzily as Cal left around 2 a.m., probably said way too much.

The alcohol had done its job and taken the edge off, relaxing them enough to openly discuss the company while studiously avoiding any personal stuff.

Lying in his bed, hands behind his head, Zac lazily blinked at the ornate ceiling frescos, the beer buzz still warming his veins. Was it before or after they'd shared their fifth drink and memories of one tenth-grade Julie Jenkins and a see-through shirt that he'd suggested advertising for a new CEO and floating the company on the stock exchange?

Cal had nearly choked. "An outsider *and* going public?" He finally got out, wiping beer from his chin.

"Yeah."

"Victor would never go for it."

Zac had shrugged. "Then you have a problem."

They'd sat in silence until Cal's phone rang. From the soft dip in his voice to the way his face had relaxed before he turned away, Zac knew exactly who was on the other end of the line. Ava, Cal's fiancée. Which, for some reason, had made him suddenly think of Emily. Curvy, luscious Emily.

With a groan he flipped to his side, punched the pillow and glared at the shadows through the half-open bedroom door.

Emily—now probably asleep—in the room next to his.

Emily, who'd kissed him so sweetly his body got hard just thinking about it.

Did she sleep on the left or the right side of the bed? On her back or front?

What did she wear to bed?

Stop.

Yet his body ignored him, his groin slowly stirring to life as a myriad of pictures flashed behind his eyes: Emily in a skimpy bra and knickers. Emily in high heels and black garters.

Emily in his boxer shorts…

With a growl, he flung the sheets off and swung from the bed. There'd be time to do it right. He'd been patient, he could wait a little longer.

But now, a cold shower couldn't.

Seven

Their 9 a.m. flight was delayed by an hour. Emily had always laughingly joked about AJ's belief in omens, but right now, seated next to Zac in Virgin Blue's executive lounge in Sydney's departure terminal, she wasn't amused.

More time in his presence, more time to feel awkward and embarrassed.

More time to rethink her decision?

On their drive to the airport Emily had shamelessly used her phone as a buffer. She'd talked with the Valhalla staff about the Point One project, texted ones who couldn't be reached…and yes, faked a few, too.

Tiredness nipped at her heels as she stared at her phone, reading the same e-mail for the fifth time. A night in the most heavenly bed in all the world and still she couldn't sleep. Her brain had teased her with various scenarios of Zac there beside her, touching, kissing, making love to her.

She frowned, reached for her cappuccino and took a sip before glancing over at Zac, who sat directly opposite.

His expression was hidden behind expensive sunglasses, but

she was directly in his sightline, even if he was busy with his text messages.

"Cal stopped by last night," Zac said suddenly.

Emily looked up. "Really?"

A small pause, then, "I suggested floating the company and bringing in a new CEO. Cal didn't outright refuse."

"That's good."

"Only if he can convince Victor."

"And the wedding? You're free that weekend," she reminded him.

"Not sure. There's lots of…" He hesitated, as if searching for the right word. "Baggage."

She nodded. "Sometimes it's better to go forward than to step back."

"Exactly." His gaze tripped over her, studying her expression (she'd gone for inscrutable), her mood (professional yet distant), her clothes (hmmm…yeah). Dark gray jacket, long skirt, plain cream shirt, sensible kitten heels.

Gray. Plain. Sensible. That's what he saw, what everyone saw. And before that kiss, she'd accepted it. How could she not, when she'd actively cultivated the facade?

But now…

He'd obviously seen something to warrant his attention.

A small twist of pleasure caught her unawares, but then their flight was announced and the moment was broken.

Twenty minutes passed, an excruciatingly long time to be on the edge of her seat. They'd boarded in silence, Zac's normal businesslike wall of confidence marred with underlying tension—tension that melted away as soon as the plane took off.

The sudden pressure drop and stomach-constricting momentum eventually eased. Yet Emily remained tense, completely aware of the man next to her, ostensibly reading the morning paper. Tension that had everything to do with last night's kiss and the dilemma she was now in.

How could she focus on her job when all she wanted to do was have Zac naked?

He turned the page and she jumped, crushing a soft curse under her breath.

He was too close and he knew it. How could he not know it after what they'd done?

She shifted her leg, angling her body toward the aisle, away from him, with casual subtlety.

Business class and still not enough room. She sighed and refolded the complimentary gossip magazine, staring at the sensational headlines without seeing them, before shoving it in the seat pocket.

The flight attendant hovered past, offering coffee, which Zac took with a smile. When he withdrew with the cup, his arm passed way too close to her chest.

She held her breath as her heart began to thump, fingers stiff on the armrest. He placed the glass in the holder between them, his hand brushing hers.

She blinked and slid her gaze sideways.

A small smile stretched his mouth…and what a mouth it was. A mouth made for kissing, with soft lips and strong teeth and— One eyebrow went up and she nearly groaned aloud. Then he leaned in and gently covered her hand with his warm fingers, and she barely managed to muffle her surprise.

"Zac—"

"Emily."

"You're…" She glanced furtively back over her shoulder. "You're holding my hand."

"Yes, I am."

His leg shifted, bumping into hers, and she nearly leaped from her seat. "Now you're—"

"Touching your leg. I know. And you know what else?" He dipped his head conspiratorially, beckoning her with his finger. With a thickness in her throat she bent forward. His warm breath swooped over her cheek and her stomach fluttered. "I think I'll have to kiss you."

His firm disclosure shocked her immobile, her eyes transfixed on his lips as they inched closer to hers.

"You can't—" she managed to choke out.

"I can." His mouth curved, the frankly seductive look in his eyes forcing her breath out in excited little puffs. "I will."

"But—"

Her protest gushed out on a sigh when his lips brushed over her cheek, searing her skin. He feathered his mouth across her cheekbone, the barest of touches, before coming to rest by her earlobe. That warm breath sent flaring heat down through her body, curling around her stomach, her thighs, before ending in her toes.

"Someone could see…" she whispered desperately.

"Yes." His teeth nibbled on her lobe and she bit her lip to stifle the whimper of pleasure.

"We…" She swallowed. "We can't do this here."

His lips skimmed the tender point where her ear met her neck. "So name the time and place."

Oh. Her breath hissed in as she struggled to vocalize what she'd been fantasizing about these last few months. Now, faced with the certainty of Zac's interest, it made her list seem… Cold. Businesslike.

He must have taken her lack of response as hesitancy, because he gently added, "Tonight?"

Tonight? She squeezed her eyes shut as his mouth moved back across her cheek in a sensuous trail of warm breath and soft lips.

"You…have that thing with Josh Kerans tonight."

He paused, an irritated frown marring his forehead as Emily opened her eyes. Yet his hand still captured hers, sending a trembling anticipation through her bones.

"Right. Client get-together at his beach house. You should be there, too."

"Why?" She pulled back, the heat in her cheeks beginning to ebb.

"Because he's a client and he invited me. And now I've invited you."

She shook her head. "This isn't…no."

"This is work, Emily, not a social outing. Jason, Mitch and June will be there." He smoothly reeled off some of Valhalla's key staff. "And your involvement with Point One means people need to see you as more than just my assistant. And I go, you go." To take the sting from the demand, he gave a small smile. "Networking is a necessity. But I promise—" his lips curved, turned slightly wicked "—I'll make it up to you tomorrow night."

His husky murmur, full of lustful promise, made her nerves groan. The air crackled dangerously between them, doing something hot and exciting to her insides. It forced Emily to swallow, but still she couldn't look away from his eyes, those dark, sultry depths that said, "I'd like to do things to you and I know you'll enjoy them."

"This has to stay out of the office," she finally blurted out. Clearly, from the look on his face, this was not what he'd expected her to say.

His mouth curved. "There goes my sex-on-the-desk fantasy."

"I mean it, Zac." At her stern look, his humor fled. "It's not you they'll talk about. You're the boss—you won't be the one labeled."

His eyes narrowed. "Why does that sound—"

"It doesn't matter what it sounds like. There can't be any secret looks, any off-the-cuff comments, any touching. During the day we're professionals."

He remained silent for so long that Emily's head began to spin from the breath she held.

Finally, he nodded and said, "I'll pick you up at eight tonight." And calmly reached for another newspaper, unfolded it and began to read.

Emily stared blindly down the crowded isle as excitement zinged through her blood. How on earth was she going to survive Monday—let alone tonight—without thinking of the coming evening?

At least, Zac thought ruefully, her skirt was above the knee— the only concession she'd made to the evening. It was still black.

It was still distorted with a boxy jacket. And she still had on a pair of horrible clunky heels.

He *had* said it was work. So he remained silent on the twenty-minute drive to Kerans's Broadbeach Waters luxury apartment, the only background noise coming from his iPod plugged into the dash.

But when he pulled into the cul-de-sac, cut the engine and saw her studying the partygoers with a frown, he paused.

"Ready?"

She took too long to commit to that nod. Her hesitation told him what she wouldn't—couldn't?—voice.

"It's a warm night. You might want to lose the jacket," he said casually.

She gave him a look that told him she knew what he was up to, but still she unbuttoned her jacket, then slipped it off her shoulders.

Her silky short-sleeved purple shirt shimmered beneath the streetlights, revealing tanned arms as she pulled the door open and got out.

When he'd rounded the bonnet, she was nervously smoothing down her skirt, a skirt that now hugged her hips, emphasizing her generous curves and indented waist.

Behind the glasses, irritation brimmed in those blue eyes. But there was also a little fear. Fear of the unknown. Fear of being judged.

He knew what that was like, even if it'd been years since he'd allowed himself to feel that emotion.

He glanced around: they were alone with only the streetlights above as witnesses. Unable to resist, his hand went to her face, but paused when she quickly rocked back. Her brow creased.

"Emily."

With great reluctance she met his eyes, her expression shuttered.

Then a car door slammed and the moment was gone. She stepped back. "We should go in."

He wanted to say more, but what? That for the first time in

his life he wanted to ditch work and instead spend the evening kissing her all over? *That* would not go over well.

Slow it down, mate. You don't want to scare her off.

He nodded, trying to ignore the growing desire warming his blood.

"Let's go."

The opulent dozen-bedroom, two-story apartment was a Valhalla triumph. Zac's signature—huge windows with intricate personalized frames and sconces that showcased the view—presented the expansive Broadbeach Waters in all its glory. Beyond the buzz of conversation, the sharply dressed and expensive-smelling people, the subtle ceiling lights and the strains of a Mozart concerto, the stunning sunset streaking across the sky commanded Emily's attention.

Red sky at night, sailor's delight.

She frowned at the childhood rhyme before glancing curiously at the assembled crowd.

Men and women greeted each other, drank champagne and chatted animatedly. Here were the über-rich in serious socializing mode. Yet how could they not notice the glorious blue-red-navy spectacle of a Surfers sunset?

She watched small waves lap up against Kerans's luxury yacht tethered at the boat ramp, studying the cerulean water before she sensed someone approaching. Zac. Only he had the power to send her body tingling on high alert.

She turned to him. "This is amazing, Zac. Another great job."

"Thank you. Champagne?" He offered the cold stemmed glass. She took it with a smile, then sipped to cover her nervousness at his direct scrutiny.

"It's—"

"Zac! You're here! *Hur mår du?*"

Delicious. The word died along with a tentative smile as a silky voice cut through the surrounding chatter. A tall, dark-haired woman stalked through the crowd, her black, sleeveless catsuit flaunting an extremely fit physique. Around her neck hung two silver chains, the handful of fashionable dangly charms chiming melodiously below a pair of impressive breasts, their curves revealed by a half-lowered zipper.

Haylee Kerans, the client's daughter. And—Emily's grip tightened imperceptibly on her glass—one of Zac's many ex-girlfriends who didn't accept the words *break up* lightly.

As Zac turned to greet Haylee, Emily stood there awkwardly, listening to them converse in melodious, singsong Swedish.

Then Haylee linked her arm through his and swung her gaze to Emily.

"Kan du talar Svenska?"

At Emily's blank look, her smile seemed to take on a condescending smirk. "You can't speak Swedish? Oh, you should. Such a *musikal* language—but then, Zac's half Swede, so I'm biased." Her striking face creased with deliberate thought. "I shall have to teach you…Emma, right?"

"Emily," Zac interjected. Emily didn't miss the way he'd firmly extricated himself from Haylee's grip.

"Oh." Haylee's eyes suddenly narrowed. "Zac's gatekeeper. You field all his calls."

Emily blinked in surprise. What, it was *her* fault Zac was an expert on moving on? Irritation bubbled up but she quickly got a handle on it.

"I'm Zac's assistant," she said calmly. "He directs, I do."

One of Haylee's eyebrows went up as her gaze swept Emily from head to toe, a silent, insulting inspection that had her flushing. But before she could formulate any kind of comeback, Zac intervened.

"Any idea where your father is?"

The younger woman's expression quickly transformed as she looked back to Zac, a perfect smile that looked a tad too bright to Emily's thinking.

"Where he normally is." Haylee nodded into the crowd. "Over near the bar, surrounded by his mates and talking business. Zac." Haylee ran a teasing hand up his arm. "You should call me. We could go for a drive in that *smaskig* car of yours."

She leaned forward, proffering her cheek. As politeness

dictated, Zac went in for the kiss, but at the last minute she turned and his mouth landed firmly on hers.

"For later," she purred, pulling back, then shooting Emily a triumphant glance.

When Zac steered Emily away, her back was rigid beneath his hand.

"She'll 'teach me'?" she muttered.

"Ignore her," he commanded as they steadily made their way across the room.

"Oh, I intend to. I'd rather take swimming lessons from a shark."

He grinned, then looked fleetingly over his shoulder. The now-unsmiling Haylee still stood where they'd left her, one elegant finger tapping rhythmically against her champagne flute.

He'd never understand women. Haylee had been fun for a month or two—impulsive and unconcerned with looking perfect, unlike many of his other exes. And growing up with wealth meant she'd been unfazed by his billion-dollar reputation. But gradually, her attentiveness had begun to chafe. Where was he? Who was he with? When would he be back? She'd gone from fun to serious, hinting about "a more permanent living arrangement" and casually wondering aloud when she'd get to meet his family.

His cue to backpedal like an Olympic champion.

"Sorry," he muttered.

"For what?"

"For putting you in the middle of that."

She shrugged, keeping pace with him as they wound their way through the crowd. "I've handled worse."

"Really?"

She paused, forcing him to stop dead too. "I answer your phone, Zac. I field a handful of ex-girlfriends' calls every week. I've been screamed at, cajoled, threatened. Some even beg and cry."

"You're joking."

"No."

The truth was reflected in her expression, prompting a frown.

But when he opened his mouth, someone clapped a hand on his shoulder.

"Zac. How was Sydney?"

When he turned to Joe Watts, Valhalla's chief engineer, his expression was neutral.

Emily stood calmly by as they chatted, fully aware of his arm, his shoulder close to hers, fully aware he could touch her at a moment's notice—but she knew without a doubt he wouldn't. This was work, and she had drawn the line. Plus...

She glanced around the room, her eyes coming to rest on a familiar catsuited woman, the center of attention in a group of men. Haylee's little display only underscored her need for the line. The billionaire's daughter didn't seem the type who liked competition. She was also someone who could make life uncomfortable with one calculated conversation with her father.

Yes, Emily realized as she watched Haylee's gaze devour an unsuspecting Zac more than once as the minutes ticked by, Daddy's little girl would come first, despite Zac and Josh's professional business relationship.

She quickly excused herself and made her way to the bathroom.

Eight

They drove home the same way they'd come, with the soft strains of music alleviating the distinctly uncomfortable silence.

Zac had sensed a change ever since their first kiss. It was as if he made her nervous somehow. Unsure. So unlike the Emily he knew.

It was oddly gratifying, knowing he could ruffle those perfect feathers, that he had this kind of effect.

He stole a glance as she stared out the window. She'd unbuttoned her shirt to reveal an elegant collarbone and smooth skin, demure yet extremely tempting. And she'd done something with her hair, loosened it up so that small strands floated around her jawline, bringing emphasis to that lush Cupid's-bow mouth.

"A lot of people are interested in Point One," she said suddenly.

The compliment he'd been reworking lay preempted in his mouth. She was still in work mode. And right now, he was her boss.

Damn. He nodded. "How are the plans coming along?"

"I've already talked with Michelle from Publicity." She crossed her legs and kept her focus ahead, out into the dark night. "If those ground-floor businesses are in by the end of November, we can utilize them for the December launch. We've already presold half the apartments. Which means we have ten left, plus five spare offices," she said as they turned off Pacific Highway and left onto Duringan Street. "I expect those to be filled in the next few weeks."

"And the launch?"

"Final estimate by tomorrow."

He flicked her a smile. "Great."

"And…" She paused as the car smoothly took the corner, passing Currumbin Surf Club on the right.

"I'm waiting on a call from Queensland Uni, to see if I can start my course in second term. April."

"They let you do that?"

"Depends on the circumstances. And I worked out a plan to pay you back."

"There's no hurry." He glanced over at her but couldn't read her expression.

"I don't like owing people money."

They finally turned into Emily's street and he pulled the car to a smooth stop at the curb. When he cut the engine, the Porsche's throaty purr died out, leaving a heavy silence in its wake.

Dark clouds hid the moon, distorting her face, making it difficult to read her expression. And he really, really wanted to know what she was thinking.

He snicked open his door and the interior light came on. Then he slowly turned, giving her no choice but to look at him.

Her face was half in shadow, half in light. An apt description for someone who guarded her secrets so very carefully.

She was the complete opposite of every woman he'd dated, someone who hadn't been born into wealth and didn't run in the same privileged circles. Yet she could handle any situation he'd thrown at her, from boardrooms to client parties to fending off clingy exes. So why did he feel the sudden urge to protect her?

"Emily."

Ignoring her startled murmur, he curled a strand of her hair around his fingers, savoring the silkiness before gently smoothing it behind her ear.

"Yes?"

He hesitated, oddly tongue-tied.

Admit it. You've been spoiled by all those other women—bold, confident women who knew what they wanted and came right out and said it.

No, not spoiled—bored. Cynical, even.

It'd been a long time since he'd had to put a concerted effort into a seduction.

That thought gave him pause. And as he sat there, trying to work out a tactful follow-up, she blinked, her lips parting slightly. The light streamed over them, revealing the tip of her tongue as it touched the inside bottom lip before she closed her teeth on it.

With an inward groan he slid his hand around her neck, cupping her head and tangling her hair.

Then he pulled her in and kissed her.

It was just as sweet, just as delicious as before. Her pouty lips beneath his, soft and pliant. That scent…conjuring up freshness and innocence. And her warm breath that came out in a gasp before lengthening into a murmur of pleasure.

His body stirred, sparked into life by one simple kiss.

He explored her mouth, tasting the curves, the creases, her soft tentative tongue that at first shied away, then bit by bit returned to tangle with his, until his blood began to pound in earnest and his breath became ragged.

He groaned. *Stop.* But Emily's fingers were teasing the hair on his nape, her gentle, almost hesitant touch only stoking the fires higher.

He had to stop before it got out of hand.

With a supreme effort he reluctantly broke the kiss, easing away with a regretful growl. She frowned and her eyes snapped open.

His groin tightened. Her blue eyes were dark and heavy with

desire, her damp mouth bruised with kisses. He could hear her
rapid breath—or was that his?—as she pulled back.

"Tomorrow night," he got out, knowing his voice was thick
with lust, knowing it wouldn't take any effort to have her here,
now. "My place."

When she glanced away with a quick nod, the light revealed
a flush on her smooth cheeks as she scrambled from the car.

Tomorrow night. His body was already keyed up just thinking
about it as he followed her out.

"Thanks for the ride."

"My pleasure." He lingered on that last word, crossing his
arms and leaning back against the car, taking a warped delight
in her flustered expression.

She turned and headed for the stairs without a backward
glance, and Zac was rewarded with a view of her gently swaying
bottom and hips as she ascended. When she paused at her door,
she finally turned to give him a nod, then unlocked the door and
went inside.

By the time he was back in his car, her living room lights had
come on, the soft glow warming the darkness as he started up
the engine.

He reluctantly pulled away, heading back into Surfers while
fervently wishing away the next twenty-four hours.

The sun was barely peering over the horizon as Emily laced
up her joggers, did a quick stretch on her porch, then headed off
down the beach.

Running was an uncomfortable, sweaty, muscle-aching affair.
She hated it while she was in the middle of it, but she liked having
done it. Liked that it kept her relatively healthy, that it was free
and right on her doorstep. And with her headphones on, no one
bothered her. She gave a few brief nods to the regulars, a smile
for the Japanese tourists who'd never seen a Gold Coast beach
before. And with the wild angry beat of Nirvana reverberating
in her head, she could block everything out as she jogged south
along pristine Currumbin Beach.

Her daily run took her through the half-filled Currumbin

Surf Club car park and Elephant Rock, then down past a bunch of sleek beachfront mansions, many of which Valhalla had been behind. Behind the grassy dunes she could see roofs, sometimes a window or two, or a glimpse of backyard as she pounded out each step on the hard, ocean-compacted sand.

An hour later, sweaty yet energized, she took her stairs two at a time, her legs throbbing with the effort.

Prior to the weekend, lots of things had been on the periphery. Now she was hyper-aware. Like instead of pulling her hair into its usual smooth bun, she looped it back into a soft ponytail. And instead of her usual lip-liner-and-balm that served as lipstick, she picked up a soft plum Revlon gloss AJ had bought for her birthday.

Two changes, two tiny things that seemed unimportant but made her feel a little more confident. And confidence meant control.

It was all about control.

It was unlikely anyone would notice, she reasoned as she walked into the office foyer. The barista at Bennetti's hadn't. Nor had the building's security. And certainly not the other workers as she crammed into the lift that sped them up to Valhalla's offices.

She had set her bag down, placed the coffee on her desk and turned on the computer before she noticed Zac's mobile phone and the sticky note on the keyboard.

"In a meeting," it read.

She placed the phone to one side, crumpled the note then opened her electronic scheduler, looking up as the mail clerk pushed open the door, smiled, then dropped a bundle of mail on her desk.

When Zac's phone beeped, indicating an incoming text, she glanced up from the keyboard.

A number not recognized in his list of contacts.

A new client? She quickly activated the touch screen and brought up the text.

"Did U get my picture last nite?"

She sat back in her chair, jiggling her leg in thought. Clients sent Zac "before" shots of their houses all the time. So why didn't he have this particular caller in his contacts? Come to think of it, *picture* was an odd word. Why not *photo?*

The phone beeped again and she nearly jumped out of her skin.

"This 1's better. Call me, K?"

When she clicked on the attachment, shock froze her fingers.

It was a very different Haylee—kissing for the camera, striking a sexy topless pose in a red G-string and garters.

Emily swiftly placed the phone on her desk, heart pounding. Her fingers twitched like she'd seared them on the stove, her breath jamming hard against her ribs.

Zac hadn't…? No, he wasn't like that. But…

He always gave his office number to the girlfriends, never his mobile. She slowly palmed the phone, then located the list of incoming calls and scrolled down. Haylee's number appeared between three and five times a day. During the weekend, she'd called him over a dozen times. If she'd sent texts, Zac must've deleted them.

Her hands were surprisingly steady as she placed the phone on her desk. Which meant there was only one rational explanation—Haylee was stalking Zac.

Work well and truly forgotten, she linked her fingers behind her head and tipped back to focus on the ceiling.

Think about it. You've met the woman. You know Zac. What else could it possibly be?

When Zac returned an hour later, she was mentally prepared.

"Any calls?" he asked with a smile as she handed him the mail and his phone.

"Cal called again."

His smile dimmed. "And Victor?"

"No. But Haylee texted your mobile."

He frowned. "What did she want?"

"It was a photo."

Her expression must've given her away because his eyes

darkened before he muttered something under his breath. "Sorry.
I thought I'd dealt with it. Leave it with me." And he turned
towards his office.

"She's stalking you."

He paused in the doorway then slowly turned back, shaking
his head. "No. Haylee's just a little…"

"Crazy?"

"Attached," he amended with a short grin. "I let her down
gently, but obviously she's taken that as an invitation to try
harder."

Zac was never rude—it was her job to buy the breakup flowers,
which he always sent with a personal note. Which was why, she
suspected, so many of his exes just couldn't let go. Emily sighed.
"Shall I get you a new mobile number?"

"Good idea." He nodded and tossed the phone. She caught it
smoothly. "Are you ready to give the update on Point One?"

"Sure." She grabbed a file and rose.

She presented her concise report smoothly, ticking off most
of the items on Zac's mental to-do list. Then she reminded
him he had a conference call at two and asked about his lunch
preferences, all while placing a steaming coffee mug by his
elbow.

When he reached for it, he accidently bumped her hand.

She made a small sound, as if he'd shocked her. And when
her eyes darted up to his, a throb of anticipation spread through
his blood at the reluctant desire in those blue depths.

Then she glanced away. "Sorry."

He sucked in a breath, sharp and ragged. How much of an ass
was he to have this gorgeous woman sorry for wanting him?

She nodded to the open door. "Megan from Accounts is
here."

"New hairstyle?" he asked.

She scooped up the contents of his out tray and stepped back,
clutching the papers to her chest. "Yes," she said.

"I like it."

She frowned, those glossy lips flattening. "That's not why I did it."

His grin called her a liar even as he remained silent.

She cleared her throat. "Shall I send Megan in?"

"Sure." Then he added, "I've got inspections this afternoon, but I'll be home around seven-thirty."

His statement hung in the silence, the subtext clear. Anticipation zinged his nerves as she glanced nervously to the door and the waiting Valhalla worker outside.

She gave him a short nod, then left.

Through his open door Zac caught the exchange—Megan commenting on Emily's new hairstyle, Emily thanking her—before Megan was standing in the doorway with a smile.

"Got a minute to sign off on the Christmas bonuses?"

He motioned her in. It was time to get back to work.

Emily sat heavily at her desk, then quickly flicked open a folder. Nervousness punctuated each flip of the page, until one finally tore at the corner.

Her hands stilled. Control. She breathed in deep, eyes closed, then let it out. *I am in control of what I do and say. It's just casual. You can walk away at any time.*

Instead of taking comfort in that mantra, it began to sound a lot like her mother's petulant whine.

Her eyes sprang open. Her schedule was still open on the computer, listing today's urgent tasks for Point One.

Right. She could either continue to moon over Zac, letting the anticipation of tonight cripple her day. Or she could get some work done.

What's it to be, Emily?

With her back straight, she picked up the phone and started dialing.

Nine

By firmly blocking out everything but work, Emily managed to get through the day with her sanity intact. It also helped that Zac had left around 2 p.m. and wouldn't return.

Apart from a few comments about her hair—all from women, she noted—and calls from both Cal and Victor, the day remained busy but uneventful. At seven she turned off her computer and locked up the office, deliberately leaving it too late to change her mind and go home.

At seven-fifteen she parked around the corner from Zac's street, killed the engine and sat in the eerie silence. As his assistant, she had full access to his elegant beachside house and his security codes. Yet she'd never had to use them for anything other than work purposes.

This was her point of no return. If she did this—

No. AJ would kick your butt for second-guessing yourself like this.

Her fingers tapped on the steering wheel as the sun gradually lengthened the shadows.

It was time.

Just as she placed a hand on the door, headlights suddenly blinded her through the rearview mirror. She hesitated, and a second later a sleek dark car drove slowly by.

Emily watched the sporty coupe crawl down Zac's street, past his house, then suddenly accelerate, leaving the distinctive scent of diesel fumes in its wake.

She shook her head then took a deep breath. Then she grabbed her handbag and scrambled from the car.

If Zac could've done a hundred and twenty down the packed Pacific Highway he would've. *Too slow, too slow,* his heart seemed to thump as the traffic sluggishly chugged along, only to stop again at the lights.

Gray clouds gathered overhead, heavy with impending rain. The steering wheel complained beneath his grip. He wanted her in his arms right now. Wanted to feel her mouth on his, her warm breath, her yielding skin.

Wanted her legs wrapped around him.

That mouthwatering thought had dominated his last few hours. He'd come that close to canceling his last meeting because of it.

Now he glared at the time—seven-forty—and softly cursed. "Come on, come ooooon…. Finally!"

Within five minutes he was home, the movement-sensitive porch light flicking on as the garage door slid up and the first fat drops of rain began to fall.

He grabbed the packages on the front seat, locked up and went through the inner door, tossing his keys on the entrance table as he strode down the hall.

He paused in the living area and placed the takeaway bag on the table.

"Emily?"

His voice echoed through the spacious silence, disappearing into the lengthening darkness.

"Yes?"

He turned. Her back was to his huge ocean-view window, the

steely clouds, turbulent sea and gently falling rain providing a dramatic backdrop to her shadowy figure.

"You've been shopping?" she asked as he flicked on a lamp.

"Food." He noted the firm grip on her handbag, held like a shield in front of her. With one finger he lifted the other package by the thin handles. "And these are for you."

She frowned. "You didn't have to buy me—"

"I wanted to. There's a difference."

"Zac…"

"Just try them on. If you don't like them, I'll take 'em back. Please," he added with a smile.

She blinked and her fingers tightened around her bag handles, eliciting a leathery squeak of protest. Then she sighed. "All right." She took his offering, carefully avoiding any contact.

"Go on up," he said, nodding to the iron-and-polished-mahogany stairs. "I'll bring up the food and drinks."

Emily took the stairs slowly, highly aware of Zac's gaze following her ascent.

She paused at the top, the small entrance stretching out into what was obviously Zac's loft bedroom. She barely registered the dark furniture, the photos adorning the walls, the beautiful bay window revealing another perfect view of the Pacific Ocean. Her heart was pounding way too hard to notice anything except the rumpled bed jutting from the wall.

It was massive, covered in a wine-colored spread with mossy-green piping, black pillows tossed casually against the simple iron headboard. The covers had been dragged from one side, which told her two things. One, he didn't have a housekeeper. And two, he slept on the left.

Zac's bed. Where he slept. Where he and other women…

No. She turned away, coming face-to-face with her reflection in the full-length mirror. This was *her,* right here, right now. Zac was a good guy. Sure, he loved women—a *lot* of women—but he treated them with respect. He didn't cheat or lie to get them into bed.

Her head reeled as she dropped her handbag on the floor, then slowly placed the designer-boutique shopping bag on the bed.

With trembling fingers she yanked her shirt free from her skirt, then plucked open the buttons until it hung loose on her shoulders. She'd packed a toothbrush, deodorant and condoms crammed in with a handful of bra and knicker sets, choosing anything remotely seductive while visions of Zac's gorgeous ex-girlfriends taunted her selection. But now, standing half-dressed in front of his unforgiving mirror, she hesitated.

He'd bought her a gift…most likely lingerie. Men were predictable like that.

She stared at her reflection. She'd picked out a red lacy bra this morning, but the thing had itched so badly she'd quickly swapped it for her favorite white cotton one with tiny blue flowers.

She pulled off her shirt, hands on her hips and studied the bra in the mirror. Clean, pretty. But still white cotton.

Swiftly she grabbed the shopping bag, frowning when she pulled out a simple white shoe box with Martinez Valero in blocked roman lettering.

Shoes. So…*not* lingerie?

She peeled the lid back, expecting something red, high and flashy—stripper shoes.

But the gorgeous strappy-sandal creation nestling in black velvet sent her feminine heart beating faster. With a gasp, she reached in and reverently pulled out one shoe.

It wasn't the tiny rhinestone-encrusted buckles that got her, nor the four-inch white-satin-covered heels. It was the fluttery arrangement of sheer silver organza petals that fell along the white leather T-strap from ankle to toe.

"Oh, my—" They were gorgeous. Quickly she toed off her black office shoes, then reverently slipped on Zac's gift.

After buckling the straps, she straightened.

Her breath caught at the sight. Wow. By some miracle her legs looked longer. She hiked up her gray skirt to mid-thigh then turned side-on. Yep. Legs definitely longer. And skinnier.

"Magical shoes," she breathed, staring at her wide-eyed reflection until her eyes came to rest on her bra.

She quickly fished out that morning's reject from her bag, swiftly got it on, then stepped back, surveying herself with a critical eye.

It was too small. The cups barely held in all that boob. She tugged, then dug her hand in, repositioning her breasts. Nope. Still about to pop out. With a resigned sigh, she focused on her hair, pulling out the ponytail, then tipping her head down to fluff it up.

The sight that greeted Zac as he padded soundlessly up the stairs stopped him in his tracks.

Emily, her butt in the air, shaking out her hair, skirt hiked up to reveal shapely muscular thighs, curvy knees and a pair of strong calves. Deceptively long legs that complemented the shoes perfectly.

But then she straightened and placed her hands on her hips, and he nearly dropped the wine.

A smooth torso, hands on her flaring hips, emphasizing an hourglass waist…and then, the most magnificent pair of breasts he'd ever seen. The lush mounds were encased in a fire-red bra, the cups sweeping so low they barely concealed her nipples.

His breath came out in a strangled gurgle and Emily whirled, wide-eyed.

As he stared, a flush spread slowly across her cheeks, hands fluttering as if deciding whether to cover up or not. Blood began to pound thickly, expectantly.

"Don't move."

She froze, fingers laced demurely in front while he took in his fill.

He ran his gaze unhurriedly down her lush body, paused on the shoes before coming back up to meet her eyes with a satisfied grin. She met his gaze, as if daring him to comment.

The only thing that gave her away were those fluttering lashes.

With slow deliberation he placed the takeaway bag and bottle of wine on his armoire. "Do you like the shoes?"

She moved, her weight transferring onto her back foot. "I

do," she got out after clearing her throat. "They're absolutely beautiful."

So are you, he wanted to add, but sensed that such an obvious compliment would only make her more nervous. Instead he poured the wine and offered her a glass.

Trepidation slowed her approach. It amused him to see his normally unflappable assistant so wary, so out of her depth. Dressed in a skirt, a bra and a pair of high heels.

It also flared something deeply male inside, firing his blood and quickening his breath.

She was all his for the night.

Oblivious to his heated thoughts, she took the glass, murmured her thanks, then took a sip. But when he reached out to run a finger over the curve of her bare forearm, she jerked back.

"Sorry," she muttered, first wiping the wine from her hand, then dragging a finger up the glass to catch the rest.

"You missed a bit."

"Where?"

"Here." With a firm hand he pulled her to him, leaned down and gently licked the drops from her bottom lip.

Her breath strangled out, her eyes fluttering closed.

Zac grinned. He took a sip of his wine before placing both glasses down and going in for another kiss.

Warmed from Zac's mouth, the semisweet liquid slipped past Emily's lips and she groaned, swallowing.

His hands on her arms firmly pinned her as he deepened the kiss, spiked with the bite of alcohol and flamed by need. Her breasts began to throb, pushed up against his chest, and she let out another groan when he wedged one hard thigh between her legs.

So hot. So, so hot.

Through the haze of desire, she felt him nudging her backward, and suddenly her legs met resistance. The bed.

They both went down, his grip tempering their fall, lips still tasting, teasing. The satin cover gave her goose bumps until Zac swept his hands over her stomach—her most sensitive spot—and she shivered in earnest.

At his deep chuckle, she forced her eyes open.

He was above her, that lock of too-long hair flopping forward, giving him a rakish edge. She couldn't make out his eyes in the shadows, but as his palm slid firmly up her belly, the slant of his mouth revealed the utter seriousness of his intent.

After months spent lusting after *the* Zac Prescott, he was finally here, in bed and touching her. This amazing, gorgeous man wanted *her*.

Then his hand cupped one breast, his thumb finding her hardened nipple, and all thought fled. The half-curve of his smile twisted the hard knot of desire inside her.

With slow deliberation, he peeled down one bra cup and her puckered nipple sprang free. His mouth swiftly covered it, the damp heat a mixture of joyous delight and shocking intimacy.

When his teeth gently scraped the sensitive flesh she gasped, her back arching, longing spreading deep into her belly, then creeping lower, fanning the blaze of arousal.

He nudged her back up on the bed, settled himself between her legs, then proceeded to lavish undivided attention on her breasts. He stroked the swelling curves, then teased the nipples into hard nubs with first his fingers, then his mouth. A myriad of sensations burst like small zaps of electricity over her skin, forcing her breath into a ragged gasp.

"Zac. Please…"

"What?" His grin was too innocent as his mouth closed over her breast. And his tongue…oh, lordy, his tongue danced a wicked rhythm over her painfully engorged nipple.

"Can…you…ahhh…"

"Keep going?" His thumb stroked her other nipple and all she could do was squeeze her eyes shut, arch back and let the sensations ride her. "Stop?"

"Yes…no… It's…" Her breath strangled out as he licked the hard nub, then gently blew on it. *Too wonderful. Too amazing. Too…*

"Too much," she managed to gasp.

"Hmmmm." When he pulled back, her eyes sprang open. With infinite concentration, he slid his hand down, over her belly, skimming the indentation of her belly button, to finally stop at her waist where her skirt had bunched.

Panic spurted as he rocked her hips, gently easing off her skirt. She hadn't had time to change into anything remotely seductive, but as he peeled off her skirt to reveal white cotton bikini knickers, she needn't have worried. His eyes were glued to her face, watching her expression, her reaction.

Like the one she obviously made when he cupped the most intimate part of her and a wave of heat roared over her skin.

He grinned again. "Too much?"

Without waiting for an answer, he ran a knuckle over the elastic waistband before gently sliding inside, his ragged groan as he tangled in her curls a mix of delight and need, mirroring hers.

The urgency in his bruising kiss was unmistakable, his lips, his tongue making her drunk with desire. She couldn't resist when he nudged her legs farther apart, his skillful fingers easing firmly inside her with a purely possessive growl that rocketed through her blood. She was so very aroused, so very wet for him. And he knew it.

When Emily's tongue tangled gently with his, it nearly sent Zac over the edge. Her teasing hot mouth, those luscious breasts pressing into him, combined with the slick warmth enveloping his fingers. He couldn't wait any longer.

With a groan he wrenched away, feet hitting the floor as he ripped off his shirt, then fumbled with his belt and zipper.

He pulled down pants and boxers, cursed as they got tangled in his shoes and socks, then finally kicked them into a corner of the bedroom with a grunt of frustration.

Emily's soft laugh dragged his attention back to the bed, but as soon as they locked gazes, amusement fled.

Those suits had a lot to answer for, hiding such a superb body beneath their severely cut angles. Perfectly rounded breasts that filled a man's hands. A curvy body with taut velvet skin. And a pair of strong muscular legs that would wrap firmly around a man's waist as he drove deep inside, again and again.

Swiftly he reached for the bedside table, pulled out a row of condoms and ripped one open.

He rejoined her on the bed, hooking his thumbs in her knickers and yanking them down, grinning as she gasped.

Desperate need bubbled up, quickening his movements as he nudged her legs apart with his knee, then took his position. And then, with a dizzying breath, he drove deep into her heat.

She gasped again, but this one felt as if it'd been wrenched from her very soul. Her back arched, head back, neck exposed and vulnerable.

He grasped her face in both hands and kissed her, urgent and hot, his blood throbbing, filling her up as he paused, fighting for dominance. Then she mewled beneath his lips, her hips bucking gently, urging him to continue.

With teeth clenched, he began to move.

Exquisite sensation. Hot friction. His breath raced, his heart pounding so hard he thought it'd explode through his chest. He thrust deep and was rewarded by Emily's hiss of pleasure, her whisper of delight ramping up his lust to breaking point. She moved with him, meeting him all the way, her hands on his hips, her ragged breath in his ear. When he gripped her butt, angled her up and plunged deeper, she cried out, her teeth sinking into his shoulder.

Just when he thought he couldn't get any hotter.

Her tiny bite stung, his skin slick with sweat and their loving. Her hips tilted up to him, her legs wrapped around his waist.

"Zac…"

She was staring right at him, her cheeks flushed, that lush mouth open in an expression of pure eroticism. "I'm…it's…"

"Hold on," he murmured against her lips as he increased his pace. She did as he asked, her legs tightening around him as she buried her face in his shoulder.

From deep inside he could feel her muscles contract, the threads of orgasm building. With a groan he went in for another kiss, unashamedly stealing her sounds of pleasure with his mouth, pulling them inside, then breathing them out.

Then it happened. With a thick cry she threw back her head,

her breath ragged and harsh. Deep inside her muscles squeezed, and in a sudden rush of incredible pleasure, he couldn't hold on any longer. With his fingers digging into her flesh, he finally let go, the scalding lust engulfing him on one almighty wave as he clawed his way through the hot depths.

The orgasm racked Emily's body with almost unbearable force. He filled every dark corner with pleasure, and her entire body shook from the force of it.

Elation bubbled from her throat as her body shuddered. She'd never been this close to this kind of…bliss. Yes, that's what it was. She felt completely alive and totally, completely spent.

"Wow." She didn't realize she'd said it aloud until Zac pulled back onto his elbows and met her eyes with a satisfied grin.

"Thank you." He gently swept her damp hair back from her forehead.

They were plastered together from the chest down, still intimately connected. Inside, she could still feel the deep erotic pulse of him, his heartbeat echoing hers. Yet his simple act of stroking her hair had her whole body in a flush, her skin tingling, wanting more.

She'd been without intimacy for way too long. And now she was overloading on it.

As if sensing her change, Zac slowly rolled from her, back onto the pillows, hands resting lightly on his forehead. And a few minutes later, with the musky scent of lovemaking still lingering, she finally heard his slow, deep rhythmic breathing.

She was glad he was asleep. It made escape easier.

Cautiously she eased from the warm bed, groped around the floor for agonizing seconds until she found her clothes, then quickly dressed, all the while with one eye on Zac.

It would be so very easy to crawl back between those sheets, back into his arms. Her body ached in a dozen intimate places, a satisfied, languid ache that eventually made up her mind.

No sleepovers. No weekends. No personal talk.

She'd made the rules, now it was up to her to follow them.

With bags in hand she crept down the stairs, across the cool living room and out the front door without looking back.

Ten

You could learn a lot about a woman by the way her hands moved when she talked. Some waved them animatedly, some used touch either subconsciously or with deliberate effect. And some liked to keep their own personal space. Emily, Zac realized, was one of the latter. She made a point of avoiding any physical contact. No brush of the fingers when exchanging files. No accidental arm contact in the elevator or corridor.

At first he thought it was her steely determination to keep that line drawn, but she retained the personal boundary even when they were alone in his office.

He stared at his closed door, then down at the remnants of his devoured lunch burger before shoving it all in the trash.

It shouldn't matter. It didn't matter. Her response was a pointed reminder of his position—him boss, her employee. Yet last night they'd been more. With him buried deep in her wet warmth, her legs wrapped around his waist as they rocked in that age-old rhythm.

Yeah, it had been much, much more.

With a soft curse, he ripped his mind back to the present. A hard-on at work was the last thing he needed, not when he had to deal with a hundred other things—like the upcoming Point One event. And then there was Cal, Victor and the whole VP Tech debacle.

He shoved back his chair and stalked to the door, yanking it open.

"Reschedule my one o'clock," he said, knowing his voice came out too harsh. "I'm going out."

Emily nodded and picked up the phone. "Will you be back for your three-thirty?"

No questions, just acceptance. Her composure rankled, her once-valued hyper-efficiency now just another thing that drove him crazy.

"Yes."

He couldn't escape the building quickly enough, the sudden desire to get behind the wheel and drive urging him on.

So he did. He drove north, up the Gold Coast Highway, then turned right onto Waterways Drive and followed the signs to Seaworld. He passed Palazzo Versace, the Sheraton Mirage, the various takeaways.

On the way he made a few calls and set up more meetings. He succeeded in not thinking about Emily or last night until he passed Seaworld itself, until the road became narrower, the surrounding vegetation thicker.

The western arm of Gold Coast Spit appeared on his left, the sandy peninsula and watery inlet filled with yachts and recreational fishermen. The road continued, through the trees that formed part of Main Beach Park, until the Spit car park appeared.

He pulled in, gravel crunching beneath the tires, and cut off the engine. The classic AC/DC song abruptly ceased, giving way to the familiar sound of pounding waves through the trees and sand dunes ahead.

Easing from the car, he breathed deep, last night's rain salty and wild on the air. He loved this spot, even more than the small strip of private beach that flanked his house.

He grabbed a bag from the boot and pulled out a wetsuit before heading toward the small board-rental shed. Ten minutes later he was jogging down to the beach toward the flags, a surfboard under his arm.

An hour passed before he finally called it a day, collapsing on the warm sand to let the sun dry him off.

Depending on which direction you faced, you could see the high-rises of Southport, the wilds of South Stradbroke Island or straight out into the vast Pacific Ocean. He'd been surfing here for years, had spotted whales, been caught in powerful storms that were a stark reminder of the power of nature and fragility of life.

How could he keep this thing with him and Emily out of the office when all he wanted to do was rip off her clothes? Hell, even in her usual office getup and those awful clunky shoes, he *still* wanted her. Yet if he wanted to keep her in his bed, he'd have to keep their after-hours affair a secret.

He hated secrets. Secrets turned people into liars, and he liked lies about as much as secrets.

With a grunt, he finally stood, his toes digging into the grainy sand as he made his way back to the car.

The soft swoosh of the glass door drew Emily's eyes up from her computer screen. Zac strode in, looking tanned and windswept. When he dragged a hand through his hair, leaving peaks in its wake, her heart did a little flip.

"Your father called."

His brow dipped as he paused, hands going to his hips. "Right. Thanks."

"You didn't give him your mobile number?"

"No."

Emily paused, feeling as if she were missing something. "He says you're not returning his calls."

"I know." Zac continued toward his office, his mouth grim, shoulders rigid. She grabbed up some papers and followed him in.

He stood behind the huge desk, his yellow smiley stress ball in one fist as he gazed out onto Broadbeach Mall.

Squeeze, release. Squeeze, release. They'd all had a laugh when one of his more difficult clients had given him that by way of apology. Everyone knew—especially the client—that Zac didn't stress.

Squeeze, release. Squeeze, release. His profile was the very definition of contained frustration combined with deep thought.

"Do you want me to give him a message next time he calls?"

Startled, he turned to her. "No." He tossed the stress ball back onto his desk. "I'll call him."

"But you don't want to."

His silent frown told her she was right, even though he'd rather she not be.

"Zac, whatever happened between you and your father—"

"—is not something I want to talk about."

The shutters slammed down so abruptly that Emily took a step back. With warm cheeks, she said, "I understand that. But when I was ten, my sister ran out, and I spent thirteen years not knowing if she was dead or alive. When she finally found me, do you think I still cared about all those stupid arguments we'd had years before?"

His eyes widened in brief surprise, weakening the frown.

What are you doing? Shut up, shut up, shut— "People make decisions based on emotion, not what's logical," she said quickly. "That's how they make mistakes. And if Victor's trying to make an effort you should at least hear him out."

She snapped her mouth shut, suddenly appalled. Then without another word, she spun and headed out the door.

Emily slapped her notepad on her desk before taking a deep breath. She didn't know what was worse, revealing that small nugget from her past or Zac acting as if last night had been a complete fabrication of her overactive imagination.

Well, she couldn't take those words back now. But was it enough to sway him?

With a sigh, she sat heavily in her chair. Yes, he had to

maintain their professional boss-employee front to throw off any suspicion. But did it have to feel so real?

She clicked through her e-mails absently.

She'd finally managed to deflect Zac's familiar non sequiturs that made her totally aware of herself as a woman, and then he went and did a one-eighty. After last night, she'd been prepared to fend off any intimate comments, to remind him they were at work and should act appropriately. But that had never materialized.

What had happened to the flirty, good-humored Zac of before, the guy she'd been able to keep separate from her personal life?

The vibe was all wrong. He was painfully polite. No, more like… She chewed the end of the pen thoughtfully. Disinterested.

Because she'd finally succumbed to his charms, slept with him, and now the chase was over, he wanted to move on?

"Emily? Do you have a minute?"

She didn't have to turn to know he stood at the door: his eyes burned a hole in her back. Instinctively, she straightened, clicking off her screen saver to reveal the Point One schedule.

"Actually, I'm in the middle of—"

"This is important."

She stilled, hand on the mouse, then sighed in resignation. *Here it comes.*

He remained standing as she walked in, then closed the door softly behind her. Her senses barely had time to register his familiar aftershave, that warm radiating body heat as he walked past her to take a seat behind his desk.

She sat, crossed her legs and waited.

He stared at her in silence. And to her credit, she stared right back.

"I don't want this to be awkward between us," he finally said.

"Awkward?"

"Us working together, given our…arrangement."

"I don't feel awkward." She gave him her best "restrained and composed" look. "Do you?"

"No."

"Because if you want out, I'll understand."

"Do *you* want out?" His eyes narrowed.

"I asked first."

A wry grin creased Zac's face. "What are we, in eighth grade?" Then more seriously, he added, "I don't want out."

Well, so much for your theory. "Well, neither do I." Her chin went up as she met his eyes, firmly ignoring the little cheer her body made.

"Good."

"Fine."

They both paused, Zac scrutinizing her with the same intensity he reserved for a particularly difficult problem.

"Do you think I'm over my head with the Point One event?" she suddenly blurted out.

He leaned back in his chair. "What do you think?"

"It's a challenge."

"Which is what you wanted." .

"Yes."

"What you've done so far is good, Emily. And we're a team here—use the staff to get whatever you need done. And keep me posted." His smile was brief. "And while we're in the office, it will always be about work. This is a Valhalla project," he added. "I know it's yours, but it's also mine. We both make this work and we both benefit."

With a nod, Emily rose to leave.

"Emily."

She paused, glancing back at him.

"Are you free tonight?"

And just like that, last night came flooding back, playing away in her mind like an erotic movie taken off pause. Despite herself, she felt excitement tingle her skin.

"Yes."

His mouth curved and suddenly he seemed like Zac again. "Then I'll see you after eight."

"Sure." She left his office way more discomforted than she'd gone in.

Eleven

The precedent was set for the next two weeks. Zac remained cool and professional during office hours. He always asked if she was free that night. Emily always said yes, except for the weekends. Those days were hers alone.

At night Zac spent hours exploring her body, learning what turned her on, what made her cry out in passion or sigh with delight. He focused on her pleasure, skillfully bringing her to the brink of bliss night after night, then taking them both over the edge. And in the early hours of the morning, Emily crept from his bed and returned to her own, exhausted. She made sure she always got to work on time, despite her growing need for sleep and the ever-present ache between her legs.

And she never let anything remotely personal slip again.

"Any plans for Saturday night?" Zac casually asked when their Friday afternoon meeting had broken up.

"Work. And I might get in a book and a bath."

She ignored the glint in his eye, then the small frown when she reiterated her plans after they were alone in his office.

Yet on Sunday, after she'd slept, read and bathed herself into boredom, she dressed in a pair of gray track pants and an old baby-doll T-shirt and opened up her laptop.

As she put the finishing touches on the launch for Point One and finally pressed "save," a deep sense of satisfaction engulfed her. *This* is what she should've been doing every weeknight instead of indulging in the joys of mutual sexual pleasure. This was her career, her life. Do this well and there was no telling the kind of contacts she'd make when it came time to set up her business.

Her hands stilled over the keys.

She hadn't thought about that in…days. Weeks, even. She hadn't heard back from the university to confirm her second-term enrollment. And, she realized with shock, she hadn't gone chasing it, either. Carnal pleasure had taken priority, pushing her goals from the limelight. And Point One had firmly kept them in the darkness.

You got caught up in the sex.

She leaned back into the sofa, grabbed a throw pillow and cradled it in her lap.

And the intimacy. And actually feeling desirable and wanted without there being an ulterior motive. For Jimmy she'd been a meal ticket. For her ex-boss, a conquest. And the others had come with their own unique baggage. Not one guy had wanted her for *her*.

Sure, she may have been clueless when it came to boyfriends, but she'd made sure to bank every single one of her paychecks. She'd always understood the power and freedom money represented.

So what would happen after Point One launched, when her debt to Zac was paid, when she got into her course?

You'll go forward with your life. Moving on, no looking back. Just like Zac always moved on, with the next eager female.

Thoughts of him with another woman sharing his bed, doing the things they'd done, suddenly made her want to gag.

She rose, threw the pillow across the room and headed for the kitchen. Grabbing the half bottle of mineral water from the fridge, she poured it into a wineglass and gulped it. The bubbles fizzed on the way down, followed by a sudden desperate need for normalcy. Her apartment, AJ, her job. They were normal, they were stable. Not this…this…crippling self-doubt.

Yet her mind was still buzzing hours later, her dreams peppered with gorgeous women vying for Zac's attention, her mother's cold, lined face and an empty room where the Point One launch party should have been.

She woke before dawn, a strange feeling pooling in the pit of her belly. After checking all the faucets, the locked front door and windows, then the lights, she texted AJ, then crawled back into bed.

No good.

It wasn't about her mother: she had no idea if Charlene was still alive, let alone where.

The Point One project?

She ran over the details in her head. No. Everything was on track, the prospectus was out, buyers were calling their sales division and the invites for the launch were going out today.

Yet something wasn't right. She rolled over onto her tummy, grabbed her glasses, cracked open the venetian blinds behind the headboard and squinted out into the predawn light.

Number seven's German shepherd was barking, as usual. Number ten had left her porch light on again. But other than that, nothing.

It had to be Zac—or more specifically, the way she felt about Zac. She knew what his life was like, the kinds of women he attracted. Who wouldn't feel inferior compared to the likes of Haylee Kerans and Trish Sattler?

With a sigh, she dragged herself up and pulled on her jogging gear.

The sun rose halfway into her run, the only other beach activity three lone fishermen and some surfers suiting up in the parking lot.

The office was empty when she got in. Zac had a site inspection that morning. A common occurrence, yet discontent dogged her routine.

AJ finally returned her text and Emily ticked it off her mental list, turning on the computer, then syncing up with Zac's schedule as she grabbed her coffee. The distinctive aroma made her mouth water, but before she could take a mouthful, the office door opened.

"Hey, Em." Zac's chief accountant, Megan Hwong, always reminded Emily of actress Lucy Liu—exotic, poised and confident. "Here's those budget figures you wanted." She put a file on the desk, then perched her Armani-clad hip on the corner with a smile.

An expectant, knowing smile.

Emily blinked. "What's up?"

Megan tipped her shiny black-bobbed head. "Just wanted to see something."

"What?"

"You."

"Why?"

Megan leaned in with a grin. "To see if last week was a fluke."

All sorts of scenarios sped through her mind. "Sorry?"

With an elegant hand, Megan gestured at Emily. "A nice hairstyle, a little lippy. You've even ditched those awful jackets," she added, eying Emily's sweater-and-skirt ensemble. "We reckon there's a man involved."

"What? No!"

"Wow." Megan pulled back with a grin. "Denial, much?"

Emily took a deep breath then said more calmly, "There's no man—it's getting warmer and I felt like a change and…and who's we?"

"Oh, Kerri and Bob," she supplied, naming the Accounts team. "Nice necklace, by the way."

Emily glanced down at the dozen long silvery strands of beads tied into a low knot. "Thanks. A late birthday present to myself."

"See? With an eye like that, I knew there was a fashion diva inside, dying to get out!" Megan grinned. "You should come shopping with the girls on Saturday."

Surprise stilled her for one second before she realized Megan was serious. "This Saturday?"

"Sure. Early Christmas shopping." She mock eye-rolled with a smile as she stood. "I'll e-mail you, okay?"

"Okay."

As the door clicked shut, silence engulfed the large office. After all her gentle refusals to social invites, all her deliberate avoidance of personal relationships in the workplace, it took just one, an invitation to shop with one of the most stylish women in Valhalla, to spark something inside, the part of her that longed to indulge in being a woman again.

She stared at the glass door as doubt surged. Was it coincidence that the offer came on the heels of Megan's casual reference to a man?

Emily gathered up some papers, walked into Zac's office, then shut the door, leaning up against the solid wood as her mind leaped to a thousand different conclusions, all of them bad.

Finally she straightened and went over to Zac's desk. No. Megan wasn't into subterfuge, unlike some. She'd asked, Emily had answered. Case closed.

Her reflection stared back from the huge tinted windows. She saw a twenty-six-year-old blonde in standard office wear—a long black skirt, sensible shoes, panty hose, short-sleeved baby-blue sweater.

She placed the papers in Zac's tray, then stepped in for a closer look. The sweater was cashmere, the V-neck showing off her collarbone, the long dangly beads drawing the eye down. She turned to the side, then front on. The material clung over her hips, a thin black belt defining her waist. Short capped sleeves showed off toned arms. With a frown she smoothed the sweater down over her belly, then her bottom.

Have I lost weight? Have I—

The door suddenly opened and she whirled, cheeks flushed. Zac.

Their gazes met and held for a heartbeat, then two. Despite herself, she felt her breath hitch as memories crammed her head.

Soft touches. Demanding kisses. Hot skin, sweaty with passion…

She felt the instantaneous heat pool low, then fan upward as he stood there, his eyes grazing her body with a slow smile.

"That color suits you," he finally said.

"Thank you."

"But I hate the shoes."

Her chin went up, a sharp reply at the ready, but his grin somehow negated her irritation.

"Maybe that's why I wear them."

One dark eyebrow lifted. "First you make a point of saying your new hairstyle is *not* to impress me, and now you're wearing shoes you know I hate?"

When he walked steadily toward her, she forced herself to remain exactly where she was. *Good, that's good. Don't show him you're affected, or how that boyish grin makes him way too irresistible.*

He stopped, so close she could see tiny flecks of gold in his olive eyes, the creases in his bottom lip as he continued to grin at her. And there was his scent, a mixture of shaving cream and some subtle aftershave that always seemed to scramble her senses.

"How was your weekend?" he asked softly. When his gaze dropped to her lips and remained there, she gave an inward curse.

Damn you, Max Factor, and your To-Be-Kissed Pink gloss.

"Fine."

"Good." It didn't sound as though he was pleased, but she let that go.

"What happened to your meeting?" she asked, determined to uphold that professional veneer.

"Rescheduled." He reached out and plucked something from her sweater sleeve, his fingers briefly brushing her arm before he withdrew. "I just sent you a text."

She nodded, letting silence command the room.

He leaned in and to her dismay, she jumped, her hip bumping into the desk.

He smiled, his mouth close to her ear, his cheek not quite touching hers but radiating warmth all the same. "Did you need something?"

Can I make a list? "Ahh. No."

"You sure?"

His breath brushed over her lobe, sending scalding heat through her veins. And when his tongue followed, she bit her lip to stop the groan from escaping.

"You don't need this?"

His mouth nibbled at the spot where her ear met her neck, then slid down her jaw.

"No…" she managed to croak out, frantically trying to ignore her body screaming *yes!* through every nerve.

"Or this?" He trailed one finger over her collarbone, then slowly into the valley between her breasts, carefully watching for her reaction.

"Zac, you can't."

His grin was full of wicked knowledge. "I can. I have."

"We're in your office," she got out as his finger edged around her bra cup, eventually finding her hard nipple. His other hand came around to the desk and settled by her hip, pinning her there, possessive yet allowing escape if she so chose.

His heat, his breath, the need in his eyes threatened to overwhelm her thoughts.

His finger rhythmically stroked her nipple, producing little shudders that she struggled to quash. His mouth—that wondrous, skillful mouth—curved, teasing her into acquiescence with one smile. And the intense heat from his body engulfed her, spinning her thoughts, negating her halfhearted protest.

She swallowed as arousal pulsed beneath her skin. No matter how hard she tried to keep their arrangement after-hours, her body betrayed her every time. Since Friday night she'd been alone, three nights that suddenly felt like three months, and now she craved him like some illegal drug.

Suddenly she didn't care that they were in his office or that she'd been the one who'd demanded secrecy. All she wanted was for him to kiss her, take off her clothes and make love to her in that plush leather office chair.

Her phone shattered the moment, the two-time ring muffled through the door before it went to voice mail.

With a gasp she twisted, away from his drugging heat, away from her weakness.

She glared at him as she quickly adjusted her glasses then smoothed down her sweater. "I told you, Zac—not in your office. What would've happened if someone had walked in?"

"Then they would've won big on the office pools."

His shrug, such a casual dismissal of her concerns, sent indignation surging. "What?"

"I know everything that goes on in this company, Emily." He crossed his arms. "The current odds of you being my next conquest are about three hundred to one."

"Three…"

As she floundered with embarrassment, his smile dropped. "Look, don't let it worry you. No one cares—"

"*I* care."

"Why?" He crossed his arms. "Why does it bother you so much what other people think?"

The familiar hot pulse of shame engulfed Emily as he stood silent, awaiting her reply. Yet she had none to give him, none that would keep him at the distance she so desperately needed him to be.

"Because I refuse to be judged on anything other than my work. And now I have to get back to it." And she was out the door.

If he hadn't had back-to-back meetings, Zac would've gotten to the bottom of whatever was really bugging Emily. As it was, he spent most of the day thinking about the deeper reason she'd been so upset and how he was going to broach the subject again.

They'd actually started becoming friends. No, not friends. The things he wanted to do to her were not friendly at all—they were downright dirty. For three long, frustrating nights he'd spent way too much time thinking about her skin, her lips, her warm, accommodating body. After such a solid beating, his restraint had lapsed that morning and he'd been unable to keep his hands off her.

You're lucky she didn't call it off then and there.

When she'd texted back a simple "can't" to his request to meet that evening, his first thought was to drive over to her place and demand to know what was going on. Yet he knew that would force her away, and that was the last thing he wanted.

So he ate Thai takeaway at home alone, absently wondering what Emily would say to a proper meal in a proper restaurant. Somewhere public where he could show her off, with candlelight, music and dancing.

She'd shut you down and you know it. So stop complaining.

Dissatisfied, he finished his food, shoved the dishes in the washer, then picked up the phone.

Time to deal with VP Tech.

He hung up thirty minutes later, flush with—not exactly victory, but close enough. Cal had been working on Victor, and while the suggestion to float the company had died in the water, he'd been making headway with advertising the CEO position. They could utilize VP Tech's young, hungry executives and keep everything in-house. Progress, yes, but Victor still wanted Zac involved, a prospect Zac refused to even discuss. At the moment, Cal was their go-between, a situation Zac felt half guilty, half grateful for.

Desperate for physical exertion, he grabbed his gym bag and headed out, taking two hours to run, row and heave weights at Surfers' twenty-four-hour gym. Yet after he showered and changed, then got back into his car, his body still hummed with energy, his brain still fixated on VP Tech.

He needed to really lose himself, not just force his muscles into screaming agony. And he knew exactly what to do.

Twelve

Emily swung her front door open but instead of the pizza delivery guy, Zac stood there, his arm resting casually on her doorframe.

"Let's go out."

She blinked. "What?"

"Out. Somewhere dark, with loud music."

"I'm… I'm…" He stepped over the threshold and she instinctively moved aside. "Expecting a pizza," she ended lamely as he paused in her living room.

He turned to face her, hands on his hips, one eyebrow raised. "Wow. Really living the high life."

"I'm also working."

She crossed her arms, refusing to let his appraising dissection of her casual sweats and bare feet affect her.

"I've just been on the phone with Cal about VP Tech and now I need to let off some steam. I thought you might like to join me."

She swallowed. *Admit it. You're thrilled you're his first choice and he came all this way to ask you. You want to go.*

And, her doubt demons added, *he could always ask someone else if you turned him down.*

"What about the pizza?" she blurted out.

His mouth tweaked. "I'll wait for it while you go change."

"I'm not sure—"

He silenced her with a kiss, a deep, blood-pumping kiss that made her legs weak and her brain fuzzy. "Emily," he finally murmured, a scant inch away from her bruised mouth. "I'm sure. We'll go someplace no one will recognize us. Trust me."

What could she say to that?

They were at Heaven, one of Surfers' popular nightclubs famous for dance music, decently priced drinks and top-notch security, and despite the weeknight, the place was packed. True to Zac's word, it was a place where no one cared who you were and how much you earned. Emily glanced around the strobe-lighted dance floor. A place where you could relax without being watched or judged. Zac could've taken her to any of a dozen private clubs frequented by the super-rich and beautiful, yet he'd picked this one.

Was it for her benefit or his?

She didn't care. Because right now the familiar, sexy throb-throb beat began to seep into her skin, teasing, tempting, making her body ache with sudden longing.

Come dance, the music beckoned as the lights flashed and the crowded dance floor moved as one. She shifted from foot to foot, suddenly desperate to get out there, to let her hair down and just enjoy the music.

Then Zac locked eyes with hers and everything seemed to fade into watercolor at the edges. For one second, the short velvet skirt and glittery silver tank top she'd dug from her closet felt way too undressed. But when he grinned, offered his hand and said, "Let's dance, gorgeous," all her self-consciousness melted away.

Linking her fingers in his, he led her to the dance floor, the heavy bass warming her blood and tingling her skin.

Bodies were everywhere, dancing and laughing, and when

the current track suddenly morphed into a familiar Beyoncé hit, the crowd roared, then surged forward, sweeping them up into the vortex.

Zac found a space near the shadowed stage and pulled her close, mashing her body up against his from thigh to collar. Emily's body responded instantaneously.

"It's not that kind of dance," she murmured, sucking in air as his arms looped possessively around her waist.

"Don't care."

His breath fluttered against her neck, delicious and warm, and slowly they began to move.

Emily laid her cheek on his chest and squeezed her eyes shut, letting the music and heat wash over her. When she was with Zac, just like this, everything else seemed unimportant. It was like closing a door, a door that held her past, her problems and her doubts at bay.

He made her feel wanted. Needed. Like she was some powerful sexual goddess in control of her destiny.

His hands slid up her back, over the bumpy fabric of her tank, his fingers teasing the soft skin under the straps. And all the while, the crowd spun crazily around them, the music echoing her rising heart rate.

"Hey, Zac! I thought it was you! How are you?"

She felt him reluctantly pull away, and when she turned, a tall, gorgeous blonde stood beside them. Emily blinked, astonishment suddenly giving way to the burn of unwelcome jealousy as the woman dropped a brief kiss on his lips.

If her smile was too stiff when Zac introduced them, he didn't seem to notice. She nodded politely as fear and irritation solidified in her stomach, the snapshot of this stunning creature kissing Zac burning away in her mind as she overtly flirted with him.

When the woman finally left, Emily was ready to pull out those glossy blond hairs one by one.

"Who does she think she is?" she muttered under her breath as she glared into the crowd. She'd obviously seen the way she and Zac had been dancing, yet she'd kissed and flirted with abandon.

She glanced up to see Zac watching her intently.

"Josie works for Scandinavian Airlines," he offered. "I met her on a flight to Europe."

"Was she—" Emily bit her lip, refusing to voice that damning question. It made her sound needy. Childish. Jealous.

But Zac had her all figured out. He reached for her, dragging her back into his embrace. Her breath surged out as anticipation began to sluggishly chug through her veins.

"Was she a girlfriend? No." He paused to study her, his eyes way too perceptive even in the strobe-lighted darkness. "Why?"

She couldn't tell him. Couldn't say that she was burning with jealousy, that the mere attention from another female sparked ice-cold fear in her stomach.

"Your exes have no concept of boundaries," she said, then ended on a gasp as his palms slid boldly over her bottom.

"She wasn't my girlfriend. But you're right," he murmured, backing up and taking her with him until they hit the edge of the dance floor. "They don't."

The massive stage curtains fell like a dark cloud at their backs, the shadows swallowing them.

His lips found her neck. She shivered as his breath tripped over her sensitive flesh, his mouth shockingly hot as he began to sway in time to the sensual beat of a familiar chart topper.

The heavy bass swirled, the throbbing pulse filling her chest, her throat. She could feel it vibrate through every muscle, echoing in Zac's heartbeat as his chest pressed up against her.

"Maybe coming here was a bad idea," he whispered.

Her heart skipped. "Why?"

"Because of this." He moved and his hard arousal pressed into her stomach.

She groaned, and for a moment she wished she could remain like this, warm and protected. But then the lights flashed, illuminating the bar crowd for less than five seconds, before dropping them back into darkness. And in those seconds, Emily caught a figure in the throng, staring straight at them.

She stumbled but Zac steadied her. When she glanced back, Louie Mayer was gone.

The enjoyment of the night fled. She couldn't concentrate on the music, on Zac's warm body flush against hers, not now.

"Can we get out of here?" she said softly.

Zac's eyes darkened, then with a short nod, he took her hand and they began the slow process of plowing through the dancers.

Emily lay on Zac's soft sheets staring at the ceiling, knowing she had a dopey smile on her face. Who wouldn't grin like an idiot when she'd just been completely and thoroughly loved by Zac Prescott?

"You okay?" Zac murmured in the moonlit darkness.

"Fine." She turned to him, propping her elbow on the mattress, her head on her hand. "But your stairs are tough on the back. And I think I have a splinter in my butt."

His grin flashed, sending a bolt of heat through her blood. "So next time, you can be on top. In fact…"

He reached for her and rolled, and she went willingly. Her body still sang with their previous lovemaking, but that didn't stop her heart from picking up in anticipation.

They lay there wedged from chest to knee, Zac effortlessly cradling her weight. Gently, he brushed her hair back, tucking the long strands behind her ears, before tugging her down for a kiss. A soft, tender kiss that made her chest contract with a longing so deep, so sudden, that it made every bone dissolve with joy.

In that moment, she completely understood why all those women wouldn't take no for an answer. Zac Prescott was like a drug. Her body burned for his touch, his skilled hands, his sinful mouth. And when they weren't together, like this, he was all she could think about.

"What do you want me to do?" His breath was warm in her ear, his lips nibbling on her lobe. She stifled a groan and sat up, her brain thick with yearning.

Her heart did another little leap as she stared down at him. Her knees firmly bracketed his waist, her bottom wedged on his abdomen. This was real. He was real.

So why did she get the feeling it could all come crashing down in disaster?

"Emily?"

Zac reached out to grasp her waist. She was like some ancient goddess of fertility, with that womanly hourglass figure, the indented waist, the gentle belly curve. And those breasts...

He reached up and palmed them, each luscious swell of generous flesh heavy in his hands.

His groin began to stir again but he ignored it, instead taking the time to thumb those rosy-budded nipples, grinning when her breath hitched and her eyes began to close in dreamy pleasure.

"What do you want me to do?" he repeated thickly. As his thumbs continued their rhythmic stroking, she began to quiver.

"Just...just..."

"Yes?"

"I don't..."

She wiggled in frustration and he swallowed a groan. "Look at me."

His command brooked no refusal. She sighed, slowly opening her eyes. The dark arousal in those depths made every muscle constrict with lust.

"You're in charge, Emily. Tell me what you want me to do."

Just when he thought he couldn't be more turned on, her white teeth nibbled on her bottom lip, the tiny pink tongue briefly flashing out to lick the spot.

A new round of flames scorched across his skin, sending his heart rate sky high.

"I want..." The warm flush spread across her cheeks as she blinked. "I want you to kiss me. All over."

With guttural triumph deep in his throat, he flipped her, pinning her to the mattress. He slid a knee between her legs, then dragged in a breath at the damp heat pooling there.

"You're wet."

She tipped back her head and closed her eyes with a mutter

of assent, and he grinned. Shocking her gave him no small amount of pleasure. Seeing her flush, watching those lashes flutter nervously, all told him he affected her, that she wasn't as indifferent as she pretended to be when they were in the office.

Oh yeah, it pleased him greatly.

He cupped her mound, the curls tickling his hand, and she dragged in a breath.

"I'm going to kiss you, Emily."

Another murmur, another sigh.

"First, your mouth." He pinned her face with one hand, the other still resting possessively between her legs.

When Zac's lips came down on hers Emily couldn't hold back her sigh of delight. Of all the things she'd missed about being intimate, kissing topped the list. Yet every other kiss paled in the wake of Zac's. He started tender, almost gentle, but soon it deepened into something hot and breathless. When he pulled back she whimpered, no longer caring how it made her sound, just needing his lips on hers.

"Relax." His mouth went to her jaw, curving into a smile against her skin. "You wanted to be kissed all over, right?"

"Yes." Although she was quickly regretting her request, because his still hand between her legs had become an almost unbearable distraction.

"So let me kiss you."

For endless minutes he lavished attention on her neck, then her breasts, before slipping down to her belly button, his hot breath creating a shivering path across her skin.

She knew where he was headed. Every nerve screamed with anticipation. Yet when his mouth closed over the most intimate part of her, the sudden shock wrenched her off the bed with a gasp.

He murmured gently and repositioned himself, cupping her bottom firmly in his palms before applying himself to the task of pleasuring her.

She couldn't breathe. Couldn't think. Couldn't do anything except feel…his strong hands, his teasing hot tongue, his warm breath. Even his chin, dusted with stubble, intimately grazed across her swollen flesh, creating an almost unbearable friction.

She squeezed her eyes shut as the ripples of ecstasy began to build. And Zac kept right on going, his tongue swirling around her hardened bud, his mouth kissing, sucking, teasing her into incoherence.

The trembling began, first in her legs, then her body, then suddenly the orgasm crashed, wave upon wave of rapture forcing a whimper from her lips.

Behind her eyelids everything went a shimmering, iridescent black. Her body twitched like she'd been shot with a thousand volts, skin throbbing with awareness. Through the thickening euphoric haze, she realized Zac had returned to her, his mouth a shocking musky combination of her passion and his desire.

Her blood throbbed through her veins, echoing deep within as Zac smoothly eased inside her, joining them in the familiar lover's dance.

He groaned, bathing her in need, before he opened his eyes and that heat-laden gaze locked on hers.

It was the ultimate act of intimacy, him moving deep inside, making love to her while their eyes held. Zac saw her every expression, every tiny move, as he slid out, then with a wicked grin, firmly back in. He heard every gasp, every murmur. And soon he was ready to explode, nerves raw from her erotic gasps of pleasure. When he finally went over the edge, she followed a moment later, their cries of release echoing off the bedroom walls.

Emily tried to catch her breath, but Zac's weight pinned her down.

"Too heavy?" he murmured, his breath tickling her ear.

"A little."

He rolled, taking her with him so she was on top, half sprawled across his chest. Beneath her cheek she felt the strong pounding heartbeat, his crisp hair teasing her skin.

This. Right here. If everything collapsed into dust right now, she wouldn't care.

The minutes ticked by, the only movement when Zac reached down to cover their cooling bodies with the sheet.

"I heard back from admissions," she eventually said.

"You got into uni."

"Yes."

"That's good."

With a smile she slowly rolled off him to settle on her back. *So why do I feel so…calm?* "Better than good. It's…" She blinked, struggling to define the burning need she'd never had to quantify until now. "It means progress. A goal achieved. It's something I've wanted for a long time."

The silence settled around them, until Zac shifted and sheets rustled softly.

"Did you like living in Perth?" he said softly.

"Not really." She moved to her side to face him, tempering her curt reply with a small smile. "Nice city, great beaches. But I prefer Queensland."

The moonlight reflected his serious gaze. "What about your friends? Family?"

"What about them?"

He said nothing, until she finally let out a sigh.

"My mother's brother died and left me his place nearly three years ago. So I moved." She shifted her weight, drawing the sheet firmly around her. "My sister AJ lives in Robina. Everyone else is…gone."

He studied her in silence. There was something serious and honest in that look. It told her whatever she chose to reveal would remain between them. And more important, he wouldn't judge.

So instead of throwing up those familiar defenses she lay back, stared at the ceiling and answered him.

"When I was seventeen I started temping for an agency in Perth." It was easier to talk in the dark, where his all-seeing eyes couldn't drag out any more than she was willing to give. "It was good money and interesting work, but eventually I wanted something permanent. So I applied for an office manager's position at Hardy, Max & Taylor."

"The accountancy firm? That wasn't on your CV."

"No. I quit after six months."

"Why?"

She was a good liar, although not as good as AJ. To get through their childhood, to survive, lying had been a necessity for the Reynolds girls. But *needing to* and *wanting to* were two different things.

"One of the managing directors cornered me on the balcony at the Christmas party and tried to feel me up. Not only was I a 'hot piece with a great rack'—sexual harassment was alive and well in corporate Australia."

Zac made a small noise, a cross between a curse and a growl. When she turned, his profile squeezed her heart. He was angry—no, *furious*—and trying to rein it in.

"Did you report it?" he ground out.

"No." At his puckered brow, she sighed. "I was twenty-two. I had no money, no power to take on one of Australia's leading private companies. Someone would've leaked my complaint and then the TV stations would've been all over it. I didn't want that kind of publicity. And anyway, it wasn't such a big deal. He didn't actually *do* anything."

"That's bull and you know it."

Abruptly she sat up, dragging the sheet with her. "Don't make this into some big emotional speed bump, Zac. I kneed him in the groin, he threatened sexual misconduct, so I quit. End of story."

"So you're saying that didn't have any lasting effect?"

"What do you want me to say? It didn't stop me dating, although my choice in men was poor to say the least. It didn't stop me marrying Jimmy," she snorted self-deprecatingly. "It didn't stop me living my life."

"Right. A life that involves secret sex with your boss?"

Zac abruptly swung from the bed, the cold floorboards on his bare feet barely registering.

"You're angry."

His jaw tightened as he glanced back to her rigid figure. "Damn right I am."

"So...what? Are you saying you want to change our arrangement?"

"I'm saying," he snapped on the bedside light, then yanked on his boxers, then his pants with sharp jerky movements, "that once in a while it'd be nice if we went out somewhere. Together, in public, instead of sneaking around like our sex life is some big covert operation."

"What about tonight?"

He shoved his hands on his hips. "That hardly counted. I'm not ashamed of us—are you?"

Zac knew his words hit home the second her breath hissed out. Her pale face humbled him, tiny barbs of guilt thickening his throat.

"Look, Emily..."

"No, you don't have to say anything." She slid to the other end of the bed, taking the sheet with her. "I... I think I should go."

"You don't have to—"

"I do." She gathered up her clothes, adding, "it's late," as if that explained everything.

"Stay."

Her face froze in an expression he couldn't read.

"I can't." She made it to the foot of the stairs. "I'll see you at the office tomorrow."

Thirteen

It was as if last Monday night had happened in a parallel universe.

Every day that week Emily brought him lunch, organized his clients and performed exactly like the efficient assistant she was. No secret glances, no tensing up when he accidentally brushed her arm. Every time he opened his mouth, her cool blue eyes remained professional and distant.

She remained in the office after he left for the night, always working. He didn't text her to come over and she didn't offer. Yet after a few days he wondered if he should've pressed the issue instead of letting it ride, because he had no idea what to say or what he could do to fix this. Her wall of silence shut him down before any words could form.

Despite her aura of back off, she still distracted him. Her black suits had finally given way to skirts that now skimmed her knees, tucked-in tops and thin belts emphasizing every dip and curve of her luscious body. To anyone else, her perfectly suitable office attire wouldn't have rated a second glance. But to Zac, who knew exactly what was under those silky shirts and soft-to-touch sweaters, it blurred the line between demure and obscene.

He'd fantasized a hundred different ways to peel off those clothes.

"So, who are you two backing?"

Daniel from HR stood at the door, the racing form in his hand. Zac didn't miss the way Emily quickly backed away from his desk, pulling the files she held protectively against her chest.

"The race. The Melbourne Cup?" Daniel said with a grin. "We're in conference room three—thanks, Em—with nibbles, drinks and a flat screen. We just need your bets."

Emily glanced at Zac, then back to Daniel, before she gave the younger man a smile. "Come on through and I'll get some money."

He'd forgotten about the Melbourne Cup, the biggest day in Australian racing, when the whole nation stopped to watch a horse race. It was a major social event in practically every business, and Valhalla was no exception. And, he thought later as he made his way to the conference room, Emily had a real talent for organizing people. As Valhalla's unofficial social director, she was the one everyone came to to organize birthdays, retirements, the annual Christmas party. More importantly, she'd jumped into the Point One launch with expert efficiency, and was currently on target and under budget.

She'd make a damn good life coach.

He mingled with his employees, chatting comfortably but always with one eye on Emily. A few times she caught him looking and every time, glanced away.

It took thirty minutes to circulate and get to the spot where she stood, but he did so with purposeful deliberation, waiting until she broke off a conversation and approached the table laden with food.

"Are you free tonight?"

A casual observer would have missed how her outstretched hand stilled briefly before she finally took the tiny quiche and popped it in her mouth. But Zac knew he had encroached on her personal space, from the way her eyes blinked to her fingers gripping the wineglass she held. Tension radiated out like an invisible force field, yet he still itched to brush back a strand of hair that had escaped her ponytail, to test the soft skin of her cheek.

Common sense overrode desire, even though he hated holding back and his muscles ached with the effort.

"You have a client dinner." She solved his conundrum by efficiently sweeping back the offending lock of hair. "Eight o'clock at the Palazzo Versace."

He frowned, mentally reshuffling.

"And I'll probably be working," she added, taking a sip from her wineglass. "The launch is less than five weeks away."

He stared at her elegant profile. "Right." The subtext was glaringly obvious. He'd crossed the line and she was backing off.

Her mobile phone rang then, which was his cue to move away.

"This is Emily."

He went over to the food, selected a celery stick and thoughtfully chewed.

She paused. "Hello?"

Another pause, then she frowned and clicked the phone off.

He moved back, ignoring her fleeting glance. He was in her space and it annoyed her.

Well, good.

She took a sip of wine, the silence between them growing as everyone buzzed with pre-race excitement. Would she say something? A thin smile flattened his mouth. Probably not.

Just then Jenna Perkins, one of his junior architects, walked over, and she gave the woman her full attention, nodding and smiling in the appropriate places. And when someone turned on the TV, he finally conceded, giving her the space she so obviously wanted.

Emily glanced at Zac's retreating back, determined not to let that swoop of regret get the better of her. She should've put the brakes on long before now, but she'd been caught up in the sex. Amazing sex.

She'd been obsessed with their illicit nights, enthralled by Zac's lovemaking. He applied himself to the task of pleasing her with uninhibited enjoyment, and while she secretly reveled in every single second, she'd crept from his bed, anxious and flustered, way too many times. And after that incident in his office, she needed to take control.

"I must be out of my mind," she muttered, shoving a cracker in her mouth and crunching down.

"Sorry?"

Emily glanced up into Jenna's quizzical face.

"Nothing. Just talking to myself. What were you saying?"

"I said—"

Emily's phone rang again. Another hang-up.

Jenna gave Emily a gentle shoulder nudge. "I was just asking about Zac…if he's seeing anyone?"

Emily swallowed back a choke. "Why? Are you interested?"

"Dating the boss? Please!" Jenna laughed, waving her glass for emphasis. "That'd just be too weird. And anyway I'm twenty-two and he's what…thirty?"

"Twenty-seven."

"Yeah, too old. No, I was just asking a question." She nodded to a guy across the room and smiled.

Emily followed her gaze. "Mal's in charge of the office betting pool, right?"

"Hmmm?"

At Emily's cryptic silence, Jenna turned innocent brown eyes on her. "What? Noooo…"

"Jen." Emily sighed. "You know how I feel about that."

"Come on, we're only having a little fun." Jenna rolled her eyes. "Zac doesn't mind."

"Betting on the boss's sex life is not my idea of fun."

"Whatever." Jenna downed the dregs of her wine with one gulp. "Jeez, you'd think *you* were one dating him the way you protect him."

Emily stared at Jenna's retreating back, her mouth open in a surprised little "Oh."

* * *

An hour later, Emily made her way back to the office. She'd picked a long shot, only one of three horses left unclaimed on the office sweeps, and no one had been more surprised than she when Total Surrender had actually won, putting a nice three hundred dollars in her pocket.

She'd laughingly accepted the congratulations and gentle ribbing before leaving everyone to finish the food and wine. Work output would be close to zero for the remainder of today. But not for her. There were simply too many things to do to justify bunking off for the rest of the afternoon.

Total Surrender. She unlocked Zac's office with a soft snort. Very apt, her winning horse. Definitely not a predictor of things to come, not when she'd put her foot down and Zac had backed off. Yet the sense of victory she'd expected to feel hadn't materialized.

She walked in the door, paused, then tilted her head with a frown.

Something wasn't right.

She sniffed the air, noting an unfamiliar scent—musky and thick, definitely not Zac. Another worker, perhaps?

Except for the cleaners, no one else had the keys.

Quickly she tested the locked drawers. Still locked. She skimmed over the blueprint cabinet. Nothing missing.

Then she went to her desk.

Inside the top drawer, next to her stapler and spare pens, a note was taped. It said cryptically, "Look out your window."

Zac was still at the party, so it wasn't him. She walked hesitantly to the office window, drew the blinds aside and stared down into busy Broadbeach Mall.

Their corner office afforded her an expansive view, from the monorail tracks stretching from the Oasis Centre to Jupiters Casino across the busy highway to the traffic-ridden roundabout directly below on Surf Parade. Nothing seemed amiss in the restaurants and eateries in the mall below. At twenty floors up, she wasn't sure she would see anything. Unless…

Her gaze snapped up, to the Sofilel Broadbeach hotel windows directly across. Almost at eye level, a sign was taped to a window.

"Just you. Where you buy your morning coffee. Ten minutes."

A thin thread of panic shot through her bones until outrage quickly overtook it. Someone had been in here, in her work area, in her things. Were those hang-ups a part of this, too?

That anger gave her courage, straightening her back and drawing her mouth into a thin line of determination.

Seven minutes later, she stalked into Bennetti's. After scanning the few customers and two staff, her gaze landed on a familiar figure sitting at a secluded table, casually sipping a short black.

When Louie Mayer's oily smile spread across his face, she swallowed a spurt of fear.

Showing fear gives them the upper hand. Another one of her mother's little life truths. Emily grimly smoothed back her perfectly contained hair. *Thanks, Mum. Handy advice when dealing with crims.*

"You're looking good, Emily." Louie smiled, easing back in his chair as he frankly appraised her. Suppressing a shudder, she gave him her best haughty look.

"Your boss got paid, if I recall. What do you want?"

The man really was huge, she realized as he stood and pulled out a seat for her. When she shook her head, he frowned and remained standing, his arms crossed, the black cotton T-shirt stretching taut until she was sure it groaned.

"Looks like you got a good thing going at work, huh?"

Emily frowned. "What?"

"Oh, just that you seem to be enjoying some personal after-hours attention from Zac Prescott."

His dirty smirk made her want to slap him. Her fingers jerked before she purposefully relaxed them.

"That's none of your business."

His grin spread wider and a gold front tooth glinted in the light. "Ah, but it is. Very much my business." He leaned in, and Emily was suddenly enveloped in a cloying musky aftershave.

"Your rich boyfriend ponied up Jimmy's debt quicker than a teenager sculling a beer at Schoolie's week. Which tells me a coupla things." He paused, eyeing two blondes as they walked up to the counter. His eyes lingered on their butts as he continued. "One—you and he are more than coworkers, especially now I've seen you both in action. And two, he has cash to spare."

White-hot panic made her heart surge. "You're blackmailing me?"

"I wouldn't say that." He reached out to stroke her hair, but she flinched away. The amusement in his smile fled. "Call it an investment. You pay up every month, and the papers won't get to hear about Zac Prescott's private life, starting with him boning his secretary and his 'compulsive gambling problem.'"

"But you took the last of my money! I don't have—"

"Use your brain, blondie." His eyes hardened. "You're sleeping with a multimillionaire. That doesn't come for free."

Her heart beat loudly in her ears, deafening her to everything else. For one split second, she could imagine herself doing actual physical harm to another human being.

She pictured herself surging to her feet and running. Running away from this café, away from this man's threats. Away from everything.

She'd started over before, she could do it again.

You can't run. Not this time. She breathed deep, once, twice, forcing calm into her limbs, her brain.

She had to stall him.

"I need time," she finally said.

Mayer shrugged and glanced at his watch. "You've got a week. I'll be in touch." And with a wink and a pat on her shoulder, he walked out.

Zac was out at a site inspection, not due to return today. Everyone else was either still in the conference room or pretending to work. The hall was abuzz with chatter and laughter, so no one noticed Emily leaving at four-thirty.

She couldn't stay at the office, not when it'd been breached so easily. Grilling the security guard and watching video surveillance hadn't brought her much joy, so now she sat in her Toyota in the basement car park, mulling through her options.

Her body buzzed with alternate flashes of outrage and panic, her skin tight and itchy. Her foot jiggled nervously on the clutch, her fingers clicking the brake button in and out, in and out, before she suddenly realized what she was doing and shoved her hands under her thighs.

She didn't want to go home. What she really wanted to do was press "rewind" and start today all over again. She couldn't afford to pay off that criminal, not even with her increased paycheck. And asking Zac for money? She'd rather earn it busking on Broadbeach Mall.

She shivered, remembering Mayer's fingers on her arm, the way his eyes had insultingly appraised her, the dirty tilt to his mouth.

She rubbed her arms then crossed them. That awful aftershave still lingered in her nostrils, taunting, smothering. It was a reminder that she was trapped, a pawn for someone else to manipulate.

No.

Her hands shot out and she grabbed the steering wheel, hard. *I will not be a victim. I will not let that thug win.* Determination surged up, charging her body with renewed energy.

He'd given her a week. Could she think of something in that time?

She *had* to.

Her phone beeped suddenly, pulling her from her focus.

U free later? My place @ 11—2 late?

It was Zac. The only person who'd been honest about what he wanted from her, who didn't lie and manipulate. A man who hadn't given up, who disoriented her with just one kiss, who made her forget the entire world when she was in his bed. Her own personal form of escapism.

Which was what she needed right now.

She returned the text, familiar eagerness heating her skin.

I'll be there.

Zac had just walked through to the living room when he heard the key in his front door, then the lock snick open.

The lights clicked off, plunging him into darkness.

He whirled. "Emily?"

The instant the figure moved from the door to the window, a dark silhouette against the full moon glimmering through his open window, he knew it was her.

Dressed in some sort of long coat?

"What are you wearing?"

She said nothing, just flicked on the small reading lamp. The soft light speared out, bathing her in gold from head to toe.

Zac's mouth went dry.

Her hair was piled up in a tousled mass, a few strands brushing her collar, one curling seductively over one eye. She was skillfully made up, her eyes wide and mysterious, her eyebrows shaped into a come-hither arch. And her mouth…

He swallowed, knowing he was staring but unable to look away. Her luscious Cupid's-bow mouth was painted a deep red, the full bottom lip in a slight pout that conjured up all sorts of erotic images.

He couldn't breathe.

She took one slow step forward, then another, hips swaying as her heels clicked on the polished floor. He glanced down. Red stilettos with a peek-a-boo toe. Long red and black ribbons that looped around her ankles, then tied in festive bows at the sides. He'd bought her those last week.

She paused a few feet away and his eyes went to her hands, to the belt she was slowly untying.

"What are you..?"

"Stop talking."

As she plucked open the large buttons on her coat, her gaze

firmly on him, he could feel anticipation building, bubbling up to heat his blood, shred his breath.

She was stripping. For him.

Unable to move, much less think, he watched her peel away one lapel, revealing a black satin strap over one bare shoulder.

He finally tore his gaze up to meet her eyes, and what he saw crushed his lungs. Even after everything they'd done, touched, tasted, she still looked uncertain.

How could she not know how desirable she was?

Man, she could bring him to his knees with nothing more than a look from those intelligent eyes. She undid him, turning every bone in his body to mush.

With a sharp inhale, almost as if she was dragging in courage, she grasped both lapels and pulled the coat apart.

A groan rattled in his throat.

The black push-up bra firmly cupped her breasts, creating an erotic valley between. He looked his fill, spotting a tiny diamanté flower perched in the center, winking in the light. Then his gaze crept lower, to the black bikini knickers tied at her curvy hips with two jaunty bows. A thin silver chain looped low around her waist, ending in a string of tiny stars hanging just below her belly button.

A rocket surge of lust sped through his blood.

Her body was flawless. Every curve was designed to be touched, every dip a perfect place for his tongue. From the silky smoothness of her thighs to the pebbly roughness of her pink nipples, there was not a section of her skin he hadn't tasted. If there were any imperfections, he'd yet to see them.

Why did she always bring out the caveman in him?

"Emily…"

Her mouth wavered, fists still bunched on the coat, flashing him. "Zac?"

Control was way overrated.

He surged forward with a rough growl, grabbed her by the lapels and slammed his mouth down on hers.

He kissed her hard and deep, a kiss born of frustration, of

passion, of desperate need. He wanted her to know exactly how keyed up he was, how much he wanted her.

Her soft exclamation muffled against his lips as she pressed up against him, her breasts hot and eager. He knew she could feel his arousal, his groin hard as it pressed into her belly. Somehow they made it across the room, but the stairs proved too much and he stumbled, sprawling backward on the steps with Emily on top.

"Ah, what the hell," he muttered as he pulled the coat from her shoulders, trapping her arms behind her. She grinned, all wicked and wanton, her hair tumbling over her shoulders.

He reared up to capture her lips and they tangled for long, sensuous moments, breath heaving, blood thumping.

Then the intercom buzzed.

"Zac…" She mumbled beneath his lips.

He pulled back and caught her soft earlobe between his teeth, grinning when she gasped.

Just as he went in for another kiss, the intercom jarred in his brain again.

He groaned. "If it's not someone bleeding from a major artery, I'm ignoring it."

Her small burst of laughter shook her body, sliding her against him. The breath he sucked in was sharp and painful.

"Hurry up and tell them to go away," she said, peeling away from him with a smile.

"Don't move." He rose, stalked over to the door, and with eyes fixed firmly on her near-naked body reclining on his stairs, slammed his fist on the intercom. "What?"

"Hi, Zac."

The woman's familiar purr cut through the air, dousing the moment like an Antarctic wind. With one sharp movement, Emily dragged the coat around her and stood.

Zac chewed back a curse. "What do you want, Haylee?"

"You never replied to my e-mails."

Emily's eyebrows shot up, hands going to her hips. Her indignation would've been humorous if he weren't so irritated.

"We broke up, remember?" he said.

Her sigh echoed over the intercom. "Look, can I talk to you for a moment? It's important."

Zac glanced back to Emily, but all she did was wave a hand, tie her belt, then walk into the kitchen.

His decision.

Emily watched from the darkened kitchen window as Haylee stalked up to the front door. She'd gone all out, dressed in a shiny leather miniskirt, thigh-high stiletto boots and a sheer blouse that left her naked underneath as she passed under the porch light. Her hair shone, the Cleopatra fringe adding sexy mystery to a striking face and dark makeup.

Gorgeous, confident and sexually aggressive.

Emily's insides cramped as she turned away.

She heard the door swing open, then Zac's curt, "What do you want, Haylee?"

There was a long pause, too long. Emily chewed on her lip. *Eavesdropping is a bad idea. Bad, bad.* Before she could convince herself, she quickly scooted back to the window, gently prying the venetian blinds apart.

Haylee had her hands on her hips, one hip thrust forward, chest out, her bold expression a mixture of smoldering and come-here. Emily swallowed. The woman knew how to command the moment, she'd give her that. But Zac...well, his entire crossed-arms posture just gave off waves of irritability, eyes firmly fixed on Haylee's face.

"I had to see you."

Zac frowned. "What for?"

"Do I need a reason? We were good together, Zac."

"I told you. You have to stop this."

Haylee responded with a pout that looked artfully practiced for maximum effect. "Do you really want to make me say it, baby? Because I will."

Zac sighed. "Haylee…"

"I know I can convince you to give us another chance. I want you, Zac. Right here, right now." When she moved in, pressing up against his chest, a thin film of fury cleaved Emily in two, leaving her breathless. Her nails dug into her palms yet she remained motionless, balanced on a knife edge.

Zac had hold of Haylee's wrists and was firmly pushing her away, his face marred by a deep frown.

"But I don't want you. Not now, not ever. Stop harassing me. Stop calling my office. Stop everything."

Then he dragged his impersonal gaze down her body. Emily almost felt sorry for the woman. She recognized the lost-all-patience-and-was-done-being-polite look. And so did Haylee, judging by her shocked expression.

"You're turning me down?" she spat out, yanking her arms back. "How dare you? Where the hell do you get off? I can name at least a dozen guys who'd be willing—no, *thrilled*—with what I'm offering."

Zac crossed his arms. "Then by all means, take them up on it."

Her eyes narrowed, darting past his shoulder. "It's someone else, isn't it? You've got someone else in there."

"That's none of your business."

When she surged forward, Zac's arm shot out to bar her way.

"Hey. Hey!" Haylee yelled into the house, straining against Zac's arm. "You do know you're only one skank in a long line? When Zac's finished with you, he'll just drop you for some other easy lay! Hey!" She squealed as Zac grabbed her shoulders, pivoted her, then gave her a small shove.

After a brief stumble she whirled, fury twisting her face into ugly lines. "Don't you touch me."

"Leave. Now."

With a foul curse and a rude gesture, Haylee spun away, then stalked down the path.

Wow. Emily pulled away from the window, then returned to the living room. Zac stood with his back resting on the closed door, concentration creasing his forehead.

"That was…" Emily began.

"Unfortunate." He sighed and pushed off from the door, his hands going to his hips.

"Do you think she'll make trouble for you?"

"With the clients? I doubt it." Zac shrugged. "But Josh…"

"You don't need Josh Kerans's business."

"No. But he is an extremely influential man."

"So are you."

"Yeah, but…" They both knew what he meant. Rich, workaholic father, spoilt daughter. It wasn't hard to do the math.

"Well." She took a breath. "If there are any problems, you can't argue with an eyewitness."

He paused, an odd expression on his face. "You'd do that?"

"Yes."

The look in his eyes blew any niggling worry from the water. And when he smiled, her heart melted.

"Come here."

She went willingly, eagerly into his arms, met his lips with a sigh of satisfaction, letting his mouth and hands cleanse the moment.

She didn't want to think about anything she'd said or done these past twenty-four hours. Zac filled her senses, her mind and soon, her body. And right now, it was all she needed.

Fourteen

Emily never thought Jimmy's old gambling contacts would've come in handy. But after a few calls and a few pointed tugs on the heartstrings, she had the most likely places Rafe Santos—aka "Joe"—would be, including a description from a former band member.

It was late Friday night, a night for revelry, dancing and shadowy assignations. After checking out five different nightclubs and two strip joints, she'd seen more than her share of excitement.

Last one. She glanced up at the familiar pink neon proclaiming Romeo's and sighed. This was one of the clubs where Jimmy's band had once played. Same indifferent young thing at the entrance, collecting her entry fee, same mirrored walls and ceilings. Same huge bouncer at the foot of the stairs. But this time, as she passed by, the man's eyes latched onto her barely contained breasts straining against the leather bustier, lingering on her until she reached the foot of the stairs. Knowing her butt encased in a short, tight denim skirt now commanded his attention, she forced down her distaste as she clicked up the neon glass stairs in her red-and-black ribboned stilettos. The closer she got to the top, the more heavily the frantic dance music pulsed in her throat and belly. Her head began to throb with the beginnings of a headache. *Focus. You're here to bargain with a bookmaker, hopefully so he will drop his blackmail attempt.*

Strobe lights, loud music and heat from dozens of sweaty dancers simultaneously hit the moment she paused at the top of the stairs. The place was cavernous as she remembered, with a split-level dance floor, a stage area and a massive bar that spanned the entire length of the room. And past the bar, in the shadows, a handful of circular lounges were cordoned off by waist-high smoky glass, a VIP area where special guests could observe the action yet still remain private.

And there Rafe Santos was.

She pulled her shoulders back, took a deep breath as a slick-looking guy in an expensive suit sidled up.

"Hey, babe, howsabout you and me—"

She didn't stick around to hear the rest of his suggestion. With her gaze firmly on her quarry, she made her way across the room, ignoring the looks, shrugging off a couple of propositions. She stared right at the group in the private booth, at the guy lounging on the comfy love seat, his arm around a stunning blonde.

As she approached, Santos flicked his gaze over her, then back to the guy standing with his back to Emily. He held up a finger, silencing his bodyguard, then returned to her, his eyes sidling up and down her body in all-male appreciation.

The guard turned with a frown. "This is a private booth," he said, stepping forward. "You need to—"

"John."

One word from his boss and he froze, a comical snapshot of menacing indignation. Santos went on smoothly. "You would send a pretty girl away without knowing why we've attracted her attention?"

The bouncer gave her the once-over with a bored look in his eyes. "You always attract women, Mr. Santos. This one isn't worth—"

"I think I'm perfectly capable of deciding who is worthy of my time, John."

Now that she was here, with one of the city's most powerful bookies a few feet away, panic began to set in. *The man is a criminal. Just what are you going to do? Who do you think you are?*

The guard's smug expression reflected all her unspoken doubts and fears as he edged aside, allowing her entry with only the tiniest of space. Her arm brushed his and she barely managed to stop herself from recoiling.

Confidence. You ooze confidence. This is just another role to play. Emily shut everyone out and put all her focus on the man she'd come to bargain with.

He's not much older than me, was her first thought. Her second was he was an extremely good-looking man. With a smooth-shaven head and dark coffee skin spread over broad cheekbones, Rafe Santos was an exotic blend of Australia's multicultural heritage. Filipino, Pacific islander…possibly some Italian in those frankly compelling eyes. He was impeccably dressed in a deep navy suit and a silk tie, ankle casually crossed over one knee as he lounged back in the sofa and appraised her.

"Can I help you, Mrs. Catalano?" he asked smoothly, the rich, cultured voice flowing over her. It was a charismatic, built-to-seduce voice, one Emily could dispassionately acknowledge without succumbing to its charms. Beside him, one arm possessively around his shoulders, the blonde woman shot her a look of haughty distain. Emily ignored her.

"You knew I was coming?"

"An attractive woman is in my clubs asking for me and I make a point of finding out who she is." His smile was all charming seduction. If she were any other woman, if he weren't a criminal who didn't exude barely leashed danger, it would've worked. "I knew your husband—"

"My ex-husband."

His mouth thinned into a smile but his eyes cooled—a powerful man displeased at being corrected. Emily swallowed. "Jimmy was a regular," he went on, taking a drag from his cigar.

"A little too erratic for my tastes, but still, good for business. Pity he died."

"Yes."

His eyes never left hers as he took another drag. "John, go and bring some more wine."

"Yes, sir."

"White, I think. Something from the Margaret River." He uncrossed his legs and eased forward, resting his elbows on his knees. "Join me for a drink. And sit." He gestured to the sofa.

Ringed by two impassive bodyguards, she could do nothing but acquiesce. He smiled as Emily slowly sat on the sofa. "A good Australian wine is so much better than overpriced French champagne, wouldn't you agree?"

She nodded, her tongue stuck to the roof of her mouth. As he studied her intently, she slid back into the lounge and crossed her legs. It eased her already-short skirt up even higher and spread Santos's grin a little wider.

"I need to ask you a favor," she began.

"Ahh. A favor for a pretty girl. I like the sound of that."

She swallowed down her apprehension. The way she worded her request was of the utmost importance. "Can we speak privately?"

He raised one eyebrow. "But we are."

She glanced at the bodyguards, at the hostile blonde. "Not entirely."

He paused, his teeth flashing in the shadows. "Intriguing. Helena."

The blonde rose elegantly, then stalked out, followed by the guards, who repositioned themselves a few feet away, this time facing the club crowd.

With a silent prayer, she began. "I know you're a powerful man, Mr. Santos. An influential man. I respect that. And I thank you for your patience while I sorted out Jimmy's debts."

"And I thank you for your prompt payment." He eased back in the sofa, hitching his elbows along the back of the seat.

Emily nodded, nerves strung out like ragged ribbons on a breeze. "So I'm wondering..." She breathed out slowly, blinked, then took a breath. "I'm *asking* you to withdraw your current request."

His eyes narrowed through the thick plume of smoke coming from his lips. "Which is?"

She met his gaze unwaveringly. "That I pay you to stay silent about my relationship with Zac Prescott."

He was still for a moment, picking her apart with ruthless efficiency.

"I see."

He took another slow drag from his cigar, blew, then watched the smoke hover gently in the thick air. Emily felt her heartbeat emphasize every dragging second, thump-thumping hard in her chest and drowning out the heavy music.

"And what did you bring to bargain with?"

His eyes slid over her face, breasts, then her legs with disturbing familiarity. She forced herself to remain still, forcing down the surge of disgust as his mysterious gaze finally reached her feet. His wolfish grin spread, spearing ice into her veins. What *had* she brought, except herself?

Suddenly Santos's focus snapped up and into the crowded club. "I think we have a visitor."

Emily turned and stared past the wall of guards to the approaching figure.

What on earth was Zac doing here?

"Nice to see you again, Mr. Prescott." Santos smiled, then nodded at the bodyguards to let him pass. "To what do I owe this pleasure?"

Zac's glacial eyes grazed over Emily, taking in her skimpy attire and expanse of leg in silence, before he returned to Santos. "I came for Emily."

Emily blinked. "You were following me?"

"I got an anonymous call."

She frowned, glancing back at the now-silent Santos as he studied his cigar tip.

When he finally met her eyes, his cold expression revealed nothing. She was the first to glance away.

"Emily." Zac's firm command brooked no refusal yet she remained seated, glaring at him.

Santos sighed. "If you two are going to fight, could you please take it elsewhere?"

"No." Emily spun back to him, desperately trying to ignore the overwhelming presence an angry, six-foot-two Zac made. "I came here to talk with you about…what I'd mentioned before," she added cryptically. Then she looked up at Zac. "Go home, Zac. Please."

"Only if you're coming with me."

"This doesn't concern you."

"I think it does."

"How do you know?"

"He's right," Santos drawled. "If I was blackmailing you to keep silent about your affair, then he has a right to know."

"What the—?" With a growl Zac surged forward, but a beefy hand clamped down on his shoulder. Emily shot to her feet the exact moment he whirled, ready to do battle, but Santos's sharp, "Enough!" froze everyone in their tracks.

"Miss Reynolds. You and Mr. Prescott may go now."

"But what about—"

His expression blanked, those dark eyes icing over, and Emily's pulse jumped in alarm. "I am not concerned with how you paid your debt, Miss Reynolds, just that it was paid. Blackmail is not my style. It's a very messy business with no guaranteed return, not to mention dangerous to my health. I like my life too much." He nodded, his small smile doing nothing to assuage her nerves. "I thank you for bringing this issue to my attention. Rest assured you will not be getting any visits from Mr. Mayer again. Understood?"

Emily nodded slowly. "Yes."

"Let's go," Zac murmured, firmly taking her wrist.

She rose shakily, relief flooding her limbs, but before she could escape, Santos's hand was on hers.

She whirled, wide-eyed, as she met his eyes.

"If you ever get bored with playing it safe…" He caressed her knuckles, smile widening as Emily felt the blush rise up.

Zac's hand tightened around hers, a deep warning rumbling in his throat. Santos flicked a glance at Zac, shrugged, then let her go, his chuckle quickly swallowed by the music.

"What the hell were you thinking?" Zac hissed, taking her elbow as they exited the club into the warm night.

She wrenched back and ground to a halt. "I was thinking I could get him to change his mind."

"Dressed like that?" He bit off a curse, dragged a hand through his hair. "It was dangerous and stupid, Emily. What if something had happened to you? What if—"

"Nothing did."

"But what if it *had?* You were being blackmailed. Why didn't you come to me with this?"

"Because *I* needed to fix it. Jimmy was my mistake, okay? My lapse in judgment, my stupid decision."

"And you're damned lucky it worked out the way it did. Bloody hell, Emily, just what were you prepared to do?"

They glared at each other, teetering on a thin tightrope. The awful truth lay in his furious gaze, laced with worry and concern. It squeezed the fight right out of her.

She took a step back. "I… I don't know. I just thought—"

"Don't do that again." He gripped her arms, tight. "Don't put yourself in danger and don't—" The gravity of the situation they'd just left crushed Zac under its weight, her confusion tangling his words. What the hell was he trying to say?

You're mine.

His expression must have given him away, because her eyes suddenly widened, a spark of lust rending the air. With a thick, frustrated growl he captured her mouth with his.

Emily's surprise quickly melted into need as her body instantly responded, lips automatically parting, her breath hitching as she grabbed his shoulders and kissed him back.

It was an angry kiss, one born of frustration and worry and desperate desire. And she matched it, letting all her tension go in this frantic meeting of breathless gasps and hot mouths.

When he finally yanked back, his heaving chest matched hers.

"No secret is worth that, Emily. Do you hear me?" He tunneled his hand in his hair, glaring out into the night. "This was about us. Not just you, not just me. At least give me the courtesy of telling me before you jump in to try and fix something."

He clamped his mouth shut as a bunch of revelers approached, moving aside as they stumbled and laughed by. Staring at their backs as they made their way into the club, he said curtly, "Where are you parked?"

"Around the corner."

He led the way, walking the short distance in cool silence.

When they finally reached her car, Emily fished for the keys in her tiny handbag, face warm, feeling utterly stupid in light of Zac's argument.

He was right. What had she been thinking? She'd gone there full of bravado, ready to bargain, but what could she have done if Santos had demanded something more?

She blinked, furiously dashing away half-formed tears.

"Emily." She jumped when Zac placed a hand on her arm, yet summoned enough courage to meet his gaze.

"Is there anything else I should know?"

I think I love you and I'm scared. Every relationship I've ever been in gets ruined. I don't want to lose you when I leave Valhalla. All those doubts and more jostled for position, but instead she said slowly, "You should go to your brother's wedding."

He sucked in a breath then rolled his eyes heavenward, muttering something incomprehensible. "Not that again?"

"You need to."

"No," he said. "I don't."

She leaned back on her car. "I see the way you react every time you deal with your father. You get all tense and jittery, like someone stuck a key in your back and wound you up too tight. He's been calling for the past few months and yet you refuse to talk to him. Look." She sighed, putting her hands on her hips. "I admit what I did tonight was thoughtless and stupid, but at least I did *something*. I faced the problem."

He said nothing, just stood there with a hard jaw and hooded eyes in the pale streetlight, thumbs hooked in his belt loops.

Finally he said, "When I was seventeen, I told my dad I wanted to study in Sweden. So he pulled considerable strings to get me into Sydney University instead. I left anyway and he disowned me. Just like that." He clicked his fingers for emphasis.

She knew verbatim his career highs and triumphs, knew he'd gotten his degree from the exclusive Lund University. But she hadn't a clue what had driven him to the other side of the world.

"So why did you return?"

His response came easily, as if he'd been expecting the question. "Five years is a long time. It gives you distance and clarity. And Australia has always been my home. I thought coming back would change things. I thought he'd changed."

"But…?"

"Victor Prescott is—" He scowled, pausing to kick at the chipped curb with one toe. "A brilliant businessman. A clueless father. My mother left when I was seven." He sucked in a breath, his troubled expression suddenly hardening. "I remember begging her to take me, too, but instead she left me with a man who divorced her within weeks, then destroyed every photo of her I had."

Emily's heart went out to him. "Oh, Zac."

"Yeah."

Zac crossed his arms. Damn. He'd let this go, had moved on. Yet somehow the bitter betrayal still clung like sticky cobwebs inside.

"Did you ever go looking for her?" Emily was asking softly.

He wrestled with the memories, indecision warring. But Emily's expression, eyes wide and open in the pale light, somehow comforted him. He trusted her with his most confidential business transactions, so why would he not trust her with this?

"Between study and classes, every spare hour I had, I looked. But she'd vanished and I barely had enough money to live, let alone offer as an incentive. Then, after I returned to Sydney I got a letter from her lawyer telling me she'd died and left me all her money." He paused, catching the mixture of poignant sadness and understanding fleet across Emily's face before her expression cleared.

It was enough for him to continue.

"You know what the worst thing was? While I'd been studying, my mother had been alive and well, living on a small farm in the next town." He clenched his fist briefly then let it go. "So Victor and I argued and I nearly punched him out. Not my finest moment," he said with a humorless smile. "I surfed my way around Australia with the money she'd left me, trying to forget who I was, who my father was. Then I started Valhalla."

Emily was silent for a moment, digesting that information as things slowly clicked into place. His confession answered so many questions, put a lot of things in perspective.

"Zac, I am so sorry," she began. "But I still think you need to do this. There's nothing worse than regret, thinking you should've done something differently. Trust me, I know."

His gaze turned astute as he searched her face. "What do you regret?"

"Lots of things." She jingled the keys. "It doesn't matter."

He stilled her hand, his fingers warmly covering hers. "It does, otherwise it wouldn't get to you." He tipped her chin up to meet his eyes. "So it matters to me."

"I don't…" Lord, she was so tired of maintaining the walls of silence. Making love with Zac made her forget the truth of who she was and where she'd come from. For a few hours she could be someone desirable, someone wanted.

Someone loved.

Yet how would that change if he knew who she really was and how she felt about him?

So instead of answering, she leaned in, grasped his neck and dragged him down for a kiss. He frowned, resisting, but when she gently pushed apart his lips and slipped her tongue in, he yielded with a frustrated mutter.

They kissed, out in the open, on the darkened street where anyone could have seen them. Emily didn't care. All she cared about was the here and now, Zac's hard, warm body pressing her up against the cold car door, not the ghosts of her shadowy past.

"Let's go," she finally murmured. "I'll meet you at your place."

"Emily…"

"Please." She lifted large eyes to his, unashamedly using every seductive trick to sway him.

He stepped back with a groan and dug in his pocket for his car keys. "Hurry."

They made love frantically, barely getting their clothes off and making it to the bed before he was on top of her, then inside her. She cried out, thrusting her hips up, wanting this, wanting him.

When they came, it was like a violent explosion, with tangled limbs, racing breaths and crashing heartbeats.

Finally, they lay replete in his bed, Zac nuzzling her neck as their bodies cooled.

"Hungry?" he murmured.

She shivered. "Starving."

"Then let's eat."

When he slid from the bed and the cool air rushed over her damp skin, she wanted to weep.

He must have caught her shiver because he gently pulled her to her feet, bringing her flush against his naked chest. Still warm, she realized, her palms automatically going to those firm muscles, gently sprinkled with dark hair. Then, to her surprise, his arms went around her, he buried his face in her neck and inhaled deeply, like he was imprinting her scent on his brain. As if she was truly desirable and he couldn't get enough of her.

He placed a soft cotton robe around her shoulders, tying it in front before giving her a wink. "Stay here." And he headed for the stairs.

They ate picnic-style in the middle of his huge bed, devouring crusty bread, dip, olives and four different cheeses. She'd expected to be uncomfortable, eating seminaked in Zac's bed after what they'd just done between the sheets. But instead, they shared stories about their respective houses and the local wildlife that dropped in on occasion.

Emily finally reclined on the pillows with a groan, an odd feeling of contentment seeping into her limbs.

"I can't fit any more in."

"Not even cherries?" He held up a bag with a grin.

Emily grinned right back. "No."

He rattled the bag. "Just one?"

His boyish charm worked its magic: with a dramatic sigh and an eye roll, she sat up and stuck out her hand. "All right."

"Nuh-uh." He plucked off the stalk then beckoned. "Closer."

She leaned in a few inches.

"Closer."

Another inch more, straining from her cross-legged position.

His gaze darted to her neckline and he sucked in a sharp breath.

Emily glanced down and noticed the robe had parted, revealing more than she cared to. Chomping down on a soft groan she dragged the robe closed.

Suddenly the comfortable moment disappeared like vapor in the air, replaced by something warmer, more heated. Intimate.

Zac crooked his finger. "Closer," then stuck the ruby-red fruit between his lips, eyes dancing.

She hesitated for one breath, maybe two. But the temptation proved too much.

Her hands went down to the mattress as she eased her legs out, shifting until she was on all fours. Zac's gaze turned quizzical but his smile remained, the cherry sitting ripe and tempting between his lips. But when she leaned forward, gave a mischievous grin and started to crawl toward him, that smile slowly dropped.

His gaze fell to her neckline, then snapped back up to her face. Oh, she knew what she was doing, all right. The heady feeling of empowerment was like a shot of pure adrenaline through her veins as she eased her way forward, finally stopping a breathless inch away. His ragged breath bathed her cheek as she paused, her mouth close but not touching the cherry offering. His whole body glowed warm, like someone had lit a fire inside. It reflected in those eyes, all-seeing eyes that probed hers, studying, cataloging, waiting for her next move—almost relishing it, judging by the way his expression tensed as she exhaled gently before inching her mouth closer.

When she latched onto the cherry and gently bit into the flesh, he choked out a throaty groan. She grinned and eased back, chewing as the deliciously sweet juice coated her lips.

The moment solidified with sudden clarity as Zac battled through the steadily growing waves of lust. Emily in his robe, her hair tousled and falling around her shoulders, the neck gaping to reveal generous breasts. Her bright blue eyes, twinkling with mischief.

And one bright-red drop of cherry juice shimmering on the curve of her bottom lip.

Her tongue was nearly out before he acted, dipping his head to steal the juice, licking, then sucking her swelling bottom lip. Her answering groan was like gasoline on glowing embers.

They sat there, joined only by a kiss, one that seemed to go on forever. Sweet, sticky, exploratory cherry-kisses in between soft laughter and knowing smiles. But then the mood changed, the kisses becoming deeper as their breath mingled, tongues tangling.

She tasted of cherry juice, white wine and olives. Zac breathed deep, dragging in the musky reminder of their lovemaking combined with the remnants of their meal. Senses reeled as his body weighed in, his groin demanding action.

It took superhuman effort to pull back from her heavenly Cupid's mouth. Her small whimper, eyes wide and dark with arousal, shattered him.

He quickly rose and stuck out his hand.

"Come with me."

His rough command made Emily shiver. Without hesitation she took his hand.

He led her into the master bath, soft bedroom light spearing into the darkness, illuminating a massive chrome and white-tiled extravaganza complete with skylight and huge corner spa, another view of the Pacific Ocean serving as the backdrop.

When he went to turn on the light, she stopped him. "Can people see in?"

His mouth quirked. "What do you think?"

"I think…no."

"Ah, but do you know for sure?" He peeled off her robe with expert hands, backing her up against the sink until her bare bottom hit the cold tiles.

Her shock drowned in a groan as his hands went to her arms, pinning her as his mouth descended. With a tiny click, he'd flicked the lights on, bathing them in a soft golden glow.

"Does it bother you, Emily?" He asked between hot kisses. "That anyone could walk along the beach and see us together? Or is it…" She gasped as his hand slipped between them, fingers going straight to the core of her heat. "Exciting? Arousing?"

"Yes." He knew her body too well, knew when she was eager for him. His rough chin grazed her neck, his mouth dipping to capture one swollen nipple.

She whimpered, hips jerking as lust exploded, those exquisite sensations quickening her blood.

"Wait, my sweet," he whispered, before grasping her shoulders and turning her to face the mirror.

She stared at her shadowed reflection, a wide-eyed, disheveled reflection, naked and bent over at the waist. Behind her, Zac swept a hand over the curve of her bottom, then across her back, his eyes heavy with desire.

"So beautiful," he murmured, before glancing up to see her watching him through the mirror. His eyes locked on hers, lingering, and suddenly Emily knew what he was waiting for.

"Yes," she breathed.

His mouth curved into a sensual grin.

Emily's breath caught when he grasped her hips and nudged her legs apart with one knee, only to explode out as he swiftly entered her from behind.

Ohhhh… The wicked delight of his hot naked flesh in hers, their eyes locked through the mirror, shadow and soft golden light shafting across his face, freezing his expression in a moment of ecstasy.

Everything felt suddenly too hot, too sensitive, yet Zac couldn't withdraw. She surrounded him completely, her hot warmth, her pliant body beneath his hands. Inside and out.

He rocked back, slowly withdrawing, and her breath hissed out. "Zac…"

His name on her lips, pleading, wanting him, nearly sent him over the edge. Instead he gritted his teeth, took hold of her hips and began to thrust.

She was exposed and vulnerable, yet she held his gaze through the mirror, bold, languid eyes watching as he made love to her.

That only turned him on more. When he eased the pace to drive in deeper, she hauled in a stuttering breath, eyes closing, head back as she braced herself on her elbows and went with the rhythm. She rocked with him, completely in sync, and it was all he could do not to lose it then and there. Instead he bent forward and wrapped his arm around her waist, planting long, languorous kisses along her spine as he quickened the pace. He felt her shudder, then gasp. And all of a sudden, she cried out, her eyes springing wide open.

When he felt the orgasm quake through her, her entire body clenched in exquisite torture around him, he finally let go, their cries echoing off the tiles.

Eventually they shared a hot bath in that massive spa, lazily washing each other between wet kisses. Then Zac wrapped his arms around her and dragged her to sit between his legs. They languished in the bubbles, his chin on her shoulder, his hands absently stroking her arms.

Emily breathed in the damp heat, the curls of steam smelling faintly of sandalwood and vanilla, and wondered if the moment could be any more perfect—lying wet and naked with the man she loved.

The frightening realization dawned just as the fiery red sunrise began to streak across the sky.

She was in love with a man who was only supposed to be temporary. A physical distraction only.

She squeezed her eyes shut, determined to hold on to the moment instead of facing the reality for what it was.

Yet how could she not think about reality when Zac's hard body was pressed against her back, his hands splayed possessively under her breasts?

"Come with me to Cal's wedding," Zac said softly, breaking the silence.

Emily paused, squeezing her eyes shut. "Why?"

"Because I want you there."

And I want to be there. More than anything. Instead, she bit her lip and remained silent.

At her silence, he gently turned her to face him, water swirling as she went. "Look, you're my assistant. No one's going to question you being with me."

Great. "It's not that."

His expression told her he wasn't convinced. "So...?"

So why did it feel...bad? As if she was breaching the line they'd drawn. She was his bedmate, not his girlfriend. They didn't share anything except their bodies.

Not true, a little voice inside reminded her. *There's trust. Professional respect. And he knows things about you, private things, and he's still here.*

Yeah. But if he knew all of it, he'd run a mile.

"It's your brother's wedding, Zac. A private family gathering. Surely they wouldn't want—"

"I want." He reached out and pulled her in, his mouth dipping down to hers. "There's no one else I'd trust to be there."

Conflict warred briefly, until his lips skimmed hers and desire swiftly replaced it. Her eyelids sagged. *Where's your list when you need it?* Yet for the first time, she felt no urge to list those pros and cons because there was only one answer in her heart.

She was sick of letting fear and doubt shape her actions. He needed her. She'd be there.

"Okay," she breathed. "I'll go."

"Good." He finally kissed her, yet despite the warm tenderness, trepidation still oozed through her body like an ever-growing toxic spill.

Fifteen

"Why is it," AJ said casually as they ate lunch at Madison's in the Oasis Centre as the March heat scorched the sidewalk outside, "that no matter how many problems a relationship is having, couples can still overlook them to have sex?"

Emily followed her sister's eyes to the far table, where the guy and girl they'd been covertly watching argue were now deep in a passionate kiss. "Is that a question or a statement?"

AJ turned her bright blue gaze back to Emily. "I'm talking about you and Zac."

"And *I* don't know what you're talking about."

"Rubbish. You love him. And I'm assuming he has feelings for you, given the fact he's been your knight in shining armor at least twice now. But you haven't really talked, have you?"

"We don't have that kind of relationship."

"Right. Let's recap, shall we?" AJ crossed her arms, pinning Emily with a firm look. "The Point One launch was a huge, glittery, publicity-laden hit. You made the man heaps of money and provided an in-depth report in favor of his new events division. He gives you a pair of the most amazing Louboutins for Christmas, which, by the way, are worth hundreds. Then you pick me over Mr. Yummy for the holidays. So okay, I'm flattered—" AJ shook her head with a comical look of disbelief "—but in God's name, why?"

"I told you," Emily muttered past a forkful of salad. "After the launch, I think people were beginning to suspect something."

"Oh, please. You've been together for…" she mentally calculated "…close to four months—"

"—twenty-one weeks."

AJ's brows went up with a smirk. "And it's just sex, huh? Right. I think you're just grasping at straws. Maybe you don't *want* it to work out." She smiled as the waiter refreshed their empty water jug and the teenager smiled back, flushing as he left. Emily shook her head.

"How do you do it?" she asked, changing the subject.

"Do what?" AJ tossed a long lock of red hair over her shoulder and returned to her club sandwich.

"Make men fall at your feet."

"Good genes, I guess." She grinned, her mouth full. "Our mother was gorgeous before the drugs and booze ruined it. But back to you—why didn't you say something to Zac at the Point One launch?"

"You're kidding, right? I barely had time to breathe, let alone deal with any personal issues."

"Okay, then…your New Year's Eve party? A perfect time after you've had a few drinks, loosened up…" AJ wiggled her eyebrows. "And there's that midnight kiss…?"

Emily shook her head. "We were in the penthouse suite of Point One—"

"Sounds promising."

"—surrounded by Valhalla staff," Emily finished pointedly. "We all ate, drank and watched the fireworks over Sydney Harbour. I avoided Zac—" or had he avoided *her?* "—went shopping with Megan and her girlfriends on the Sunday after, then came home a few days later."

AJ snorted and sat back in her chair. "That's just dumb. Why hasn't he said anything?"

"Er, probably because he's fine with the way things are?"

"How could he be? What's not to love about you?" AJ's righteous indignation made Emily smile. "And why haven't you asked him?"

"You know why. I'm gutless about this stuff. I don't want to spoil the time we have left by ruining it. And anyway, I *know* him. Zac loves women. He never falls *in* love with one."

AJ tossed down her sandwich and reached for a napkin. "Well, now you're just not giving the guy enough credit."

"We agreed it's just about sex."

"Since when is something 'just about sex'? He makes you glow, Em. Look at you." She eyed Emily's floral shift dress with approval. "All this *and* a decent pair of shoes. There's hope for you yet."

Emily rolled her eyes. "Thanks."

"You're welcome." AJ gently shoulder-bumped her sister. "And we both know it's more than clothes and looks. People can change—just look at me."

Emily grinned despite herself.

AJ grabbed her water glass with a leisurely smile. "If a juvie runaway can come back from the brink of a glorious criminal career—" she waved her glass theatrically "—her sister can find a good guy who truly deserves her. Right?"

Emily shrugged, pushing a piece of tomato around on her plate in silence.

AJ sighed and covered Emily's hand with hers. "Em. This isn't something you need to pro-con, okay? Sometimes you just have to listen to your heart and leap right on in, regardless of the consequences. And—" she arched her eyebrows before spearing Emily's tomato with her fork "—that stupid office betting pool means squat when you're leaving in less than a month."

Half an hour later, Emily avoided her reflection as the elevator returned her to the office. AJ had a point. Well, she amended as she unlocked the office door, AJ *always* had a point. But this time, Emily began to wonder if she was actually right.

She sat at her desk, then placed her purse in the drawer.

The months leading up to the Point One launch had flown.

Two weeks prior, she'd relocated to Sydney to oversee the preparations, and even with that temporary move she'd felt the keen stab of loss. Sure, she'd spent those fourteen days living and breathing work, yet with the breaking dawn, in the split second she struggled from deep sleep to slow awareness, she'd felt it in the huge hotel and the cool sheets: emptiness.

It was almost painful, the launch night. She'd watched Zac circulate, his powerful presence and barely contained elation commanding her eyes every time she glanced over. And when he'd singled her out, praising her work and congratulating her in front of that rich, influential crowd, his perfunctory kiss had seared a path across her burning cheek.

Hours later, just before sunrise, his exhilarating euphoria had only heightened their passionate reunion.

Tell him how you feel.

With a sigh, Emily grabbed a notepad and pen, then checked her phone messages. After noting the calls, she flicked the page and slowly drew a line down it, filling in the two columns with the familiar "pro-con."

Every night her body rejoiced in his arms. During the day, the cracks had begun. The strain of the facade was beginning to tangle with her mind, winding her up into a tight mass of nerves.

Yet in public Zac was flawlessly—almost effortlessly—the epitome of the platonic boss.

What if she put it out there and he responded with indifference? Pity? A polite "thank you"? Worse, what if he called their arrangement off? She swallowed a spurt of panic. If time had flown these last few months, the weeks she had left would surely drag if he rejected her, especially when she'd agreed to go to his brother's wedding in two days' time.

Which reminded her… She clicked open a folder on her computer. She had to make a recommendation to the selection panel for her replacement.

When the office door swooshed open she glanced up, head crammed full of things to do, a pleasant smile on her lips.

That smile froze as a uniformed policeman walked in.

His bars indicated someone high up…a senior sergeant, or maybe a local area commander. Nervousness hit her stomach as she darted through worst-case scenarios.

Keep calm. Act normal. She gritted her teeth. Great. Now she was channeling her mother.

"Can I help you, Officer?" she said calmly, shoving those memories aside.

The cop tucked his cap under one arm. "Is Zac around?"

"Let me check. Can I get your name?"

"Senior Sergeant Matthews."

Emily rose fluidly, walked over to Zac's door, knocked, then went in.

"You have a policeman here to see you," she said when he dragged his gaze from the computer screen.

He glanced past her shoulder and the small frown quickly spread into a smile.

"Tim!" Zac rose, hands braced on the desk. "What can I do for you?"

As the policeman walked past Emily, his expression grim, Zac's smile slowly dropped.

"Close the door behind you, thanks, Emily," Zac said.

She did as he asked, then returned to her desk. Dread pooling in her stomach. This wasn't about her. It couldn't be.

And yet… She drew in a short breath. Something more serious than, say, a parking ticket would warrant a personal visit from a Senior Sergeant.

She heard Zac's muffled exclamation. Moments later, the cop emerged, his mouth flattened into a severe line.

Emily watched him leave, then swiveled back to Zac. His head shaking in disbelief as he stared at the papers in his hand.

"What's wrong?"

He pivoted and she quickly followed.

"Haylee issued me with an AVO." He slapped the restraining order down on his desk, one hand on his hip.

"What?" She swiftly closed the door.

"An Apprehended Violence Order."

"I know what it is." She paused, struggling to remain calm

as outrage scorched the back of her throat. "This is payback, for the night she turned up at your house."

He crumpled up the papers, hurling them across the room with a foul curse, but when she made a move toward him, the radiating waves of fury brought her to a stop.

"She's lying, Zac. We both know you didn't do anything."

His jaw clenched, eyes blazing. "That won't matter—the accusation alone will be damage enough. I have to call Josh." Zac had picked up the phone and was dialing.

"Zac," she said louder. He ignored her.

She moved, swiftly cutting off his call, eliciting a furious scowl. It was painful to watch him struggle to get a handle on his emotions. Despite everything in her past, every crappy thing that had happened to make her who she was, she'd never wished she could turn back the hands of time so fervently as right now.

"I was there, remember?" she said. "And I'll sign whatever needs to be signed as your witness."

His expression changed as the words sunk in. "You'd do that?"

She nodded. "Yes."

"Why?" He frowned. "After we've gone to such lengths to keep us a secret?"

Because I love you.

Fear slammed into her with such a force that she took a step back, desperate to avoid his gaze. Instead she homed in on the discarded AVO.

"Because it's the right thing to do." She walked over, picked up the papers and began smoothing them out, seeking calm in the rhythmic movement.

Zac stared at the papers she held out, his thoughts spiraling. She was actually going to step up and risk her privacy, possibly unveil her personal life to be scrutinized and gossiped about.

Yes, he wanted entry into that private room, but not like this.

He shook his head and took the papers. "No."

"What do you mean, no?"

"I have a solicitor. He can deal with it, make it go away."

"How?" Her hands went to her hips. "You have to go to court, unless she decides to drop it—which I don't see happening. She's a woman scorned, Zac, and she wants to hurt you. And she'll do that by hurting your company."

"You're giving her way too much credit." He tossed the papers onto his desk. "Now, if you'll excuse me, I have a call to make."

When she just glared at him and refused to budge, he glared right back. Yet beneath his irritation, a shot of admiration sparked. Her cheeks were flushed, eyes dark with righteous anger, her hands on her shapely hips, one leg thrust forward. Damn if she didn't look absolutely adorable right now.

"Emily," he began.

"Fine." She sighed before whirling and stalking out the door.

As expected, Josh Kerans was unavailable. So Zac called Andrew, his solicitor, who directed him not to approach Josh or Haylee. When Emily stuck her head in and asked for a long lunch, he nodded absently before trying to get back to business.

But a horrible feeling hijacked his thoughts, encroaching into work. He hated doing nothing, yet nothing was exactly what Andrew had instructed him to do. "Lie low for the rest of the week," he'd said. "Go to your brother's wedding. I'll get us an expedited hearing date and we can refute everything in court."

Which didn't placate him one bit.

They boarded their Sydney-bound flight early Friday morning, then an hour later switched at Sydney for the small country plane that would take them west to Parkes.

Emily remained silent as they drove through Gum Tree Falls, then down the dirt road to Jindalee, the outback spa resort where Cal and his fiancée were holding the ceremony. Sure, she'd anticipated Zac's mood wouldn't exactly be joyous, but this complete emotional shutdown was ominously disturbing.

Twice, she'd asked, "you okay?" and he'd replied with a nod and a short "yeah."

Which did absolutely nothing to calm her worries.

Finally, at the end of a long dirt road, Jindalee appeared. The homestead sprawled across the land, the green corrugated iron roof glinting in the sun atop large slabbed and roughly mortared walls. The iron porch railing was decorated in loops of white and silver-blue organza, sprigs of silvery gum-tree leaves serving as bouquets in between. Large earthenware pots filled with banksias and waratahs flanked a blue carpet that ran across the small grassy yard, up the stairs and stopped at the huge wooden double doors.

Past the main homestead she caught a glimpse of the skeletal frame of a massive extension. To the left, another blue carpet led to the wedding marquee and beyond that, a handful of guest suites.

When Emily opened the car door, the late-afternoon heat slammed into her, stealing her breath. She paused for a moment, then exited, the familiar strains of classical music floating in on the warm breeze.

"Mozart's Concerto for Two Pianos," she murmured, shoving a loose lock of hair behind her ears.

Zac looked up as he took their bags from the boot, the first real look since they'd started this trip.

"You like classical music?"

"I like Mozart," she replied, shouldering her handbag. "I saw *Amadeus* about a billion times. I'm told it was my uncle's favorite movie."

"The one who left you the apartment?"

She nodded. "I never knew my mother had family until his solicitor contacted me." She closed the car door with a solid thunk. "From what the neighbors tell me, he was a pretty good guy. He used to watch movies with Kitty from One B every Saturday night."

She let him digest that little piece of information as they mounted the steps. Then the doors swung open and Cal and his wife-to-be stood in the entrance.

Emily watched Zac smoothly make his way through Ava and Cal's warm welcome and the inevitable wedding-guest introductions. If his smile appeared too tense or his shoulders too rigid, she said nothing. Just having him here was a major step.

They were shown to their rooms, two elegant side-by-side suites decorated in cream and gold with a huge four-poster bed in the center. As Zac placed her bag on the bed, Emily's gaze slid over the opulent coverlet, the whispery canopy. It was so massive, so in-your-face, it felt like a huge elephant in the room. It tauntingly reminded her that everything had changed.

She hung up her suit pack, the wardrobe door blocking her from Zac's view.

"What time's the ceremony?"

"Seven." He dragged off his tie, then undid the top button of his shirt, the tanned skin at his neck forming a tempting V. She swallowed.

"Are you going to talk to Cal and Victor?"

"I can hardly avoid them."

"That's not what I meant."

He gave her a small smile. "I know."

She let it go, instead flipping the top of her suitcase open. Why on earth had she said yes to this? This was a wedding, a celebration joining two people in love. If that wasn't a slap in the face, what the hell was?

"I'll let you unpack."

One glance was all it took. One glance to see the uncomfortable tension riding his body as he stiffly grabbed his bag and made for the door, and her reason became clear.

She was here for Zac, to be whatever he wanted her to be this weekend—his date, his support, his emotional sounding board. He trusted her with his family secrets, a trust that simultaneously humbled and shamed her. What had *she* trusted him with?

She was sick of hiding—behind unspoken truths, behind awful work clothes. Even behind the possibility of a broken heart. She'd spent years protecting herself, making decisions based on fear.

She sank to the bed, staring unseeing at the closed bathroom door, at the polished golden handles and white glossy wood until spots danced before her eyes.

A mixture of dread and excitement rushed in, making her

limbs tremble. She was actually going to do it. After the wedding, after the reception. She'd pick her moment and then…

Then she'd tell him how she felt. Damn the consequences.

Sixteen

"Callum Stephen Prescott, do you take Ava Michelle Reilly—"

Emily's eyes skimmed over the bride, a shimmering, smiling vision in off-the-shoulder white satin, a tiny tiara of diamonds holding back waves of black hair, and her throat caught. Well, what do you know—brides *did* glow.

Then she looked over to Cal. Dark and gorgeous in a sharp gray dress suit and sky-blue cravat. But it was his expression that held her: a rapt look of such happiness and pride as he gazed on Ava that it actually made her breathless.

She swallowed thickly, forcing back unexpected tears.

"You okay?" Zac whispered beside her with a frown.

She nodded, unable to speak.

When he silently offered her his handkerchief, she took it and carefully dabbed under her eyes. "It's just a little…" Fanning herself with her hand, she gave a short, self-deprecating laugh. "I've never been to a wedding before."

"Really?"

"Shhhh!" An impressively decked-out woman to their left frowned. Emily gave her a watery smile, mouthing an apology.

Zac bent in, his lips close to her ear. "What about your own?"

She sighed, her eyes fixed on the beautiful picture Cal and Ava made as they recited their vows. "We signed papers at the town hall. Hardly cause for tears of happiness."

When Cal and Ava finally kissed, their joy was so palpable everyone laughed, then began cheering as the kiss just kept on going.

She shook her head. "I didn't think it would be so…so…"

"Emotional?"

"Exactly." She offered him his hanky back and he took it, eyes never leaving her face. She smiled nervously. "What?"

"I love your shoes."

She choked out a laugh. "Thank you for them. I think I'll concede I'm hopeless when it comes to buying footwear."

He glanced down at her feet, at the soft leopard-print high heels, the tiny pearl strands looped around the ankle. "Did I tell you how beautiful you look?"

She flushed. "You don't need to."

"I want to."

With a grin and a wink, he swung his gaze back to the ceremony, leaving Emily to swallow the lump in her throat. Hope bloomed low in her chest, a tentative bud curling around her heart. "Zac…"

Their conversation was cut short by the arrival of the bride and groom. As Cal and Ava accepted congratulations, posed for photos and smiled their way through the small gathering, Zac couldn't keep his eyes off Emily. She was no longer his conservative, efficient assistant. Dressed in a short flippy lemon skirt, a silky white tank and a cap-sleeved tangerine-colored cardigan that emphasized her womanly curves, she was elegant yet mouthwatering.

She'd even ditched her glasses. Her hair was swept up at the sides, the blond curls tumbling down her back. Unable to help himself, he ran a hand up her back, tangling his fingers in the soft waves.

She glanced up at him and her mouth stretched into a smile, her eyes shimmering from still-damp tears.

And that's when it happened.

The sounds of the wedding, the nesting rosellas, the clink of the caterer putting down the final settings, everything just fell away. His heart leaped as emotion slammed into him with such power it left him struggling for breath.

He was hopelessly, totally in love with Emily. His assistant, who couldn't stand a messy filing system. Who harbored a secret love of cheesecake and mocha lattes. Who accessorized her desk with hot pink and sky blue. Who danced in the dark. Who had woeful taste in shoes yet chose lingerie that made his eyes roll back in his head. Who kept her past locked down, allowing no one entry.

He'd never been so hell-bent on discovering what made a woman tick. She was more than just a challenge: those tiny pieces of information she doled out just made him hunger for more. He'd managed to piece together the basic framework, but she hadn't offered more than he'd asked.

Craving movement, he went in search of the circulating waiter. He was fully aware he was living on borrowed time. She was leaving Valhalla next month, and by leaving the company she'd also leave him.

No going back, just moving forward. Like she'd been doing all her life.

So where the hell did that leave him?

He watched in brooding silence as his stepmother approached Emily. Emily returned her smile, and soon they were deep in conversation. Unbidden, Zac's mouth tugged up. Isabelle had a way of putting people at ease, which he suspected came from her honest, working-class background, devoid of the polished sheen of wealth. His gaze lingered on Emily's face, the way her eyes creased when she laughed, the way she held her hips, one forward, one back, her back straight.

Then Victor joined them and familiar panic snaked through every muscle, urging him forward.

"You're Zac's assistant and his date?" Victor was asking as Zac approached with two glasses of champagne.

"Yes." She glanced up at Zac, smiling her thanks as he offered her a glass.

If Zac hadn't been watching the man so carefully, he might've missed that brief expression. But when their eyes met, Zac knew.

You're sleeping with your assistant.

The faint aura of censure accompanied an eyebrow raise, judgment quickly masked behind an impassive expression.

Zac scowled. Nearly thirty years old and he was still proving to be a letdown, tainting the exacting standards of the Prescott name.

His fingers involuntarily tightened on the glass stem before he downed the contents like water.

Well, Dad—screw you.

"I'm starting uni in April," Emily said.

"Doing what?"

"Small-business degree. I'm going to be a life coach."

Victor's bushy eyebrows went up. "A what?"

And here it comes. Zac shoved a hand in his pocket, forcing back an irritated growl.

"A life coach. You help clients determine their personal goals, then help them achieve them," Emily said.

"Like a career consultant, darling," Isabelle explained. "But more…"

"Broad," Emily added with a smile. "Holistic."

"Right. And there's a demand for it?" Victor asked.

Zac frowned. He'd been expecting Victor's usual halfhearted interest laced with thinly veiled skepticism. Instead it sounded as if the man was almost…interested.

"A huge demand," Emily said. "And it can be business-oriented, too—large corporations, government departments have life coaches under long-term contracts, which means a steady client base." She glanced at Zac. "Working at Valhalla has given me some excellent experience in the field."

"I'm sure it has." Victor's face was the epitome of politeness, yet annoyance still wound its way around Zac's chest. He had no doubt his father knew more about Emily than even she did. He was hard-core through and through, leaving nothing to chance, no sudden surprises lurking in the background. He knew this because of the way Victor watched Emily when he thought no one was looking. A calculated study, as if weighing up his options before deciding on appropriate action. The look was as familiar to Zac as every traffic light along the Gold Coast Highway from Surfers to Broadbeach.

It was Cal's wedding, for heaven's sakes. He should be happy for his brother. Dammit, he *was* happy. The man had everything—a lovely wife, a cute baby and a burgeoning business out here in Sydney's far west. Yet every time he spotted Victor, every time he thought about dealing with VP Tech, he cramped up. Like now.

"You two need to talk," Cal had said earlier in his suite. "Despite whatever he's done, he has changed. Hell, he's even agreed to consider our suggestions. Once he realized it'd give him more time to focus on his new pet projects—"

"I didn't come here to discuss business, Cal."

"Right." Cal had lifted one eyebrow as he tied his cravat with smooth precision. "So what did you come here for?"

"You're my brother. You're getting married, remember?"

"And Victor is your father. You can't ignore him forever."

"That's what Emily says." Zac muttered, absently fingering the wedding bands Cal had entrusted him with.

Cal straightened his cuffs. "Smart girl, that."

"Yeah." He couldn't help but smile. "She is."

When Cal finally held out his hand, Zac dropped the rings in his palm. "Ready?" Cal said.

"Are *you* ready?"

Zac saw the look flicker in Cal's eyes, his chest imperceptibly swelling as he nodded. Who would've thought his cool, workaholic brother would get emotional at his own wedding?

"Mate, I've been ready for months. Let's go."

Now, as the sun finally set and everyone gathered under the wedding marquee for the reception, Zac hung back on the porch watching the proceedings. Lounging against the railing, cast in the half shadows of the dying sunset and nursing a drink, he watched the man who was his father make his way slowly through the throng, smiling as the local townsfolk congratulated him in breathless awe, bailed him up to chat or simply bathed in the cast-off glow of a billionaire legend.

Victor actually smiling?

He took a slow sip of his drink. Maybe the surgeons did more than remove a tumor.

When Victor finally broke away, strode up the steps and disappeared into the house, Zac swallowed the last of his champagne, clamped a lid on his emotions and pushed off the railing. Perfect timing.

Yet just as he approached the door, he heard a voice from inside.

"Oh, I'm sorry!"

It was Emily—he'd recognize her voice anywhere.

"No, my fault," Victor returned. "I've actually been looking for you."

Zac hesitated, curiosity overriding purpose.

"For...?" He heard the smile in Emily's voice.

"I find your business venture very interesting."

"Really?"

Wow. Victor making small talk. Zac stayed still, wondering where the conversation was heading.

"And you're actually quitting work to study?"

Zac frowned. Victor never asked a question he didn't already know the answer to.

"Yes," Emily said slowly.

"That's a bold move, considering the current economic climate."

"I know. And uni fees aren't cheap."

"How's your start-up capital?"

"I have enough," she said cautiously.

"Which means you don't. Most small businesses fail within five years, you know."

"Yes. Mr. Prescott—"

"Emily. Let me cut to the chase. I don't know what Zac's told you about me—"

"Zac doesn't talk about his family."

"Really."

Zac could imagine Victor's raised bushy eyebrows, a picture of skepticism.

"Really. I work for him. We don't…have that kind of relationship."

"But you *do* have a relationship."

There was a slight pause, then Emily said, "I don't think that's an appropriate question."

Despite himself, Zac grinned. *That's my girl.*

Victor snorted in amusement. "No, I guess it's not. So let me get to the point. I'd like to offer you this."

Another pause, a small rustle and a gasp.

"That's a lot of money, Mr. Prescott," Emily said faintly.

Zac's grin fled.

Unthinkingly he surged forward, shoving open the doors in one almighty heave. In the long hallway, both Victor and Emily turned as one, a perfect visual of surprise. It took only one second for Zac to register the check in Emily's fingers, her flushed cheeks, Victor's scowling countenance.

"What the hell do you think you're doing?" He grabbed the check, staring down at the bunch of zeros before returning slowly to a now-inscrutable Victor.

"Zac," Emily said calmly. "Your father was just—"

Zac rounded on his father. "Just couldn't help yourself, could you, Dad?"

Victor crossed his arms. "If you just slow down one second, everything can be explained."

"Maybe you should take this out of the hall."

Zac whirled at the sound of Cal's voice. He and Ava stood in the doorway holding hands, wearing twin expressions of concern. Behind them, a hushed blanket of whispers spread across the wedding guests who'd stopped to blatantly stare at this exciting development.

Zac gave a curt nod and strode past them, into the reception area.

He struggled, trying to rein in his fury, but it was a losing battle. The past surged up to scorch his throat with painful, crushing memories and a desperate desire to be free of Victor's suffocating influence.

The doors closed, underscoring the moment with finality.

"I've had enough of secrets. He," Zac stabbed Victor with an accusing finger, "was offering money to Emily. A lot of money."

Emily gasped. "Just what are you implying?"

Zac raised one eyebrow, glaring at Victor. "Why don't you tell them, Dad?"

"Zac…" Cal warned.

He ignored his brother, instead turning to Emily. "Were you going to take it?"

Are you completely insane? Her wide-eyed stare mirrored that thought, her mouth dropping for one second, just before she snapped it closed and placed her hands on her hips.

"What do *you* think?"

Of course not. He pulled his back straight, struggling with the dark ghosts of his past, but the automatic answer on his tongue was a second too late.

"You," she breathed, giving him a glacial look, "are an idiot, Zac Prescott."

With supreme dignity she turned on her heel and strode for the door.

Zac swallowed in disbelief. *What have you done?* "Emily. Wait."

As Cal opened the door, she turned back to him, eyes eerily calm, expression neutral. "You need to deal with your family, Zac."

Then she was out of the room, and Cal closed the door behind her.

No. This was wrong. Zac surged for the door, but Victor's voice stopped him in his tracks.

"She's right, you know," Victor said calmly. "You can be an idiot."

Zac felt the fury burn from the inside out as he rounded on the older man. "You do not get to—"

"Shut up, Zac," Cal butted in. "Let him explain."

"What's there to explain?" Zac lashed out. "He was giving her money to walk away because she just wasn't good enough for a Prescott. That's the kind of stuff you do, Dad, right?"

At everyone's frowns of confusion, Zac laughed, the bitterness hot in his throat. "'Money always talks loudest.' Isn't that what you've always said, Dad? You paid Mum to leave, just like you did a bunch of my unsuitable girlfriends. And let's not forget you bought me a place at Sydney uni, right?"

"I think," Ava gently said from the door. "I should go and check on Emily." When she took her husband's hand and squeezed it, Zac's anger deflated.

"Ava…" His gut pitched in self-disgust. "It wasn't my intention to ruin your wedding."

She waved a hand. "Not ruined, just…made it more entertaining. It seems we've started a tradition." Her lips curved as she and Cal shared a joke before she nodded. "Just don't kill each other, okay?" With a smile she swept the doors open, then closed them firmly behind her.

The room plunged into thick silence. Zac glowered at Victor, memories and past grievances fusing to form a heavy stone in his gut. *I dare you, Dad,* he glared. *I dare you to deny the truth.*

"Look, most of those girls were more interested in themselves than in you," Victor began.

"Way to go, Victor," Cal muttered and threw himself down into a one-seater.

Zac scowled. "So that made it okay, Dad? You had no right."

"I had every right! I was protecting you!"

"From what? From leading my own life? From my own mother?"

"She was sick, Zac!" Victor exploded. "You were barely a year old when I came home one day to find you alone in the bathtub! God knows what would've happened if I hadn't been there."

Zac sucked in a breath, the icy shards piercing his heart. "No."

"Yes. She couldn't cope—with a baby, with being my wife, with the constant scrutiny and attention, the expectations that entailed."

Victor's craggy face creased for one second before he quickly composed himself and went on.

"She wanted to leave and I let her go. The settlement was generous."

"And then she disappeared."

"Yes."

"You know," Zac said, "it took me a long time to come to terms with what you'd done." He dragged a hand through his hair. *Liar. It's always been there, eating away at you.*

"I kept the truth about your mother from you, and I'm sorry." Victor's brow dipped and he stepped back, a sudden picture of remorse. "I didn't want you to think it was your fault she left."

"But you never explained *anything*. I asked, but you either ignored me, said 'she's not coming back,' or changed the subject. Jesus, Dad, you not only tossed her things out, but destroyed every single photo!"

"I was angry," Victor ground out. "And okay, in retrospect, I should've handled it better. You were a withdrawn, solitary child, and your mother was not well."

"So you just cut her loose?"

"No!" Victor barked. "Your mother just wanted privacy. So I let her go on the condition she got help and you stayed with me. Yes, I was angry. Yes, I blamed her for a long time. But there was nothing more I could've done. She didn't want to be found—not by you, not by anyone. And my job was to make sure you were safe and well taken care of."

"I needed a *father,* Dad." When Zac felt his voice crack, he stopped, swallowing thickly. "But you were always working. I didn't need the latest PlayStation, I just needed *you*. I needed you to tell me the truth, to let me make my own mistakes. I needed—"

He choked, the past saturating every corner of his mind, overwhelming, suffocating. He shoved one hand through his hair, head downcast. *Dammit, mate. Get. It. Together.*

With gritted teeth, he finally lifted his head. "Do you know I've never heard you say 'good job, son'. Not once."

Victor frowned. "I'm sure I—"

"Not once."

Victor's craggy face reddened. "Then I'm sorry, Zac," he said stiffly.

Zac's eyes widened as they met Cal's, mirroring stunned surprise.

"And I don't want VP Tech," Zac added, on a roll. "I design houses, Dad. I love my job and I'm bloody good at it. I just don't understand why you're so hell-bent on involving me in a company I have absolutely no interest in."

He paused, the cool air stilling as both brothers waited for Victor's answer. When no one said anything, Zac glanced at Cal. His brother just shrugged.

"Because it was the only way you'd ever talk to me," Victor finally said.

"What's wrong with the phone?"

Victor's eyebrows shot up. "You refused to take my calls. It took a threat to get you down here."

Damn. Zac scrubbed one hand across his face. The man had a point.

They both fell silent until Victor said, "Look, after I was diagnosed with that tumor, I began thinking about things…regrets, mostly. How I'd do things differently. And you topped the list, son." He smiled, a thin humorless smile tinged with remorse, before exhaling heavily. "The way I handled things with you was inexcusable. My major regret."

Shock rooted Zac to the spot as reality suddenly tipped sideways. This was crazy. Victor didn't apologize, much less talk about his feelings. What kind of world was it where Victor Prescott recognized he was wrong?

The same one where Cal gave up the Prescott legacy, apparently. And one where Emily walked out on him.

Emily. He paused, breath shallow and garbled. What the hell had he done?

"So what was that check for?"

Victor crossed his arms. "My new project. I'm looking for a few good small businesses to help off the ground. I offer silent financial partnership, they do the work, and we both benefit."

Zac glanced at Cal, who nodded. "He's right."

"And if you hadn't burst in," Victor added, "I would've explained that to her."

Zac studied his father with a critical eye. His hair was thinner, grayer. There were darkening circles under his eyes, eyes that normally held such authority and command but now were simply those of a man who'd experienced life and all its ups and downs, had worked murderous hours for something he passionately believed in.

Looking at the man with whom he'd fought so hard for so long, he realized that now that everything was out in the open, he was more sad than angry. Sad that things had turned out the way they had, sad for all those lost years.

It didn't hurt quite so much. For once, his mind was clear with purpose.

Zac shook his head. "She wouldn't have taken it."

"Hmmm. Well." Victor slowly loosened his tie with a sigh. "I *was* trying to do something nice."

Zac's eyes narrowed. The past had taught him to refute it. Argue. Deny. Yet the truth lay heavy in the air, truth that couldn't be denied or ignored.

For the first time in a long time, Zac actually believed him. It was a start, however small.

He gave Cal a contrite look. "Sorry about messing up your wedding, mate."

"You didn't. And I'm not the one you should be apologizing to," Cal said pointedly.

Zac nodded. Could he be a bigger idiot?

He surged for the door, grabbed the handle and wrenched it open. "I've got to be somewhere."

Seventeen

When Zac's phone rang as he strode along the path to the guest suites he had half a mind to ignore it. But then he glanced at the display. His solicitor. "Andrew."

"I texted you but you didn't call back."

"Sorry. Patchy reception," Zac said. "What's up?"

"Good news," Andrew said. "The AVO's been dropped."

Zac paused, rubbing his temple as relief washed over him. "Mate, thank you. I really owe you for this one."

"Oh, it wasn't me. When I fronted up at the station, it'd already been taken care of."

Confused, Zac thanked him again, then hung up. The only way that could've happened was if Haylee had withdrawn the charges. Which meant...

He pounded on Emily's door, a faint thread of relief mingling with overwhelming trepidation the longer the seconds grew.

Finally, the door opened and Ava stood there. She said nothing, just gave him a small smile and a pat on his arm and left.

Emily was zipping the top off her suitcase and shoving it open. Seeing her flushed and barefoot, her shoes kicked across the room, quickened his heartbeat, forcing every single thought from his brain.

She barely glanced up when he gently closed the door.

"Leaving?" Zac said softly.

"Well, I hardly think it's appropriate to stay, do you?"

In silence, he watched her scoop up a pile of neatly folded clothes, then stuff them into the bag.

"Emily." He paused to clear his throat, then started again. "Look, I—"

"You don't have to explain yourself, Zac." She kept right on packing, refusing to meet his eyes. "That's quite okay."

"No. It's not. Can you—" He frowned as she disappeared into the bathroom. A few seconds passed before impatience sent him to the door, only to barely avoid a collision when Emily came barreling back out.

When he grabbed her arms, she gasped.

He dropped his hands. "Can you stop for a second and just talk to me?"

She took a step back, her toiletry bag pressed up against her chest, her eyes cool. "About what?"

"About what an idiot I am."

His lips tweaked encouragingly, but hers remained flat.

"Okay." He grasped her arms more gently this time, and felt the tiny shiver she tried to suppress. Slowly, he guided her from the doorway, across the room and down onto the solid pine chair before taking a seat next to her on the edge of the bed.

"I hesitated back there, I admit it. And my only excuse is… well." He sighed with a shrug. "Okay, I have no excuse. I'm sorry."

She finally met his eyes, giving him a thorough going-over. "You actually thought I'd take the money? After everything that's happened?"

"Not for one second," he said firmly. "It was just shock, seeing Victor pull that stunt. I choked and I'm sorry. He's used money as a bargaining tool all my life, and watching you two at the reception, chatting so easily—"

"I was doing that for you."

"Me?"

She tossed her toiletry bag on the bed and eased back in the chair. "Calming the waters. Putting your dad in a good mood. For you."

He started. "I didn't realize."

"Well, I was." She firmly crossed her arms and legs, the overt body language telling him he wasn't out of the woods yet. Not by a long shot.

"And did you go and see Haylee for me?"

A small frown passed fleetingly across her brow. "No. I saw Josh."

The look on his face tilted her chin up. "I offered to help, you refused. So I called Josh's assistant and found out where he was having lunch."

"What did you tell him?"

"The truth. We talked about a few things. Apparently Haylee's been acting out since her parents' divorce last year. She has a bit of a problem letting go of her exes."

"She…"

She stared at him, daring him to make an issue of this. Hell, he should be delighted to be in the clear, but instead, all he could think of was that she'd sacrificed her privacy to help him.

This time, she'd been the one to charge in and save *him*.

And by doing that, she might as well have taken out a full-page ad about their relationship. Which had to mean something. Surely it meant something?

"You really are quite extraordinary, do you know that?" he murmured with a smile. "What on earth would I do without you?"

She stilled, her bright blue eyes capturing his for long, agonizing seconds before they suddenly began to flutter.

"I'm sure my replacement will do a great job," she said softly.

"That's not what I meant."

They stared at each other as the air practically crackled with unspoken words. But as Zac took a breath and opened his mouth, Emily got in first.

"My mother was a cokehead, a drunk and a welfare cheat," she blurted out. "I don't know who my dad was—my mom had an affair with some guy, then went back to Pete, my stepfather. AJ is actually my half-sister, six years older. My mother taught us to shoplift when I was five. When we got caught, Charlene and Pete did a runner and we were shipped off to the Department of Community Services, then foster care when DOCS couldn't find any relatives to take me. I was ten." She paused, gauging his stunned silence before continuing. "AJ ran off and I didn't see her again until I was twenty-three, when she tracked me down through my uncle's obituary. Yes, I've had it tougher than some, but I would never take money from your father. Never."

She finally stopped to take a breath, clamping her mouth shut. Yet past her defensiveness, the bright eyes that held his so steadily, Zac could see the turmoil. Turmoil that had been shoved down deep, then covered over by hyper-efficiency.

Chaos, uncertainty and disorganization—they all scared the crap out of her.

"I'm not telling you this for sympathy," she added quickly, her face reddening. "I just… I thought you should know."

His silence, his expression laced with concern and sympathy, ripped at Emily's composure, the walls she'd built crumbling as she wrestled with tainted memories. Her mother's booze and drug-soaked hangovers, the constant hunger-filled days. Charlene and Pete screaming at each other. The dead-of-the-night departures. Too many goodbyes.

She hadn't planned on saying this much, but it was like her mouth had yanked the steering wheel from her hands and had floored it. Zac did that to her, made her feel crazy, out of control. He'd invaded her life, challenging her self-preservation, demanding she open up to him, and now she couldn't reconstruct her defense no matter how hard she tried.

"I'm a foster kid who was given up by her parents—no wonder I suck at relationships. For years I kept everything in a suitcase. Ready to leave in minutes. It took me ages to actually buy furniture. I've never…" *Felt I've belonged anywhere. Until now.* She swallowed, her stomach fluttering.

His expression softened.

"Your past doesn't define who you are."

"But it does influence you. You know that. Which is why I said yes to you. It was about sex, not emotion."

He flinched as if she'd landed a physical blow. "Do you think that's all we are?"

Her breath hitched. "Isn't it?"

His expression was a tangle of emotions she couldn't quite unravel. "You tell me."

This was it. He wanted the truth and she'd never lied to him before. But instead of leaping into that abyss of uncertainty, she took a shuddering breath. "I find myself—" she glanced up at his unreadable face, then quickly away "—wanting more. Feeling more. Look, the fact is, I think I'm in love with you, and it's a strange, scary thing. But this doesn't have to mean—"

She ended in a squeak of surprise as Zac surged forward, ending up on his knees before her.

Her wrists captured by a pair of strong hands, silenced by those intense eyes as they searched her face, she could see the dark edges of his pupils, the small lines bracketing his mouth.

"Emily." He paused to breathe in deep, his eyes closing for a brief second before they returned to hers with burning intensity. "I know there's comfort in predictability. And I know you hate chaos and disorder. But that's what love is—it's crazy, unpredictable and full of mistakes."

"Look, you don't know... What?" She frowned. "Are you saying... What *are* you saying?"

"I said," he slid his hands down to capture hers, "I love you." He gave a wry snort. "I've actually been in love with you for months."

She was totally and utterly speechless.

"Em? Sweetheart?" He gently shook her hands, his mouth curving into a slow smile. "Can you say something?"

"No one's said that to me in a very long time."

Zac drew in a long breath. Lord, she was amazing. She may be compact, fitting under his chin, yet the power she wielded was infinite. She could destroy him with a few mere words.

"Then let me repeat it. Emily Reynolds, I love you. I love the way you're so hyper-organized, I love the way you blink and chew on your lip when you're nervous…the way you're doing right now," he added with a grin. "I love your loyalty, your sense of right and wrong. And—" his mouth swooped down, so close he could feel the warmth from her cheek on his "—I love kissing you, making love to you. I love every single inch of your gorgeous body."

All the words Emily had prepared, silently rehearsing over and over in her head, disappeared into a delicious haze as Zac kissed her slowly, tenderly, thoroughly.

When he finally pulled back, his hands still cupping her face, swelling elation threatened to choke her. It was like she'd been soaring a thousand feet off the ground.

"Do you want to add anything?" he murmured, eyes dark with flickering arousal.

"I think I found someone to fill my position."

His laugh rumbled through her, shaking her entire body. "I don't think anyone could ever do that, my love. And while we're on the subject of you leaving…"

"Yes?"

His arms tightened around her. "You should at least consider Victor's offer. He knows a good investment when he sees it."

"Really?"

"Yes." A myriad of emotions passed over his face until he settled on one Emily recognized. Peace.

When his lips gently met her upturned mouth again, it was like their first kiss all over again. Desire rampaged through every vein, arousing her, filling her with such a need that she thought her heart would explode from it.

Was it possible to be any happier right now?

"Marry me, Emily." His lips moved across her neck, little flares of heat on her skin. "I won't lose you. Be my wife."

Yes. Yes, it was.

Her breath hitched as she pulled back and stared into his face. His eyes may have been languid with desire, his mouth curved into a sexy smile, but his expression was deadly serious.

This was so much more than she ever deserved. Ever expected. Ever hoped. Joy surged until she was sure her face would crack from the huge grin.

"You're not going to lose me. And yes, I will marry you."

In between laughter and a few tears, they kissed again, until suddenly, kisses were no longer enough.

Their clothes were quickly discarded, the bedcovers yanked off, and they fell to the mattress in a tumble.

"I love you, Emily," he murmured, loving the way her eyes widened and her full mouth curved.

"And I love you, too, Zac."

And then, suddenly, words were no longer necessary.

* * * * *

LET'S TALK
Romance

For exclusive extracts, competitions
and special offers, find us online:

Want even more
ROMANCE?

Join our bookclub today!

'Mills & Boon books, the perfect way to escape for an hour or so.'

Miss W. Dyer

'Excellent service, promptly delivered and very good subscription choices.'

Miss A. Pearson

'You get fantastic special offer and the chance to get books before they hit the shops'

Mrs V Hall

Visit millsandbook.co.uk/Bookclub and save on brand new books.

MILLS & BOON